The Lady And Mr. Jones

The Lady And Mr. Jones

ALYSSA ALEXANDER

This book is a work of fiction. Names, characters, places, and incidents are the product of the author's imagination or are used fictitiously. Any resemblance to actual events, locales, or persons, living or dead, is coincidental.

Copyright © 2017 by Alyssa Marble. All rights reserved, including the right to reproduce, distribute, or transmit in any form or by any means. For information regarding subsidiary rights, please contact the Publisher.

Entangled Publishing, LLC
2614 South Timberline Road
Suite 105, PMB 159
Fort Collins, CO 80525
Visit our website at www.entangledpublishing.com.

Amara is an imprint of Entangled Publishing, LLC.

Edited by Alethea Spiridon
Cover design by Erin Dameron-Hill
Cover art from DepositPhotos

Manufactured in the United States of America

First Edition November 2017

To Joshua
Thanks for still thinking your mom is cool

To Joe
For everything

Chapter One

Spring 1819

Jones rubbed a thumb along the faint line running the length of the pistol's barrel. He couldn't remember now the origin of the scratch, but he had never been able to polish it out to his satisfaction.

Nevertheless, he tried. A man took care of his weapons.

There was very little light in the hidden nook of his commander's office. Curtains blocked the candlelight from the main room, so it fell just shy of the flintlock pistol. But Jones needed no light for this work, as he knew the feel and shape of the weapon, every ridge in the wood, every curve of the iron. Still, bringing out the small, soft linen square he kept in his pocket, he began the meticulous process of rubbing the iron and wood.

And he listened to the conversation occurring beyond the secret alcove he had been assigned to.

"The Flower is no longer yours to command, Lord Wycomb. Nor has she been this last half year." Sir Charles

Flint spoke carefully to the man standing on the other side of his desk. The light was bright near the two of them, from the fire and the windows and the candles. It shone on the broad, barrel chest of Sir Charles and the lean, elegantly clothed agent challenging him. "The Flower is now under my direct command."

Ah. They were discussing Vivienne La Fleur, the opera dancer who had captivated London between visits to France and breaking into the homes of the *ton* at Wycomb's direction. She excelled at thievery, with her quick fingers and elegant grace. She was also damned good at lock-picking, as her new husband, Maximilian Westwood, had become aware.

But Henry Taylor, Lord Wycomb—the bastard—had mistreated her and lost Sir Charles's good will.

And Jones's respect.

"I trained her." Lord Wycomb's voice was as cool and careful as the spymaster's behind the desk. "I found her in the rookeries as a child, trained her for espionage, and commanded her assignments for a decade. She *is* my agent."

From his hiding place, Jones glanced at Wycomb's back, at the set of his shoulders and angle of his head. Jones couldn't see his face from this vantage point, but there did not seem to be any sign of untoward anger.

Jones refolded the linen square and began to polish his pistol anew, focusing on that single scratch he could not smooth out.

"The Flower *was* your agent. I have reassigned her. Again, I now control her missions," Sir Charles answered. There was no hint of his anger at Wycomb's treatment of the Flower—but Jones knew, if Wycomb did not. Jones had seen Sir Charles months ago in this very office, had witnessed the mingled fury and pity. "Why is it that you require her expertise?"

"An assignment that is not under your command, *Sir*

Charles." Haughtiness. Presumption. Precedence. All echoed in the room.

From his hiding place, Jones narrowed his eyes. A man didn't disrespect his superior officer, regardless of social titles. Tempted to stand and reveal his presence, Jones flattened his hand over the pistol to steady himself. He had his own assignment, and allowing his irritation free rein was not it.

"I have a need for the Flower's particular talents." Wycomb leaned over the desk slightly, bending at the waist by only the smallest of angles. He expanded his chest on an inhale, creating an indentation in the back of his coat that clearly outlined the pistol hidden there. "I want access to her."

Wycomb's movement was not significant, but the linen in Jones's hand paused in its steady rhythm as he watched. Waited. Jones suspected even that small angle over the desk would not be tolerated by Sir Charles. Still, his forefinger slid against the trigger, palm cupping the stock.

It was only a precaution, a moment to prepare for action, if need be.

But there was no need. Sir Charles's chair scraped against wooden floorboards. He stood slowly, eyes never leaving Wycomb's face though Sir Charles was nearly a head shorter. The flame of the candle flickered over the tight features of both men as silence reined for a beat, then two.

"Vivienne is not available to you." Sir Charles spoke softly, his voice dropping to a whisper. "You will need to use another of the spies you command. Not the Flower."

Wycomb did not move, his head and shoulders steady as he stared at Sir Charles.

Neither did Jones move. He continued to observe the faint crease running the length of coat and the pistol between Wycomb's shoulder blades. Perhaps Lord Wycomb expected Sir Charles to yield immediately, the lesser title giving way to old blood. But old blood and titles held no sway with Sir

Charles. If they did, he would not be spymaster.

The pistol's trigger had warmed beneath his finger now. Jones held his hand steady, knowing this moment was one reason Sir Charles had directed him to be here, in the shadows.

He suspected the other reason was he would soon be hunting a fellow spy.

Finally, the crease running down the center of Wycomb's coat smoothed out as his shoulders eased. Only the smallest of movements revealed that he'd conceded. Jones imagined it grated. But that small movement told Jones what he needed to know. His finger relaxed and slipped from the trigger. He lifted the linen square that had fallen to his lap and set it once more to the metal barrel.

"I don't have an agent with the Flower's talents available to me. The other agents I command are good, but not good enough." Wycomb set his hands on the edge of the desk. His tone was not persuasive, necessarily, but it was too sociable for Jones's liking. "Give me Jones, then. He's a close second to the Flower."

"Jones is not available." Sir Charles's tone mirrored Wycomb's falsely friendly words.

"Surely you understand their particular talents," Wycomb said.

"I have given you my orders, Lord Wycomb. The Flower is no longer yours to command, and Jones is not available." Sir Charles held Wycomb's gaze for another moment. Jones recognized impatience in the slight narrowing of Sir Charles's eyes and the downturn of his mouth.

"You may regret this, Sir Charles." It wasn't a threat, precisely, but Jones heard the warning clearly enough in Wycomb's words.

"I may," Sir Charles answered. He picked up his quill and ran the feathers through his fingers once, twice. "My agents are not at your disposal. Though you may be of higher social precedence, when it comes to espionage, my lord, it is my decision that is final." Sir Charles did not sit, but he moved papers across the desk and riffled through them, his focus clearly shifting to another task.

It was a dismissal, and not the friendly sort.

Wycomb didn't answer, but he stiffened, and his shoulders—clad in what Jones assumed was the most fashionable coat available—straightened and pulled back.

"Good day." Wycomb turned away with slow, deliberate movements so that Jones was able see his face as he strode toward the door. Shadows lay beneath his eyes and the creases along his mouth had deepened in the last months. He was angry, but not desperate.

Desperation was something Jones recognized well enough. It made men do things they would never contemplate otherwise. There was no despair in Wycomb's eyes, only exhaustion and worry, so there was no need for alarm.

Yet.

The door to the hall fell closed with a loud *snick*. Sir Charles did not look up at the noise, instead settling himself in the chair he'd recently vacated. The quill he'd been holding dipped into the inkwell, as efficiently and calmly as though there had been no confrontation between spymaster and titled senior agent.

Jones continued the soothing rhythm of linen over wood, linen over iron as he cleaned the pistol. He did not leave his dark corner. Experience told him Sir Charles was not ready, and he was not certain of his own thoughts on the matter at any rate.

It was a full five minutes of quill scratching on paper before Sir Charles spoke.

"Do you understand why I called you in?" He did not look up from his documents, though the writing instrument no longer fluttered a path along the page. It hung suspended in the air, as if waiting to add punctuation to their conversation.

"Yes, sir."

"Wycomb is bordering on insubordination." Sir Charles muttered it, pushing away the paper and tossing the quill aside.

His words did not particularly require an answer, so Jones continued his work in the corner. The pistol was no doubt perfectly clean, but productivity was better for thinking than idleness.

"I don't care for Wycomb's methods. I never have. But he is effective, and I wasn't aware of the lengths he went to achieve such effectiveness." Sir Charles pinched the bridge of his nose between forefinger and thumb and let out a long sigh. "The Flower suffered at his hands, and I don't intend to let it happen again."

That *did* require an answer. "No, sir."

"I don't trust Wycomb." Sir Charles looked up, and though it was unlikely he could see into the hidden corner, his eyes seemed to pierce right through Jones. "I'm not sure I ever did."

"Agreed, sir." Jones tucked the linen into one coat pocket, the pistol into the other. He stood, stepping into the room and letting the heavy curtain that had partially hidden him fall closed. "What is your direction?"

"Watch Wycomb. Find out what he is working on that requires the Flower." Sir Charles leaned back, propping his elbows on the arms of the chair. He pressed his fingers together to form a triangle. "You've done this before with our own agents, so I know I can trust you to see it through, no matter the outcome."

"Yes, sir." Jones slipped into the bright circle of candlelight near the desk, his own instinct humming as much as Sir Charles's.

Sir Charles's fingertips tapped together once, twice. A third time. "I don't believe Wycomb is working on an assignment. I would have been informed directly or as a courtesy by another spymaster. I haven't, so whatever he is involved in, I suspect it's outside the service."

"Understood, sir."

Jones would be hunting his own. Again.

He would set the Gents onto Wycomb first. That would be a simple and effective method of gathering facts. The Gents were small, smart, and unnoticeable. More, Wycomb had yet to be introduced to the rascals Jones had gathered.

"Do you have any suspicions?" he asked, thinking of which threads to begin tugging at. "Any suggestions as to where to begin?"

"I would suggest beginning in areas not involving espionage." Sir Charles paused, one brow twitching upward. "Still, I want no part of his life left unturned. He has considerable freedom as a senior agent, but there are lines. I need to know if he has crossed one."

Jones ran a hand over his coat pocket, instinctively checking for the recently cleaned pistol. A quick shift of his shoulders told him the second pistol hidden beneath his coat was also there.

"And Jones," Sir Charles added softly. "The lines do not exist for this assignment."

Chapter Two

Cat flattened her hand over the smooth surface of the letter, satisfied her temper didn't translate to trembling fingers.

> *My deepest apologies, Baroness Worthington. I was unable to secure approval for reconstruction of the tenants' roofs. The trustees determined the mills require modernization for increased efficiency and profit, and believe the roofs will withstand another winter.*
>
> *Yr. Humblest Servant,*
>
> *Matthew Sparks*

"The mills." Disappointment warred with fury. She had made a promise to the tenants, once last summer and again just this past February before she'd left for London. Now it seemed she would not be able to fulfill it.

The quiet rhythm of a lightly tapping foot stilled. Its owner looked up, her aging gaze unfocused for a moment as she switched it from her most recent needlework to Cat's face. "Hm? Did you say something, Mary Elizabeth?"

"I was just talking to myself, Aunt Essie." The darling woman wouldn't be interested in roofs and mills, though she would listen if she knew they were important to Cat. But Cat would shortly be angering her guardian—who was also Aunt Essie's brother—so perhaps it was best to keep the problem of the promised roofs to herself.

"I understand, dear. I sometimes do the same." Essie's brown eyes blinked behind the round lenses of her spectacles. "Though you do look a might put out. Is something troubling you?"

Cat looked down at the letter again as thunder roared beyond the townhouse walls. "It is nothing serious, aunt." But she did not intend to let it pass. Pushing to her feet, she carefully folded the note. "If you will excuse me, I need to respond."

"Yes, of course, dear." Aunt Essie turned back to the pretty pale-blue linen spilling over her lap. The embroidery needle pierced the fabric, its trailing white thread slipping through the cloth.

"Thank you." Cat strode to the door, already formulating strategies for dealing with the trustees and the mills. No doubt the mills could use modernization, but the roofs were more important. The well-being of the people *under* the roofs was more important. "I shall see you at luncheon, then, Aunt Essie?" Cat didn't pause in the doorway to look back.

Essie's words floated through the door and into the hall. "Do send Mr. Sparks my regards."

Cat stiffened, pausing mid step to look behind her. "I beg your pardon?" She set her slipper on the parquet hall floor, leather *shushing* on wood.

"I recognize Mr. Spark's handwriting, Mary Elizabeth, which means you have news from the Abbey." Essie didn't look up and the needle didn't pause in its journey through the center of the embroidery hoop. "Don't anger *him* too much, will you? Your uncle is not easily pacified."

"Apparently, my face and my correspondence are easily read." Cat turned in the doorway, narrowing her eyes on white curls piled high and the two simple gold combs holding them into place. "What do you want to know?"

"Nothing at all. What is between you and Wycomb regarding Ashdown Abbey will not be changed by my opinion."

"But you have one."

"An opinion? No, I would never presume. Only—" Now Aunt Essie's hand paused as she looked up. "Mary Elizabeth, you cannot win. You are wedged between the trustees, your uncle, the estate, and the husband you will soon find. Whatever happens, you cannot win."

Cat knew this. Every breath and every fiber of her being echoed this immutable fact. There was no victory and no freedom for her. "I've lived with that knowledge nearly every day of my life, Aunt Essie, since the day I realized being born female meant I couldn't inherit both the earldom and the barony."

She imagined her distant cousin was none too pleased with the higher-ranking title but lesser estates. Nor was *she* pleased that to ensure the barony's estates remained in her family she had to marry and provide an heir. Still, she thanked all the fates and all the gods of every religion that the barony was the older title by writ and held the more profitable land.

Ashdown Abbey was still hers.

Cat clutched the letter from home in her fist, thinking of the mills and roofs and trustees. The paper gave way and crumpled in a satisfactory manner. "If I hadn't known I was trapped before, I became quite aware after my father died."

Essie let the embroidery hoop fall into her lap, abandoned.

"I know, dear. I'm sorry your father put the barony into a trust. That's typical—only, you seem to fight it so very hard."

"I don't know how to do anything else." She wished she did. She had trained to be Mary Elizabeth Frances Catherine Ashdown, 13th Baroness of Worthington. Fought to prove she could carry on the legacy of the first Mary Elizabeth Frances Ashdown, who had been granted the barony five hundred years earlier.

Fought and lost, she thought fiercely.

"You are you father's daughter in character." Essie sighed, gaze flicking over the features of Cat's face one by one. "I see it every day."

"Yet my father did not believe in me enough to let me inherit the entail and lands outright." Bitterness filled her throat even as she tried to swallow it. "A five-hundred-year-old peerage, one of the few allowing a woman to inherit by writ, and he put everything into a trust so I cannot touch it until I am thirty-five or married."

"I'm sure he had his reasons," Essie murmured. Hollow words, echoing those she had spoken when they first learned of the trust.

Cat breathed deep and let out any betrayal with her exhale so only sadness remained behind. She could not change what her father had done. "What of my mother? Am I not her daughter?"

Essie smiled softly. "Oh yes. Yes, my dear. You are her very image, and you have her spirit, too."

"Do you miss her?" Cat couldn't bring herself to move back into the room. An ache grew just below her breastbone, making it difficult to draw breath. It was her mother who had called her Cat and taught her that Mary Elizabeth Frances Catherine Ashdown was her own woman, no matter what the barony required of her.

"Every day. I could not have asked for a more loving,

joyful sister." Essie searched Cat's face again, for what exactly, Cat couldn't say. There was a sort of pride shining in Essie's eyes. "Go, then. Fight whatever battle you are fighting today."

"I will." Though she was afraid she was embarking on yet another crusade she could not win.

On the floor below, the door to the front hall opened. The ferocity of driving rain sounded briefly on the air before it closed again. Cat didn't need to look over the banister to the ground floor see who had come in. The butler's murmur of "welcome home, my lord" told her exactly who had arrived.

When footsteps began to ascend the staircase, Cat prepared to face the newcomer with a bland expression and polite smile.

It seemed the battle had come to her.

Chapter Three

"Uncle."

"Mary Elizabeth." Lord Wycomb's head and shoulders appeared first, then the rest of him dressed in the most elegant of coats. He paused when he reached the top of the steps, though his hand still rested on the banister.

"Might I have a moment of your time?" She gestured toward the nearest unoccupied room, which, to her dismay, was the ballroom.

Wycomb's dark brow rose. His hand fell away from the banister. "Only a moment. I have many demands on my time."

Clearly she had no demands, if his expression were correct. But she wasn't ready to start the confrontation yet, so she did not argue.

"Yes, of course," she murmured.

The letter from Mr. Sparks was still crumpled in her hand as she led Wycomb to the door. He let her enter first as propriety dictated, then stepped into the shadowed ballroom with no more sound than the sighing displacement of air.

It was quieter here, as the windows faced the rear garden rather than the street. Drawn curtains let in only filtered streams of light dimmed by rain and clouds, both of which seemed absent of the thunder that had rumbled just minutes ago.

"What is amiss now, Mary Elizabeth?" Wycomb tugged briefly at his left cuff, twitching it into place without bothering to meet her eyes.

"I have received news from Ashdown Abbey." She squeezed the letter tight in her fist and set it behind her back so he would not take it. "The trustees have decided not to provide the tenants with new roofs this year in favor of improvements to the mill."

He stilled, letting his cuff slip from his fingers. "I was not aware Mr. Sparks corresponded with you privately," Wycomb said softly, failing to comment on the roofs. His eyes flicked over her, as though there would be some mark upon her that screamed *corresponds with estate managers*.

"My father never neglected his duties." Did Wycomb think she would have no interest in her inheritance? "I will not either."

"It is not your duty, Mary Elizabeth." His head angled slightly so that the pale light from the windows slanted over sharp features and the few silvered strands at his temples. "The trustees make the decisions with my participation and, occasionally, guidance." He did not step forward, did not make any movement at all.

Somehow she felt as though he had.

She narrowed her eyes, refusing to give in to his subtle intimidation. "The trustees may make the decision, but *I* am the only Ashdown left, uncle. *I* am Baroness Worthington."

"Indeed, but your inheritance is not yours to control."

That did not mean she was not helpless.

"I met with the tenants last spring." She felt each rigid

point of the crumpled paper fisted in her hand, as though all of her body's sensation had centered to that single spot. "They were passed over then for the improvements to the smithy and the chapel. I promised them I would see their roofs were repaired this year. It is only a handful of cottages, and my fortune is more than—" She broke off, realizing that she was no longer certain what state her fortune was in. It was one of the hazards of having trustees. "It is not insignificant. I'm one of the wealthiest women in England. Surely there are sufficient funds for a few roofs."

Wycomb clasped his hands behind his back and strolled away to the window, his boots ringing quietly on the parquet floor.

He'd set his back to her. As though her concerns were of no importance.

Oh, she would not tolerate such indifference. She went after him.

"Surely, there is enough," Cat said again.

"Whether there are sufficient funds is not at issue." He did not turn around to face her, but set a hand to the curtain and pushed it aside. "What *is* at issue is that your trustees and your guardian have assessed the situation. We have decided."

"I made a promise." Cat dug in her heels, the letter in her hand nearly forgotten except that it gave her something to squeeze.

"Mary Elizabeth." Wycomb's words were soft. Very, very soft. A shiver ran up her spine. "You do not have the power to make any such promise to the tenants." Now he did look at her, turning his head and dropping the curtain. Cold blue eyes met hers.

Anger rolled through Cat at the statement. She let the heat of it swell, grow, and though she attempted to use her mother's training to ease it, she could not. The sting of his words remained, as sharp as any needle.

"No, I suppose I do not have such power," she said. There was no denying he was right, and it scraped at her.

"I don't expect you to understand these estate matters, but I assure you, the proper decision has been made." He turned to face her fully so that the white of his cravat shone in the dim light.

"And the goodwill of the tenants?"

"We don't need it. If they choose to leave, there will always be more tenants."

Cat sucked in a breath, ready to rail at him for such sentiment, but he again walked away. Simply walked across the room and set his fingers on the door handle.

"It is none of your affair, Mary Elizabeth. You need only concern yourself with navigating the Season to secure a husband. There are not many gentlemen worthy of your birthright. You would do well to entice them."

He was gone, through the door and into the hall, leaving her with no answer.

Someone cursed.

It was her.

Frustration was a hot, hard ball in her belly, one that did not ease as she made her way to her chambers. She resisted the urge to slam the bedroom door. Control required more willpower than temper, and if there was one trait she possessed, it was willpower.

Turning to face the room, she looked around the space. It had been hers since she was old enough to be out of the nursery. Someday, when she was married, she would sleep in the baroness's chamber below. For now, she'd chosen to stay here.

She moved instinctively to the dresser, her gaze focused on a slim glass bottle there. Painted pale blue, it was smooth against her palm when she picked it up. Removing the cork stopper, she inhaled deeply. The scent of violets calmed her.

Even the feel of the bottle against her skin soothed her.

Mother.

A lady has better weapons than a man, my darling. Subtlety wins more wars than brute force.

"I'll pay for the roofs myself," Cat said into the room, quiet now that the rain had tapered off and no longer tapped against the windows. Replacing the stopper, she went to the escritoire and pulled out a sheet of paper. "I made a promise."

Dear Mr. Sparks,
Please use my pin money to replace the tenants' roofs. There is a significant amount available in the same location my father held his personal funds. More will be available as the new quarter begins.
Respectfully Yrs,
Mary Elizabeth Frances Catherine Ashdown
Baroness Worthington

There. Mr. Sparks would see it done, as her father's will ensured he could not be removed from his position beyond illness or legal incompetence. The new roofs would anger the trustees, perhaps, when they found out, and her uncle as well. By then the work would be complete, or partially complete. There would be nothing they could do but deny her pin money—and that they could not. It was hers by the terms of her father's will, and it was more than she ever needed in a single quarter. Cat folded the letter into the proper shape. Lighting a candle, she set the end of the white wax she favored to the flame until it was soft. Pressing it against the paper, she closed the flaps. Quickly, before it cooled, she pressed her seal into it.

Her father's seal.

Fortitude. Courage. Generosity.

Generations of Ashdowns had lived by those words—and

she was the last one, which meant the duty was hers alone. If Wycomb discovered she was mailing the letter to Mr. Sparks, she would be failing in that duty.

Standing quickly, she went to the wardrobe for her pelisse. It was March in London, and the air would be damp and chilly after the rain. She started to pull the garment over her gown, then sighed heavily and rang for her maid. The girl would be horribly disappointed if Cat readied herself to walk to the Receiving House.

It was only a few moments before Eliza arrived, so there was little delay in her plans.

"Thank you for coming so quickly." Cat smiled at the young, round-cheeked girl she'd brought to London from Ashdown Abbey. "I have an errand, and have need of my pelisse and bonnet as well as a companion."

Eliza's eyes brightened as she bustled toward the garment Cat held out. "Of course, my lady. I would be honored. Shall I send round for a carriage?"

"No, I'd rather walk." Cat shrugged into the pelisse Eliza held out for her, then moved to the dressing table to sit on the cushioned stool. "There seems to be a break in the weather after days of rain, and I'd like to take advantage of it."

"I shall be ready in a trice, then, milady. Here, I think the bonnet with the blue ribbons would be best. It's nearly the same shade as your eyes and compliments your gown as well." Taking the bonnet from the shelf, she held it up for Cat's approval.

"Yes, I think that is a good choice." Cat smiled at the girl, though inwardly she wondered what difference it made. At a ball, where she was to meet her future husband, one was careful about accessories and color choice. She was only going to the small haberdashery she favored because it doubled as the closest Receiving House.

A lady didn't meet her husband at the Receiving House.

Chapter Four

There was nothing unusual about Worthington House, aside from the fact that it was on Park Lane in London. The very end of Park Lane and the poshest area, it seemed to Jones. He would have never dared to approach this place in his youth. Now here he was, strolling past Worthington House.

Life was a study in the unexpected.

As he examined the street, with its row of townhouses and neatly kept cobblestones, Jones mentally reviewed what he knew of his target.

Henry Taylor, Lord Wycomb. Senior spy, with others at his command. No legitimate issue, no bastards, one living sister, one deceased sister, one niece and ward, Mary Elizabeth Frances Catherine Ashdown, Baroness Worthington. His financial situation was as yet unknown, but Jones would be determining some of that information shortly and had sent ambassadors to ferret out the rest.

Jones knew it was the baroness who owned Worthington House. She was wealthy. Beyond wealthy. Even after the earldom had gone to a distant cousin, she still held the vast, multi-property barony and its more than 100,000 acres.

It was baffling to him that one person could own so much land. His space as a babe had been a blanket in a foundling hospital. As a boy, a corner in an alley. As a youth, a small bunk with other spies on the cusp of manhood. Now his space was one room in a townhouse owned by another spy.

Nothing like the vast Worthington House. The building was made of brick, as the other townhouses were. There were small balconies in some windows, which only made them easier to break into, and curtains at every one. It lacked the iron-fenced area and stairs down to the kitchen of the neighboring townhouses, but as it sat on a corner and took up twice the street as the townhouse on its left, he imagined the kitchen was on the intersecting street.

Shoving his hands into the pockets of his greatcoat, Jones resisted the urge to whistle idly as he approached the space where he would cross the front door. Whistling was never as unnoticeable as it seemed.

He glanced behind, quickly, to determine the length between streets and how many townhouses were between Worthington House and the next street, then back again to the building. His mind cataloged the building's facade. *Eight windows across, four floors and the attics. Double front doors. A short walk to the street. Standard casement windows with curtains—*

"*Oof.*" Whoever it was that hit him was soft and womanly, with hips that were nicely rounded. He knew, because he gripped the curves to steady them both.

"Oh my goodness, sir!" The woman stepped back, smiling that friendly, polite smile strangers gave one another.

His hands fell away from her body as though they'd been scorched. Even as an accident, he had no right to touch a lady, and every feature told him she was one. The faint scent of violets and vanilla and lily reinforced it, as no woman of the street would wear such perfume. Jones lowered his head and touched one still-burning hand to the brim of his hat in acknowledgment, assuming it would shade his face and she would move on.

She didn't.

"I do apologize, sir. I wasn't watching where I was walking, I was in such a hurry." She tipped her face up so that he seemed to be looking at her through the tunnel of her bonnet.

It occurred to him just how private a bonnet could be. In that moment, no one could see her eyes beneath the brim but him.

Blue.

Color was all he could understand. Blue eyes in a shade he'd never seen before. Brilliant and iridescent and bright and—no, he had seen a color like this.

Only once before.

Now he had to say *something*. She stood on the walkway emerging from the courtyard of Wycomb's house and was most likely his niece, the Baroness Worthington, a person who should not notice him, lest she compromise his mission. Yet saying nothing would only pique her interest. Turning the moment into something memorable would serve him no good.

"It is my fault, my lady. Good day." Tugging at the brim of his hat, Jones continued to stroll down the walkway as though he had not just passed his target's home—and his niece.

Later. He would conduct reconnaissance later. There was always time to observe, but only a few moments to escape.

Damn if he wasn't curious as to her purpose. Maybe it was the red hair that made her brave the dull gray skies, though the locks were just shy of flaming and more the warm, glowing shade of a banked fire.

All the more dangerous in his mind.

There was no telling what was happening beneath the surface of a banked fire.

"Interesting," Cat murmured, watching the man's broad back disappear around the corner of Park Lane onto Oxford Street. She couldn't say why he was intriguing, exactly, but the man had been both ordinary and extraordinary all at once, with eyes that saw only her and a jaw both rigid in bone and soft with light stubble. "I wonder who he was."

"Beg your pardon, my lady?" Eliza moved to Cat's side, gaze skimming over Cat and likely cataloging imagined bruises and scrapes. "Are you hurt?"

"Oh no. Not at all." A man with shoulders that appeared ready to bear any burden—but clad in the most ill-fitting greatcoat—was nothing of importance. There was no need to notice him, other than he had been polite.

And very hard and strong beneath his coat.

Cat set her hand on Eliza's shoulder and squeezed lightly in reassurance. "It was nothing. Let's be off, shall we?"

It wasn't far to the haberdashery, but somehow the walk seemed long. Cat looked down at the sealed letter in her hand, loosened her grip, and forced her shoulders to relax. She had a letter to deliver—an important one that would change the lives of her tenants.

The interior of the haberdashery was brighter than the sky outside, which had become a bit more ominous than before. Perhaps she had been premature in assuming there was a break in the weather. "I'll just be a moment, Eliza," Cat called to the maid waiting on the street before letting the door fall shut.

Cat paused to let her eyes adjust. Candlelight turned buttons and thimbles into twinkling stars and glowed on ribbons and lace and pretty, embroidered stockings. She smiled at the large clerk standing amidst the cacophony of women's frills. The man leaned on the countertop and focused happy brown eyes on her face.

"Hello, Mr. Roundman. I've a letter to post, please." She set the wrinkled letter, then the fee, onto the smooth wood counter separating them.

"The Bellman would've been by later or tomorrow, m'dear. Or your uncle would frank it, I'm sure." He scooped up the paper and coins, then turned away to complete the business.

"Yes, I'm certain he would, but I enjoy the exercise." She also didn't want her uncle to know what she was about. Still, she couldn't leave without buying something from one of her favorite shopkeepers, so she pointed to yards of lace draped over a cord stretched between two shelves. "May I have a length of that gorgeous lace as well?"

"Of course, milady!" Mr. Roundman measured and cut, his large hands surprisingly delicate on the intricate lace. "Do y'know, this is straight from the Beer lace ladies in Devon, and is the very best you can buy."

"Is it now? I wouldn't expect less from you, Mr. Roundman." Cat searched her mind for details of his life, then leaned against the counter just as he had done a moment before. "And how is Mrs. Roundman?"

"She's well enough." He turned away to wind the lace and called over his shoulder, "And the little ones, too." After he'd handed her the bundle, she smiled at him.

"Do say hello to Mrs. Roundman and the children."

"So I will, milady." He grinned, showing a blank space somewhere on the left. He'd had a tooth pulled since she'd last seen him.

"Thank you, Mr. Roundman. Now, I must return home. Good day." She nodded, waved, and pushed open the outer door. Only to find rain pelting the street and her maid nowhere to be seen.

Cat pressed her back against the stone building. Angling her head to keep the cold rain from her face, she searched the street. It seemed the deluge had caught everyone unawares, as those on foot were scurrying for shelter. Lightning flashed and thunder roared a moment after.

"Brilliant." Even if she had brought an umbrella, it would do no good in this storm.

Water began to seep through her pelisse and she shivered, then put her hand uselessly over her head to hold off the rain. She would have to go back into the haberdashery. Already her skirts were wet and her bonnet would be completely ruined. The street had emptied of foot traffic, so she spun on her heel to return to the shop to wait out the storm.

"Come wit' me, milady." The patter of hard rain nearly washed away the hoarse whisper and she almost missed the words.

But a knife streaked through the drops, shining dully inches from her face. It was quite noticeable, as was the patched clothing and worn cap of the ruffian.

She was being robbed in the middle of Oxford Street.

Chapter Five

Panic rose up, bright and hot, so that her heart clattered against her rib cage. Her gaze focused on the knife. It seemed alive, ready to strike. She fumbled with the drawstrings of her reticule as she tried to extract it from her wrist, but her gaze did not leave the knife.

She thrust the beaded bag at him. "Here, take my reticule."

He shook his head, and Cat saw nothing but a scruff of dark whiskers beneath the brim of a cap pulled low. "Come wit' me, milady."

"No, no. The money, it's all in the reticule." The knife was so close to her belly. She could not breathe. The blade was just there, only inches away. Rain beaded on the metal, drops swelling as large as her terror.

"'Tisn't the blunt I'm after," he rasped.

Wind gusted, lifting her skirts and whipping them around her ankles and calves. Thunder roared through the air again.

"Then what?" She cast about the street for a rescue, but the rain had become a horizontal assault. The street was empty save for a few carriages careening through mud and manure, occupants probably focused on returning home rather than an abduction on the street.

Where was her maid? Anyone?

"'Tis you I'm after," the ruffian said. Fingers gripped her upper arm hard, pressing into the flesh. He tried to push her forward, shoving his unwashed body against hers so they would move down the street.

She balked, instinctively pushing back.

But the knife.

The knife.

She felt it now, a slight pressure against her pelisse, but not a cut. There was too much fabric between it and her ribs. *For now.* Her mind reeled, terrified that such things could happen on Oxford Street. In daylight. But it was not daylight. The gray rain had forced an early twilight and she was alone. Which meant she could only rely on herself.

Cat let the man pull her forward by the wrist, let him think he had her cowed. Let him become complacent. Then—

"Bastard!" She drove her free fist into his jaw. Pain sang through her arm, mixing with rage and power.

He'd not expected it. She saw that in his shocked eyes clear enough. The man's head snapped back, revealing missing and blackened teeth beneath the whiskers and cap. She gasped as his knife went through the pelisse, just far enough to know she was lucky to be spared death.

Jerking away from him, Cat stumbled over her own skirts as she tried to run. Gentlemen down the street rushed from a carriage to a club to avoid the rain. She gathered her breath for a scream, but the ruffian's arms snagged her middle, pushing the air from her lungs before she could make a sound.

Suddenly *he* was there. The man she had bumped into on Park Lane.

His greatcoat swirled around him as he lashed out at her

captor. She stumbled as the ruffian freed her unexpectedly and she went down hard on her hands and knees. Even through her gloves, she felt the sting of the pavement on her palms. Struggling past her skirts, Cat staggered to her feet.

The man from Park Lane kicked out his foot in a fast arc. The ruffian had no chance against him—he was untrained and unskilled, that much was clear when he failed to even attempt to dodge. The foot of the man from Park Lane caught the ruffian mid jaw and he dropped to the walkway.

Cat had half a mind to assist in some way. She leaped forward with no definite plan—and stopped short when the man from Park Lane leaned down and grabbed the ruffian by the lapels, then jerked him to his feet.

"Who sent you?" The question was terrifying in its lack of emotion.

"No one!" The ruffian struggled, his hands gripping the fists of her savior.

"Don't lie." The man from Park Lane slammed the ruffian against the nearest wall. Once, twice. Held him there, feet dangling inches from the ground.

Cat flinched with each hit, but did not look away. She wanted to do the same.

"Don't matter," the man gasped, breath heaving as he looked up into the falling rain. "They aren't after her. She's just leverage, they said."

"What do they want?" her savior asked softly. Menacingly.

Cat stepped forward, pushing into the driving, whipping wind, unsure exactly what she was doing. But her would-be abductor shook his head and the man from Park Lane pulled him higher off the ground. The ruffian's feet scrabbled in the air, useless appendages against raw fury.

"They want the gov'nor to fall in line," the man gasped. "He's not delivering what he promised."

"What did he promise?" It was another question delivered

in a low, soft voice that gave Cat chills. Then it was drowned out by a crack of lightning and a roar of thunder.

"I dunno. But—well, they don't tell me."

"I see. You just do the work." Her savior stood unmoving, greatcoat swirling about him and still holding the man in the air. "Tell them she's not to be touched or they'll answer to me." With that, her savior dropped the man onto the walkway. The ruffian stumbled, recovered, and ran. In seconds, he was swallowed by the streaming gray rain.

"I don't understand." Cat's bonnet lifted in the wind, caught, and was ripped from her head. Rain pounded against her face, her body. She could barely see beyond the water clinging to her lashes and forcing her to blink. "Who are you? Who was he?"

"I'm Jones, my lady." The man set a respectful finger against his bare head in introduction, as his hat had fallen somewhere in the scuffle. Water plastered dark brown hair to his skull.

"I don't understand what he wanted." She shouted it above the howling wind. It nearly lifted her from her feet and pushed her straight toward the man called Jones. He caught her, arms going around her and folding her in.

"You." He looked down at her, eyes fixed on hers. The irises were brown—a deep, dark, rich brown, with no hint of green or gold. One of his arms fell away. The other ushered her toward the haberdashery, guiding her body with only a touch of his arm against her waist. She nearly turned into him, hoping for his arms to come back around her.

"I don't understand," she shouted again into the wind as he led her against the brick building. It was not shelter, precisely, but if she pressed herself close enough to the rough surface the rain seemed less inclined to pummel her.

And then he was there in front of her, blocking the rain so that it pounded on his back instead of on her. He leaned close, almost over her, the heavy fabric of his greatcoat cocooning her.

The cold water on her skin heated in the strangest way. The scent of man and rain surrounded her and she breathed deep, unable to help herself.

"I cannot guarantee they won't try again, my lady." He spoke so quietly, so intensely, it was almost to himself. If he had not been so close, if she had not seen his lips move, she would not have heard him above the wind and rain. But his eyes never left her face. "Do you know why he wanted to abduct you?"

"No." Unease rose and grew in her. She gripped his shoulders without any thought of the impropriety and felt his strength beneath the heavy greatcoat. "Do you? Tell me, what is happening?"

"I don't know." He shook his head and pulled away from her slightly. "Go back in the shop and get warm. Then go home. I'll follow and see he doesn't bother you on the way."

"My maid—I don't know where she has gone." Breathless, she only stared up into the dark eyes of the stranger who had become less of a stranger in these past minutes.

"Wait in the shop. She will find you, no doubt, when the storm is over."

With that the man, this Jones, left her. The rain began its relentless pounding again now that she was not protected by him. Cold pinpricks pelted her face and neck. He stood a few feet away, waiting, then he jerked his head toward the haberdashery.

"Oh. Yes." Her mind had gone blank. She'd heard his words, but the loss of his heat and protection had distracted her. Cat turned and ran into the shop, pulling open the door and tumbling inside. She glanced over her shoulder as the door fell closed behind her.

Jones was already gone.

"My lady!" Mr. Roundman exclaimed, drawing near and clucking over the state of her wetness.

Cat heard the shopkeeper's words, felt the drying cloth he placed around her shoulders. When her maid arrived later she was full of apologies. She had been at the window of a different shop and ducked in when the rain started. She hadn't come out until the rain slowed.

Cat barely heard her. Someone had tried to abduct her. *Why? And what should she do?*

Jones's words echoed in her mind.

I cannot guarantee they won't try again.

Chapter Six

Jones smoothed a hand over the worn pages of the first book he had ever purchased. He'd pored over the pages, examining every word, every brush stroke of the paintings. That mankind could learn something and share the knowledge through the printed word had been a marvel to a boy from the rookeries.

Even a marvel to a man who had scrimped and saved and gone to bed hungry to have enough money to buy something so frivolous as a book. But this naturalist's handbook contained a painting that had captivated him long ago. Two butterflies sharing the page, the one at the bottom had small, spotted brown wings—a sad little species compared to the brilliance glowing above.

Morpho helenor achillaena in Latin, or as he had first read it, *Lepidoptera I. Papiliones I. Nymphales VIII. Potamides C. Conspicuae d.*

He didn't know what any of those words meant, but he knew what he saw—an exotic butterfly native to the warmer climates. The color of its wings was just as he remembered, though it had been months, perhaps a year, since Jones had last looked at the page. Those wings were a dazzling blue he'd never seen anywhere in his life. Iridescent. Incandescent. Brilliant. Luminous.

None of those words did the color justice.

None of those words could accurately describe *her* eyes.

He had followed the baroness and the maid back to Worthington House, as promised. No one looked at them twice along the way, even though the baroness was wet and bedraggled.

She was beautiful even then, though she looked a proper mess.

Jones touched a fingertip to the stunning butterfly wing dancing across the page. He could only say that her eyes had been like this. So blue they sent a man's heart soaring and his knees to the ground.

Yet he had made a mistake.

She had seen his face twice now. The baroness knew what he looked like, had spoken to him. He had even defended her in the street. He would not be able to hide from her easily as he investigated Wycomb.

He supposed it did not matter now. She was already in danger. Whoever Wycomb was involved with—and whomever he had angered—knew of her.

She's just leverage. They want the gov'nor to fall in line.

For a moment in the street, Jones had thought to take her away with him, to protect her. His intervention would do nothing but alert Wycomb of the investigation.

Being among the bosom of the *ton* was probably the safest place for her, at least for now. The *ton*'s prying eyes could often be protection enough, and if she were in danger from Wycomb, he would have long ago attempted something. Still, it was time to take the next step. The gov'nor was involved in something right enough.

"Not *that* book again, Jones. Don't you think you've read

it enough?"

Jones stilled, his hand frozen over the wings of the butterfly. That was the voice of the only man who knew what the book meant to Jones.

"At least I read, Angel." He closed the book, setting his hand over the smooth leather cover for one more moment to regain his equilibrium before facing his mentor.

"I read, too. Quite a bit, in fact." The man facing him grinned smugly as he sat on the edge of the study desk. He crossed his legs and cocked his head, the leather thong holding his hair in a queue shifting against his back. "I read recently that a certain someone is on special assignment." Golden brows rose. "No details were provided."

"No." Jones stood, picking up the naturalist handbook to slide it back onto the bookshelves. If there was a slight pang in his chest because he had not been ready to close the cover over the blue butterfly, he was confident it didn't show in his movement. "And I can't tell you about it."

"Ah." Angel only grinned more broadly. "One of *those* assignments, then. I won't pry, but do have a care for your hide when you're hunting one of your own. British spies aren't stupid. More, Lilias would like you to join us for dinner in the coming weeks and I'd hate to tell her you died because you were spying on another spy."

"How is your lady?" Angel's wife seemed like a more prudent topic than his current assignment.

"She's well, as you would know if you visited more often." The Marquess of Angelstone's lips curved up in a wry grin. "Which she told me to tell you."

"Please convey my apologies. I've been busy." Guilt sat uncomfortably on his shoulders, so he rolled them to release the tension. "I'll try to visit soon."

"Oh, stuff it, Jones. We all know you're not one to sit down to a family dinner."

How could he when he didn't know what family was? "Still, I should—"

"Not be concerned." Angel waved Jones's future absence away with an elegant hand. "Lilias's confinement is drawing near and she was simply hoping for company other than my mother and sisters-in-law."

"I'll make time to see her, then." It was a jolt, remembering that the woman who fought on the fields of Waterloo was going to have a babe. He'd seen Lilias only a few times since she'd begun to swell with child and it was both awe-inspiring and terrifying.

"There's more, Jones." Angel's tawny eyes sobered, and the laughter faded from his voice. "I have to go to Italy, probably for a few weeks."

"An assignment?"

"Yes, there's an informant there who is in some trouble. With Lilias so near her time—" He broke off, breathed deep, then started again. "I know she'll be well. She has two months yet and she is healthy. My mother and sisters-in-law are there, and the physician and midwife will attend. But…" His voice trailed off as he straightened his shoulders. "Jones, I never really thought about what fatherhood meant, until I realized I might not come back from this mission. If I don't—"

"You will." Jones said it calmly, because if a spy doubted for even a moment that he would return home, then he never would.

"I know. But if I don't return, I need to know someone is watching out for Lilias and the child." Angel breathed deep and looked straight into Jones's eyes. "Will you?"

Something burst through him, something bright and powerful. Pride, though that seemed too pale a word. Perhaps it was gratitude, except he did not deserve such an honor. "The Earl of Langford would be better suited," Jones said, referring to another spy. A peer. A trusted friend.

"And I know Langford will take care of Lilias, too, but he also has his own family to protect. I want someone else—someone I trust implicitly—to watch over her while I'm gone and if…Well." Angel rubbed a hand over his jaw. "Will you?"

He asked as if Jones didn't owe every second of his life to the man. "Of course."

"Good." Angel looked down at gloved hands and spread his fingers wide. After a deep breath, he closed his fists again and looked up at Jones. "Good."

He seemed so vulnerable just then, in a way Jones had never seen even when Angel was falling in love with Lilias. It wasn't fear, precisely. Nor was it worry or sadness. It was a strange combination of all of it.

Which was why a spy should never fall in love.

"Truly, Angel, I'm sure Lilias could protect herself well enough." Jones decided he wanted a brandy to lighten the atmosphere and strode to the decanter. "She almost brought down a trained assassin, after all." He gestured to the golden liquid, then stopped.

He was offering Angel his own brandy.

Angel didn't hesitate, but simply nodded his acceptance. "She probably would have bested the bastard if it hadn't been raining and dark. More, she was wading through the Serpentine. At least she wasn't wearing skirts that day." Angel snorted and his scorn seemed to bring everything back to recognizable ground. "Well, if you do visit, she'll stop pestering me. She's unbearable with all this inactivity, and if you're not careful, you'll be her next project."

"Project?" Jones handed a snifter to Angel, who swirled it and sniffed before sipping.

"Every day it's something new. New drapes for the morning room, folding gowns for the baby, searching for the perfect set of tin soldiers our child won't be able to play with for years yet." Angel shrugged his shoulders and pushed away from the desk to study the shelves. "Lilias is bored now that the physician has restricted her activity and she can't ride or fence or—in her words—have any fun. By the way, where are my field glasses? These are all yours." Angel was frowning as he studied the sets lined up on the shelves.

Jones shifted uncomfortably, the muscles inside his belly and chest going tight. He'd made a decision he had no right to make, surely. "I put your pair upstairs. In your old—in your room."

"Oh good. I rather like that pair. I'll have to collect them before I leave." Angel tossed an easy smile over his shoulder that made the tight muscles inside Jones relax. "We both know I'll not be staying in this house for many more nights, Jones. I'll need to visit, but with Lilias and the babe—no. I'll not be here."

It was what Jones feared. Not the lack of a roof, as he could rent a room easily enough with his pay and the money he had diligently set aside. But this house, Angel's bachelor quarters, had been a mainstay in his life. It had been the only safe place for too many years.

"I can begin moving out my items tomorrow, my lord, if you intend to rent or sell soon." The very words drove a hole in Jones's heart, and he hoped it did not show on his chest.

"What are you talking about?" Angel spun his body around, his eyes wide, mouth turned down in a frown. "I'm not selling or renting this house."

"But if you're no longer staying here, then it's not needed. Training has moved to other locations." He supposed the house had outlived its usefulness.

"It has, but you're still living here, aren't you? I'm not selling it as long as you're willing to stay."

Pride roiled in Jones's chest. "You don't need to pay for me. I can find my own place."

"Why the hell would you? This house is ideal. The

locks, the training room, the weapons store." Angel spread his arms wide, as though by doing so he could gather up the entire house and all its contents. "You've lived here almost as long as I have, longer now that I've moved to my family's townhouse. It isn't my place any longer, Jones. It's yours. And we may still need it in the future."

"I can't pay for the upkeep," Jones said flatly. "My salary doesn't run to this kind of house, and I won't allow you to pay for it."

"The service will pay for it."

Hope could wound as much as drive fear into a man's heart, he decided, dropping into a chair. "What?"

"Sir Charles approved it months ago. The house is yours to use, Jones, as long as you're working with the service. After that, it reverts to me. But Sir Charles—well, let's just say he wants the spy hunting his spies to be happy."

He should not feel such relief and joy. It was only a house, one that didn't belong to him. But he could remember the night Angel had brought him here, and that he'd been warm, well-fed, and comfortable for the first time in his life.

"We should use it for more training, then." He leaned forward and set his elbows on his knees. He didn't want to have other people underfoot, along with all the emotional maintenance and bickering that required appeasing. But emptiness was a waste for a building such as this. "I've no experience in training, but we have space for it."

"Jones." Angel's voice held more command than Jones had heard this past year. "It's yours, for the foreseeable future. There may be training required at some point, but for now, the space is yours."

Jones looked at the shelves, at the instruments he'd laid out there. He thought of the training room and the hours he'd spent honing his skills, the room he'd slept in and made his own after his training was complete.

The townhouse was a gift, for however long it lasted.

"Take it, Jones."

It wasn't that simple. A man didn't accept gifts of this magnitude. But—

But.

"For now." Jones looked up into Angel's amber eyes and felt twin spires of gratitude and elation. Only Angel would know what this gift meant. "For now."

Chapter Seven

Cat set her palm on the handle of the study door, but did not turn it. She simply let her hand rest there a moment as she stared through the midnight gloom at the inlaid rectangular panels of the closed oak door.

She had heard what the ruffian in the street had said that afternoon. She was leverage so the "gov'nor " would fall in line.

There was only one man in her life who could be called gov'nor. With no father, no brother, there was only one person close enough to her, in theory, that she could be used to such advantage.

What was her uncle doing that a lowborn thug had been dispatched to keep him in line? In truth, she didn't care what happened to Wycomb—unless it touched her lands and her people. Her abduction would most definitely put Ashdown Abbey and all the rest at risk.

She turned the door handle without any conscious connection of brain to hand. Still, the handle moved, the door opened. Her decision was made.

Her father had commanded this room before his death, though Wycomb claimed it for his own when he'd moved into the townhouse, stating until there was a new lord, he would see all would be kept in order there. Coals burned in the grate beside the desk, banked beneath a thick layer of ash for the evening. The low, red glow and occasional lick of flame emitted enough light for her to recognize furniture, though it did not penetrate the shadows covering the dozens of shelves ringing the perimeter of the room.

She paused, letting her eyes adjust to the darkness and her bare feet warm themselves on the thick rug. It wasn't difficult to see her uncle's things scattered over her father's desk once she studied the play of firelight over wood and paper and glass. Correspondence, a pair of spectacles Wycomb rarely used but refused to discard, an inkwell and quill.

More important, somehow, the room was losing the scent of her childhood. It had once smelled of old leather and dust from ancient books, of horse and out-of-doors. All of the things her father had loved. Now the room smelled of her uncle's bay rum cologne and—she sniffed. No, it was not just her uncle she scented. Some semblance of out-of-doors and man remained, but it was something not quite her uncle, nor her father.

Perhaps because the room did not belong to either of them.

Sadness welled, but she pushed it away. She had a task to accomplish.

Cat moved to the sturdy desk, a great affair with heavily carved legs and a dark finish. Family legend said the desk belonged to the first Mary Elizabeth Frances Ashdown, but Cat did not believe it. Either way, her fingers curled around an elaborate brass handle and she drew out the top right drawer. She couldn't see the contents clearly, but she had no desire to light a candle and draw attention to herself. Reaching for the poker, she shifted aside the ashes in the fireplace behind the desk and stirred the logs to let off enough light to see by.

The drawer was filled with quills, paper, and various sundries. Nothing of any use. A snap and the drawer was closed again. She reached for the next one—then her hand jerked on the cold metal as a sound ricocheted through the silent house.

Footsteps in the hall. Hard and sharp, as if their maker were ready to poke holes in the parquet floor. She knew the beat of those steps. She also knew every squeak of wood and shift of the house, and precisely where her uncle walked in the hallway.

Panic streaked through her. *He was nearly to the door.*

Her gaze darted around the study, searching for the best location to hide. There were chairs and curtains, but none of these would be big enough.

The door pushed open, hinges silent and well-oiled.

There was no more time.

Cat dropped to her knees behind the desk, grateful the rug masked the thud. Hoping her uncle wouldn't sit at the desk and discover her with a swift kick, she scrambled into the nook between the massive drawers propping up each side of the desktop.

And came eye to eye with a man who had no business being beneath the desk.

Cat drew in a lungful of air to scream, but the man covered her mouth with his hand. An arm banded around her waist, drawing her forward in a rush of linen nightshift.

She could not breathe. The arm was too tight about her waist, the wide hand over her mouth. Fear clogged her lungs. She was pressed against the man, against a strong, hard side, and though coals in the fireplace shed enough light she could see, panic blinded her.

Her uncle's footsteps drew close, driving two holes of terror into her. Terror of Wycomb, and of the stranger.

Cat stared at the man beneath the desk.

Jones.

That was the single name her savior had given her.

Her mind wheeled and swooped and spun, trying to connect all the facts. The street, the ruffian, Jones—who was now here in her home—hiding.

Yet so was she.

Wycomb moved more loudly than usual, his feet shifting swiftly over rug, wood floor, then rug again as he crossed the room.

Trapped against Jones, Cat could only look at him. Her heart drummed against her rib cage, loud enough Jones would surely hear. She was practically on his lap, the structure of his coat pressing against her skin through the thin linen. His ungloved hand was still over her mouth—warm, but dry and strong. Also very male and foreign. She wriggled against the arm holding her in place and contemplated biting the hand covering her mouth.

He shook his head once, sharply, his message clear enough.

Don't move. Don't speak.

Wycomb's polished boots appeared in the opening beyond the desk. Tassels still slipping over the surface, the footwear planted themselves right in front of her. A clink sounded as a candle was set down on the desk above, throwing an additional glow to the space beneath the desk.

She should scream, loudly, but then Wycomb would know she was there. He would ask why she'd been in the room, why she was hiding beneath the desk.

With *him*. The stranger. Jones. The very man she had not immediately revealed.

She was doomed. It was too late; she could not explain her behavior.

Cat stared into Jones's eyes. They were dark, haunted by

the flickering shadows from the glowing coals nearby, and focused on her face. The rough pad of his thumb stroked once against her cheek, leaving a sensitive trail along her skin.

Strong brows rose in question.

Conscious of the *shoosh* of papers above, of the tassled Hessians crowding the opening, Cat nodded her head, slowly, so Jones would understand she would not scream. A moment passed, his hand still pressed against her mouth. Then it fell away, and with it a sense of warmth.

But he did not otherwise move. Her nightshift pooled around them, Wycomb's boots whispered against the carpet, and still, Jones did not move. He only looked at her, evaluated her.

Oh yes. Even in the semi-darkness, she could see he was thinking.

But so was she.

They were very close. His leg pressed against hers, an arm still circled her waist, hot on her skin with nothing between them but her nightshift. She could smell some combination of man and fresh air. It was drugging, that scent of his.

She jerked as a drawer above opened. The underside wood was pale and unfinished, nothing like the deep glossy brown of the rest of the desk.

Jones also studied the drawer, but she believed perhaps he was listening more than looking. His eyes were narrowed, his head tilted slightly to one side. He looked intelligent, and not the least bit like a thief. Nor did he look like the savior she'd thought him in the street, with the air of watchful danger that hung about him now.

The space beneath the desk seemed suddenly to be shrinking, even as the heat rose.

The drawer above slammed shut and Wycomb muttered a curse. "It must be here." Another drawer opened, this one to the right. Jones turned his head toward the drawer, held there, again cocked to one side. Listening. Then that drawer, too, slammed shut and Cat jumped. Jones set a hand on her arm, perhaps to steady her, perhaps to quiet her.

A small piece of paper dropped onto the coals in the fireplace just beyond the desk. Jones surged forward as though he intended to burst from their hiding place. His fingers tightened on her arm, pressing against her skin. But it was too late for whatever Jones wanted. Wycomb's hand came into view, the poker he held shoving the paper into the coals.

In seconds, there was nothing left but glowing ash.

Wycomb's Hessians disappeared, leaving only two oblong imprints in the thick rug. Cat let out a long, nearly silent breath as her uncle's footsteps faded across the room. Another moment and his boots sounded in the front hall, then a quiet opening and closing of the door leading to the street.

Wycomb had left the townhouse at nearly three in the morning. Which left her alone with Jones.

She twisted away, expecting him to tighten his grip. But his arm loosened, leaving behind nothing but quickly fading heat.

"Wait, please." His voice was pitched low and held neither command nor plea, but a confident steadiness that calmed her racing heart. "Only a few minutes, as he may return."

"We're simply to sit here under the desk?" she whispered.

"Yes." She couldn't decide if she should laugh at Jones for suggesting it, or herself for agreeing with him. They didn't want to be caught now.

It was also disconcerting to realize *she* had become *they*.

Jones was not an ally of her near-abductor or he would not have saved her. He was not an ally of Wycomb's, or he would not be hiding beneath the desk.

Which meant he was the closest thing to an ally she had.

"Well." Drawing in a deep breath, she murmured, "Hello again, Mr. Jones."

Chapter Eight

"My lady."

He looked at her upturned face, at the cheekbones highlighted by the glow of the coals. Authority and dignity angled her chin. *Lady* and *haute ton* were all but visible in the baroness's flawless skin. Her hair, though tied at the nape with a ribbon, was free to riot down her back.

He had been right. Banked flames.

"Why are you here? I am not so foolish as to believe in coincidence." Baroness Worthington whispered her question into the semi-darkness beneath the desk, accusation rather than fear edging her words.

"Neither am I." He raised his brows. "It is interesting to make your acquaintance again under these circumstances."

"Mm." The sound she made was combined irritation and disbelief, but she did not argue. She might not have revealed his presence to Wycomb, but she was also hiding.

Which begged the question, *why?*

As silence spread its quiet, waiting wings around them, Jones slid his gaze to the nearby fireplace. Delicate ash clung to burnt wood, lightly waving in the air as though some unseen breath moved it. Disappointment gathered beneath his breastbone, then faded away. The document was lost, and there was no benefit to dwelling on its contents. It was enough to know Wycomb would enter his study in the early hours of the morning to burn it.

"Are we finished under the desk? I would like to stand, please. My legs are aching." There was a dry humor to her words, and he wondered if she were amused by their situation. Certainly the two of them hiding beneath a desk, one after the other in order to avoid discovery, would be comical to witness.

"It's probably safe." Etiquette warred with protection in his mind, as he debated allowing her to leave the cubbyhole in advance as a lady should, or leaving before to ensure her safety.

She did not wait for his direction. She solved the dilemma by shifting to her hands and knees amid the swish of linen.

"This is so odd," the baroness muttered as she crawled from beneath the desk. Her nightshift caught beneath her knees and she wrestled to free the fabric. He was treated to the most delightful pulling and stretching of thin linen over her bottom. "It's also embarrassing," she finished.

"I'm finding the view enjoyable." The words fell from his lips before he could stop them. It was the most ungentlemanly comment he could make. Surely she would see, with a single statement, that he was nothing but a boy from the streets.

"I beg your pardon?" On her hands and knees, the baroness turned to look over her shoulder at him. She narrowed her eyes, but did not move. That lovely bottom stayed in front of him. Taunting him.

"My apologies, my lady."

She scooted out from beneath the desk, movements quick and sharp.

"My words were inexcusable." He did not look anywhere but into her eyes as he crawled from beneath the desk, refusing to allow his gaze to stray to any other part of her anatomy.

He hoped it would put her at ease and make him feel less like a clod.

"It was." But she did not sound panicked or prudish, only drew in a long breath and let it out again. "You should not say such things."

"No, my lady."

But time mattered, so he unfolded himself to his full standing height, leaving her sitting on the study floor and looking up at him. She hesitated, then began to struggle to her feet.

"Please, allow me." He spoke softly, holding out a hand and hoping she would not be so disappointed by his lack of finesse as to refuse his offer of assistance.

She stared at his hand with an expression he could not read. He looked down, expecting to see something frightening or strange attached to him, but he saw only his hand, gloveless to ease his search. It was not smooth or elegant as a man of her station's would be, but wide, with blunt fingers and calluses.

Still, she set her hand in his and let him assist her to stand. Soft and smooth skin moved against his hand with none of the roughness marking his own flesh. He wondered if she could feel his base birth through his very skin.

Then she was standing and he let go of her hand.

"Does your uncle often burn items in the fireplace?"

"No. Yes." A long, heavy sigh filled the space between them. "I can't be certain. Why is it important?"

"Mm." He squinted at the fireplace and saw that a corner of the paper Wycomb had dropped into it had fallen well outside the coals. There would likely be nothing of note on such a scrap, but he could not ignore it. He bent over the coals, searching between flame and shadows.

From behind him, he heard a soft voice full of command. "I have waited quite long enough for an explanation, Mr. Jones, considering our previous encounters."

"There is no need to call me Mr. Jones. Just Jones will be acceptable."

"Very well, Jones, I would like the truth." She sounded more suspicious than she had before, but she bent over as well so they stared at the fireplace in tandem.

He turned only once from his task to study the curve of her cheek and the long, slim line of her neck as she looked into the fireplace. Setting aside any thought of how the light glowed on her skin, he went back to his task. Reaching toward the edge of the hearth, he retrieved what was left of the document and studied the charred edge.

She peered at the small scrap in his hand. "What does it say?"

"Nothing. It is blank." Jones slipped the fragile paper into his pocket to examine carefully later. He looked down into her pretty face, at the arched brows and serious mouth. "What now, my lady?"

She did not move but stood before him, face drawn and concerned, body taut with worry. "I don't know."

"Neither do I."

When she inhaled and straightened, he did the same. They simply stared at each other, with nothing but the hiss of coals and sound of breathing between them.

Finally, the baroness said softly, "You aren't a very good thief."

"Apparently not." A smile tugged at his lips, though he chose not to free it. "Neither are you. I wasn't the only person caught."

"True, I suppose." The baroness shifted uncomfortably, drawing her shoulders in. He imagined the creamy skin over her cheekbones would be beautifully flushed. "It cannot be coincidence that you are on Park Lane, then again on the street to rescue me, and now here in my home. I know my uncle, Lord Wycomb, is involved in something dishonest—or at least suspicious—or I would not have been almost abducted. But leaving me with no information places me at risk. I cannot allow that."

It was possible she was an ally of her uncle's, or perhaps a pawn. Perhaps she was innocent. Circumspection, then.

"I'm looking for information about your uncle's activity." He cocked his head and gestured to the desk, with its drawers she had searched not long before. "Much like yourself, I believe."

"'Information' sounds ominous." Curiosity rang in her tone along with a certain satisfaction, as though her own thoughts were proved correct. But there was no surprise on her face or in her voice. "What kind of information?"

"About your uncle. I believe he may be"—Jones paused, searching for words that would not overly alarm her, nor provide too many details—"experiencing some difficulties. I would like to know what they are."

"Why?" The baroness breathed in slowly, then out again. Her nightshift swirled about her ankles so that it came alive in the half light.

"I work for a group of gentlemen who have an interest in determining whether your uncle is acting within the confines of the law." He chose his words carefully. "Though occasionally unorthodox, they are within the confines of the law themselves so there is nothing to fear from them."

"Hm." Her eyes narrowed, displeasure at his answer clear on her face.

"What were you doing in here?" he asked, flicking his gaze toward the desk. "What were you searching for?"

"I don't know. Something. Anything that might indicate what he was doing and if the barony is at risk." She let out a frustrated sound, then gestured toward the fire, then the drawers. "I have a feeling you are better at this than I. Don't let me stop you."

He paused, considered her words. "Well played, my lady," he said softly. He could not force her to leave while he concluded his search, and if he left now she would certainly continue hers and might find evidence he needed.

"I rather thought so." The smile she flashed was satisfied and well pleased.

There was little left for him to search in any case. He had been nearly through the desk when the baroness had stepped into the study. All that was left were secret partitions.

Jones tugged at his sleeves, pulling up the cuffs before beginning a methodical search of the last drawer Wycomb had opened. It was difficult to pretend the baroness was not standing only a few steps away, watching carefully with eyes the color of a tropical butterfly. Still, training won out over the hum beneath his skin and he ran his fingers across the inside of each drawer, searching for a spring or lever.

"Are you looking for a hidden compartment?"

Jones spared a moment to admire her quick mind. She was most definitely not a fool. "Yes, but I believe Wycomb just emptied any such space."

"Hm." A quick glance revealed she was studying his every movement. But she also seemed to be thinking carefully. "If we are both looking for information regarding my uncle, perhaps we should join forces."

His fingers stilled in their path across the underside of the desk, then resumed with renewed speed. "No." His mind was also moving with renewed speed.

"I want to know whatever you know."

"That is not possible. What I know is only suitable for my superiors."

"Superiors." She held herself still and though her face did

not change expression, he knew her mind was spinning and whirring. Finally, after a moment of intense thought, her lips curved up in a sly smile. "And what *I* know?"

"You?" He paused, fingers hovering over the tiny spring he knew would open the space Wycomb had already emptied. She had a point, he decided, moving again to locate the spring and press it lightly. Satisfaction welled in him as a small panel opened along the front of the drawer. It had taken longer than he'd expected to find it, but Wycomb had been a spy for as many years as Jones had been alive.

The baroness gasped and bent over to peer closely at the drawer. She brought with her the delicate scent of violets and vanilla, and he leaned closer to bring it into his lungs and his memory.

Her hand slid over wood, bumping against his lightly. She paused, fingers resting on his own. Holding. She looked at him quickly, lips parted. "My apologies," she murmured, her gaze not leaving his.

"It is nothing." But her touch was much more. Soft, stirring.

Long fingers slid away again as she searched the drawer.

"It's empty," she said after a moment, her mouth turning down in disappointment. "It seems you were correct. My uncle has removed everything."

Jones stayed silent as he slid the panel closed again and shut the drawer. A space recently relieved of its secrets still contained knowledge. In short, Wycomb had a secret worth keeping, much as he had a document worth burning.

She must have realized that fact as well, as her body straightened and quivered as though she were a plucked bow.

"I want to know what he is doing," she said sharply.

Chapter Nine

She had believed Wycomb was involved with unsavory creditors or a business arrangement that soured, predicaments solved by money and time. But this no longer appeared to be true. There was more, much more, or Jones would not be searching the room on behalf of his "superiors" and Wycomb would not be hiding documents behind a secret panel.

Gripping the edge of the desk, Cat let fear and panic run their course, the emotions solidifying inside to form a ball in her stomach. When it had hardened, when she could control both, she looked back at Jones.

A stranger. Handsome with his lean features and sharp cheekbones, even with the serious expression he always seemed to wear. She could not trust him, but her options were limited at the moment.

"Am I in danger?" she asked, letting the darkness quiet the words. "Real danger?"

"I do not know, my lady. Not for certain." He shoved his hands into his breeches pockets, and though she heard regret in his voice, she did not see it in his broad shoulders or resolute face. "I've already taken some measures to protect you."

"Measures?" The word felt comforting, but not enough. Not nearly enough.

"A watch." Jones paused, looking around the study at the combination of her uncle's and father's possessions. "When you leave this house, I or one of my watch will follow."

"Your watch." Not a guard, but a *watch*. It was not a guarantee of any protection. "What of my uncle?"

"If you were in danger from Wycomb, my lady, he would have struck earlier." His face was very grim, the full lips turned down and brows angling in. "I doubt there is concern from that quarter at present."

He sounded as though he were attempting to convince himself as much as her. In the end, though, they both knew there was no protection from her guardian inside the walls of Worthington House.

"And the men he has dealings with?" That was the crux of it, wasn't it? Where and when would she be safe? "The one who abducted me on the street?"

"I don't know."

"I could leave." Whirling away, Cat stalked the shadowed corners of the room. She needed the privacy those shadows would afford her, if only to mask the burgeoning terror in her. "I could hide. I own hundreds of acres with cottages and villages. I could go anywhere in the world."

"You *could* hide." He didn't disagree and his voice held no reproach. Nor did he admit doing so might alert her uncle, though she guessed he understood that as well as she.

She felt the censure nonetheless—not from Jones, but from herself. She could not run. Doing so might protect her life in the short term, but it would not protect her lands or people, nor would it end whatever was happening here. And of course, Wycomb had every right as her guardian to force her to return, should he find her.

Staying was the only choice she could make.

"I have no method of defense, Jones. Even if I should take to carrying a knife or a pocket pistol in my reticule, I have no experience using them." She turned to face him as she came to terms with that. When she could be certain her shoulders would be straight and her chin could be lifted, she did so and looked through the gloom toward Jones. "But I am not defenseless. I have my own weapons. My eyes and ears, my knowledge of his habits and access to his life within these walls."

Jones was silent as he leaned over to stir the coals again. Something caught and flared in the fireplace so that the room began to glow more brightly. When he stood, the light gilded wide shoulders and a strong jaw. He still did not speak, but only watched her, waiting for her to finish.

"Jones." Cat said it decisively, knowing that if she made this pledge, she would have to stand by it. "I will give you any information I can learn or discover in exchange for what you know."

"No." The word did not come out of his mouth harshly, but she flinched nonetheless. "I cannot make that bargain, my lady, nor will I lie to you about it."

Her inhale was very, very controlled. She restrained any impulse to blurt out an answer, choosing her response carefully. "What is your offer, then, Jones? Because I will not provide what I know without reciprocation."

"I will tell you as much as I can."

"That is not good enough. Not nearly good enough." The moment hung suspended in time, their gazes piercing the pale light to meet.

"I will give you the information that will keep you safe, and more where I am able." He pushed away from the desk to stand straight again. "I will not do anything to subject you to danger, and I will protect you with my life if need be."

Cat could not think of more to ask from him, nor could she accept such statements as false, as this man had shielded her once already.

Would it be enough?

"I appreciate that you did not lie or make a promise you did not intend to keep." That would have to hold her, she supposed. "But I have much to protect. I will not leave my lands, my title, and my people in jeopardy."

"And yourself?"

"Protecting my life is what will protect the rest." She ran a finger along the edge of the drawer with the secret compartment. "How will I contact you, Jones?"

"You cannot. You will have to wait for me to find you."

"When?"

"As often and as safely as I can."

It did not seem like enough, but she chose to accept it for now. It was too late, too unsafe, to continue here. She took a step backward toward the door, her nightshift billowing around her, and she suddenly realized she had been wearing next to nothing during their exchange. The very idea heated her skin in an oddly delicious way. "I suppose I should say good night."

"I suppose so." He smiled, his lips tipping in a way that was intimate and amused all at once. "I bid you farewell, my lady." He bowed, quick and efficient, without flourish despite his flowery words, then turned toward the windows.

When he twisted the lock and pushed open the casement window, Cat realized what he must be doing.

"Lock the window behind me," he said, before slipping over the sill into the darkness beyond and lowering himself a few inches.

Cat strode toward the opening and looked out. His face, pale in the light of the slivered moon, seemed to hang suspended in the night. Squinting into the darkness, she saw his fingers scrabble along the brick and stone, his boots wedged against the lip at the top of the window of the floor below. She curled her fingers around the edge of the windowsill.

"You are three levels above the ground!" she whispered as he began to scale the side of the building.

"Lock the window behind me."

As she watched, heart in her throat, he pressed himself against the brick. A moment passed, then another. He seemed to draw from some well of quiet stillness before he moved his feet again and began a steady descent.

"Good night." Her whisper floated into the darkness.

She wondered if he could hear her.

Chapter Ten

"Thank you very much for the dance, my lord." Cat sent her partner a warm smile and relinquished his arm as they reached the edge of the dance floor. She tried hard not to look over her shoulder for Wycomb. Observing without being observed was more difficult than she'd expected. "It was a lovely idea for the countess to host this impromptu ball."

Her partner, a fourth son who—however nice—would not be a proper choice as husband for the Baroness Worthington, bowed and looked at her with hopeful calf's eyes. "I'm grateful I had a chance to dance with you, my lady."

Perhaps coming from a dashing rake of the *ton*, the words would have had a different meaning. From this agreeable, eager fourth son, they were simply sweet.

"Very kind of you." Cat inclined her head, quite aware that if she showed him particular attention the gossips might make too much of it. "I must return to my guardian, however, as I believe we shall be leaving shortly."

"Of course. Please, may I escort you?" He offered his elbow, which she was honor bound to accept and did so with a pleasant smile.

"Thank you." She glanced around the room, gaze flitting over the dispersing dancers and the milling guests. It was ridiculous to be watching for Jones or the ruffian from the street. Neither would appear. But it was not amiss to watch Wycomb. There was surely no danger lurking here in the ballroom, but she did not intend to ignore him.

"Is something the matter, Baroness Worthington?" The fourth son angled his head and she felt the arm tucked beneath hers stiffen. "Your, ah, grip indicates there may be a problem."

"No, of course not. My apologies." She loosened her fingers and waved her other hand toward Wycomb, the painted fan she carried bumping lightly against her wrist. "My guardian is just there, deep in conversation, as per usual. Thank you for your company and the dance," Cat said to her escort, who took his leave with a nod of his head and a nervous flick of his gaze toward Wycomb.

Her uncle seemed particularly absorbed on this occasion. Dark brows angled fiercely down as he leaned toward his companion, a nice enough looking gentleman with clever green eyes and a face much younger than Wycomb's.

"Hello, uncle," she murmured as she stepped beside him and into a pause in the conversation. "It was a most lovely country dance, and my partner was superb."

Wycomb did not look at her at first, but held himself still enough to impart displeasure. She heard his long, slow inhale of irritation. Then he shifted his shoulders and tilted his head just slightly to the left, as though he'd heard her but did not want to acknowledge her. It was a stance she had seen more than once, but she refused to be considered a nuisance and stayed her course.

With a twist of her wrist, Cat grabbed her dangling fan and flicked it open. Deliberately, she smiled at her uncle's companion. "Have you tried the punch yet? It's quite delicious."

There would be no choice now but for Wycomb to introduce her. She nearly smiled at her uncle, but decided it would be baiting a predator. Still, a lady could always employ her social weapons.

"Baroness Worthington," Wycomb said smoothly, though she heard the underlying impatience beneath the proper introduction. "May I present the Marquess of Hedgewood?"

"A pleasure to meet you, my lady." The marquess smiled and bowed, his eyes as amused as the lips that curved up as he spoke. "My apologies, we were discussing business. But there is surely no business so important as to forget your loveliness."

She nearly laughed at the platitude, but it was so typical of these gatherings she easily dismissed it. Cat extended her hand and let the marquess bow over it. "Lord Hedgewood."

"I've not had the pleasure of trying the punch, but I shall make certain I do. I believe there are additional beverages to be had. Anything I should try, particularly?" He cocked his head, seemingly prepared to consider her answer. His eyes were still twinkling at her and she wondered if they shared a joke Wycomb wasn't part of. It certainly seemed so.

She pursed her lips. He was rather charming, this marquess. "I would suggest the pink champagne, but stay away from the lemonade. It's ghastly."

"Wise advice, then. Lord Wycomb, let's postpone our business and take advantage of the social whirl. Good evening, my lady." He bowed once more in that short, half-amused way men did when they took their leave, as though they expected the lady to stay their departure. Cat did not, and he turned into the crowd and faded away between bright gowns and somber jackets.

"The Marquess of Hedgewood would be a good candidate

for your husband, Mary Elizabeth." Wycomb nodded politely at a passing acquaintance while he spoke and did not look at her. "You would be wise to curry his favor, as he is looking for a bride."

Unease slid over her skin as quietly as a cool breeze. "Lord Hedgewood?"

"He has all the necessary attributes. Old blood, wealth, property. His family is not as old as your own, but it is quite as good as you will get."

She was not interested, not even the least bit, despite how charming the marquess was. Cat also knew better than to outright disagree. "I shall take your recommendation under advisement, uncle."

"You would do well to accept it as more than a recommendation." Wycomb turned his head to look down at her with a gaze that did not pierce her skin, but felt as though it had. Blue and cold, his eyes ranged over features tight with control. "You must marry, and soon. There is more at stake than even your considerable fortune."

Unease gave way to discomfort, the air that had been cool on her skin turning into a chill rippling up her spine.

"I don't understand." Her hand tightened on the thin wooden handle of the painted fan, and she wondered if a soldier did the same on the hilt of his sword as he went into battle.

"Nor do you need to." Wycomb angled his head and gestured to the ballroom at large, pulling every giggling female and smooth politician and charming rake into their conversation. "I have made an extensive study of those unmarried peers with wealth and lands to match your own, as well as those who will be entering society in the next few years."

"The next few—" She choked on the words. Did he think she would marry an untested boy, simply to secure her fortune?

"You cannot wait until you are thirty-five to break the trust, Mary Elizabeth." He looked away again, leaving her with only his profile as a method of determining what he was thinking. "There is too much uncertainty. Too much could go wrong. If you die without an heir..." He let the words trail off, and she knew it was because he assumed that blow would strike her the hardest.

So it did. If she did not have an heir, the barony and all that it held would pass out of the Ashdown bloodline to a branch so far removed there was no Ashdown blood left. In short, it would follow the way of the earldom her father had held and which could not pass to her.

"I realize I must provide an heir." She'd known and resented it all of her life. She wanted to huff out a breath in frustration, so she inhaled and held it instead. "I don't intend to create an heir with just anyone simply so I can secure the title. I have centuries of history to think about, both before and after my lifetime, uncle."

"Which may not last as long as you believe, my girl," he said softly. His hands did not touch her, but she felt imprisoned all the same. "Consider his suit," Wycomb continued, gaze as piercing as if the cold blue had become spears. "If not him, I shall find another man for you. But consider his suit, Mary Elizabeth, to secure the future."

"I suppose life is fragile," she said carefully. Fighting the urge to swallow hard, Cat looked out over the laughing *ton* swirling around the ballroom amongst candles and sweet flowers. Perhaps the flowers were so strong they could not scent danger or fear. "Illness could strike at any moment, I know. But I'm in good health."

"Life is still fragile, as you said." Now he did touch her, setting his hand on her shoulder. His fingers did not vise over flesh and bone, but were soft. Yet they were no less menacing for it. More, perhaps, because he could hurt her if he chose. "Accidents happen more often than you think. A wrong step, and such an unfortunate event could happen to you."

His voice barely carried to her beneath the strains of the violins and chatter of the guests.

The threat still echoed beneath the words.

The chill in her spine became fear, then fear became terror as she looked into very cold, steady eyes showing not a shred of compassion, nor even humanity. *What had he become?*

This was wrong. All wrong. An heiress did not secure a husband by threat, and no uncle threatened his niece with…she could barely think it. She would have thought it a misunderstanding.

Except this man was so much worse than she'd expected.

"Good night, Mary Elizabeth." He bowed, a proper and elegant movement, then smiled slowly. "Do enjoy the rest of your evening, my dear. I have some people I need to speak to, but please let me know when you are in need of an escort home and I shall oblige."

He stepped away from her as a pair of breathless young ladies ambushed Cat from either side.

"Oh, my lady, isn't it all exciting?" One chirped, her fan fluttering near her flushed face.

"So many interesting persons this evening!" The other followed suit, her eyes sweeping across the room.

Cat looked to either side at the vapid girls fluttering about her. She was trapped in the ballroom, gooseflesh prickling her arms and fear thrumming beneath her skin.

There was no escape.

When she left this room, she would take the fear with her.

Chapter Eleven

"Your report, Jones?" Sir Charles's command was delivered from the center of Angel's study—now Jones's study—rather than an official building on Crown Street.

"Sir." Jones glanced once at the chair behind the desk. It was his seat, his study, even his townhouse now that Angel had given it to him and the service was paying for it. Perhaps Sir Charles expected him to take the chair, as Angel would have done even with his commander present.

Jones stood in front of the desk.

"As we suspected, Wycomb must be driven in part by a need for funds." He smoothed the grubby paper he'd jotted his notes on. It had already been used once on the opposite side so he could save a few pence. "I was able to obtain information on his finances from the bank housing his accounts—"

"Indeed?" Sir Charles said dryly. He swung his greatcoat off and laid it over the back of a winged armchair. The sword cane he favored already leaned against the upholstery. There was a time Jones would have manned the door and acted as butler for such outerwear, but now he lived alone—and Sir Charles chose to forgo ceremony.

"It is not difficult to enter a bank to review the ledgers, if one is of a mind to do so." Jones held back the amused smile threatening to curve his lips. He'd had the skill as a boy and had honed it, along with the ability to know exactly how much missing gold would send up an alarm. Only now, as a grown man, he didn't abscond with money, but information.

Not that the money didn't call to him on occasion, but he had set that boy aside many years ago.

His hands twitched on the paper, as though their flesh recalled long ago thefts in forgotten rookeries, when he craved money nearly as much as he craved food. The only difference between the two was that one could buy the other.

"I truly don't want to know how you do it," Sir Charles murmured. He held out his hand and Jones set the paper into it. Sir Charles tipped it toward the window to read it. The document was little more than a mass of wrinkles in the streams of spring sunlight.

"No, sir." He had methods that might not be considered conventional, but they suited him. He squinted at the simple script marching across the mangled paper, but recalled the information easily without reading his notes. "Wycomb was in debt. Significantly deep in debt, in fact, just a year ago."

"And now?" Sir Charles ran his fingers down a column of numbers, paused, then let out a long sigh. "That is quite an increase in only a year."

"Yes, sir, and without a clear direction of where the funds originated from. His few properties were heavily mortgaged and he'd lost significant income in the markets." Jones shook his head and paced away from the desk, running his fingers absently along the bookshelves. He'd read everything in this room, marveled that one man could have so many books—and that Angel would share them with an ignorant boy.

"I don't know what other expenses Wycomb has, but his accounts have been bleeding pounds for the past few years. And as we know, spying provides little true income."

Sir Charles slid a gaze toward Jones, speculative brows raised, as he set the paper on the desktop. "Are you asking for additional funds, Jones?"

"No, sir." He fumbled with his coat, tugging it more securely into place as he straightened his shoulders. He knew exactly how fortunate he was to receive his salary. "Only noting that Wycomb was in debt, and espionage would not provide the income he needed to dig himself out of that deep a pit. He was close to losing his modest family estate. He was never wealthy, his family has been living on credit for generations, as they are simply a branch of a larger family and are connected to the Baroness Worthington and the Ashdowns by marriage." Jones set his hand on the scrap of paper.

He scrubbed his thumb over the digits. They were only numbers, of course, yet numbers translated to acres and houses and farmland. To tenants and servants and others who depended on the lord. More, those numbers, acres, and tenants belonged to *her*. "I also found out—with a few discreet inquiries of his stable boys—that his tenants on his small estate have been leaving for years. As his financial condition worsened, they've begun departing in droves. They claim mistreatment."

"Hm." Sir Charles set his hands behind his back, rocked his barrel-shaped body back onto his heels. Jones guessed they were both remembering the Flower and Wycomb's mistreatment of her. "The Baroness Worthington? His ward?"

The sharp snap of wood and flames ricocheted around the room as logs in the fireplace broke apart. Sparks flew, and Jones looked toward the fireplace, somehow expecting the baroness to be there.

"I believe she knows nothing of the details," he said finally, looking at the dancing fire and thinking of the baroness's hair. "Wycomb has not asked her for funds because she does not control them—or at least, that is how it appears. Her inheritance is in trust and what income she regularly receives quarterly would not have been enough to settle his debts, though she does receive a significant amount."

"He would have had to approach the trustees, then." Sir Charles walked toward the fireplace himself. Picking up a poker, he adjusted the logs so recently broken apart. The sides of his mouth turned down in a hard frown. "I wonder if that is where the income originated."

"I don't know. Yet." But he could find out. "Someone paid his debts, sir. Once those were paid, Wycomb began to grow his wealth. He is flush."

"Which means we risk his escape."

There was no need to respond to the truth.

"I've set the Gents to keep watch on him." Jones folded his notes into a small, neat square as he contemplated his answer. Slipping the paper into this pocket, he knew he would be retrieving it later. Wycomb wasn't the only spy who enjoyed a good fire late at night.

"The Gents?" Sir Charles pursed his lips. "Good. He's not aware of them, to my knowledge, though I can't imagine he would notice those ragamuffins if they stood in front of him."

"Likely not. Also, I don't believe bringing in other agents, even on a limited basis, would be beneficial. I don't know of any who might be working with him outside of their assigned capacities, but it is a risk I'm not ready to take."

"Agreed." Sir Charles prodded the wood again, the movement idly contemplative rather than managing the fire.

"Finally—" How to admit to his commander he'd been caught by the baroness? "Sir, there was an incident with Baroness Worthington. A series of incidents, in fact."

Sir Charles carefully settled the poker into its resting place before turning to face Jones. "A series of incidents." There was no question in the tone, only a demand for explanation.

"As I was engaging in reconnaissance, I followed Baroness Worthington to Bond Street. She was nearly abducted."

"By whom?" he asked sharply.

"A hired lackey. He said it was to force the 'gov'nor' to fall in line and deliver what he'd promised."

His commander was silent for a long, long moment. Then he softly asked, "How do you know this?"

Now for the difficult moment. "I had no choice but to act, sir. I could not allow a woman—a lady—to be abducted by a criminal."

"No. You would not." Sir Charles strode toward a wingback chair, picking up the greatcoat draped over the muted leather back. "But you have also revealed yourself to Baroness Worthington as well as Wycomb's enemy."

Jones did not speak. There was nothing to say.

"And Baroness Worthington?" his commander asked. "How did she respond?"

"Shock, as you might imagine, but she recovered well. She punched him."

"What?"

"Punched him, right in the face." Why that amused him, Jones couldn't say. "The lackey never saw it coming."

"Isn't that interesting." The corners of Sir Charles's mouth quirked up. "The second incident?"

"I was discovered by Baroness Worthington while searching Wycomb's office." Failure tasted sour on his tongue and burned in his belly. Yet he could not have prevented it from occurring.

Nor was he certain he would have, if he could.

"Discovered." The many capes of Sir Charles's greatcoat slipped over the chair back as its owner deliberately, slowly, set it back down. "This is no small incident, Jones. She could compromise the entire investigation. This entire office," he said softly.

Sir Charles was right—and worse, he did not yet know of the bargain Jones had struck with the baroness. Jones squared his shoulders, ready to accept both blame and responsibility.

"Sir, she was searching the office herself, looking for evidence of what Wycomb is doing. I had been doing the same. Wycomb entered the office and she discovered my hiding place. I—" He broke off when Sir Charles's hands gripped the back of the chair, fingers turning white.

"I beg your pardon?" his commander bit out. "Wycomb nearly discovered you both?"

"I have provided her with as little information as possible, and she has agreed to assist in the investigation." It was not an answer to Sir Charles's question, but there was no answer that could explain the circumstances. Mentally flailing for purchase on the slippery slope leading to discipline, he squared his shoulders. "I believe she will be an asset."

"Assuming she doesn't reveal herself to Wycomb." Cool brown eyes remained level as Sir Charles released his hold on the chair. With that same stare, he raised a brow and said, "Tell me how you intend for the baroness to assist you?"

A steady voice. A respectful gaze. His mind knew what was required, no matter the layer of panic spreading through him. A single misstep and his career would be ended—and he had nowhere to go but back into the rookeries.

"I don't have access to the *ton*, sir." The breath Jones drew in was deep and calmed the fear slicking a layer of sweat on his forehead. "The baroness does."

"And Angel? Or another spy, such as the Shadow? They are both in that world, Jones, though the Shadow has primarily chosen inactive status." One hand settled on the arm of the chair, large, blunt fingers tapping lightly against the leather.

"She has access to the household, in the open, without subterfuge or lockpicks. And since she had discovered me, I had little choice. Dismissing her might have led to the baroness revealing my presence to Wycomb."

"'Discovered' you," his commander repeated. "Are you losing your skills, Jones?"

It was a valid question, one Jones knew the spymaster had to ask. Jones drew a deep breath and fisted the hands he held behind his back. "No, sir. It was poor timing and coincidence, that is all."

"Neither is an acceptable excuse."

Jones nodded once in agreement. He held Sir Charles's considering gaze, waiting for the moment when judgment would fall.

The silence stretched out, thin as the paper he'd folded into his pocket. He did not want this assignment removed, nor did he want a formal reprimand. But he had made a mistake—two, in fact—and agents had been reassigned for far less.

"It is too late to rectify the situation. You will have to use her." Sir Charles picked up his greatcoat, decisive now. "We must prepare for an error that reveals the investigation. One word, and Wycomb will either run or attack."

Attack, thought Jones. Wycomb never ran.

"I expect a report each day, Jones. *Each day.*" Sir Charles swung the greatcoat around his shoulders so the capes whirled out before enclosing his wide chest.

"Yes, sir." Relief flooded him, fueling his body so that he stepped forward without intending to. He opened his mouth to say more, but Sir Charles had already turned his back and was through the doorway into the hall.

Jones was dismissed.

He was *not* reassigned, or worse, returning to the rookeries.

Chapter Twelve

"Good morning, uncle."

"Hm." The cup of coffee on a path toward Wycomb's lips did not pause, nor did he raise his gaze from the newspaper open before him. The slight angling of his head, however, told her he knew exactly where in the room she stood.

Cat had not expected him to do anything out of the ordinary. The noise low in his throat that *did* acknowledge her arrival was all she usually expected in the way of a "good morning."

She could not say she particularly cared if he greeted her. She didn't on any other morning. Yet this morning she was conscious of the suddenly dangerous strength and breadth of his shoulders in the elegant coat, of the way his eyes flicked toward door and window—even the movements of the footman in the corner of the room warranted a second glance from Wycomb.

Had he always done so? Cat rolled her shoulders to ease the tension in them and turned toward the sideboard and its waiting eggs and sausages and scones. Perhaps her uncle had always been observant of his surroundings and she had simply never noticed because she had never looked.

She was looking now.

Stabbing a thick, round sausage with her fork and transferring it to her plate, Cat tried to ignore the roil of fear building inside her. She fought to keep her hands steady as she chose a scone from the sideboard. Perhaps Wycomb was watching her even now, noticing that her breath was shallow and her hands fumbled with the serving forks. Perhaps he was thinking how best to force her to marry, what incentive would drive her in that direction. But when she turned, his gaze was on the newspaper. He did not glance at her as she moved toward the table and took a seat a few chairs away. It was as though she did not exist.

Cat decided that was acceptable, though her fear had not lessened. He could stare at his newspaper while she ate. She had much to occupy her mind. Ball gowns, a trip to the milliner's shop, the roofs of the tenants. Jones. Calming her racing heart. But her attention was still focused on the man to her right, sitting at the head of the breakfast table. Each shift in the lines of his face as he absorbed the articles, the rustle of paper as he turned the page.

Then his teacup rattled as he dropped it into the saucer, porcelain clinking against porcelain. His gaze focused on the newspaper as though nothing else existed, brows angled in concentration. He did not lean forward, did not betray by the slightest additional body movement that something in the newspaper meant a great deal to him.

But Cat knew.

Her fork paused in its ascent to her lips, breakfast forgotten, as she studied Wycomb. He never reacted quickly. *Never.*

When he dropped the newspaper beside his plate, Cat quickly shoveled cold eggs into her mouth so she would not be caught staring. He stood, but she did not look up or make eye contact lest he notice her.

"Brown," he called to the butler, striding to the door and through it without a glance behind him. "Send for the unmarked carriage."

Cat willed her bottom to remain in the chair and her feet to stay planted on the thick rug beneath the table. She most definitely did not want to be noticed. Cutting carefully into her blood sausage and setting the bite into her mouth, she ignored the surge of anticipation thrumming through her veins. She chewed slowly, listening to the silence in the breakfast room and the clatter in the front hall.

Wycomb had not left the house yet, as she could hear him speaking to Brown. She could not take the newspaper at least until then, and she could not allow the footman standing in the corner of the breakfast room to see her rush to the newspaper, either. Trying not to exhibit any of the impatience bubbling up in her, Cat slathered jam on her scone and ate that as well. It was dry as dust in her mouth, though she knew cook's scones were the best in England.

She could practically hear the newspaper calling her name and fancied the footman could as well. But she ignored it until her plate was empty and the front door had closed behind Wycomb. Then she slowly and carefully stood, pretending today was like every other day. She started to stroll from the room, moving around the table to the door.

Pausing at Wycomb's chair as though a headline from the open paper had caught her eye seemed natural, as did taking the newspaper as if absorbed in the article and wandering from the room. She might have done it any other day of her life, Cat thought, quite satisfied with her performance. Climbing the stairs to her room, she tried equally as hard not to run and give the paper more importance than she should.

Then she was alone in her room, the paper spread over

the pale-blue coverlet of her bed. Smoothing her hand over the page Wycomb had been reading, she studied the various notices listed there. Births, deaths, travel news, markets, advertisements for goods and the prices of corn. She could not determine what part of it had caught it his eye.

But something had.

Carefully tearing the paper so that she kept only the page Wycomb had noticed, she set the rest in the fire burning low in the grate. She did not want anyone to know she had torn out that particular page, as she did not know if anyone in the household would report such items to Wycomb. After folding the remaining page, she fisted it and watched the fire lick at the paper on the hearth. Flames rimmed the edges, growing brighter as they worked their way to the center. Then there was nothing but ash floating in and around the flames.

She would have to decide what to do.

Chapter Thirteen

"Mary Elizabeth, do have a care for my feet, dear. I'm not able to walk as quickly as you." Aunt Essie's voice floated toward her and Cat turned, taking in the buildings and bustle of Piccadilly. Essie puffed along a few yards behind her, cheeks pink from exertion.

"My apologies, aunt." Cat smiled at the woman and waited on the walkway while Essie drew up beside her. "My mind was wandering."

"I gathered." The older lady blew out a breath, fluttering the curls around her face. "What has distracted you enough you've passed Hatchards?"

"I passed Hatchards?" Cat looked down the street through strolling ladies, prancing bucks, and young street sweepers and realized she had, indeed, passed the bookshop. Frowning, she looked down at her aunt. "You should have called out."

"I did, dear." Essie raised her brows. "You ignored me."

"Oh. Well, let us go back." Cat set her fingers to her forehead, hoping to realign her mental maneuvering to avoid any thought of Jones and focus on the moment. After all, she could not wish Jones into appearing before her. She'd been trying since yesterday morning, the newspaper page foremost on her mind.

Then again perhaps she could.

There he was, across the street, strolling as though he had no cares at all. He moved easily, his gait unhurried but also not leisurely. The soft morning light seemed to focus on the planes of his face, on the well-made body cutting through the crowds unnoticed.

His gaze was on her. She felt it even from across the street. The awareness that his eyes were tracking her slipped over her skin so she was conscious of her every movement. Foot to pavement, foot to knee and hip. The chemise and gown touching her body were suddenly heavy, almost uncomfortably so. Her skirts swished around her ankles, the ruffle of the petticoat brushing the points of the bones there. The pelisse over her gown felt strangely stiff and restrictive, pressing unsettlingly against her breasts.

Even the April breeze, full of London's smells, seemed to be warmer, stronger, even sweeter as it passed over her face than it had only a moment before. Was it always this way, when a woman knew she was being watched? Perhaps a woman's body gained such strange knowledge after being pressed so closely to a man's.

She met Jones's gaze through the carriages and wagons on the street, trying to convey with her eyes that she needed to speak with him.

"We should be quick," Essie huffed. "Your uncle will likely finish his business shortly and return for us."

"Yes." Cat did not turn to look at Essie as she spoke, but continued to hold Jones's gaze as he moved down the street. He was nearly abreast of her now on his side of the street and she felt a slight panic. Would he cross over? Should she find a way to go to him?

Then he was past her, and though he no longer had his eyes on her, her skin still felt marked by his gaze.

She slipped into the bookshop to browse the aisles as a lady would, Essie at her side. But her gaze was on the large windows beside the door. Stacks of books were displayed there, the muted leather covers set beside quills and chocolates intended to entice customers.

She stayed near the window, looking over the nearest shelf.

"What do you think of these, Aunt Essie?" Cat flipped through the pages, fanning them to create a light breeze. Her gaze flicked toward the passersby crossing the square of daylight offered by the window.

A man with the correct color of hair strolled by, then another with the correct build, each of them sending her pulse leaping only to have it dip again when it was not Jones.

"They seem interesting," Essie said, peering at the fluttering pages. "Is it for one of the properties?"

"What? Yes. Of course." Cat had no idea what she was saying. No idea at all—because Jones had just appeared in the window. As he passed, he turned his head as if the books displayed in the window caught his eye. He paused, bending to look more closely.

Cat blinked and the handsome face was gone from the window, leaving a space quickly filled by a pair of ladies and a moment later, farther away, a crested carriage.

"I had better begin my hunt for a publication on embroidery patterns." Essie looped a ribboned pale-green reticule over her forearm. "Do be quick yourself." She drifted toward the area set aside for books on household management and various ladies' pursuits.

The bell over the door tinkled and Cat instinctively looked toward the sound. *Jones.* His gaze touched hers for only a moment, enough that she knew he had seen her. Then he turned and stepped into a corridor flanked by bookshelves, disappearing between the pages of history and geography.

Jones was here, hidden between mountains and towers of books.

Heart thumping, Cat wandered the aisles, gloves running along the well-worn shelves as if considering the titles. The scent of leather and paper circled her, musty and fresh all at once. Sunlight from the front windows dimmed as she moved to the interior of the shop and into the stacks and rows of books. The patrons and bustle from the front of the shop quieted, each step taking her away from reality and closer to *something*. Mindful of the silence of books, she turned into another aisle.

And saw him.

He leaned against a shelf, his brown coat and pantaloons fading into the background of worn wood and leather-bound books. One of those books was in his hands, the pages opened so their secrets were reflected in his eyes. She tilted her head to read the title of the slim volume, taking in the tan cover and the dark lettering inlaid there. *The Scientific Study of Blades as it Relates to Plows, Also Containing Observations on the Scythe.*

Something in her heart smiled to see the title. She had read that herself only a year or so ago. He looked up, focus shifting from the book to her. He smiled faintly, full lips curving up just a little at the corners.

"My lady."

"Jones." She smiled in return, conscious of the dim solitude of the shelves, the hum of voices quieted by the twists and turns of the aisles.

"What has happened?" With a gentle *shoosh* he closed the volume, then slipped it onto the shelf. "You have something to tell me?"

"Yes." She drew a deep breath, pulling the collar of her pelisse more closely around her. There would be no turning back now. "Wycomb read something in the newspaper that caught his attention."

"Ah." Brown eyes lit with interest. "Progress."

• • •

He tried not to notice her gloved, elegant fingers brushing against her own skin as she fiddled with her pelisse. Or the way that pale skin rose above her bodice and peeked between the squared edges of the outer garment.

He *had* noticed, and now his fingers tingled. Shoving them into his pocket, he said, "What newspaper was it?"

"*The Times.*" She released the pelisse, fingers fluid and graceful as they moved to her sides. Whatever emotions might be running through her, she still moved and stood as a lady. "I took the page he was reading. I've read it over and over, but I don't know what part of it meant something to him."

"What day was it delivered on?"

"Yesterday, Tuesday. And I was cautious in taking the newspaper." Her voice held a note of satisfaction that matched the tilt of her chin. "I burned what was left, so no one would know I ripped out the single page. I thought it might raise someone's curiosity."

"That was clever." She was cautious and careful, as he'd hoped she would be. "Where is it now?"

"Hidden in my chambers."

"Mary Elizabeth?" The voice was quiet, curious.

"My aunt," the baroness gasped.

Jones angled away, turning body and face so that her aunt would not identify him. It was too late, he knew. She would have seen his face.

"Is this the one you wanted, my lady?" He spoke the

words loudly enough that the elderly woman at the end of the aisle would hear. He reached up, retrieved a book at random on the topmost shelf.

"I believe so, yes." The baroness accepted *The History of Beekeeping*, flipped open it's binding. "Just a moment, Aunt Essie."

"Hurry, dear. Wycomb has arrived and he is in a temper." The woman stayed where she was, watching.

"We must meet again." Jones kept his face turned, pretending to be reading the spines.

"Where, then?" the baroness said softly. "And when?"

"Where will Wycomb be tomorrow evening? At home?"

The baroness glanced behind her, as if the space between her and her companion would reveal her uncle's plans, then back at Jones. "We are scheduled to attend a soiree. If I plead illness, he will likely go to his club until the early hours of the morning and I will be free. We can meet in the garden once the servants retire for the evening."

"Be ready for a sign, my lady. It will be late."

"Late, then. I will watch for you." She raised her voice, closed the book. "Thank you for your assistance, kind sir. It is not what I am looking for, however."

He set it back on the shelf, nestled between brown leather binding and blue.

"You are most welcome." He nodded his head in farewell. "Good-bye."

He turned his back on her, leaving the bright green gown and white pelisse alone among the books. As Jones went around the corner, a voice shot down the aisle and made his insides curdle.

"Mary Elizabeth." Cool. Controlled. *Wycomb.* "I am disappointed in your tardiness."

"I do not feel well." Cat set her head against the upholstered back of the chaise longue in the drawing room of Worthington House and closed her eyes. "I'm sorry, uncle. I know tonight is important, but it would be worse to attend the soiree and be ill than to simply not be there." She set her hand to her stomach, and though she was feigning severity, there was no need to *pretend* her stomach was roiling and pitching.

She imagined even great actresses were nervous before a performance.

"You cannot afford to be absent from the social whirl, even a single night, if you intend to marry this Season."

She opened her eyes to find Wycomb studying her carefully over the rim of his brandy glass. The look in his blue eyes was sharp, but the lines around his mouth had deepened and there were shadows smudged beneath his eyes.

It was difficult to face a man when there were secrets running just below the surface. His words, her words. Actions. Undercurrents and innuendos. The knowledge that her uncle was involved in something disreputable lurked beneath everything, but *he* did not know she knew of it.

"I am aware of the effect of too many absences, uncle, but it is still relatively early in the Season. A missed soiree shall not set back my prospects." Offering a half smile, Cat laid aside the slim volume of poetry she had been reading and tightened the paisley shawl draped over shoulders. "I do bring the Ashdown fortune with me. This Season or next, or even three or four Seasons from now, I will be quite eligible. And I will attend an event tomorrow, of course."

But not tonight. Tonight, she wanted to be at home when Jones came looking for her.

"You do not want to wait until next Season to marry, Mary Elizabeth." Wycomb swirled the brandy in the glass, a strange emotion flickering over his features. Her imagination marked it as ominous.

It disappeared so quickly she might have been mistaken.

"Perhaps not." Cat sighed and turned her head, pretending it was all too difficult. He would see through her ruse, as he knew her well enough to know there was little she could not manage, including illness.

He did not toss back the last of the brandy, but swallowed it smoothly and slowly as though savoring every ounce. Then he held up the crystal snifter and stared into it, seemingly intent on ensuring every drop had been consumed.

"Do not forget the Marquess of Hedgewood."

"He is—"

"Your future husband." Wycomb set his glass onto the sideboard with a sharp snick. "He will offer for you before the Season is over if you prove your worth to him."

"Prove my *worth?*" Oh, that sent her temper spiking. But she did not give way, nor bend to his will. "I don't intend to prove my worth to anyone. I am woman enough to stand on my own, and my inheritance and lineage are beyond compare."

"They are not as important as yourself."

Cat gaped at him, shoulders settling against the cushioned chaise. Never once had she believed Wycomb cared about her, specifically. Feigned illness, abduction, investigation—they all rolled away.

"Uncle."

"Hedgewood has aspirations that demand a wife with specific skills." Cool eyes narrowed, gaze flickering over her from head to toe. "You fulfill his requirements. I expect you to meet his expectations, which include hostessing, political adeptness, social niceties, and doing your duty—in all respects."

"I see." She supposed affection was too much to expect. "I am not well enough to attend to Hedgewood or the soiree."

Hedgewood was not her concern. Only Jones mattered

for the moment. She would deal with her marital prospects tomorrow. Nerves thrumming, Cat let her eyes drift closed again, hoping it appeared she was simply too tired to converse with Wycomb, let alone attend a soiree.

After a long pause, he finally spoke again. "Your color is good, Mary Elizabeth, so I trust whatever ails you will remedy itself by the morning."

"I'm sure it will." Cat did not open her eyes, but heard him stride across the room in that strong, fast gait he used when he was angry. "I hope you find something to amuse you this evening in place of the soiree."

"I shall. My club will no doubt offer more pleasure than squiring a young lady who does not value her place in society." The door to the hall opened, hinges emitting a faint squeak. "Good night." Then he was gone, leaving behind nothing but a controlled, quiet click as the door closed.

He was furious. Livid. She had never been frightened by it before.

She was now.

Chapter Fourteen

The words *"Take me to White's"* floated between Wycomb, the coachman, and Jones on a warm night breeze.

Slipping farther into the shadows of Hyde Park, Jones watched Wycomb ascend the carriage steps on the other side of Park Lane. He was leaving for his club, which meant the baroness and her aunt were alone in the townhouse with only the servants for company.

It made Jones's work easy. It was a simple matter to steal into the walled garden through the mews. A simpler matter to pick his way through benches and shrubs and urns to the windows. The baroness sat alone in the first room he looked into, and he wondered if she had kept to the ground floor because she knew he was coming.

The space was informal and more comfortable than he'd expected, a small drawing room with warm tones, plush pillows, and a slight untidiness. Books were scattered over surfaces, a pale, rose-colored shawl draped over a chair. Even the miniatures placed about the room lacked organization.

Perhaps this was her space, or at least family space, and

thus more often used. He hadn't expected to find untidiness in a lady's house with servants—a spy's residence, yes. But not the household commanding the largest wealth in the nation.

Somehow this room suited the baroness, which was stranger still. Seated on a chaise longue, feet curled beneath her, she was as elegant and informal as the room around her. Only a single row of lace edged the yellow gown spilling over the seat. Instead of piled atop her head, the warm, rich red of her hair was restrained with a narrow ribbon at the base of her neck. The remainder curled and spiraled down her back, taking on a life of its own as she tipped her head toward her book.

She was beyond lovely. A painting—still life given breath.

When she turned the page, her ungloved fingers slid over the paper. Softly. Skimming the surface as if it were precious.

Something inside him tore.

As precious as that book might be, a few dozen more lined the shelf behind her. Yet more would be in other rooms of the house.

He owned fewer books than he could count on one hand.

Jones set aside the ache in his chest and tapped on the window, disturbing her peace. Combined regret and pleasure twined in him when she lifted her head and stared out, gaze fogged with introspection.

He was close enough to the glass she should be easily able to see him, so he simply pointed to the rear of the townhouse. She nodded once and uncurled her legs, dropping the book onto the chaise. Purpose, grace—each filled her movements so it seemed she danced beyond the window.

Whatever her dance, it was not his.

He stepped back from the glass as she left the room, flattening his back against the brick wall. Silvering moonlight filtered between trees, marking the rear door of the house. He watched. Waited. Minutes passed, time slipping through the dark. When she finally emerged from the house, she moved slowly and carefully—almost as silent as a spy.

"My lady," he whispered into the dark as the door closed behind her.

She turned toward him, light from the window beside the door slanting over her face. Furrowed brow, pursed lips—both softened when she saw him.

"Jones." She stepped forward twice, quickly, boots crunching over the stone path.

"Not on the path," he said, then jerked his head toward the rear of the garden. "Away from the house."

"Yes, of course." She stepped onto the damp, silent grass and followed him. She'd added a shawl before coming outdoors. The swirling pattern rippled over her shoulders, coming alive in the half light, then turning to shadows on shadows as they retreated toward the garden wall at the rear of the yard.

Lanterns swayed in the work-roughened mews beyond and light from the windows of Worthington House crisscrossed the ground—but between the two was a place where light from neither location could reach. The darkness deepened, pulling them into that cocooned space.

It was there he went, faced her. On the edge of two realities. Jones knew this place well, between the elegance of one locale and the harshness of another.

Darkness could be safe.

"My lady," he whispered, looking down into a face he could just barely see. It was soft in the dim light of the narrowed crescent moon, but resolution firmed her lips.

"I wasn't sure how long I should wait." She tipped her face up to meet his gaze. "I have the newspaper page."

"Thank you, my lady."

She turned away, head bowing as she fiddled with her bodice. A moment later she drew a long breath and offered a square of paper as she spun to face him again. "Here."

Folded small and pressed flat, it was little more than the size of a large coin.

It had been tucked into her bodice.

He did not want to take the paper from her. He had done such things before, with other ladies. Other women. Women of his class or fellow spies, even ladies passing their husband's political secrets. Often, the paper held the woman's scent, the heat of her body.

But this was *her*. It would be the heat from *her* skin that would warm the paper, and it might carry the subtle scent that rose when she was near. Yet there was nothing else he could do.

Reaching out, he took the small square of paper, careful to avoid brushing her fingers. They were both ungloved—she, because she had been at home, he, in order to work. He tried not to think of the skin that had warmed the paper. Of the pale, white breasts beneath her gown and chemise. Of pretty pink nipples pressed against her stays.

Jones swallowed hard. The paper was warm. Hot, even. He did not need to bring the newspaper to his face for her scent to reach him—it rose from her skin. Breath shaking in his lungs, he willed his body under control. Lusting after a lady was beyond acceptable. Beyond anything a man of his kind could justify.

"I am not certain what to say." She ran the tasseled ends of the shawl through her hand, fingers tangling in the fringe.

He did not answer. There was too much to say. Too many lies and too little truth. Silence hummed between them as much as the trees and flowers whispered in the night.

"Jones?" The tassels fell away, free to dance in the night air unencumbered by long, slim fingers.

"Has your uncle ever asked you for funds?" He blurted the words, as he could think of nothing else to do or say.

She was so close, her scent stronger now and full of some mysterious mixture that made him itch to touch her. "Or the trustees?"

"No." Frowning, she looked back at the house, then to Jones again. "I don't know if the trustees would grant such a request if he did. Is he in debt?"

"Not now, but I believe he was previously." His mind cast around for more. "His debts were considerable and were recently settled."

"I did not know." Her gaze narrowed, the shape barely discernible in the dark. "How did you find out?"

"I have—" He broke off, considered his words. "Methods."

She paused, looked up into the blanket of night and stars, as if searching for the veracity of his statement. "I shall accept that, I suppose, though it seems to me there must be an explanation there."

He did not answer. Could not. So he simply leaned against the rear garden wall and waited, letting the rough stone pressing against his back ground him. He fingered the newspaper in his pocket, wondering what information it might convey. It felt promising, this small scrap of paper and ink. As if something were starting, as if progress had been made, even if it was only a small step.

It was a step forward.

"How shall I contact you if I discover something such as the newspaper again?" Her fingers came near to touching his arm, searching for an answer, then fell away again before contact occurred. That almost-touch burned as much as a brand. "I cannot sit at Worthington House in the evenings, waiting, without raising my uncle's suspicions. As it was, he was skeptical about my excuse for staying home this evening."

He had thought of this, evaluating possibilities. He could not—would not—tell her of Angel's townhouse. She might be observed entering it, which would ruin her reputation. More, she might see or hear more there than he wanted her to know.

"My apologies, my lady. There is no quick method of contacting me." He stepped closer to her, wishing to offer some reassurance. "But I will not be far."

"There must be a way." Turning, she began to pace the path before she remembered to step back into the grass.

Jones stared at the place where she had stood. Perhaps the simplest solution was right there in front of them. He crouched before the stone wall, ran his fingers across the rough surface.

"What are you doing?" Her voice floated toward him from somewhere above and behind.

"Looking for weakness." His index finger traced the mortar between the rocks, moving along the irregular surface, until he found what he'd hoped for.

"Do you know, Mr. Jones, your conversation is not as revealing as I'd hoped. You are looking for a *weakness,* but I do not know what you mean. You work *within the confines of the law* for *gentlemen* you do not name." The words he'd spoken to her when she discovered him beneath the desk echoed in his memory. "Again, I do not know what you mean."

He smiled into the darkness. "Not Mr. Jones, my lady. Just Jones."

"I had forgotten. Just Jones." Then she was crouching beside him, bringing with her the violet and vanilla scent of danger. "I maintain, however, that your conversation is not revealing. So many vague answers you have given me."

"My apologies." He did not intend to become more revealing. Reaching down, Jones slipped a thin-bladed dagger from his boot.

The baroness sucked in a breath through her teeth, held it. "You carry a knife in your boot?"

"Yes." The boot didn't fit well when the knife was

removed.

Jones studied the foundation of the wall. The shadowed shape of the rock contrasted against the lighter outline of the mortar, defining his path even in the faint moonlight. Turning his knife, he gripped the base of the hilt and used the horn handle to scrape at the loose mortar. Chunks fell away to disappear into the grass below.

He turned his head to speak to her, to explain what he was doing, and discovered her gaze fixated on his working hands. Faltering, he looked down at the stilled dagger. The blade was shaped like a diamond at the hilt and tapered to a point as he preferred. There was little light here, beneath the trees and in the shadow of the wall, but still the iron caught the moonlight. Flashed.

When he looked up again, her gaze had risen to his face, but her fingers reached slowly out to settle on his forearm. Not a plea, not a staying hand. He could think of no reason she would touch him. *But she had.* Her hand was warm through his shirt and coat, but pale in the moonlight. Soft touch, without pressure.

A butterfly's touch.

His breathing went ragged, blood humming, hunger pounding through him. Then her hand tightened on his arm, and her intention became clear. It was a warning.

"*Within the confines of the law,*" she said softly. "I shall hold you to that, Jones."

He did not answer because her lips were so close, her scent so compelling in this secluded cocoon—and he did not want to make a promise he may not keep. Not when his mind was bent upon espionage but his body focused only on her.

Her grip loosened, then her hand fell away. He held her gaze, wishing those iridescent blue eyes were visible in the dark. They were not, and whatever churned inside him, she would not feel the same.

He called upon all he had to beat back the desire. To remember his purpose. What flooded through him had no place there.

He won the battle, forcing his mind and body to focus on cautiously scraping at the mortar. Chunks fell away, a few at a time, then a few more, until Jones could grip the stone. Slipping the dagger back into his boot, he curled his fingers around the cool, rough surface and began to jiggle it. When it came free, he brushed as much of the mortar as possible from the oblong stone, then set it in the grass.

"If it had not already been loose, this would be impossible." He said it not as an explanation, but rather a way to fill the silence. A way to calm his racing heart.

"We can be grateful the mason has not repaired the wall." Her words were light and meant to be amusing. He heard that clearly enough. But the warning still edged her tone. "What are we doing with the stone?"

"If you need to get a message to me, you can leave it here." Jones put his hand into the cavity and brushed away yet more bits of loose mortar. "The stone is not large, so you'll be able to easily remove and replace it."

She shifted forward to look into the dark space left by the absent stone. The movement caused her skirts to rustle, a sound both foreign and stirring.

"You will check it regularly?" she asked.

"Yes. In the early morning or late at night. In darkness, certainly."

"Good." She nodded, shifting back again. "Good."

"Put nothing meaningful in writing," he added, lifting the rock and returning it to the cradle of the wall. "All I need to know is that I must find you, and I will contrive to do so."

"What should I write, then?" She stood, taking away the heat of her body he had been too distracted to notice until it was gone.

"A note between lady friends." It was all he could think of that would be innocuous. "Perhaps where you plan to be of an evening, the color of your gown. It would assist me in finding you."

"A letter of that nature would be messengered or franked. There would be no need to hide it." She shook her head, the hair spilling down her back shifting and twisting to form new and lovely coils. "Wait."

She looked up into a sky both studded with stars and clouded by London's fog. After a long, deep breath, she looked back at him. "Love notes."

"I beg your pardon?" The earth had shifted beneath his feet, surely.

"A lady would have no need to hide a letter unless the receiver were unsuitable in some way. Love notes." Through the distance and dark that separated them, Jones felt her eyes on him. "They would not be true."

"No."

"If I leave a note—any note—you will know that I have information. If the note were to be discovered, the only consequence is that I would be forbidden to see the man again."

"If Wycomb forces you to give a name?"

"I shall say a handsome man I met on the street. I do not know his family or his direction, but only leave messages for him."

"It would be true."

"Yes, which would make Wycomb believe me."

She had the makings of a very effective spy. She had grasped the concept of surviving an interview—tell a lie that is also the truth. It wouldn't hold through torture, but it would through most interrogations.

"My lady." Jones looked down into her pale face. Her eyes were wide, but not frightened enough to ensure her safety. "Be careful. So very careful. Say and do nothing that would cause suspicion or put your life in danger."

"No. I shall simply write love notes." Irony rang in her tone, matched by the knowing purse of her lips. Glancing behind her at the brick and glass of Worthington House, she pulled her shawl close. "I should return before I am missed."

"Yes." He should offer some word of advice, or perhaps gratitude for what she was about to engage in. Yet nothing he could think of seemed useful, so he whispered, "Good night."

"Good night."

She disappeared into the dark, leaving behind nothing more than the promise of a love note.

Chapter Fifteen

Jones spread the newspaper across the study desk, mindful that his informants were waiting for direction. Shifting the paper closer to the window, he scrutinized it for any sign of what might have disturbed Wycomb. Bits of gossip lined the page. Town news, financial information. Any of these might catch Wycomb's attention for any number of reasons—even legitimate ones related to his proper assignments or life in the *ton*.

"Tuesday," he muttered under his breath. "What did Wycomb do on Tuesday?"

"Went to the docks, sir," a young voice piped up from behind him.

"The docks?" He hadn't followed Wycomb himself yesterday, being engaged elsewhere, and hadn't yet received a report from the Gents in the interim. But—ah yes. He saw it now. "Did he visit the *Anna Louisa*?" He tapped his finger against the page, considering the ramifications.

"Yes, sir." Another voice, this one older than the first and just beginning to crack, answered him.

He turned and surveyed the three boys in front of him. They'd ordered themselves by age, as they usually did: Rupert, Angus, and Young John. He had once been like them, searching for purchase in a world where there was none. He'd wanted nothing more than stability and food. These boys wanted the same.

He couldn't save them if they didn't want it. He could only offer an alternative to theft and gin—the same alternative Angel had given him.

"The *Anna Louisa*. You're sure, Rupert?"

"Yessir." Rupert stepped forward, his shock of red hair glinting over freckled cheeks and a thin face. He'd grown tall the last few months but hadn't yet filled out his new frame. "He was down at the docks, talking with the cap'n. Was right angry, to be sure. T'was to be part of my report today, but I s'pose you already know." His shoulders slumped slightly.

"I wouldn't have guessed the *Anna Louisa* if you hadn't told me he'd been at the docks." Jones offered the statement as truth.

"Oh?" Rupert's head lifted, and he grinned, revealing teeth too large for his narrow face. "Well that's better'n being late."

To hide his own grin, Jones glanced down at the newspaper and the notice in it.

The Anna Louisa. Departed India November 1. Arrived London March 22. India. What was the significance of that? Or was it the captain or crew that held significance?

"How long was he at the docks?"

This time it wasn't Rupert who answered, but Young John, the smallest and newest member of the Gents.

"Sixty-two minutes, sir, give or take if I counted too fast." He was only eight, but he had a meticulous nature that lent itself toward such factual details. "But he t'weren't on the docks the whole time. He went below, too."

"Aye," Angus agreed, though looked to Rupert for confirmation. He was still shy, despite working with Jones for over a year. "'E went below for summat like twenty minutes and came back up right mad."

"Didn't shout at the cap'n, though." Rupert grimaced. "More like he froze him with his eyes."

"Eyes like that, them is scary." Angus shrugged his shoulders as though shrugging off the memory. "Reminds me of me da, and 'e t'weren't a nice'un."

No. None of the boys had nice'uns, which is why they'd taken to the street.

"Good job, Gents." Reaching into his pocket, he took the three coins he'd promised and flipped one to each of them. Young John missed catching his and it plinked onto the floor and rolled away. He chased it with a delighted hoot, as though something as simple as a good run was a little-experienced joy.

"What of today?" Jones asked, pushing the newspaper to the side of Angel's desk.

No, his desk now.

The boys exchanged glances, a little hesitant. Concern etched into their faces, eyes widening. He could almost hear them mentally debating who was going to be the harbinger of bad news.

Rupert pulled himself up, apparently having decided it would be him, and tugged at his grubby shirtfront in preparation. "I been wi' ye the longest, so I'll tell ye, sir. 'E gave us the slip, sir. Went into a pub—"

"A right nasty one!" Young John added, standing up onto his tiptoes to add emphasis. "In St. Giles."

"But then 'e didn't come out. Not from the front, nor the back, neither," Rupert concluded. He snorted in frustration. "Waited hours, we did, until we sent Angus in to see what was what. The gov'nor t'weren't inside, neither."

"He t'weren't anywhere, sir!" Young John shook his head a little wildly, his red-blond curls shaking. "But I 'as an idea 'bout where 'e went."

"Is that so?" Jones raised his brows and leaned against the desktop, settling in to hear whatever idea Young John had concocted. "Go ahead."

Young John wiped dirty hands on dirtier breeches and glanced once at the other boys before beginning. "Well, I think as how 'e changed 'is clothes inside the pub. 'E was carrying a leather satchel when 'e went in. I was thinkin' as how 'e might have changed into other clothes so's we didn't notice him come out."

Jones cocked his head, considering this bright child with the earnest eyes. "Young John, that's a good theory. A very good one." If Wycomb wanted to disappear, a disguise would be an efficient method. Jones rubbed his jaw, noting the slight stubble that he should have taken care of that morning. "If he did change his appearance, where did he go afterward? And why?"

"Dunno, sir." Angus tugged at the shock of dark hair that fell over his forehead. "Mebbe back down t' the docks."

"Hm." Jones looked back at the paper. It seemed he'd be paying a visit to the docks himself. "Well, gents. I have another assignment for you."

All three of them straightened, expressions bright and eager.

"There is a loose stone in the wall at the back of the baroness's garden. Check it in the morning and at night—but only in the dark." He wouldn't risk the boys being seen by Wycomb from a window. "If there is a note there, bring it immediately to me. Understood?"

"Aye, sir." Young John grinned and hopped from foot to foot, too energetic to stand still. "I've never been in a posh garden!"

• • •

Whatever her uncle believed about the lords of the *ton*, a single night's absence clearly did not hurt her marital prospects.

Flowers began arriving in mid-morning. Notes accompanied them, full of well-wishes for her quick recovery and disappointment she had not been part of the social whirl the night before.

Callers arrived next, leaving their cards in the front hall. At first, Cat indicated to the butler she was not at home, but Essie insisted she receive them. She sat in the drawing room, waiting for the sound of footsteps on the stairs as callers arrived.

"My dear baroness!" Two simpering girls and their equally simpering mothers arrived amid flowered bonnets and rustling skirts. "We hope you are feeling better today."

"Yes, many thanks on your inquiry." Cat remained seated, hands lying in her lap, and smiled politely at the ladies. "Did you enjoy your evening? I was disappointed not to attend the balls and soirees last night."

They launched into enthusiastic descriptions of gowns and dances, perching themselves on settees and chairs. Aunt Essie's embroidery needle dove in and out of the fabric as she listened. Cat held her smile, though her cheeks ached from the effort. Ten minutes later, Brown brought another visitor. He bowed, announced the guest.

"The Marquess of Hedgewood." The butler's tone held no censure, no emotion. "Lord Wycomb informed him you were at home."

Cat's smile froze, but she rose and held out her hand with all the grace her mother had taught her. "My lord."

"My lady." Hedgewood removed his hat and bowed over her hand, green eyes laughing up at her. "I had hoped to see you last evening."

Her other visitors shifted and sighed and tittered. They would not stay more than a few additional minutes, even less now that they could spread the news that Hedgewood had called on her.

"I was unwell, I'm afraid."

"Yes, your uncle sent word to me." He squeezed her hand once, easily, then let it go and smiled. "I trust you are better today?"

"Indeed." It was too late to stop the gossip. The ladies were standing, making their curtsies to the marquess and Cat, then bustling out of the room and down the stairs.

"Well, that should hold them."

"I beg your pardon?" Cat raised her brows at the marquess, not certain what he meant.

"They were hoping for a bit of gossip and I thought to provide it." His lips tilted up in a half smile on one side. "I plan to offer for you, my lady, and your uncle indicated my suit would be accepted. I thought we might have a little fun as we went along."

"Fun?" She spoke calmly, refusing to allow her voice or face to show her disquiet. "You have yet to offer, and I have yet to accept."

"True." His smile didn't falter, but broadened to reveal a dimple on the left side. "We can always cite a difference of opinion if our union fails to come to fruition. But I doubt it will."

Aunt Essie cleared her throat, held up her embroidery frame. "I've forgotten my yellow thread upstairs, dear. I need it for this flower pattern. Do excuse me."

"Aunt Essie."

"I shall return in five minutes. Less. I promise." Essie disappeared through the door as quickly as their guests had, her skirts moving in the same rhythm.

"Well." Hedgewood gestured to the bottle-green settee.

The tailoring of his coat was flawless. Still, brass buttons shifted over his lean chest and striped waistcoat. "May we sit?"

After a final glance at the doorway, Cat murmured, "Yes, of course."

What was her aunt planning?

Hedgewood sat easily, propping himself on the arm and setting his hat on his knee. Cat chose the chair opposite, perching on the edge and straightening her spine just as her mother had taught her.

"We do not need to stand on ceremony, do we?" The marquess cocked his head, eyes not laughing now. "I hoped to find a companion who was not too tight-laced. I thought you might be such a lady."

She most certainly was. Yet becoming comfortable with the marquess felt tantamount to an acceptance of marriage. That, she was not ready for.

Still, she smiled at him. A genuine smile. "I appreciate the sentiment, Lord Hedgewood. I am not one to strictly follow the rules. It is only that my uncle has moved forward without informing me."

"Ah." Shadows came into his eyes and a frown tugged at his lips. "I see."

"That being said, I am not adverse." She suddenly found she wasn't. Marriage to Hedgewood would not be the great love of her lifetime, but she could see it would be tolerable. "I simply wasn't prepared."

"Good. Very good." The frown on his mouth tipped back into a smile. "I am glad to hear you are not adverse."

"I know little of your family, my lord." Keeping her spine straight, she let her hands go lax in her lap. A small concession. "Where is your country seat?"

"Dorset. Not near the water, however. My family holds land west of Shaftesbury." Hedgewood's gaze did not stray from her face, but flickered over it as though gauging her interest. Or, perhaps, her knowledge.

"I know the area well." If she were to marry him, it would be best to begin their association as she hoped to continue. "My father and I often passed through Shaftesbury as we traveled to our properties in Somerset."

He was serious when he spoke, all signs of charm dissolved into a firm, smoothly shaved chin. "I have heard you were involved in the management of your father's estates."

"Yes." She would say no more.

Everything pivoted on this one moment. The extent of her battle with Wycomb, her lands, her future. Silence drew out between them, strong as the spring sun beaming through the tall drawing-room windows.

"There are some things," he finally said, words slow as if he were choosing them carefully, "that you would not be involved with in the future, though I would willingly take notice of your advice on your family's estates."

She spoke just as carefully, lifting her chin a degree. "I am not yet certain if that is acceptable."

"I see." He did not seem angry, or even surprised, particularly. Handsome features remained neutral. Assessing.

"My lady." Quiet words slipped into the room, preceding the silent Brown by only a moment. "A letter has arrived for you. It is marked urgent."

The envelope was wrinkled, torn on one corner, but she recognized the handwriting of Mr. Sparks slanting across the paper. Thin lines, fast strokes, but heavy and dark.

"Thank you." Accepting the envelope, she slid it into the space between her leg and the chair.

Silence stretched as Brown left the room. Longer.

"Do you need to read the letter?" Hedgewood's neutral features had tipped down into a frown now, instead of the laughing smile she had become accustomed to.

Escape was Cat's only thought. "I'm sure it is urgent—"

"A few minutes won't hurt." Aunt Essie was standing in the doorway, white hair piled higher than usual and sporting a comb with a paste bluebird. She glanced at the clock. "Why, at home hours have barely begun."

"True," Hedgewood said, standing and setting his hat on his head. "If you will excuse me, however, I must be going. I've business to attend to yet today."

"My lord." Aunt Essie stepped forward and held out her hand. "It has been a pleasure."

"Miss Taylor. Lady Worthington." He bowed, lingering over Cat's hand. As she expected—as any lady anticipating a proposal would. "Farewell, my lady," he murmured over her fingers. He let them slip out of his grasp and strode to the door. Through it.

When his footsteps faded down the stairs to the ground floor, Cat spun to face her aunt.

"What in the blazes was that? Leaving me alone with a suitor?"

"I—ah—" Aunt Essie blushed, the pink riding high on her cheekbones. "I thought, as he is soon to be your husband, that you might enjoy a few minutes alone. Hedgewood is very handsome, Mary Elizabeth."

"I suppose." Amusement could soften irritation easily enough.

"Forgive me? I know a proper chaperone would never have left, nor would your mother." Excitement hovered around the corners of Aunt Essie's eyes. "Only, Hedgewood possesses good humor and such a lovely mouth. Surely, a discreet kiss would not come amiss?"

"I am sorry to disappoint you, Aunt, but he did not kiss me."

Aunt Essie's face fell. "That is unfortunate."

Chapter Sixteen

"Well, then," Cat murmured to herself, having made her excuses to her aunt. "We shall see what news Mr. Sparks has sent."

She ducked into the nearest door and realized it was her uncle's estate room—once her father's estate room.

Also a place to hide with a man, as she had so recently discovered.

Shutting the door, she quickly tore open the envelope from Mr. Sparks and read the note.

Baroness Worthington,

The roofs are being replaced at a rapid pace. They will easily be repaired by winter, if not fall. A few roofs would last another year or so, but as your pin money would pay for the repairs, I chose to repair them in advance to keep ahead of the trustees. I hope this meets your approval.

The tenants are grateful, my lady, and know full well

where the funds were derived from. Their goodwill and loyalty are the highest I've seen since your father's death.

I will soon leave for an accounting and observation of the other properties. I shall send word of their state to you as well as the trustees, as usual.

The trustees visited Ashdown Abbey, and will be visiting your other large estates as well. Be well, my lady, and stay strong.

Yr. Humblest Servant,

Matthew Sparks

Cat crumpled the letter in her fist. The trustees knew what she had done, which meant Wycomb would soon know as well.

"Bloody buggering hell." She leaned her head against the polished panels of the door and tucked the ball of paper into the pocket of her gown. Closing her eyes, she took a deep breath. Another.

The roofs were being built. Whatever happened after, whatever the trustees did or didn't do, the roofs will be built as she promised.

There was pride in that. Honor in that.

Her eyes flicked open to examine the estate room, the partially drawn drapes. The musty books her father collected. Art was here, too, on the walls and surfaces. Every vase and painting a testament to love of life rather than value. The massive desk allegedly belonging to the first Mary Elizabeth Frances Ashdown anchored the space.

Wycomb had emptied a secret drawer in that desk.

Jones had hidden beneath that desk.

She looked down at the letter in her hand. Mr. Sparks

had given her the warning—the trustees and Wycomb would be approaching her soon. But there was more here than an unruly ward and her guardian.

She crossed the room, heeled slippers moving over wooden floor, rug, and floor again, just as Wycomb had the night she had discovered Jones.

Quickly pulling open the drawers, Cat gave a cursory glance to their contents. She attempted to open the secret compartment Jones had discovered, but could not locate the spring or lever. With hurried movements, she completed her brief search, then circled the room for anything out of the ordinary.

She found nothing.

But there must be something. *Anything.*

There was.

Late afternoon sunlight slanted over the desk, wavering as clouds shifted over London. Over the stack of fresh paper lined up precisely with one corner. Thin shadows crisscrossed the surface of the top sheet, tiny black dots dancing between them.

Narrowing her eyes, Cat scooted to the desk and stared down at the paper. The shadows and dots—lines and inkblots left from a quill used on the now-missing sheet above. Picking it up, she held it in front of the window, then shifted it so the light struck it differently. Over and over, shift and tilt and study.

7p. A_____ Louisa.

The markings weren't perfect, but it was enough. She had pored over the newspaper page her uncle had found so important and she distinctly remembered a ship called the *Anna Louisa.*

Was it seven tonight? Tomorrow night? Another day? Thoughts swirled, unfolded, reformed.

Wycomb would not be seeing her and Essie again until very late in the evening. He planned to be out until they met at a ball, despite his insistence the evening before that she make her *ton* appearances. If she knew her uncle, there would be little that would keep him from personally seeing she met her obligations.

It must be tonight.

She whirled, seeking the round, yellowed face of the clock on the mantle. Five o'clock. She had two hours to hide a note for Jones without Wycomb seeing her—anyone else would accept an excuse, but not he.

Cat picked up the quill lying silent but ready, slid an unmarked sheet toward her. She looked down at the instrument resting between her fingers, at the tiny feathers lining the hollow shaft, the sharpened nib.

The paper beside it seemed very white. Very empty. The feathers of the quill trembled, each white, downy barb fluttering.

It would be her only weapon against Wycomb.

She firmed her wrist and breathed deep, dipping the quill into the inkstand.

Dear Sir –

I miss your countenance, my darling. The handsome lines of it have haunted my dreams these past nights. I would be most honored if you allow me to gaze upon you once more. I should like to meet before half past six this evening, when I must leave. If you cannot come to me, then I shall leave the time and manner of our meeting to you.

I will have much to share.

Yrs. With Affection,

C

There. It was written—poorly written, but it was complete.

Quickly, before she could change her mind, Cat blotted the note, folded it, sealed it. She did not use the seal with the Ashdown crest, instead, she melted and pressed a simple red wafer against the paper—a wafer like thousands in and around London.

She might not engage in such clandestine behavior regularly, but she was not stupid.

The blotting paper she tucked into the pocket of her gown. She would burn it—not here, as the embers in the fireplace had nearly cooled during the day. In her chambers, where the fire would be ready for curling tongs.

The love note she would leave for Jones.

If the note was still behind the stone by half past six, she would go to the docks herself.

• • •

The stench of the docks was sharp in his nostrils, as biting as the spring rain on his face. But the rain was a boon, despite the water already soaking through his coat and into his skin. People in the rain looked to their feet so their faces stayed dry—no one looked up into a raining sky, or at a spy.

Jones huddled against the wall of a bricked warehouse, biding his time as he studied ships through the watery half light of dusk. The *Anna Louisa* was only one of many vessels moored on the Thames, queued up like so many doxies lining the wall at the nearby taverns.

Dock workers and sailors darted through the rain, climbing up rigging and loading and unloading everything from kegs of ale for the crew and crates of wool and silk to be sold, despite the late hour.

The *Anna Louisa* was quiet, however, her goods already

unloaded and the crew on leave—probably making the acquaintance of the doxies. No doubt the ship would sail out again soon, but for now, there were only a few sentries posted.

A wagon trundled by, the work horses straining to pull the mountain of barrels piled in the rear. Jones pressed himself against the building, a habit of training rather than a need to hide.

The Gents were certain it was the *Anna Louisa* Wycomb had visited, and the newspaper the baroness provided confirmed. What had Wycomb wanted with the vessel? Shipment records, bills of lading for goods on board—Jones could access those through official channels. It was more likely an undeclared person or goods that were of interest to Wycomb. Such things happened with regularity.

Jones rubbed a hand over his jaw. Perhaps he would work the local taverns, determine what he could about the ship. Sailors were an exuberant lot after months on the ocean. Pulling his collar up against the weather, Jones started down the cobbled street.

Light footsteps pounded against the street, then drew level with him. Rupert, freckles almost invisible under the flush of his cheeks, nearly barreled into Jones. The boy bent over and set his hands on his knees, panting.

"Sir—" he huffed out. "Sir—"

Jones touched his shoulder, concern washing through him. "Take your time, Rupert. Catch your breath."

"Aye, sir. But—the baroness—"

Concern spiked to fear, and he could not stop his hand from tightening on Rupert's shoulder. "What happened?" The words whipped from him, fast and dark.

"She left the town'ouse an' 'ired a 'ackney, sir." Rupert straightened, chest still heaving. "She's—"

But Jones didn't need to listen.

He could see her, not fifty yards in front of him. She wore

a dark hooded cloak and leaned against a brick building just as Jones had done minutes before. Despite her attire, he recognized warmly red curls peeking from beneath the hood. Her face was pale and blurred by rain, but he knew her even from this distance.

"Bloody hell. She's here."

"Aye, sir." Rupert jerked his head in agreement. Not one of the sodden orange hairs plastered to his skull moved. "She went ta the garden wall first, though, an' checked the stone. There were a note there—we 'adn't seen it yet, sir. T'weren't there this morning."

Jones heard Rupert's words, absorbed them, but his gaze never left the baroness.

She wasn't looking at him, had yet to hear his boots beating a tattoo on the cobblestones as he crossed to her. Rupert trotted along beside him, shoving at the hair streaming water into his eyes.

Jones knew the precise moment the baroness recognized him. Her face turned his way and her eyes widened. For a moment, even though he was moving, stepping carefully along the street and through the gloom of evening rain, it seemed the world slowed. The dockworkers ceased their shouts, the casks rolling down the gangway stilled in mid roll, the wagons carting goods stopped.

The earth ceased to spin.

Then it all started again as he reached her.

"Jones?" Her breath puffed out in shock.

"Baroness." No doubt he should not growl at a lady, but it was too late. "This is no place for you."

"I would not be here, but it is an urgent matter." She bristled, shoulders tightening beneath the expensive cloak, chin tilting up. Her eyes narrowed, the iridescent blue taking on a sheen of anger. "I found something on Wycomb's desk this afternoon. It was only indentations on paper, as if someone wrote on the page above it. I believe it said '*7pm, Anna Louisa.*' Someone needed to be here, and you had not found the note yet—so I came."

"In a cloak anyone from the docks would steal off your back." Panic clawed in his chest. He reached out, gripped her narrow, graceful shoulder. "When they see what is beneath the cloak, you will be lucky to have your body intact when you leave this place. *If* you leave."

"I don't intend to risk everything I hold dear because I am afraid." Her words were quiet but forceful. Her chin tipped up, though he had not believed it possible to lift it higher. "Wycomb should be here at seven o'clock, and I intend to find out what he is doing."

She shrugged her shoulder to dislodge his hand. He gripped harder, trying not to hurt her with the force of his fingers, but wanting to keep her safely in place.

"Let me determine why Wycomb will be here," he said. "Hire another hackney and return to Park Lane."

He looked down at her face, the lines of it shadowed by the hood. She was magnificent—a red-haired siren risen from the sea to lure men on the docks. He leaned forward, closer, to block her from view of anyone that might be passing by. Water sluiced from the roof, falling into the gap between his collar and neck to chill his skin, but he maintained his position.

"No, I—"

"My lady. Baroness." He gentled his tone. Perhaps he had been too harsh. "It's not safe here for a lady, and Wycomb might recognize you. Please."

She breathed deep, a slow inhale that held as much consideration as her gaze. Droplets of water clung to her lashes like so many diamonds, and a light flush moved over the delicate line of her cheekbone. She pursed her lips, and he knew a man would have to be dead not to find her beautiful.

Beautiful and unattainable and a thousand times removed from his life.

Frantic fingers scrabbled at his waist, tugging at the edge of his coat.

"Sir." Rupert's insistent whisper layered with the patter of rain. Jones looked down, saw freckles stark against skin that had lost all color. "'E's 'ere, sir. The carriage." Rupert jerked his head to the right.

Jones whipped his head to the side, the baroness doing the same. They stared at the carriage not fifteen feet away and the man exiting it. He moved carefully down the steps of the hackney, hat pulled low to avoid the rain and greatcoat swirling around him. There was no mistaking him for anyone but Wycomb, not with the dark hair edged with the silver, elegant clothing and handsome features.

He was so close Jones heard the click of his boots as they touched the stone street and the swish of his greatcoat as he spun around to pay the jarvey.

The baroness sucked in a breath, her hand vising around Jones's upper arm, fingers digging sharply into muscles. "It's him," she said, words almost unintelligible.

"Turn away!" Jones whispered, angling his body so his back was to Wycomb. He had no greatcoat to cover her with, no method of blocking her entirely from Wycomb, so his body would have to do.

She did as he asked, spinning away so her back was pressed against his chest. He put his arms around her, set his hands on her forearms. He could not feel the heat of her body, nor even the shape of it through the fabric of his coat.

But he wanted to, as much as he wanted to breathe.

"Rupert, go," he whispered to the boy, who scampered off almost before Jones finished speaking, footsteps scuffing on the stones. He would be safe enough, being accustomed to navigating worse than the docks.

Jones kept his body angled, shielding the baroness from Wycomb's view as best he could. She had bent her head and pulled the cloak around her, so there was little Wycomb would see beyond the hem of her skirts.

But they did not look as if they belonged. As if they had a reason to be there.

He set his hands on the baroness's shoulders, turning her so she was pressed against the side of the building. Then he shifted so he was in front of her.

"What are you doing?"

"Attempting to make us look ordinary." He leaned in, trying to make his body appear amorous.

He did not have to try hard. With her face turned up to his, those butterfly-blue eyes wide and her lips rosy and parted, he did not have to try at all.

"Jones." Her hands gripped his forearms tightly. "What is ordinary? Who are we trying to be?"

A crystalline droplet fell from the edge of her hood onto her cheek, tracking down the pale skin to the corner of her mouth. The tip of her tongue darted out to claim it, and his belly clutched in reaction.

"Lovers." He could barely say the word. It did not pass easily through a throat tight with need. "A sailor and his lover. I don't know how else to make you indiscernible from other ladies here, and indiscernible is all that is required."

"Yes, of course. Ordinary lovers on the docks." Her gaze flicked over his shoulder briefly before focusing again on his face. "I can't see him well. The carriage is beginning to move away, but my uncle is looking around—for someone, I would expect."

"Good." Jones resisted the urge to look over his shoulder, knowing better than to even hint they were focused on their quarry. He would have to rely on the baroness's limited view for information. "Good," he said again, searching the lines of her face for some knowledge she might not have put into words.

Her hands clutched at him, a quick, involuntary spasm. "He's looking this way." Her panicked whisper was accompanied by tensed shoulders and she began to move, prey scenting danger and bracing to run.

Jones did the only thing he could think of to hold her in place and shield her from Wycomb, though it was not a new thought. He had been thinking of it for minutes already, hours, days. At that moment, it seemed he'd been dreaming of it the whole of his life.

He kissed her.

Chapter Seventeen

Her lips were soft and cool. They trembled once, then firmed beneath his. She did not part them, nor did she angle her head to encourage him, but the loosening of the hands gripping his arms told him her fear had eased.

Then she did the unimaginable, sending a heady and unholy lust tearing through him. She rose on her toes to bring their mouths into better alignment. A simple gesture, one that probably meant very little to her.

It meant everything to him.

He could taste her more perfectly, her scent rising into the air to mingle with the rain. She stepped closer, cloak falling open to draw him between wings of expensive velvet. Her lips parted on a soft, quiet breath, body rising as if there had been a sudden shift in her awareness. Had she been kissed before? He thought not—she was a lady, not a doxy.

He would do well to remember who he shielded her from, and more, the status of the woman who had moved from a few inches away to fully within the circle of his arms.

With regret, Jones released her lips and angled his head

so that he nuzzled somewhere near the graceful curve of her neck. He caressed temptation as much as regret.

"Do you see him?" he rasped, wondering if she recognized lust in a man's voice. "Is he still there?"

"Yes, but he is not looking at us. Jones—" She broke off, lips close enough he could feel the heat of them.

She pressed her mouth to his, chastely, lips together, but hard enough he felt the hunger in her. He couldn't read the lines of her body, the planes of her face or curves of her lips, but he felt urgency. Her hand fisted in the edge of his coat, strong, small fingers twisting the fabric.

He wanted to cup her cheeks, to taste her fully, but—

Holding firm, he let her kiss him again before she pulled back, and when she looked up at him, he was certain she'd carved out a small part of his heart.

"Is it— I was not ready for this, Jones." There was no trembling, no fear in her. "I am not prepared for desire."

"Neither am I," he murmured, belly clutching.

He ought not to have touched her. He should never have begun this pretense, Wycomb or not, because he had known what it would lead to.

Perhaps in his heart of hearts, it was why he had.

She was something he could never be. No matter that he'd craved the taste of her, that the stunning blue of her eyes haunted his sleep. He could never have her, not in any reality. Under the pretense of espionage, he could pretend for only a moment—yet there was no honor in that.

He did what he should have done in the beginning. Sliding his hands around her waist, he lifted his head away from hers so there was no promise of a kiss between them. He pressed her more firmly against the brick wall of the tavern. With the right positioning, he could block her body entirely, and if he were strong, if he controlled himself, he would avoid her temptation as he should have done.

But her eyes, oh, those wide, hungry eyes, stared at him. *What had he done?*

"Do you see him, my lady?"

"Yes," she whispered. "The carriage is gone. He's standing next to the wall, just as we are, to stay dry."

"There is no one with him?"

"Not yet." She shook her head, her eyes still wide, but now a light smile tugged at her lips. "Do you know, Jones, this is the second time you and I have stood in the rain like this."

"I remember." He had not kissed her that time, though he had wanted to then as much as he did now. "It was wet."

"'It was wet.'" Her smile bloomed, as bright as if the sun had pierced through the dull, variegated gray of the clouds above. A laugh slipped between her lips, the hands still holding the edge of his coat tugging slightly. "Oh, Jones, you have a way with words. Do all the ladies swoon at your feet when you speak such love-words to them?"

"I do not speak to ladies." He did not have any experience with—what had she said? *Love-words?*

"Do not worry. I was only jesting." Her lips were still curved as she flicked her eyes to Wycomb. The smile died away instantly. "Someone has met my uncle."

"Tell me."

"They did not shake hands," she murmured. "They're only talking, standing side by side. The stranger is shorter than Wycomb and his clothes are not of the same quality. He's wearing only a coat, no greatcoat, and a cap like yours." Her eyes returned to Jones's face, then moved up to his cap, then back to the two men. "Yes. Just like yours."

"Can you see their faces?"

"Only from the side. Wycomb is—" She squinted, thick lashes nearly touching. "He is not angry, but he is not happy, either. The other man is frowning, and he is quite angry. He's gesturing with his hands and arms, and is even pointing at

Wycomb." Her eyes widened and her mouth fell open.

"What?" Rain poured from the slate roof above, tiny waterfalls pounding onto his shoulders rather than craggy rocks.

"He poked Wycomb in the chest with his finger." Incredulity swelled in her tone. "And Wycomb took a step back."

"Does he look scared?" He wanted to see for himself—*needed* to see it for himself—but doing so would risk exposing her.

"Not scared. He's furious." She frowned as she studied the scene.

"What is he doing?"

"Nothing. It is how I know he's furious." She rose up to see better over his shoulder. "He's not moving, and his head is angled to one side as though he's amused at the other man's ranting. When he stands so perfectly still, he is beyond furious. And, well, he becomes colder and colder as he becomes angrier—which sounds ridiculously foolish."

"No." Jones shook his head, looking down into the pale face beneath the hood. A faint, embarrassed flush tinged her cheekbones. "You know him, how he reacts."

"I don't recognize the man, but, Jones, he's no dock worker or sailor. He's not dressed in the same quality of clothing, yet his mannerisms, the way he moves and his skin, his teeth—he's not lived a rough life. He's of the aristocracy, or at least a merchant or of the gentry."

"You'd make a passable spy, my lady."

Her smile was quick, showing that she, too, had good teeth. "Thank you, Jones. I find that quite a compliment." There was silence for a moment as she carefully studied Jones's face, leaving him wondering what she saw when she looked at him. Then she turned back to the scene unfolding behind him, again squinting through the rain. "The other man is right in Wycomb's face, leaning very close, and—can you hear it?"

"Oh yes." The words were clear enough, though the wheels of a passing hackney did their best to drown out the noise.

"One week, Wycomb! One week is all you'll get from us!" the stranger shouted.

Jones needed to see the second man's face. He might be a spy or an informant. It would be exceedingly negligent to the mission—not to mention detrimental—and his commander would tan his hide if he found out.

He tugged her hood forward, fingers brushing against damp red tendrils.

"Keep your face turned down toward the ground. Do *not* look up." When the baroness did as he'd instructed, Jones turned his head and upper body enough to get a good, clear look at the men behind them.

The stranger stepped back from Wycomb, though there was nothing defensive or submissive about the movement. Jones saw his face at three-quarter view and committed the brown hair, wide set eyes, and thin lips to memory. Then he turned back to the baroness, quickly hiding his own face again.

"I don't recognize him, either." But Jones wouldn't if the man were of the *ton*.

The baroness tipped her face up again and the hood fell back slightly to reveal a loose curl flirting with her jawbone. Before the idea solidified in his brain, Jones reached up to twine the lock about his finger. The red was bright against his skin, soft against the calluses of his fingers.

When he realized what he was doing, when he heard the sharp intake of her breath and her eyes met his, he dropped the curl and tugged the hood back up.

"What are they doing now?" he asked, trying to pretend

he could not still feel her smooth, silky hair on his skin.

"The other man is leaving and my uncle is looking around." She averted her face, then a moment later flicked her gaze back up. "Now he's walking toward the Thames. He's—yes, he's walking down the dock toward a ship."

"Which one. Can you read the name?"

She shook her head. "It's too far."

"Is Wycomb facing us?"

"No."

Jones turned only his head to confirm Wycomb was where he expected—jogging up the gangway and slipping over the side of a ship. He disappeared, but Jones needed nothing more.

The ship was the *Anna Louisa*.

"Hell." He needed to follow, quickly, but he couldn't leave the baroness leaning against the side of the building. Alone.

The rain had slowed to a sprinkle, but dusk had grayed the air. Still, the blue of her eyes was bright.

"Come with me." He held out a hand for her, palm up. "I'll protect you."

She looked at his fingers, then his face, and set her gloved hand in his ungloved one. The fine kid leather was softer than anything he could think of.

Except, perhaps, her skin.

Jones pulled her along with him toward the *Anna Louisa*, moving at a half jog. She kept pace with him easily, half-boots lightly pounding the cobblestones. Water sloshed around her skirts, turning the remaining bits of dry fabric a dismal shade as water seeped into the fibers. Determination sculpted her features.

They moved across the wooden dock, reaching the gangway of the *Anna Louisa*. Standing there, surveying the planked path through the gloom, he knew he should not bring her onto the ship.

He was going to do it anyway.

He'd just have to ensure she was safe.

Jones studied the deserted deck, the gangway, the docks. No one would notice two strangers in the gloom of a wet dusk, but if they lingered too long, they *would* draw attention to themselves.

"Please, do as I say, my lady."

"I'm not a fool." Sharp words, but he heard the fear beneath them. She nodded once, pulling at the edges of her sodden cloak. "I am well over my head now."

He had not expected her to admit it. "You certainly are not a fool."

Tightening his hold on her hand, he scaled the gangway of the Anna Louisa, fingers of his free hand digging into rope guards and booted toes planted firmly on the wood.

His feet were silent out of habit. Hers were just as silent. No sound met his ear but water against the hull, the scrape of leather sole on wood, and distant shouting on the docks.

"Wait." Jones let her gloved fingers slip from his hands when they reached the head of the gangway. He dropped onto the deck, grimacing as his boots made a soft, dull thud on the slatted wood. Jones crouched, waiting for her to join him. When she did, he slid himself into the shadow between rail and decking, and waited for her to do the same.

There was nothing unusual about the rigging or the deck, nor the masts or the wheel. Rope snaked in all directions, coiling in corners and twisting over the wooden planks. More hung from above, or were pulled tight to secure the sails. Crates were stacked, barrels lashed together, ready to be lowered into the hold.

There was nothing here to see beyond the typical workings of a ship.

Except it wasn't deserted.

The ship's watchman sat on a barrel not thirty feet from them. He was turned away, enthusiastically stabbing his dinner with the tip of a knife. Chunks of meat, thick slices of bread. Simple fare. Judging from the barrel with its top removed beside him, ale was being just as enthusiastically consumed.

He didn't need to tell the baroness to be quiet—wide eyes stared from beneath her hood, their whites glowing in the gloom.

Chapter Eighteen

Terror could steal breath and freeze muscle, while still setting the heart thundering.

She wanted to run, to slip back over the side of the ship and simply run. But Jones bent over, pulled a knife from his boot, and stood again—all in one movement, as if it were as natural as breathing.

Clearly, terror had not affected him.

His free hand was warm when he took hers, despite the chill of the rain. That heat stole through damp gloves to her numb fingers. He tugged gently, pulling her behind him as they moved across the deck. They crouched behind a stack of crates, but she knew it couldn't possibly hide them.

Jones set his lips to her ear. "Stay close. We're going to the captain's quarters. There." He nodded toward the stern of the ship.

Small mullioned windows stood sentinel on either side of a doorway, flanking it with glass diamonds glowing gold from the light within. Shadows moved beyond, voices little more than water lapping against the hull.

"If the watchman turns around, you run."

"And you?" she whispered, trying to ignore the man happily guzzling ale from the tankard he'd just dunked into a barrel.

"I'll use this." The light from the captain's quarters shone gold on the knife blade. Cat shuddered, but there was nothing to do but follow.

Only she didn't follow. Jones pushed her forward, keeping himself between her and the watchman. She did not have to look to see if the knife was out, or if Jones was behind her. Both would be true.

They were out in the open now, though night was nearly upon them. Scrabbling across the decking, she led them to the cabin and crouched beneath the windows. Back against the wall, gasping, she looked out over the deck. The watchman picked his teeth with his knife between sips of ale, still oblivious to them.

"Idiot." Disgust coated every consonant and vowel. Jones grappled in his coat for something. "Here, take this. Keep it trained on him. If he moves, shoot."

A pistol was shoved into her hands.

"What?" She tried not to shout. As it was, the word was well above a whisper and sent her gaze toward the watchman. She fumbled the weapon, prayed she wouldn't accidentally press the trigger, and finally held it steady.

"I need a few minutes. We're too far for a knife throw to be deadly. At the least, the sound of a shot will give you time to get back to the docks."

They were going to die.

"What are you doing?" Her hands were steady with the pistol and Cat counted that a boon.

"Cracking the door so we can hear." He spun on the balls of his feet and reached for the handle. "Do you have my back?"

His eyes were dark, the planes of his face hard—but it was him. The core of Jones was here, as if someone had lit a candle to reveal his soul. Whatever and whoever he was, this man was in his element.

"I have your back, Jones."

She pressed her body against the cabin wall and trained the pistol on the watchman. He'd yet to notice them, and she didn't know if she should thank God, Fate, or Dionysus.

From the corner of her eye she saw Jones scurry forward, reach for the handle. There was a soft *click*, barely noticeable against the light breeze and the water around them. Jones pushed open the door.

A scant half inch of light speared over the deck. Gold. Bright.

Cat raised the pistol, waited for the watchman to turn. He didn't—but words filtered through that open doorway.

"You only provided half the order." Wycomb's voice was low and cold, as it was when he was furiously angry.

"Aye." Temper fueled the other man's words. "T'was all I could get. The Indiamen were hustling it past customs."

"My customers are unhappy." A pause. "Shall I direct them to you?"

"Blast it, Wycomb!" A thump, a metallic rattle, as if a fist pounded on a tabletop and shook the silverware. "I did ye a favor, as his lordship asked me to. But damned if I'm going ta get mixed up in yer mess." His voice rose to a shout, streaking through the gap in the air and across the deck.

"He's seen us." Cat gasped, fingers convulsing on the pistol.

"Oy!" The watchman staggered to his feet, dropping the tankard to the planks below. "What are you doing there?"

Jones made a guttural sound deep in his throat. "*Run.*"

She did. Back past the crates, half-boots flying over wood and rope, to the side of the ship. She was climbing up the rail, pistol still in her hand, when she realized Jones was not behind her.

He'd intercepted the watchman. Fists flew, flesh met flesh, a blade flashed—and the watchman was down. Blood spread across his shirt, a crimson flower blooming over brown worsted. Jones leaped over him and Cat didn't hesitate. She was over the side of the ship and on the gangway before she'd thought to move.

Running on the narrow spit of wood, Cat didn't spare a glance behind. She could hear Jones behind her, feet pounding. They flew over the wooden dock one by one, onto the cobblestone street and through the softening rain.

The shot chased them.

...

It rushed through the air only inches from his head, the ball thudding into the bricked wall of the nearest building.

"Hell." He ducked instinctively, pulling the baroness toward him. Spinning around, he pressed her against the building so she was protected by his body.

Another shot pounded into the brick beside them and the baroness let out a shriek, her body jerking so that every bit of her pressed against him. He had only an instant to register thigh and breast and hip before she moved away again.

"Who is it?" she asked, breathless.

Jones glanced over his shoulder, then back—one swift look so his face would not be recognized. *Bloody hell.* It was Wycomb, a pistol in each hand, running down the gangway.

"We need to hide. Now." He dared not look behind him to see how close Wycomb was or if he were aiming again. The risk of being recognized was too great.

Spinning the baroness away from the wall, he seized her hand and started to run. He had to slow to pace her shorter frame, but the panic that caused her ragged breathing fueled her feet as well.

He knew these streets, having run here as a boy looking for cargo to steal and sell. He turned right into an alley, then left onto a street and right into another alley. A few more turns and in the moments when dark fell fully, they were well away from the docks. Eventually, Jones pulled the baroness into a shop doorway set into the bricked side of a building.

They stood side by side, panting, hands still clutched together.

"Well," the baroness said between gasping breaths. "I don't think I've run so far or fast in a long time." Her hand gripped his hard, rubbing the bones together. "Are we safe? Is he gone?"

"Yes. He's gone. Or—" He looked about at the street again, at the well-shod men and women passing by, then the windows above and their respectable curtains. "Or at least he's unlikely to follow us this far."

"Are you sure?" Her voice quavered, the tremor nearly imperceptible.

"No." He spoke the truth, because he found he could not lie.

Her hand nearly crushed his as her head jerked up, the hood of her cloak revealing a face brilliantly white in the settling darkness. "Did he recognize me?" Her whisper was harsh, blending with the clatter of a passing carriage.

"I don't know."

What if he had? Jones could not send her alone into Worthington House. She would have no protection from Wycomb if the worst had happened.

He looked down at her, at the wide eyes, knowing he could have led a lamb to slaughter. He'd not brought her to the docks, but he *had* brought her onto the *Anna Louisa*. She should be sitting in a drawing room sipping tea from little porcelain cups, not running for her life.

"My apologies, my lady. I should not have—"

The hand folded in his jerked away, leaving nothing but cold, damp air in his fist. He swung his head around to look at her and found eyes bright with temper.

"*You?* As though my uncle did not bring me to this place?" The words were soft, but dangerous as any thunderstorm brewing behind dark clouds. "I will not allow my lands to be at risk, nor allow my uncle to participate in something immoral. No matter what it is, I will not avoid the fight. Do not think to shelter me."

"I beg your pardon?" The ground had shifted quickly beneath him. He stepped back to find the steadiness of the cobblestones again—only it didn't feel as though anything beneath his feet had solidified.

"You are more than a man who simply works for business gentlemen." The night hid the color of her eyes, but not the fierce expression on her face. "I saw you on the ship. Your knife, the pistol—the watchman. Did you kill him?"

He opened his mouth, closed it. Knifing was not polite conversation. Then, "Probably not, if he receives medical care. I've sustained worse."

"That is something." She gripped his coat, pulled him closer. "Who are you? Mercenary? Soldier?"

He shook his head, casting around for an excuse. A cover.

"Spy?"

He jerked, his body moving of its own volition.

"Ah." Full lips tipped up in satisfaction. A faint glow from a corner gas light shone over her features. She stepped forward so the space between them was no wider than the layers of cloak and coat. Her gloved hand settled on his cheek and a soft expression moved over her face. "I see."

"My lady," he said. "I could not tell you."

• • •

"I suppose not." Facts fell into place as the truth became clearer to her, each piece fitting together to form a single mosaic.

"You must not tell anyone, either." His face tightened into grim lines. "There is more at stake than you know. Some of which I can tell you, but much I cannot."

So serious, this spy, and so full of honor. Her hand dropped away but she moved even closer, suddenly craving the heat and scent of him now that the pieces of him were in place.

"I trust you, Jones." She tipped her face up, wanting his lips to take hers. *Willing* them to. This tight, unbearable sensation in her belly would surely break her if he did not kiss her again.

But he didn't. Only the London night air touched her lips, cold and quiet. His gaze fastened on hers as though committing the shape and color of her eyes to his memory. He stepped away from her in a sudden, decisive movement, his hands coming up as though warding her off.

"Forgive me." The words were a whisper from his lips, snatched by the wind a moment later. "I should not have kissed you earlier."

"There's no need for forgiveness." She looked down at her own hands, rubbed a finger over the small, neat stitches of a glove seam. She felt much less ordered than those stitches, as though someone had plucked at her and pulled her out of the prearranged line. Breathing deep, she looked up again at those dark, dark eyes. "I wanted it."

It was truth. A truth she should not say, but the words could not be stopped. Something inside her had soared when he'd kissed her, and another part had become golden and warm and liquid—more, though, was a place inside her heart that had bloomed.

"I still want it, Jones."

He was quiet for a long moment, in which time became darkness and yearning and chilled rain. "It cannot be, my lady," he finally whispered.

"No. It cannot." She was constrained by class and duty even for something so small as a kiss. Chained by them, with the chains of duty forged in tradition. Whatever Jones and his kisses had given life to inside her could not withstand law and custom and her father's trust. "But I wish it could be."

Jones said nothing, the planes of his face smoothing out until he became unreadable to her. He held her gaze, conveying nothing that soothed and everything that raked at her heart. Then he turned away, eyes examining every nook of the street.

He led her out of the hidden doorway, taking her elbow to steady her over the doorstep. "Come, we'll find a hackney." He scanned the street, angled toward another—then stopped, his hand tightening on her elbow. "I cannot let you return alone."

"What choice is there?" Bitterness edged each word. "If Wycomb didn't recognize me and I don't return, he will send an alarm and begin a search. It is impossible for me *not* to return."

"If your uncle did recognize you?" He spoke as if he knew the answer and was waiting for her to arrive at it, his focus still on the concealing shadows around them.

Cat studied his profile. His nose was strong and straight, his mouth set in resolute lines. When he raised his hand to call a hackney, the muscles of his shoulders and back shifted beneath his jacket. The tight feeling in her belly grew, spreading through her body to warm her cheeks, her thighs. He was not as elegant and refined as the men of the *ton*, but there was no denying his masculinity or his strength.

She knew what she must do. Taking a deep breath, Cat lifted her head and tipped her chin high. "There is only one way to find out."

"So there is."

A moment later they were bundled into a hackney together, he on one seat and she on the other. Their need to taste each other—and the inability to do so—sat squarely between them.

They didn't speak as the carriage made its way to Park Lane, but she was conscious of every shift of his body, every soft breath. His gaze nearly pinned her to the carriage cushion, dark and sharp and as corporeal as the rest of him.

"Don't look at me like that," she finally whispered.

"Like what?"

"I don't know, but it makes me—"

"You haunt me, my lady. Everything about you, but most especially your eyes." Even as his sentence trailed off, he pressed his lips together. "Forgive me. I should not have spoken."

Her eyes. How strange. Unsure what he meant, she looked away and down at her hands, resting quietly in her lap. The supple, tan kidskin was pale against the dark cloak surrounding her.

"I will not let you enter Worthington House alone, my lady. You may need protection."

"How can you—"

"The same way I entered your uncle's study. It's past sunset and approaching night. If I am quick, I will be able to enter and exit with no one the wiser."

"And myself?" Her fingers flinched. "My uncle had planned to meet us later at a ball, after an appointment, though I suppose we know what appointment now."

"Yes." A wry half smile moved his lips.

"Aunt Essie will be expecting me to—oh no." She rubbed

her temples, knives and pistols fighting with gowns and curling tongs in her mind.

"What?"

"I'm late. Considerably." Cat puffed out a breath. The carriage began to slow, and her panic to rise. "She'll want to know where I've been."

"Lie," he answered brusquely. "Feign illness, as you did before, so that you do not go out into the *ton* tonight. Go to your room to rest—then, we wait."

"For Wycomb to come for me?" To beat her, perhaps. Or kill her. Terror wove through her, though she struggled to force it out.

Until Jones spoke and the terror lodged in her chest.

"Yes."

Jones stayed in the carriage as she descended the steps, quickly so Brown would not see who was inside. She heard Jones thump the ceiling of the carriage and the hackney moved off.

Cat swept up the steps, chin held high. She was the lady of the house, after all. Even if her insides were swirling and twisting with need for Jones and fear of Wycomb.

Aunt Essie was hovering in the hall, white hair piled high and dressed in a frilled evening gown.

"Oh, Mary Elizabeth. I was so worried!" Warm, plump arms encircled Cat, the closest to home and mother Cat could remember for some time. "Where have you been?"

"I was out. I'm not feeling well, Essie." Cat set her hand on her aunt's cheek. "I went for a walk and started feeling sick, 'tis all. I'll be well enough tomorrow, I promise."

"What of the ball?" Essie drew back, looked at Cat—and her eyes narrowed. "Very well. When my brother arrives to meet us, I shall tell him you took ill. But be careful, dear. He is not patient or forgiving."

So Cat knew, given the pistols aimed at her that night.

Chapter Nineteen

The room was dark. Only the faint, reddened glow of coals shone in the hearth. Somewhere in the darkness Jones waited, unseen and unheard.

But she knew he was there. Beyond the mounded coverlets, beyond the bed curtains standing sentry on either side of her, a man filled the room with his unseen presence.

He'd slipped into her room just after she'd blown out the candle. A shadow in the corner, behind a chair and drapes.

Fear should be weaving through her. Instead, Jones was a comfort, out there in the dark of her room. He'd not left her alone to face the terrors of the night.

Trust wandered in and out of the dark as well. Trust in Jones.

The house settled into silence. She could not hear Jones's breath, nor any movement. Not the shush of boot against floor, or even a rustle of clothing.

She could not say the same for herself. Her breath sounded harsh in her own ears, though her body made no noise. Each muscle was tensed, unable to move, ears straining for Wycomb's arrival as much as a sign from Jones. Everything hummed beneath the surface of her skin, a slow, unseen rush of unease and disquiet.

"Where are you?" She barely spoke the words, the whisper lifting from her lips before her mind knew she'd said them.

"I have not left." It was not an answer to her question, and she smiled in the dark to hear it.

"What will you do if he comes? If he recognized me and he comes here?"

"Protect you."

The words floated through darkness and time, not anchoring her to this room or her fear, but something different. She pulled the coverlet up to her chin and let it wash over it her, let Jones's presence fill the empty places in her so terror could not hide there.

A scuff of boot on floor filtered through the darkness, then a scraping sound. "I'm opening the window, my lady, to better hear the noises outside."

Cat breathed in as cool night air slipped into the room, still carrying the scent of rain. Distant carriage wheels rumbled over cobblestones, overlaid by raucous laughter as people moved along Park Lane. Each sound echoed in the small, inset courtyard below her window.

She would not have thought to open the window to hear Wycomb coming.

"How long have you been a spy?"

He was quiet a long time, and she thought he had not heard her. Then his murmured words filled the dark.

"Since I was a boy."

"A boy?" Surprise rippled through her body, and her voice rose as she shifted in the bed. "Is your father a spy, then?"

Again he was silent, but she knew now that he had heard

her. Perhaps he was weighing his words, or thinking on them at least. It seemed so when he finally, slowly, said, "I don't know my father. Or my mother."

Sorrow etched a mark into her heart, as did shock. She could not imagine living without that knowledge.

"I was abandoned at a foundling hospital, my lady."

More shock. More sorrow. And tears, she discovered, gathering behind her eyes. She opened her mouth to speak, but the words did not come. There was more here, more for him to say. More to Jones himself than being a spy or an abandoned babe, but she would not pry further.

He didn't continue for a long moment, so she asked a simple question.

"How late will you stay tonight, Jones?"

"Until Wycomb returns. If he identified you, he will not wait until the morning." He moved now, though she could not hear him, precisely. But the air moved and awareness slipped over her skin.

Suddenly she saw his shadow, above and to the right. Broad, square, straight. Blackness against darkness. She sensed he was looking down at her.

"I do not ask for pity," he said softly.

"Nor would I give it." Sorrow, yes, but not pity. Pushing up to seated, she let the coverlet fall where it may. "Where you come from is important, but only in so far as where it sends you."

"I suppose that is true." He stepped forward and moved as though he would sit beside her, then stepped away again. Still he stood above her, looking down at the bed. He would not be able to see her, any more than she could see him beyond vague shadows that were darker and lighter than each other. "Where did your past send you, my lady?"

They existed in a different place now, somewhere outside of time. Outside of the separation of class and society, of his life and hers. So she answered with truth.

"To unhappiness. My past is a burden and joy, Jones, though I would not change it. I am trapped, and I cannot see a way out."

"Trapped by what?"

"The trust. The only escape is to marry—and marry well. The Marquess of Hedgewood has already indicated he would offer." She looked down at her legs, at the two mountains of fabric they created as she folded them inside her arms and rested her head on her knees. "The trust will not end until I am thirty-five or married. I must either let the trustees control lands and people without understanding their hearts, or I must marry and give that same control to a man who will not have the understanding I do."

"Are the hearts of the people so important to you?" The question was soft, nearly lower than a whisper.

"Yes." Her father had taught her this. He had understood the value of each person on his lands. They were all part of the fabric of life. "Without the tenants—every farmer and housewife, every fishmonger and blacksmith—the whole would not exist. Each is a part of the whole."

Her words stretched thin, becoming only silence. Jones, hidden in the darkness, said nothing, and she wondered if perhaps she had said too much.

"I know enough about the *ton* to know you could wait until the trust is broken and inherit. Your title can be held by a lady in her own right." There was a shifting in the shadows, as if he had repositioned himself.

"In the interim, the trustees could drive away loyal tenants. I would lose touch with all of my property. They will not allow me access to information nor listen to my suggestions. I have no choice but to marry someone with my views."

"My lady—"

"I could do it alone—all of it—if only my father had allowed it." The bitterness in her belly betrayed her, rising to choke her words. Refusing to give in to it, she smoothed the coverlet over her legs and swallowed hard.

"My lady, a trust is customary, is it not?"

"I trained for years with my father. I worked, read, memorized accounts and figures—anything he did, I would do. I *know* how to run the estates, crops, work with tenants, and manage investments. All of it." In the end, custom and tradition won over her experience. "He let me *believe* I could do it, allowed me to think that it would all be mine once I gained my majority. When he died, he put it in the trust and took it all away."

Disappointment ran deep. Deeper than she had thought.

Looking up at the shadow above her, at the indistinguishable face of Jones, she sighed. "I suppose all of that sounds silly and spoiled. Here I am, lamenting that acres of land and thousands of pounds did not come under my control outright, when so many others have so little."

Including Jones.

The silence and dark spun out, and she wondered what he thought of her. Perhaps that she was petty and small-minded. Spoiled, as she had said.

"I have never known a lady like you." The mattress shifted as something heavy pressed on it.

Jones. There on the edge of her bed. Beside her.

He'd twisted his body to face her, hip just brushing her thigh. She could see him more clearly now, though he was still shadowed. The strong edge of his jaw, the lean cheekbones. His expression was hidden in the dark, in the night, but she felt the focus of his gaze as if it were physical.

The soft, gentle stroke of thumb across her lips made her breath shake.

"You have such heart," he murmured. "You see so much

more than any lady I've met."

Warm, strong hands cupped her cheeks. Held there.

"I don't—it's nothing." She didn't understand what he meant, couldn't think beyond the hitch of her breath and the gentleness of his hands. Her hands searched for purchase on the coverlet.

"It's everything." His lips found hers in the dark. Yearning and need spiraled through her, tangling in her belly.

Arms circled her, drawing her in. Every inch of her body warmed, tingled, throbbed, but it was his mouth that held her. Magic whispered there, in his taste, the touch of his tongue. Careful, hesitant.

Adoring.

It was as if he could not believe she was real.

Her body was hot. Waiting. His mouth was sweet when it pressed against hers. She felt his need, as well, but the gentleness held sway.

She set her hands on his forearms, ran them up his biceps to his shoulders. She let those shoulders ground her, let herself feel protected. He'd removed his coat and there was nothing between her hands and his body but thin cotton. Not the soft, expensive linen that a lord would wear, but simple fabric. Beneath that, muscle shifted as his arms swept around her. One hand splayed against her back, hot and strong through her nightshift. The other tangled in the hair at the nape of her neck, just at that spot before it wove into a loose braid.

His tongue swept along the seam of her lips. She parted for him, shock and desire spinning through her as his tongue met hers. He tasted of man, of rain. Of safety and danger. All of him centered in her, filled her with a swirling, heady tangle of want and pleasure.

Suddenly Jones stilled.

His arms were around her, his mouth on hers, but his body, his breath, had stilled.

He moved away from her, fast and quiet, leaving her cold and alone on the bed.

Loss. Confusion. Both welled in her until they were replaced by fear as the sound of hoof beats grew louder, louder still, then stopped so near the open window there could be no doubt the animal and its rider were in front of Worthington House.

...

"Oh God." Cat scrambled up, nightshift tangling around her knees. "Is it him?"

"Lay down." Jones was already gone from the edge of the bed, moving toward the window. The curtains were partially pulled, and he flicked one back to see the street. "Pretend to be asleep, and *do not move* unless I say. Do you understand?"

"Yes." Cat was already burrowing beneath the coverlet. It wasn't protection against a weapon, but she felt safer buried beneath the cotton and silk.

Through the open window, Cat heard the front doors of the townhouse open and the murmur of a sleepy footman. Wycomb spoke sharply, though the words dissolved before reaching her ears. The door closed, its sharp snap echoing in the courtyard.

Then, silence.

She expected her uncle to call for her, to come running upstairs and through hallways. Cat waited, unable to breathe, staring into the darkness above her.

"I can't hear him." Licking lips made dry by her own harsh, hot breath, Cat forced her fingers to ease their clutching grip on the coverlet.

"I am right here, my lady. He will not hurt you." Jones was close to the bed. His tone was mild, but the words hard-edged. "Just stay in the bed so that I know where you are."

The silence outside her chamber walls was broken by light footfalls measured by purpose. They paused outside the door. Cat went rigid, every fiber of her body fighting not to run.

The door opened a sliver. Candlelight shone through the gap, crossing the bed at her waist. She closed her eyes, pretending to sleep as Jones had asked—and waiting for something else.

Death, perhaps.

Time became interminable, a breath she could not breathe.

Wycomb did not enter but continued to stand at the doorway, looking in at her. Then, slowly, the door closed with a quiet click.

Still, she could not breathe.

More footsteps, fading away now, until there was nothing beyond her door. No one in the room beyond Jones.

She did not know how long it was before Jones spoke. It might have been hours. She thought she dozed as exhaustion gripped her, but if so, it did not last long. When he finally spoke, she discovered he was near her, just beyond the edge of the bed.

"I think it is safe, my lady. But if you do not mind, I shall stay a little longer."

"Yes." The word shuddered out. Fear could steal one's breath, she realized, not because one could see the threat, but because it was brutally difficult to wait for the threat to arrive. "Yes, please. I don't—"

She didn't know what to say. Cat turned on the bed, pillowing her cheek on her hands so that she faced him. She realized now he was seated in a chair he'd moved beside the bed. She had not heard him repositioning the furniture, but he was clearly there, leaning forward with elbows resting on his knees. Shadow among shadows. The line of his back was strong and straight, and his shirtsleeves were rolled up to reveal his forearms.

Some small, new part of her thought perhaps it would be easier to fight without the encumbrance of a jacket.

"I won't leave you. Not until dawn." Jones raised his head, and though she couldn't see his eyes, she felt the intensity there. "Wycomb did not recognize you, or he would have entered the room, but I don't intend to take a chance he's waiting."

"What of tomorrow? What if he waits?"

He rocked forward, looked down at his clasped hands. Despair seemed to hang as a weight about his neck. Reaching toward the bed, he whispered, "I cannot stay in this room in daylight, my lady. I would, if I could. I promise I will be watching, as best I can."

She took his hand. There was no thought in her mind beyond the fact that it was there, solid and strong. *He* was there, for whatever might or might not happen tomorrow.

"Jones." She gripped his fingers, unsure what to say, but knowing that this large, rough hand was comfort and reassurance. "Thank you."

"You're welcome, my lady." His hand did not move, but remained as solid as before. His fingers curled inward, enfolding hers and warming them.

It was then she fell asleep.

Chapter Twenty

When she woke the sun was high in the sky. Dawn had come and gone, and it was near to midmorning.

She was alone.

Her arm was still outstretched over the cooled sheets, as if waiting for Jones to return. Foolish thinking, foolish thoughts. She was not thinking of her safety, but only of his presence. Of his gentle kiss. And of the words between them—words of childhood and loss and heartache.

Yet, those few words might hold the heart of him.

I was abandoned at a foundling hospital.

Cat pushed aside the thick blue coverlet, slipping from the bed and into the bright sunshine streaming through the window.

It was still open.

She smiled into the breeze now filled with light, baking bread, and the shouts of hawkers. Somewhere on the other side of the window and listening to the same sounds, would be Jones.

The soft tap of knuckles on wood filled the air and

Cat whirled, all sense of protection dissipating. Her breath clutched in her throat as the door opened. Blond curls beneath a small cap appeared around the edge of the door, a pretty face following. Cat's shoulders sagged as relief permeated the bone and sinew of her body.

"Eliza." Her ladies' maid. *Not Wycomb.* "Good morning."

"Good morning, my lady." The girl smiled and stepped into the room. "You were sleeping so deeply when I came at the usual time, I thought it best to leave you."

"Yes, thank you. I was not feeling well yesterday evening." Cat moved toward the night jacket thrown over the chaise across the room and shrugged into it. "What time is it?"

"Half past—"

"It is time to discuss this evening's soirée." The interrupting voice raised the hair on Cat's arms and sent an icy ball into the pit of her belly.

Wycomb stood in the doorway, handsome face set in lines that allowed no latitude for argument—but she did not see death in his eyes. She hoped if death had chosen this lovely morning to take her she would at least see it coming.

"Uncle." She inclined her head, holding it at an angle that meant *you're not welcome*. Her mother had taught her that one to ward off unwelcome attentions in the ballroom.

Her father had told her to use her fist or her knee, but that didn't apply in this circumstance.

Gripping the front edges of her night jacket, Cat stared at the man she no longer knew. Any trace of the docks was hidden beneath an elegant coat and waistcoat, anger lost in the nothingness behind his eyes.

"The Marquess of Hedgewood has asked for your hand in marriage. I have accepted his offer."

"Accepted?" *He could not have done so.* Numb fingers fell away from the cotton night jacket. Cat stepped forward, feet uncertain as to their course but body unable to stay still.

"I have not agreed to wed him," she said sharply.

"I do not require your agreement." Her uncle held her gaze steadily. "I signed the contract last night."

The little maid fluttered somewhere near the armoire, gown and petticoats frothing over her arms. The excitement gathering in that portion of the room did not ease the dread gathering within Cat.

Wycomb had committed her to marriage—a lifetime—without her consent.

"I will not marry him."

"You do not have a choice." He spoke as if her words had no meaning. He shrugged his shoulders, shifting his coat so he could properly situate his shirt cuffs.

"What will you do? Lock me in my room and starve me until I obey?" She had heard of such things, but had never believed them. Nor would she allow it. A door made of wood could be broken, as could a glass window if a person were desperate.

She would be desperate.

"No, Mary Elizabeth. I do not need to lock you in."

The maid ceased her fluttering, the rustle of clothing stilled until silence hung between the shadows and sunlight.

"Eliza, please allow me a moment to speak privately with my uncle." Dimly, Cat heard the girl slip into the hall and shut the door behind her. Just as dimly, Cat thought of the docks, of pistols, of balls thudding into brick. Palms slicked with sweat, Cat straightened her shoulders. "I do not wish to marry Hedgewood."

"I am your guardian, Mary Elizabeth." Wycomb lowered his voice, stepped forward. He was close, so close she could smell his soap. He was taller, stronger, and loomed over her frame.

"You will not always be my guardian. Only until August."

"True," he said. "For now, the law shall be on my side."

Curse the law. "I cannot be made to say the words. The church requires consent."

"Also true." Wycomb began to walk, footsteps soft but creating a circle around her—one that tightened and squeezed her breath without touch or words. She did not speak as he stepped behind her and set her lips near her ear. The scent of bay rum was strong, as was the light brush of his breath against the curls laying over her neck and shoulders. "Yet I signed the contract, which includes a clause that in the event of a breach of promise—in short, should you break the engagement—a good portion of your fortune will be forfeit as well."

"A good portion." Hate slipped and slid beneath her skin. "What? How much?"

"Complete the ceremony and sign your name to the parish register, and Ashdown Abbey will be your separate estate." He stepped beside her and looked down at her. "It will be in trust under the Chancery Court until his death—untouchable by Hedgewood or his creditors—then revert to you or your heirs. He will have no part of it."

Her hand fisted, rose, then fell again. "If I don't marry him?"

"Ashdown Abbey will become Hedgewood's by law." Triumph twisted his lips as he met her gaze. "Forever."

• • •

A soft breeze filtered through the air. Barely a ruffle of time and space.

From the desk chair, Jones could see the door of the study, which remained firmly closed.

The Flower, then.

"The door is not nearly as difficult as the window." Jones pulled his pistol from the waist of his breeches and set it on the desktop, just beside the newspaper he was reading. "If you insist on entering by that method, I suppose I cannot stop you."

He did not look up, but kept his fingers moving along the printed lines of the page. The Flower would not expect more, at any rate.

"Your window locks—they are nearly as ridiculous as Maximilian's once were." Her voice was both laughing and efficient as she shut the study window with no more noise than a sigh.

"They are the best, as you well know." He grinned at the page he'd been scouring—unsuccessfully—for information on the *Anna Louisa* and her next voyage, though the lines blurred now that he had lost his focus. "I know of no one else who can pick them."

"*You* can, no?"

"Of course." He looked up, abandoning his reading. "But not as quickly as you."

A lean, taut female body prowled the study. The hair tucked beneath her man's cap was dark and curling, though Jones could see little more than a few stray locks. But he knew the woman and that wild hair well enough: Vivienne La Fleur, child of the streets, opera dancer—and spy.

"It is always a pleasure, Flower, but what brings you here? Why are you not settled at your home, cozied up to your new husband, and playing matron?" The teasing words were for form, as it was Jones himself who'd paved the way for Vivienne to find love, but he did enjoy seeing the Flower's embarrassed flush. She had not yet become used to being married.

The flush faded, as did the slight smile on her pretty lips. "Henri."

There would be no more teasing between them.

"Wycomb." Jones stood, setting aside the paper with no

more thought to its contents. The pistol stayed where it was, gleaming on top of the study desk. "What did he do?"

"He came to Maximilian's last night demanding that I assist him. Maximilian nearly retrieved his dueling pistols from their case." The Flower huffed, her shoulders moving beneath the man's coat in a Gallic gesture both dismissive and irritated. Still, fear lay beneath the words. "I will not go back to him. Sir Charles has said I do not report to Henri. *Alors*, I do not. I could not."

"No." Jones knew the reasons were many and started when the Flower was a girl, though the most recent was she had fought her commander and bested him. Wycomb would never forgive such insubordination, no matter that Sir Charles had championed her.

"Henri was different than I remember, Jones, though it has been a half year since I have seen him." The Flower cupped her fingers around her elbows. It was not a gesture of protection, but it tugged at Jones just the same. "Confidence, he has always had. Command, as well. He was even a little charming, a part he has always been able to play as necessary, though he knows I can see through the charade. But there was something beneath that I have never seen."

"What?" Jones itched to pick up his weapon so the worn, comfortable stock would press into the palm of his hand.

"I do not know." Her dark, nearly black eyes snapped beneath the cap she wore. "Desperation and agitation, perhaps. It was not right, Jones. I have never seen this in him, not in all the years he trained me."

"Do you know his niece? The baroness?"

"Niece?" The Flower frowned, dark brows curving over her face. "She is young, no? He speaks of her on occasion, but as if she were young and of little use to him."

She was old enough to marry, too young to own property. "She is not so young."

"I know little of her, as he rarely spoke of anything to me beyond assignments." The Flower plopped into the chair opposite him and stretched booted feet toward the fire. "Life is never what you think, is it? He we are, sitting in the West End of London with the *ton* all around. The rookeries are far from here."

"Farther in substance than distance." He cleared his throat. "What time did Wycomb arrive last night?"

"Not long after ten o'clock." One corner of her lips tipped up. "I remember, as I was arguing with Maximilian. I wanted to go to bed, to make a baby, you understand? He wanted to work on a document from the Prussian ambassador."

"Idiot." Jones laughed, though the idea of the Flower—a fellow spy his own age—creating a family made some small part his heart ache.

"So I told Maximilian." She cocked her head to one side. The cap covering her hair shifted and she swiped at the long lock that tumbled free. "It would be impolite of me to say I won the argument, seeing as you and I made love once, all those years ago."

He snorted. "That doesn't seem to have stopped you."

"*Non.*" She shrugged. "We both understand there was nothing there but friendship. As a friend, Jones, I would have you know that family and spying can exist together, if you want it enough."

"Ah." There was nothing more for him to say. He didn't believe her.

"You advised me once when I was at odds with Maximilian to take love, even if it was fleeting, because it could not last for a spy." She rose from the chair, raised her small, quick hands as if to say *take it*. "It can, if you want it to."

"I don't know that I do." He did. He knew it in every fiber of his being. He breathed deep, closed his eyes, then opened them again to meet the Flower's dark gaze. "If I did, now is not the time for me to fall in love. Lord Wycomb has arrived on your doorstep, asking for your assistance. Why come to me?"

"I know there are things you cannot tell me." The Flower paused, casting her eyes around the room. Her gaze landed on shelves, field glasses, a compass, then finally met his. "I thought to go to Sir Charles, but if there is an investigation—or if one should be started—then it is you I must come to."

She did not know of the investigation already started, then. There was more he could not tell her. Jones stood and paced toward the Flower, then away. Wycomb had arrived at the Flower's home after Jones and Baroness Worthington had been at the docks, but before Wycomb returned to Worthington House. That left two questions. Why did Wycomb need the Flower, and where else had he gone?

"Why did he come to you, specifically?"

"I do not know." She leaned her forearms on the back of one of the arm chairs Angel had set in front of the desk long before Jones came to live there. He'd not moved them, as they were a reminder of the many times he'd been praised and chastised there. "I wish I did."

He would have to tread lightly. Wycomb was a spy under investigation. The Flower could not know until Sir Charles indicated she could. Yet, what connection might she have with the *Anna Louisa*?

Wycomb had been the Flower's commander, taking her from the streets and turning her into a spy. He'd broken her spirit and terrified her, then rebuilt her and taught her what she needed to know to survive. The Flower was fashioned of strength and tenacity, a testament to the heartache and training she endured.

The Flower knew Wycomb better than anyone.

"There has been a change in him," she said again, still leaning on the chair. She eyed her hands, turning them over to look at her palms. Her eyes were grave, brows lifted high to form two pointed arcs of emphasis.

"Did he tell you what he is working on?"

"*Non*. He did not say exactly. But, Jones…" She narrowed those focused, nearly black eyes. Pushing away from the seat, she crossed the small space between chair and desk. "He said if I agreed to assist him, I would not need to leave London to perform the tasks."

That was *something*. London was large and complicated, but it was still a manageable geographic area. More manageable than the whole of Britain or the Continent, at any rate.

"Do you understand the significance?" The Flower asked sharply, setting her hip on the edge of the desk and planted her booted feet firmly in the patterned rug beneath.

"The problem is here in London," Jones answered.

"Yes, but more than that. He requested my assistance." She leaned forward, arms folded in front of her. "Henri does not request. He demands. Commands. Subtly bribes or threatens, depending on his quarry. He does not request."

"Ah." He saw it, as clearly now as if he had stood beside Vivienne when Wycomb arrived. "He was all charm and persuasion."

"*Oui*, but he always is. Only this time, there was no threat of reprisal under his words. No demand. He was nearly begging." She shook her head, grasping the cap with one hand to keep her rioting curls contained beneath. "I do not like this Henri. Perhaps it is only that I am not in his command that caused him to act so, but whatever his reason, it made me uneasy. If he wants something so badly to *ask* me for help, instead of demanding it, then he is in trouble."

"I understand." Jones turned away from her to stare into the fireplace. He watched as flame devoured wood, then coal fed flame. A give and take that fueled the light and heat in this room.

The Flower's words were only one piece of a puzzle he needed to build. One piece would fit into the next if he gathered enough pieces.

"I appreciate you telling me."

Black eyes became fierce, snapping and darkening further as she stepped toward him. "The line is important. What we do so often wavers between right and wrong, but there is still a line that cannot be crossed."

"Yes, but—"

"There is justice in you, Jones. You understand both sides of the line. It is why Sir Charles has chosen you to spy on other spies. It is not easy." She gripped his shoulder, her strong, clever fingers a comfort and a loss at one time. "Justice is never easy, but it is right. There must be someone willing to hold others to the line. And I—Maximilian and I—appreciate that you do. We would not be together, or even alive, if you had not investigated my actions last year. I nearly crossed the line."

It was true. They both knew it, though she had not said the words before. The value in them, the value in what he did each day, seemed to coalesce even as her words faded on air.

"Thank you, Vivienne."

"*Oui.*" The small, competent hand released his shoulder. She turned away, moving toward the window. After shoving open the casement, she swung a leg over the sill, then paused. "If I hear more of what Henri is doing, I shall pay you a visit."

"Do use the door next time, won't you?"

With a laugh, she slipped out the window and into the night.

Chapter Twenty-One

"What do I do, Aunt Essie?" Cat dipped her knife into the jar of blackberry preserves, then spread the rich, purple-black fruit over her biscuit. "Uncle signed the contracts."

"I don't know, dear." Aunt Essie dragged her teacup to her mouth and set its rim against pursed lips. "He is your guardian, and they are legally binding marriage contracts."

Cat stared at the biscuit in her hand. She knew it would be fluffy and light, the preserves sweet and tart and thick—but she could not bring herself to eat it. Her mouth was dry and tea already roiled in her stomach. She dropped the biscuit onto the patterned Wedgewood plate.

Wycomb had trapped her.

"My dear." Essie reached over and set wrinkled, plump hands over Cat's wrist. "I worry for you. Are you ready for marriage?"

"No." Even if Jones discovered Wycomb was doing something illegal, the contract was still binding. Ashdown Abbey would be Hedgewood's. "I suppose I have no choice."

"I am happy to hear our earlier conversation has changed

your mind, Mary Elizabeth." The voice sliding from the shadows was wily and low. Wycomb strode through the hallway door and into the breakfast room. "The wedding will take place before midsummer."

"Before mid—" Cat whipped her head up to stare at the man in the doorway. Her uncle appeared as unconcerned by her wishes as the well-cut coat sitting on his shoulders. "It is not even May."

"The marquess does not wish to delay the ceremony." Wycomb perused the sideboard, though he had no doubt breakfasted earlier as per his habit. He chose a ripe grape grown in the hothouse at Ashdown Abbey. "Hedgewood wishes to evaluate each of the newly acquired properties prior to the winter."

She recognized the set of Wycomb's shoulders and purse of his lips as studied disinterest. It felt as though something small with many legs skittered across her skin when he acted in this calculating manner.

"You lie," she said, slowly coming to her feet. Essie squeaked and china tinkled. "You lie. It is not the marquess who has chosen the date. It is you, so that I will not yet have reached my majority by the date of the wedding."

Silence fell, broken only by Aunt Essie's nervous intake of breath.

"True." Wycomb lifted a plate from the sideboard and leaned over biscuits to inspect them, not bothering to look at her as he spoke. "You are my ward, Mary Elizabeth, until August." Now he turned his head and looked at her, as though she were no more interesting than the biscuits. "Before then, I legally control you."

"Only if I allow it," she said softly. Her heart bumped inside her chest, an erratic beat she could not control.

A cold light flared in his eyes as they narrowed on her. He straightened, chest expanding with the force of his fury.

She braced herself for whatever assault he intended. Openly challenging him was a step he would not tolerate—they both knew it.

The onslaught of his anger never came. Wycomb pivoted to face the hall as a shout echoed, followed by running footsteps.

A man barreled through the doorway wearing a filthy homespun coat and breeches stained with black, sooty streaks. Wide eyes flicked frantically around the room—but whatever he intended to do was cut off by Wycomb as he leaped forward. Her uncle's body twisted with ease and elegance, arms whipping through the air as though he regularly practiced slamming men into walls. Pictures rattled and one crashed to the floor as the man cried out.

"Milady! Mr. Sparks—" He was cut off by Wycomb's forearm pressing against his windpipe.

"Wycomb!" Cat surged toward them, ignoring Aunt Essie's short shriek and the clatter of her chair as it toppled to the floor. "He's from Ashdown Abbey!"

She didn't think, only curled her hands around Wycomb's shoulder and tried to tug him back. He let go, jerking his arms in release. Cat ducked to avoid being hit and stumbled.

"Speak," Wycomb commanded.

The stranger slipped to the floor and opened his mouth, gaze shifting first to Cat, then Wycomb, then Cat again.

"The granaries, milady. My lord." The man slumped against the wall, rubbing his throat. "They've caught fire. When I left, they were nearly half gone." He sucked in air. Wide eyes stared at Cat. "Mr. Sparks, he said he thought they would all go."

Her heart rose into her throat. She swallowed hard, hoping it would slip back where it belonged. Crouching down, she brought her face level with the man's. "Was anyone hurt?" Cat set her hand on the man's shoulder—a gesture that had Wycomb lurching forward, then back again.

"No, milady." The man shook his head and straightened, and she saw that it wasn't dirt on his face, but streaks of soot. "When I left, only a few were hurt from burns an' such, but no one badly."

"How long ago?" she whispered.

"Early this morning. I rode hard, changed horses to be here quick." Scrubbing a hand over his face, he smeared the dirt and soot over weary creases. "I 'as to get back, milady."

"Go to the stables. Use a fresh horse for the return and tell them to ready the carriage. I'm going, too," Cat said firmly, already spinning toward the door.

"You shall not." Wycomb's voice shot through the room, command a sharp edge on his words.

Cat stopped, drew a deep breath in through her nose and let it out through her mouth. It steadied her, that breath. "No?"

"Mr. Sparks will do what needs to be done. You are needed here, to secure your inheritance. Hedgewood will be announcing the engagement tomorrow."

Cat turned to look at her uncle. His coat was wrinkled and lopsided on his shoulders from his efforts, but his hair seemed as elegant and his face as controlled as ever. His will was nearly palpable, weighing heavy in the room.

"Sir?" She looked at the sooty tenant, then her aunt. "Essie? Please excuse us, if you would."

"Of course, dear." Essie swept out, herding the tenant before her and leaving silence in her wake.

A clock ticked somewhere nearby, it's rhythmic signal counting the seconds between Cat and—something. Wycomb ran a hand around the circumference of the plate he'd dropped onto the sideboard, finger tracing the outer rim in slow, thoughtful movements.

Finally, his words soft and careful. "You cannot help

them."

"Perhaps not, but I should be there." It was her duty. They were her people, her tenants, and she would not fail when they needed hope. "My father taught me that in times of need, the tenants will look to the lord. Is he there? If not, they will despair and, perhaps, lose faith. Loss of faith breeds dissension and difficulties."

Wycomb's lips lifted at the corners with mocking amusement. "These are not feudal times, Mary Elizabeth. Nor are you the lord."

She would not let his words rankle. "I may not be a lord, and no, these are not feudal times. The fact remains that my tenants look to me as the last Ashdown to lead them. Failing to do so fails them." She squared her shoulders. "I will strike a bargain with you."

"I am listening." His fingers paused in their movements around the edge of the breakfast plate.

"I will say nothing more about the marriage to Hedgewood." It was as if the jury at Old Bailey had ordered her death. Her skin became clammy, her ears buzzed, but she was bound by contract. She had little to lose. "I will not fight it."

"You will say the words and sign the register?" He took a step forward, cocking his head as he approached. She fought the urge to retreat. "Do your duty by Hedgewood?"

"Yes." The shudder tried to wrack her entire body, but she refused to give it rein. "Yes, I will do my duty."

Something flickered in Wycomb's gaze.

She'd won.

"*We* will leave shortly," he bit out. And oh, she could see the words were bitter. "Be ready."

Chapter Twenty-Two

The advantage to one's family seat being a long day's ride from London was one needed to pack very little.

The carriage waited on the cobblestone street, rolling forward and back as the horses pranced restlessly. Beyond them, Hyde Park and London moved and thrived and lived, unaware that her freedom was gone and her tenants' livelihoods at risk.

But there was more. She knew it.

"Aunt Essie, I need a moment." She tucked the short note she'd written to Jones more firmly into her palm. "I'll return shortly."

"Wycomb will be angry if you're late." Essie clutched the handles of her reticle, knuckles whitening as they became sharp little points. "He said—"

"Yes, I know what he said." Which was exactly why she wanted Jones to follow them. "It will only be a moment."

She left a frowning Essie in the front hall and slipped through the townhouse to the rear garden. It was difficult to leave a note behind the stone in daylight without being seen.

She reached down as though there were something wrong with the leather half-boots dyed to match her pale pink gown and did her best to hide the stone behind her skirts. From there, it was little effort to push the stone out of place, tuck the scrap of paper into the hollow of dirt, and nestle the stone back in place.

Still, she could not just walk into the garden, check her boot, and leave again. If anyone were watching she would appear suspicious. Perhaps Wycomb was watching from a window.

Perhaps Jones was watching.

She glanced around, her heart thumping a little—though from fear of Wycomb or the kisses of Jones, it was not clear. But there was no one at any window that she could see, nor anyone watching from the gate at the rear of the garden.

She took a moment to snap the stems of a few bluebells carpeting the lawn. Holding them to her nose, she thought perhaps she could use it as an excuse if it was needed.

It was needed.

"What are you doing, Mary Elizabeth?" Wycomb stood in the rear doorway, his gloves fisted in one hand and his hat already perched on his head. "The carriage is ready."

"Yes, thank you. I just needed a moment to calm myself. I'm quite worried, as you might imagine." Her words sounded just like the lie they were, so she decided to stop speaking altogether. "We should go." Clutching the bluebells in her fist, she strode toward Wycomb and the house.

Though he watched her carefully, he turned aside and let her through the door to the rear kitchen. She hoped he did not look behind her.

• • •

Jones trotted along the walkway of Park Lane, then through

Hyde Park, trying to keep the carriage in sight. But he could not keep pace with horses, even in the midst of slow-moving traffic on the street. When the vehicle disappeared, he simply changed course and returned to Park Lane.

Whatever they were doing, it was not a quick foray on Bond Street or to Gunter's. The urgency of body movements, the speed of the coachman's start—something was wrong.

It was an hour before an opportunity to check the stone arrived. Jones slipped through the gate leading from the mews and knew in an instant the stone had been moved— fresh earth and mortar littered on the ground beneath it.

He itched to jerk the stone out of the wall and see what the baroness had left for him. But he couldn't simply dash forward. Raising his face to the summer sun he checked windows in the surrounding townhouses. There was no way to entirely protect himself from view except at night, but the trees and vegetation at the rear of the garden still provided some cover.

He couldn't do anything about the sunlight.

Drawing a deep breath and scanning the garden and mews again, Jones prepared himself for the jolt of her handwriting.

He slipped forward through the gate, moved the stone and retrieved the note in less time than a dandy needed to pry off his boots. Then Jones was back in the protection of the open street and its pedestrians, walking away from Worthington House.

Her home.

The note clutched in his fist was hot. He should loosen his grip, but he couldn't bring himself to do so. If he did, the note could be plucked away by the wind. He tightened his fist and moved through the streets, searching for a place to stop and read it.

It was in the shadow of the mews, tucked between two doorways, that Jones finally smoothed the note open. The paper was heavily weighted but soft between his fingers. He was compelled to sniff it, but thought the baroness might find it unseemly, so he simply rubbed the paper between his fingertips as he read.

My Dearest –

We are traveling home. The granaries caught fire and much of the remaining store is gone. The tenants are quite worried, as this year's harvest is looking to be less than usual. I must be with them.

We shall return in a few days' time, I'm certain, and I would enjoy seeing your handsome countenance. I shall continue my duties, of course, but I wish that you were with me for your advice and company.

I shall miss you.

All my regard,

C

Her script was neat and precise. It didn't march across the page, nor did it flow easily. It was careful. Jones smudged a thumb over the dark ink. Careful and deliberate, as her movements and words were until she forgot herself.

He wondered what the *C* represented.

Folding the note, he buried it deep in his coat pocket. He would burn it later, as he had done before. There would be no record she had ever written him a note.

Any pang he might feel at that loss was pushed aside. He needed to pack his belongings.

He was going to the country.

His own townhouse arrived in his vision not long after, as did the carriage resting in front of it. Angel's carriage. His mentor was in the hall, a set of books in one hand. He was reading the spines, head ducked down, gold queue at the base of his neck shifting over a dark coat.

"Ah. Jones. I was looking for my copies of—" He stopped, cocking his head. "What is the matter?"

"My investigation." No details. No specifics. But he could make a request of this man—the one he trusted above all others—and know it would not be repeated. "It's Wycomb. I don't have authorization to tell you, so—"

"Understood." Angel's lean face went hard, the softness marriage and impending fatherhood had wrought there fading as if it never existed. "What do you need from me?"

"He's going to the country with his niece for now, and I will be following him." The request rankled, but only because he *should* keep the investigation to himself. "Anything you see or hear in my absence will be appreciated."

"Of course." The books dropped onto the nearest table—a spindly one appearing to be barely tolerant of their weight. "Anywhere I should be specifically listening?"

"Anything outside of the *ton*, particularly related to ships."

"I will let you know if I discover anything." Amber eyes narrowed in thought, then widened again. "Why do I feel as if you in are over your head?"

"I have no idea."

Chapter Twenty-Three

"I'm sorry, Mr. Sparks." Cat kept her voice low so the men clearing away the sooty rubble wouldn't hear. "We'll rebuild the granaries, stronger and larger, using new methods."

"It is not the loss of the structures that is worrisome, my lady." Mr. Sparks scrubbed a hand over his soot-covered chin, dislodging black dust from untidy stubble. She'd never seen him unshaven before. "It is the loss of the grain. The tenants were depending on it for livestock until the harvest."

"We'll rebuild the store of grain, as well. The trustees will purchase enough to feed the livestock." They would. They *must*. "They'll understand what is needed."

"Yes." Mr. Sparks's sigh was heavy, the strong chin at odds with the defeat in his eyes. "Yes, they will."

Dread fell into the base of her stomach. "You don't think so," Cat said flatly. She turned to look up at him. The wind had shifted while she traveled home and the breeze was cool and sharp on her cheeks.

"Actually, I do. The trustees will do what is necessary, but nothing more." He angled his head to return her gaze with hooded green eyes behind round spectacles. "The trustees will protect your inheritance, my lady. Make no mistake about that. But—" He went silent.

Cat did not need the words.

"The tenants will worry there isn't enough to go around," she said softly. Cat breathed in and trapped the air in her lungs just as she was trapped. Anger boiled beneath her skin, but she let the breath out slow and smooth. "I know many tenants will have a bit set by of their own grain, but not enough."

"Aye. Not enough for the livestock and their own bellies." Mr. Sparks rubbed the back of his neck and surveyed the men working together. Diligent laborers and farmers beside blacksmiths and shopkeepers. "That sort of worry causes difficulties between neighbors and friends."

"Use my pin money, Mr. Sparks."

"You have little left until you receive next quarter's installment." He looked sideways at her. "You spent it on the roofs."

"I will ask for more." She huffed out a breath. "I will tell the trustees I need new gowns."

"My lady." Mr. Sparks's smile was kind, but resigned. "If you raise the issue, the trustees may request to review the dressmaker's bills. Or they may speak to your uncle."

He was right, and her stomach burned with that knowledge.

"But didn't you hear? I'm to be married." Bitterness rode on her tongue, sharp and acrid. "The Marquess of Hedgewood. Surely that deserves new gowns."

"I had not heard." She felt more than saw Mr. Sparks become motionless, think, then move again. "My felicitations."

"It was not my choice." She lifted her face to the sky, breathed deep of the charred air. That, too, was bitter. "Wycomb signed the contract without my knowledge, and furnished Ashdown Abbey as payment in the event of a breach."

"Ah." A world of knowledge lay in the single sound. "When is it to be?"

"Before my majority." She looked over the steaming desolation in front of her, the wooded area beyond and, in the distance, the walls of Ashdown Abbey. Cheerful spring sun bathed all of it, gilding even the ruins with gold light. "I agreed to proceed with the wedding so that I could keep the Abbey."

"I see." A deep sigh. Another. "This is not what your father intended."

"I wouldn't know. He never saw fit to tell me his intentions." Her fingers curled into her palms and she turned away from the sunlight. Toward truth.

"Your father—"

"Had his reasons. I know. I have been told time and again. Bugger that." The words slipped out before she could think. Mr. Spark's eyes widened so they were nearly as big as the lenses of his spectacles. Cat was instantly contrite. Not about the sentiment, of course, but his shock. "My apologies, Mr. Sparks."

"Er. Yes." He coughed, and she heard the amusement there. "I imagine you learned it from your father, my lady. It was his favorite, ah—turn of phrase."

"So it was." Her lips twitched, remembering her father ranting in his office about unfair taxes or a bad crop. He always waited it out, because he believed if one worked hard, life would turn out all right it the end.

Silence moved between them, punctuated by the grunts and calls of those clearing the mess of smoking wood and thatched roofing.

"What do we do?" Cat raised her face to the sky again, to the blinding sun that refused to dim despite the wreck of the granaries it shined upon. Fear would be building among the tenants already.

"Nothing, my lady. We let the trustees determine when to rebuild the granaries, and we let them determine how much wheat and corn to purchase or import from your other estates—the cost will be dear, no matter which choice they make, with the price of grain being high at present." Mr. Sparks rubbed the back of his neck, conveying soot to one of the few clean places left. "The coffers will withstand the loss, my lady, as long as we can get the release from the trustees."

"Will the tenants' hearts withstand the loss?" she murmured into the sunshine, offering her fears up to the shining beacon. There was no response. Not from the beams warming her face or from the man standing beside her.

She needed to think. To settle. The walk back to the Abbey was short, if she went over the open fields rather than the lanes and roads crisscrossing the land, but those moments could be used to gather herself.

Her father had always said a good walk would solve most of life's problems.

"Excuse me, Mr. Sparks." Turning to the man, she smiled into the bespectacled face. "I'll return this afternoon, but I need to be at Ashdown Abbey."

...

Jones had never seen anything of such magnitude.

From the innyard on the edge of the village he could see all of Ashdown Abbey, the valley it was nestled in, and the surrounding farmland. More was hidden beyond trees, beyond the river ribboning in the distance.

"Oi! Sir!" The innkeeper called cheerfully, wood and iron bucket smacking against his calf as he strode past Jones. "The mail coach won't be by for another three hours at least, if yer lookin' to travel."

"Thank ye, sir." Jones lapsed into the local patter, nodding his thanks. "I'm jest lookin' for a bite to eat on me way through."

"Where's yer horse, eh?" The innkeeper smacked his buckets down in front of the water pump set in the center of the courtyard.

"Down at th' blacksmith's. 'E threw a shoe." It was true enough. He and the horse had spent the night in a thatch of woods, one of them rolled in his greatcoat and the other snorting out his disgust at the lost shoe. "Helluva great house, there." Jones set his hands in his pockets and nodded toward the Abbey.

"'Tis. One thousand, six hundred four acres. And a half." The innkeeper surveyed the valley view, chest puffing out as if he were the owner. "The half being part of a land dispute back in 1513. Those ruddy Froggans—neighbors ta the north in those days—stole that half acre and the Ashdowns ne'er did get it back."

"Shame." Jones's lips twitched. Ruddy Froggans.

"Aye. There ain't no male heir, neither, which is even more of a ruddy shame. Earldom went to an idiot cousin, so the family only kept the ol' barony. 'Course, 'tis the richest in Britain just the same." Huge hands worked the pump. Up, down, up, down. Water splashed, clear and sparkling in the sunlight, cascading into the bucket. "The baroness, she's a right good sort though. Rumor is she used 'er pin money ta pay for cottage roofs, as she'd promised they'd be repaired this year."

Jones didn't speak, but simply took in the tiny cottages north of the expanse of stone that was Ashdown Abbey. Beyond that, field upon field of green and gold patchworked over the countryside.

All of it hers.

Every haystack, every tree, every blade of grass—and

every person living and working there. Hundreds of people.

How did she live with that responsibility?

"Does she—" He stopped, not sure what he wanted to say.

"The baroness?"

"It is not important." Jones shook his head, looking back to the Abbey and its surroundings. It was a vast, immeasurable estate she was protecting—and more acres in other parts of England.

It might as well be another country, another world.

"Shame she weren't born a man." The innkeeper huffed. "Though if she had been, she might not have that sweetness about her."

Jones turned around. The pump still moved, up, down, driven by those competent hands. Cheeks pink from exertion, the innkeeper exchanged one bucket for the another.

"I beg your pardon?"

"Got 'er father's mind and 'er mother's sweetness." Up, down, with arms corded with muscles. "Ne'er saw someone take ta the earth and the people the way she did, even as a girl."

The innkeeper stopped pumping, let the last of the water run into the second bucket. Puffing out a breath, he wiped wet hands on the grayed, worn apron tied about his waist.

"You knew her as a girl?"

"And her father before her." The innkeeper bent over, grasped the bucket handles. Water tipped over the edges as he stood again, landing on his boots and recoloring the leather a darker shade. "We were boys running the same land. Me father's a cottager."

"Ah." There was a great deal Jones wanted to know, to ask. But he did not. There were so many words they stuck in his throat, vying for a release.

"Come in for that bite, eh? Me missus has a good a thick

stew and bread today." The innkeeper sloshed away with his buckets, whistling through his teeth. He entered the inn through the rear door, bellowing for a bowl of stew before he was over the threshold.

Jones threw one final glance at the great house larger than the War Office. Larger than even than the Royal Pavilion or Carleton House. Perhaps even Westminster.

This was where she had been born.

He been left at the front door of a foundling hospital.

Hunching his shoulders, Jones set his course to follow the innkeeper's and ducked into the common room. Half a dozen men ranged at the counter, another half dozen at the tables. Locals, by the looks of the conversation passing between tables and stools.

Jones took a seat at the counter between a man half his size and twice his age, and a young man who looked as if he'd grown a foot in the last week and forgotten to eat. He nodded to each, then to the innkeeper behind the counter.

"Thet stew will be right out, sir." The innkeeper reached toward the tankards lining a shelf behind the counter. "Ale?"

"Aye. Many thanks."

"Ya be needin' a room?"

"No." Jones accepted the tankard and drank deep of the bitter ale. "The horse should be ready soon, I think."

"Horse threw a shoe." The innkeeper leaned to the side to explain the circumstances to Jones's new companions. "Down at the blacksmith's now."

"Well, sir, you couldn't have found a finer village or pub to throw that shoe." The old man cackled. "Though things'll be a mite tight around here soon."

Black looks all around. Counter patrons to innkeeper to tables patrons.

"Eh?" Attention pricked, Jones cocked his head in question.

"The granaries of the big house burnt down. Right down ta the ground." The old man thumped his tankard down beside his empty stew bowl. Uneasy murmurs rippled through the common room. Silence rippled in their wake. "Grain'll be scarce soon. Them trustees were jest here not more'n a week past, but the muckworms won't help."

"Muckworm sounds—" He wanted to say ominous, but he wouldn't have known that word without Angel's books. "Not good."

"'Tisn't." The innkeeper leaned down, ready for a bit of unfortunate gossip. "The old earl put the estate in trust, see? Typical, o'course, 'cept our baroness knows what's what. She could have managed it all—would do better than Prinny at managing the country. Right smart girl, our baroness."

"What's that to do with muckworms?" Jones set his arms on the counter, as if ready for his own bit of gossip.

"Oh, they don't care none about us, see?" The boy to Jones's left had his face nearly in the stew bowl, shoveling it in as if it might be his last meal. "Them trustees, the uncle—the uncle is the worst. He's our baroness's guardian, but he's less smart than the trustees."

"Uncle?" This was what he'd come for. News, information, opinion. All of it would be important.

"Aye." The boy swung to face him as he spoke, the old man doing the same a moment later. Jones leaned back so he could see both. "That uncle, he's tricky," the boy continued. "They say he disappears in plain sight and drinks blood. It's why his eyes is so scary. And I seen him riding late at night like demons was after him."

"Codswallop." The innkeeper wiped the area in front of Jones. Again. Once more. Nothing changed on the bar top. "The uncle is a bastard by choice, begging yer pardon." He nodded to Jones. "The old earl was fooled, as the bastard's nature t'weren't out until the old earl died. Eh, but our baroness is an Ashdown. She knows what's what, and she'll do what's right."

"Aye, she will, if she has the chance." This was shouted from a table behind them.

"True enough." The old man to Jones's right moved closer, opened his mouth—and stopped when the kitchen door swung open to reveal a tall, wide woman with rosy cheeks and a bowl of stew in her hands.

The previously attentive patrons listening to the conversation suddenly became attentive of their meals. Nothing but quiet and the clink of spoons against bowls was heard as the innkeeper's wife plunked a bowl in front of Jones.

She studied the room. Frowned. "What bit of mischief are you all up to now?"

"Nothing!" The innkeeper started rubbing the bar top yet more vigorously. "Just letting our newcomer here know what's what about the big house."

"Well, that's a simple tale." Chafed and red hands settled on the woman's hips, gripping their ample girth. "The old earl had a choice. Give the baroness everything outright and hope some rapscallion didn't turn her head, or protect the barony so she could marry a man she loved. He protected it—only them trustees and thet uncle are in league or summat. Our baroness is a good girl, but they don't give her leave to do what needs doing."

"Don't the trustees do it?" He knew the answer of course. The baroness had said as much—but he wanted to know what these people thought. Those who bore the brunt of the trustees' short sightedness.

"Them?" The innkeeper's wife snorted. "They don't understand as much as a flea. 'Tis all numbers back in London."

He couldn't disagree. Dipping his spoon into the bowl,

he retrieved beef and carrot and potato. When they hit his tongue, his mouth exploded with flavors he couldn't have imagined—herbs, spices, onion, butter. It was home and flavor, heart and comfort. All in a single mouthful.

He must have made a sound, because the innkeeper's wife laughed.

"You'll do, sir." She folded those work-reddened hands over her apron. "The door is always open to a man who enjoys my stew."

"It's—it's—"

"Aye, 'tis. My missus is a fine cook." The innkeeper beamed first at Jones, then at his wife, round face splitting with the grin. "She's also clever, an' she's right about our baroness. Why, she were out just this morning, standing over the granaries."

"Helped carry water, too!" Came a shout from one corner or another of the common room. "I saw her wit' me own eyes. Our baroness does right by all the generations of Ashdowns, going back to the first Mary Elizabeth Frances."

"She does," the innkeeper agreed. "Thet uncle of hers, though—don't trust 'im a wink. He'll put a knife in yer gullet as soon as look at ya."

Jones dipped his spoon into the stew again, blew on it to cool the heat. "What's 'e like in London, I wonder."

"Dunno." The old man next to him leaned forward. Bushy brows rose, their lengthy hair bristling with the movement. "But I 'eard tell 'e turns into a demon with red eyes. Nine feet tall, they say, and 'e can freeze you with a look."

"Oh, thet's foolishness," the innkeeper's wife scoffed, waving away the tale with both hands.

"'T'isn't." The old man sat up straight and jabbed his fork at Jones. "I 'eard it from me wife's cousin's son's nephew, who came up from London just last month. A demon, they say in the rookeries."

"What the hell was he doin' in the rookeries, I'd like to know?" The innkeeper settled his arm on the bar top, squinting at his customer.

"The boy? Or Wycomb?" The old man held out his empty tankard, jiggled it from side to side in an unspoken request.

"Both, eh?" The innkeeper accepted the tankard and began to fill it from the barrel spigot behind the counter. He didn't take his eyes from his customer, though he seemed to know just when to turn the spigot so the tankard didn't overfill.

"Boy was paid a ha'penny to deliver a message. 'E takes on odd jobs on th' docks from th' East Indiamen, 'oping 'e'll get a job when 'e's older." The old man shrugged. "Dunno why Wycomb was in the rookeries."

Jones continued to spoon the stew into his mouth, but his ears were buzzing. It wasn't the red eyes or ability to freeze that caught Jones's attention.

Rookeries.

Chapter Twenty-Four

Only a few gray tendrils of smoke drifted up into the late spring air. Still, they were visible against the brilliant blue sky above. Cat stepped over charred wood, over ash waving in the slight breeze.

So much loss—so much fear for her tenants and laborers. Would there be enough to feed them? She had walked over the Ashdown lands yesterday. Dreamed of fire in the night. Walked again in the late morning light. But she still had no answers.

The only solution seemed to be marriage. If she married, the Abbey was hers, as were the expenses. As were the tragedies.

She breathed in, choked on the stench of smoke and burnt wood. Standing in the midst of the rubble, avoiding the spots still steaming and emitting an occasional flame, Cat could only mourn the loss of her people's security.

Then she saw them, beneath fallen beams but just far enough away from the flames they might have survived—burlap bags.

They would be filled with grain. At least three bags lay in that triangle of charred wood and earth—sideways, fallen, but unburnt. Water marks marred one bag, but not the others. How much good grain might there be hiding in that unplanned cave?

Feet moved without thought, half-boots crunching on scorched timber. She scrambled over beams, tripped over partially burnt thatching. Yet she could not stop her feet from running, her hands from windmilling as she moved.

Hope lodged beneath her breastbone, compelling her feet.

The fallen beam lay over the bags, driving them into the ground so the once round shapes were now oblong. Grasping the nearest bit of burlap with ungloved hands, she tugged, pulled. But there was no movement. Nothing. That semi-wet sacking was lodged beneath a joist wider than her own body. But that didn't mean a few inches wouldn't make a difference.

She crouched, uncaring whether the pretty sleeve of her lavender gown would be salvageable or her skirts were dusted with ash. All that mattered was the grain.

She set a hand to the timber, then her shoulder, and shoved.

She hissed out a breath. Rough, partially burned wood scraped against her arm through the thin capped sleeve of her gown. Digging her feet into the rubble, she pushed harder. Teeth gritted, muscles straining, elation shot through her as the beam shifted.

Releasing her muscles, Cat stood, let out the breath she'd been holding. After a moment to recover, she crouched again, planted her feet in ash and set her shoulder once more to the wood.

"Here. Let me."

The beam moved with a sudden jerk as someone with more strength shoved at it. She nearly lost her balance, but she dug in, centered herself, and pushed again—knowing without looking that Jones was working behind her.

The beam shifted, groaned, then fell into the rest of the burned wreckage with a splintering sound. Ash and blackened remains exploded, shooting into the air. Small projectiles rained down, rattling against their brothers, leaving only light ash still floating.

"Oh!" The sound escaped her lips without permission. She straightened, puffed her cheeks, and let out another heavy breath. Waving away the ash, she took in the unburned bags of grain.

But it was Jones she wanted to see now.

Black streaked over the shoulder of his coat. Bits of gray dust clung to his sleeve, dancing merrily in the breeze as if they weren't part of the destruction. Cat reached out and brushed them away, keeping her gaze averted from Jones's face.

She didn't know what she would see there. The last time she had spoken to him, it had been in the dark. She had kissed him, held his hand as she waited for death.

But she *did* have to look.

What she saw there was all the fierce gentleness she'd felt from him that night. It burned from those deep brown eyes, needy but restrained. He stood away from her, head angled up as if he could not look at her directly, either.

Or would not.

They stood there, not looking. Breathing.

Then his deep eyes met hers. He didn't touch her. Didn't need to. The heat in his eyes flared, and she felt the answer in her own body. Desire, lust even. She felt it now—that delicious sense of awareness, the warmth between her legs, the tightening of every muscle.

He turned away. Drew in a ragged breath. She never heard the exhale, as either pride or fear sent her reaching for the burlap.

"The grain." The words were awkward to her own ears.

Coarse threads brushed against her skin. She gripped the nearest bag, tugged. It loosened, but did not come out. She stepped around, angled her body, tugged again. It came free and a pair of large, competent hands were there to relieve her of her burden.

"How many bags are there?" His words were no less awkward than hers had been, accompanied by a choked sound that might have been a grunt as he hefted the bag onto his shoulder.

"Five, total." The next bag was there, the others past it and still under rubble. She scrabbled with fingers already black with soot, pivoted her body for a better position.

A quick glance showed the swing of Jones's brown jacket as he carted the grain away from the burned area. Only his back was visible, the breadth of it. No muscle could be seen through his coat, but it was there beneath cloth and skin.

A hitch in her lungs, another in her belly. She turned away and gripped the bag in front of her to drag it from what was left of the smoking granaries.

"Wait!"

She reeled, lost her footing, regained it, and looked up— Jones sprinted toward her. He peeled his coat off as he ran, leaving nothing but the cotton shirt moving over his body.

"Jones. What—?"

The coat rose high in the air above her, whipped down again as he swept past her. She spun, choking back air and words. Coat smacked against wood, through fresh smoke and flames leaping up from the beam they'd moved. She stumbled away—from the fire, from the swiftly moving coat as Jones worked to smother the flames.

The flames moved with her.

Her gown.

Shock scored her throat as flares of yellow and gold rode the cotton hem. The scent of burning cloth rose into the air, riding on curls of light, nearly white smoke.

With no weapon, no coat, she fought with her hands. Smacking at the flames, shaking the fabric. The burn on her palms and fingers made her breath hitch, but it was less than the burn of panic rising in her.

Tumbling to the ground, she tried to stomp on her gown and petticoats. A cry ripped from her throat. "Jones!"

He was there, throwing his coat over her feet, enveloping her legs in simple brown wool. Face grim, he spoke not a word. He only wrapped and bundled, gloveless hands working fast. Beneath the wool, beneath the cotton and muslin, the muscles of her thighs trembled with the need to run.

Yet running would only be worse.

When he pulled the coat away stray twists of smoke still rose, but the brilliant gold flames had disappeared. Every muscle of her body wanted to go limp, but waves of terror still rolled through her.

"Get out of this wreck." Jones stood, moving toward the still smoking beam. His foot lashed out, spreading embers and coals apart. "To the grass."

"I need to help." She scrambled to her feet, stepped forward. Half-boots crunched on the rubble, and she looked down, searching for flame.

"Your skirt—" He stopped, glanced once at the blackened hem. Brows lowered, mouth tipped down. He went back to spreading embers, smothering flame. "It is too likely to catch flame. I can't save you and the grain. Take your pick, my lady."

She did, scrambling out of the wreck of granaries and to the brown, dead grass ringing it. Part of her wanted to reenter, to pull the burlap bags free. Instead, she watched as Jones hefted each one to his shoulder, hurrying to bring them out to the safe, grassy area.

Five burlap bags of grain. One by one, they landed at her feet.

As if they were a gift.

When he was finished, Jones bent over, hands on knees. His breath heaved in and out, but he did not hang his head to regain the rhythm. Instead, he watched the smoking beam, the embers.

"It happens," he murmured. "The heat deep in the wood catches flame once it meets the air."

"Yes." She knew, and stared at the broken sections he'd spread so they would cool. The faint glow of red still burst to life in places.

"Your hands?" He turned his head, his focus on her now.

"Tender, but no lasting damage." The vague sting of her hands didn't matter just now. "Jones."

He straightened, tall and sure, but those deep, clear brown eyes did not leave her face. "I thought—" Throat working, he swallowed hard. "My lady."

"Don't. Not anymore."

"I beg your pardon?" The faint lines on his face became more prominent as he frowned.

"Please. Call me Cat." It was everything to ask. He would not know it, but everything inside her opened just to ask.

Cat." He breathed in once, a long, slow breath. "Why Cat?"

She was still for a moment, very still and silent, her gaze searching his face. Finally, carefully, to keep that open place from being unhurt, she said, "Mary Elizabeth Frances Ashdown was the first Baroness Worthington. Every firstborn daughter is named the same, in deference and in tradition. But my mother gave me another name, so I wouldn't forget I am *me* before I am the baroness. Mary Elizabeth Frances *Catherine* Ashdown. I'm Cat."

Did he see her? Her throat was tight, her heart racing

beneath the confines of her stays. No one had seen Cat since her parents died.

That she wanted this spy, this Jones, to understand her, was something she could not think of now. So she pushed it away and concentrated on today. Just today, right now, in the bright light of a sunny morning.

Today, she wanted Jones to see Cat.

"Catherine." He whispered it, the word barely a sigh on the air. His hand came up, blunt fingers reaching for her face, then falling away before he made contact.

"My parents only used Catherine for important occasions. When it was just us, it was always Cat." She rubbed her hands on her skirt, however filthy it might be.

He was suddenly close to her, his lips just there. So very close she could barely breathe. "Yes, I can see Cat in there."

She flew at him, at the arms already open for her. At the lips pressing against hers before she could think. Around her swirled the scent of burnt wood and grass, but inside her heart there was only Jones.

Need, sweet and painful. Sorrow, because they could never be. Gratitude, for all that he was. They rose and swamped her, as much as his arms enclosed her and his mouth consumed her.

Through all of that was relief and the vision of her blackened skirts.

"I am not kissing you because you saved me." She said it against his mouth, pressing him closer as she rose to her booted toes. "I am kissing you because I want you."

"Cat." His single word was lighter than a growl, darker than a whisper.

...

His legs gave way.

She didn't know what her words did to him. *Couldn't* know.

She could not feel the heat and pain and bloom of love that stirred in him.

Jones released her and staggered, righted himself, and faced Cat. Her chin was set, the stunning butterfly-blue eyes trained on him. The flush kissing her cheekbones was as alluring as her reddened lips.

But she was not his.

He spun away and walked through fire-browned grass, eyes intent on the bags of grain. He could not look at her now, or he would forget the choice that must be made. Yet some part of him was left behind, pulled from his body as he brushed past her. A piece of him he could not name or see, but would always be missing from his heart and residing in her.

The burlap grew large as he came close, yet the slumped shape and textured fabric blurred in his vision. Just for a moment. As if a bit of rain had obscured his vision.

He blinked. The rain ceased, leaving his vision clear and vivid.

"Jones." The ragged whisper flew on the air, piercing his heart. "Do you not want me?"

"*Not want you?*" Pivoting, every muscle of his body fighting him, Jones wheeled on her. "I can't breathe when I look into your eyes. I can't think."

Suddenly he was in front of her again, hands cupping her cheeks. Her skin was warm, smooth. Everything a young lady's skin should be.

Everything his rough hands were not.

He stepped back, tried not to kiss the lips parted on a deep breath.

"Go to the Abbey, Cat. Or the cottages. Bring someone back to retrieve the grain. I'll wait until I see you coming back—but I can't stay to assist." He raised a hand, palm up. "Wycomb."

"Yes. Of course." She wasn't trembling, but vibrating. Rage, lust, fear—any and all of them might have coursed through her. He could not know which, based on the bright light in her eyes. "I'll bring someone to retrieve the grain."

"Good." There was a tree beside them, and he found he needed the substance of it to support him. "Good."

She didn't move.

"Wycomb has signed the marriage contracts." Everything about her was suddenly bleak. Eyes, mouth, shoulders, body. "Hedgewood."

A knife had been plunged into his heart. A second time in his belly. It was the only explanation for the pain that ripped through him.

She reached toward him, let her hands fall again. "I feel as if I should never see you again, and yet cannot do without you."

"I feel the same, Cat." He laughed, though it was mirthless to his own ears. "But you are Hedgewood's."

"I belong only to myself, and I don't understand love. I don't." She shook her head, then stared straight at him with iridescent eyes that arrowed into his soul. "But if I did, it might be you."

He couldn't speak. He could only kiss her with everything in him, all of the heat and pain and love that swirled in a rioting mass he could not control.

Soft skin met his palms as he cupped her face. Ripe, ready lips pressed against his and turned his heart inside out. He breathed in and his body shuddered as her scent—violets and vanilla and lily—crowded his mind.

"We cannot stay here." The words tore from his throat, but he did not move. "If anyone sees us—"

"I know. My uncle." She turned her head so that her

cheek lay against his heart. She would hear it beating, hear the frantic need in him. "I know you are a spy, Jones. But why are you spying on Wycomb?"

She lifted her head and set those eyes on him.

"He is a spy as well." He didn't hesitate. Trusting was idiocy for a spy—a fact he knew well. Yet this was her. Cat. Trust had slipped through cracks before he could stop them up. "I will not say more about it, but know your uncle has fought well for this country. He has also—" Jones stopped.

"I don't need to be told." She stepped away from him, the arms that had pulled him in falling away. "He has done horrible things as well. I know Wycomb."

He couldn't speak. If she thought Wycomb had committed horrible deeds, what would she think of him? He had committed unspeakable acts himself. Jones stepped away, hoping she would not think of his actions.

She had. He saw it clearly in her eyes.

"I do not judge, Jones." Lashes fluttered over blue irises. "I cannot know what is required of either of you. But I know your heart, and I know Wycomb's. I see your actions, and I see his. There is no comparison."

"You cannot possibly understand, my lady."

"I know *you*, Jones." A small, ungloved, filthy hand gripped his shoulder. "And bloody hell. Call me Cat. I didn't kiss you so you could revert to 'my lady.'"

He laughed, because there was little else to do. She brought the laughter in life, even when it was hard. He dipped his head, kissed lips that were waiting for his. "We are stupid to linger. I cannot stay here to ensure the flames are out and still take the grain somewhere dry."

"No. Others will move the grain if I call for them." She stopped and stared into his face. "Once they do, you will be gone to me again, won't you?"

"Yes."

"Well." She laughed, though the sound was pained. "Do not mince words."

"My lady. Cat." He wondered if he could ever say "Cat" without feeling as if he were an interloper. "I must always remember my country. Before family, friends, heart, and home, my country must come first."

"You realize your country encompasses family, friends, heart, and home, yes?" She shook her head, a small half smile lifting a corner of lips that were perfect for kissing. "Go, Jones. I will procure the men needed to move the grain and extinguish whatever flames are hiding beneath the ash."

. . .

Jones could not leave the shadows.

It stung, hiding this way. Removed from the men shouldering the bags of grain, from the smoldering wood once again being spread out and doused with water for safety.

Removed from Cat.

Wycomb stood at the edge of the wreckage, polished boots embedded firmly in the heat-deadened grass. Arms clasped behind his back. The specks of silver in his dark brown hair glinted under the mottled sky above.

Jones dared not move.

"Thank you, Mr. Hopwood, for having your boys cart the bags to the village." Cat's voice floated to him. A small hand, still covered with soot and without a glove, lay softly on the sleeve of a wizened old man.

"'Tis our pleasure, m'lady." The man scrubbed a hand over his face. The next words slipped away in the wind.

Whatever they were, Cat's smile bloomed in response.

His heart seized. Hands gripped rough bark. He could not step into the open and bask in that glow, could not assist Hopwood's broad-shouldered sons haul the grain to the cart.

Wycomb stood just there, straightening his cuffs and standing at the edge of the scene as if it were his property.

Rookeries. What was he involved in?

"Mary Elizabeth." Wycomb's sharp words carried above the wind and activity. "Come."

Her head turned toward him, her shoulders tensed. But Cat did not move. Instead, she spoke again to Mr. Hopwood, gesturing toward the cart now swarming with large boys situating bags of grain.

Jones smiled at her refusal to heed Wycomb's instruction, his light laugh fluttering the fern inches from his face. It died again as Wycomb gripped her arm and tugged her to the horses they'd arrived on. She didn't fight, but her chin lifted — and the long fingers curling around her upper arm pressed sharply enough that she winced.

Jones swiveled, set his back against the tree. He could not watch. His body strained with the need to wrest her from those biting fingers, every muscle vibrating.

He could not show himself.

Fisting his hand, he pressed it into his thigh. Hard. Harder. Pain would be his reminder to focus.

If Wycomb saw him here, in the wilds of Oxfordshire, he would know he was under investigation.

Chapter Twenty-Five

The floor was frigid, despite the warm night and the soft glow of the tall candelabra. The rough flagstone scraped her bare feet. She'd walked the cloisters as a girl, as her father had—as the monks had, centuries earlier. Meditation and prayer, estate problems to solve, family quarrels. All those thoughts and more were thick in the air under the domed ceiling.

Cat sent her current concerns winging into the night to join those that had come before.

Beyond the arcing mullioned windows lining the corridor, Jones would be waiting in the night. In the house, behind stone walls carved for the original abbey, Wycomb was seeing to his own business. Aunt Essie would be embroidering or netting, perhaps reading. The servants and Mr. Sparks—as much her family as Wycomb and Essie—would be busy with their evening tasks.

She could only pace past stone columns, past elaborate windows, past columns again, and through dim light. So much swirled inside her. Need, temper, fear, sorrow—all of it building. Pressure pushed against her rib cage, against her lungs.

Her home. Her people. Wycomb. Marriage to Hedgewood.

Jones.

And her father.

Fingers curling around a carved stone column, Cat stopped walking to stare into the night beyond the windows. She could see nothing except her own reflection, and vaguely, the reflection of the intricate walls of the original abbey behind her.

"Why couldn't you trust I would do what was right?" The whisper rose from her lips. Words and sound torn apart. They would go unheard, because her father was not there to hear them.

He had never told her it would all be held under trust. She had run everything in his last year of life. She and Mr. Sparks. Yet her father had never told her the properties would be withheld for so long. A little while she might have suspected. She was not yet of age when he died. But *thirty-five*? Now she was contracted to Hedgewood.

It could be worse, but it could be better.

It could be Jones.

Whether he owned nothing more than the clothes on his back or an estate larger than hers was unimportant. She knew his measure.

He'd saved a stranger from abduction, before he knew her.

He accepted the task of spying on another spy when he knew it would be difficult.

He put out fires and saved strangers' grain, because it was right.

She also wanted him. Everything in her body ached, exquisitely tight and ready for something. That moment. The one she'd heard the maids whisper and giggle about.

She breathed in, held it. Skin hot, belly taut with need, she stood in the faint wash of candlelight and wished for Jones.

"The tenants' roofs are much improved." Cold words slid into the night, raising the hair at the nape of her neck.

She whirled, resisting the urge to flee as Wycomb stepped from the shadows into the light from the tall candelabra set at the end of the long alley of cloister.

"Uncle." The light Kashmir shawl she wore over her gown was not enough protection from his frigid eyes.

"I discovered a group of laborers finishing one of the cottage roofs, and noted that nearly all of them have been replaced." He moved slowly down the long, narrow hall, boots striking the flagstones with precise measure. "How do you suppose the roofs were paid for, Mary Elizabeth?"

She did not answer. She was not inclined to lie, but she did not care to answer with the truth.

"Did you countermand my direction and approach the trustees?" He stood directly in front of her now. Close, so close, looking down at her. He did not touch her, but he did not need to—fear spiked just the same, sending her stomach twisting and churning.

"No." She swallowed hard, but raised her chin to meet his gaze. She was standing on the floor thirteen generations of Ashdowns had stood on before her. That floor had survived war, famine, politics, bloodshed. There was strength beneath her feet, if only she was willing to use it. "It was my pin money—mine to use as I see fit, with no one to direct how I spend it."

"I see." Soft words, no less icy than before. "Yet it was against my command. You *deliberately* deceived me, doing what you chose."

"Doing what was *right*." She set her bare feet, straightened her shoulders. "Eventually, Ashdown Abbey and all the rest of my inheritance will be mine to control."

"No, it will not." He began to circle her, slowly. She felt his blue eyes on her, never letting up, never leaving her. "You will marry the Marquess of Hedgewood."

"Yes, and then it will be mine." She turned on a bare heel so she faced him. "You signed the contract stating that if I marry Hedgewood, Ashdown Abbey will be mine."

He stopped his circling, eyes narrowing. Then, very softly, "But still under trust."

A knife was suddenly at her throat, the flat surface sliding across her skin. Smooth. Cool. His eyes glittered in the semi-darkness, never leaving her gaze as he sent the weapon over her skin. Again. Her breath jerked in, held—but when she exhaled that breath was fueled by fury.

"Do you think to control the Chancery Court as you control the trustees now?" She gritted her teeth, waited for the knife to slash across her throat. To feel her life's blood spilling down the front of her nightgown.

"No." The knife stopped its path across her throat. "I will control you."

"You—" Fury coursed through every fiber of her body, rising and biting flesh. "No."

"I will, because I am willing to take risks." The tip of the knife pricked her skin. Just there, in the hollow at the base of her throat. It stung, but it was small in comparison to the panic skittering inside her. "Are you?"

She could not speak. Terror was huge inside her chest, blocking every syllable.

He leaned toward her, slowly, eyes fixed on her face. Setting his lips against her ear, he whispered, "How, exactly, did you move the bags of grain to the grass this afternoon, Mary Elizabeth?"

Jerking back, she met Wycomb's eyes. Not quite blue in this dim light, but the expression was clear. Menace. Death. Easily recognized in the blank stare.

Humanity had left him.

"I dragged the bags." Swallowing was near impossible. She spoke no more, did not breathe.

"Mm." The blank eyes flicked over her jaw, her mouth, each eye. Searching for a lie. She knew this, without needing to see beyond expressionless eyes. "Dragged them."

The knife moved away from the small cut, then changed course to slip across her flesh in the opposite direction. She dared not swallow, dared not move.

"Yes." There was nothing to hold, nothing to grip to keep herself from crying out. "Dragged them."

"I saw no drag marks."

A lie discovered by details, but she would not admit it. Admitting meant sacrificing Jones. "Do you doubt me?"

"I do. You've proved you do not follow direction—the tenant roofs, if you recall." The knife slipped away. He stepped around her and began to circle her once more. "But we are leaving Ashdown Abbey tomorrow, so whomever assisted you—"

"Tomorrow?" She forgot the knife in his hand. Forgot safety. "The damage to the granaries isn't repaired. We must locate outside sources of grain and rebuild for the fall harvest. There is so much to be done."

The knife was suddenly at her throat again. Her mouth opened, breath heaved in. And then nothing. No part of her body moved save fingers scrabbling at empty air.

"I know you had assistance at the granaries, which leads me to wonder why you have not told me who it was. It is not a woman, or there would be drag marks. The bags are heavy. It must be a man, one you have not told me about." He did not press his body against hers, but she felt him just the same. Stronger. Larger. Danger lurked in the small space between his body and hers. "And it is true I cannot make you consent to marriage and say the words in front of a man of the cloth."

The point of the knife did not move as he angled his head. "But I can—and will—make things more difficult for you if you do not. Whoever you are fucking, you will cease."

She jerked, the course language striking her as if it were the knife. "I am not—"

"I don't care for your excuses. You were with a man at the granaries, and if it had been an innocent meeting, you would give me his identity." His face moved close to hers, so that she could see each furrow of anger in his skin. "You will pretend to be a virgin on your wedding night."

Cat didn't argue, couldn't, as the knife moved to that hollow between her collarbones again. Pressed against tender flesh just beginning to bleed.

"Hedgewood wants a virgin wife and many sons. You will give them to him." He murmured the words.

"Why Hedgewood? Why are you so intent that I marry him?" She still did not act, but her mind whirred, propelled by fear and anger and calculation.

The knife dropped away, though the threat was no less real.

"Good night, Mary Elizabeth." Wycomb leaned down, pressed thin, firm lips to her forehead. She shuddered at the touch, unable to help herself, but he did not pull back. Instead, he moved toward her ear, set his mouth there once again. "We shall see what tomorrow brings."

He pulled back, lips twisted in a satisfied smile.

Then he was gone, leaving her alone in the cloisters with the echoes of her ancestors.

Chapter Twenty-Six

"Don't turn around, Cat." His voice was quiet, the assured confidence sweeter to her than the soft morning birdcalls.

"Jones." She did not move, but let her arms remain wrapped around her curled legs, let her face continue to rest on her knees as she watched the sun steal over Ashdown Abbey—only now her body hummed and heart leaped.

Somewhere behind the stone bench she sat on, in the thicket of tree and brush and shadow, was the man she wanted to see more than any other. Only she could not turn to see him lest someone from the Abbey observe them.

"Are you well?" They were solemn words, weightier than the fog lifting from the great pond spreading in front of the Abbey. She could picture Jones's solemn expression as if he stood before her—eyes deep and focused. Jaw tight with concern. "After yesterday afternoon by the granaries."

She could not answer that question. She didn't know.

Kisses. Fire. Threats.

All of them equally compelling.

"Wycomb held a knife to my throat." She said the words

in an even tone. Anything else would break her.

Underbrush rustled once, then went still again. "Cat."

"I'm safe, Jones." Her mind knew this, but the alarm rattling around inside her chest did not. "He did nothing more than threaten." The light prick of the knife wasn't a true injury—there had only been one small bead of blood.

The silence behind her was solid and heavy. It drew out so long she wondered if Jones had disappeared into the trees at her back.

"Why?" The word was choked, as though it were difficult for him to speak.

"For one, Hedgewood." She tightened her arms around her legs. Ashdown Abbey was lovely at dawn. Pink and gold light shot from the horizon, turning the stone of the house a beautiful rose. Bright flowers bordering the pond danced as if greeting the early morning sunbeams rippling across the ancient moat.

There was no hint of the danger sleeping inside the building.

"Will you marry Hedgewood?" A rustle of branches again, a whisper of leaves. Jones was not far from her, probably not ten feet from the stone bench she sat on. Yet he seemed to be well beyond her.

"I think I must." It would be bitter. Jones had stirred something inside her, and nothing would ever be quite the same.

"I shall look into Hedgewood." A hard tone, but she heard something else coating the word. Not panic, not fear—something, though.

She spun on the stone bench, setting her bare feet down on the dewy grass and searching the foliage in the wooded area behind her. She could not see Jones, not even a boot or a flash of jacket.

"Are your feet cold?" he asked. She couldn't determine

what direction the words came from. They seemed to echo against wildflowers and fresh green leaves.

"Yes, but I've done this since I was a girl."

"What?"

"Walked barefoot at Ashdown Abbey." She smiled as memories floated in and out of her consciousness. "My father once said I understood the estate more than anyone else because I was always barefoot. I've walked every inch of the estate, curled my toes into the soil." She did so now, gripping the grass and dirt. "I have felt the blood and bone and dust of my ancestors, felt the future. I know what it is to toil in the dirt, day in and day out, because I did so as a girl. I worked beside the laborers so I would know."

Heat, dust. Aching back and arms, legs that shook as much as cook's pudding. Welts from plants whipping her calves and blisters on her palms from the scythe handles. The frantic need for water.

"I know what it is like to work in the fields, and I know what it is like to have tea with the Prince Regent in the drawing room." She looked over her shoulder at the many stories and outcroppings and additions to the Abbey. "*It's mine.*" Fierce propriety filled her. She loved every stone, every blade of grass and drafty window. It was hers to protect, along with all the other properties. But none were as dear to her as this one. "I will not let Wycomb take it from me. Never. It is mine."

She hadn't known how much she would fight for it.

Last night, rooted in the ground of her ancestors and waiting for death, she'd learned.

"My lady. Cat." The hand came from nowhere. Wide, callused, and just there in front of her. She looked up into Jones's face, into eyes that were softer than she'd seen before. "Quickly."

She set her hand in his and stood. He pulled her into the trees and brush, past ferns and branches full of early summer growth.

The eyes of Ashdown Abbey faded away.

They were alone.

Sunlight shown through new leaves, tinging the air a pale green. He stood among the trees and brush just as if he were on a London street. Feet solid on the ground, shoulders back, gaze flicking around. Always on guard.

The hand holding hers tightened, rich chocolate eyes targeting her throat. His breath hissed out as his free thumb came up, pressed lightly against the mark between her collarbones.

She'd never felt anything so gentle. So reverent.

"I would take you away from Wycomb if I could." The vicious tone was one she'd not heard from him before. It scraped at her heart, digging into a place already weak. "I'd take you across the world, if it meant you were safe."

"I can't leave everything in the hands of Wycomb." Stepping closer, Cat looked up into his face. Lean, even common features—grim. Tension edged his unshaven jaw, temper drew his brows down. Every plane of that face tugged at places inside her she could not allow free rein.

"Kiss me, Jones. Please." The words spilled from her before she could think to stop them. She didn't care. "Please."

• • •

"Cat." He was not certain what he wanted to say. He was not even certain if his heart was beating.

The sun slipped between the leaves above, illuminating her face, her eyes, with such brilliance he could not breathe. Each curve, the shape of her mouth, the lashes fringing her eyes. Each was gilded by beams of light that turned the beautiful into the exquisite.

There was nothing he *could* do but kiss her.

But not yet. Not yet.

The hand reaching for her belonged to him, and yet he did not recognize its movement as being directed by his mind. "You are not what I expected."

Her skin was soft beneath his thumb when he feathered it over her cheekbone. He slid his fingers into the bound curls feeding into the braid tracing the line of her spin, let the loose strands slip against his skin. Those renegades, too, were soft and fragrant.

"What did you expect, Jones?" Her eyes were bright, but not with shock or fear. With need, even longing. It echoed in him, calling up all the need and longing he did not want to give voice to.

Sometimes the heart had its own voice.

"I don't know, but not you. Not this woman who sees the people on her lands so clearly. Who loves them so much." His other hand now moved of its own volition so that he cupped her face. "Your heart is lovely, and I had not expected it to be so."

He leaned close, thinking only to taste her. Here, where the silence of the morning met the thrumming inside his head, inside his heart. Where the cool air fought the heat in his blood, and where there was no one to know but the two of them.

Her mouth was sweet, her lips inviting. They opened for him on a sigh—a contented one.

"I was waiting for you, Jones." She pulled back, looked up at him with eyes so blue he could barely hear. Could barely see. Everything stopped, even the earth on its axis. "I was waiting for your kiss."

"*Cat.*"

He had to have her. To taste her. Fire and lust swam in his head, in his belly. Something else—something deep and pure—moved in his chest.

His arms went around her, pulled her close. She was warm and soft against him, but filled with a power and resilience that defied everything he knew. Small, strong hands snaked around his back, gripped tight in the folds of his coat.

She rose up, simple cotton gown and Kashmir shawl nothing against the bulk of his clothing. He wished he could feel the length of her against his body, narrow hips, small breasts, but the clothing he wore made it impossible.

His hands roamed down her sides, covering rib cage, waist, hips. She wore no chemise, no petticoat. Dawn must be too early to dress properly for the day. Her skin was hot through the featherweight fabric, the barrier leaving almost nothing between his hands and her body.

It was she that deepened the kiss, sending her tongue over the seam of his lips. Tongue tangled with tongue and he could not hold back. With a light groan, he moved his lips to her throat, feathered kisses down that lean line until he reached the edge of the shawl. He tugged at it, let it drop to the ground, so he could press his lips to the smooth skin between the curve of her collarbone and line of her bodice. The dress was loose without stays and he was able to push the sleeve down to reveal her bare shoulder.

Pale. Curved. Strong.

"You are so lovely, Cat." Skimming a finger along the line, he marveled at the freckles there. Pale gold, as if her shoulders had been kissed by the sun. "Inside and out."

He set his lips to those freckles. Beneath the hand still gripping her hip, Jones felt her body tremble. His heart thumped in response, his blood thundering with need.

Bending close, he ran his fingers along the edge of the bodice. His mouth followed the line, nibbling, kissing. She tasted as subtle as her scent, and as mysterious. Her hands dove into his hair, tugged just a little.

"Touch me."

Dark lust roared in him at her words, desire mingling with yearning, hunger for her overwhelming him. He pressed her against the tree just there at her back and took her mouth. He had to taste her again. *Had* to, even as he pushed that loose bodice far enough to expose her breast.

She was beautiful. Small, round, and perfect. Nipple pebbled in the cool morning air. He brushed his thumb across that point and heard her gasp. He looked to her face, searching for fear or shock. Neither was in her eyes. Instead, that iridescent blue seemed to burn into his soul. Her lips were parted and reddened from his kisses.

Suddenly, as if in a dream, he felt her fingers twine with his and bring them to her breast. He cupped her, brushed his thumb across her nipple again. The elegant fingers moved with his but her gaze never left his face.

"Yes," she whispered.

He was lost in her. Suddenly frantic for more, he slid his free hand down to her thigh, lifted it. Her leg curled around his waist, held there, as natural as if they had done this before. Only they hadn't. *She* hadn't.

He should go. Leave her.

He couldn't. He wanted to devour her, so that every part of that sweet, feminine, fiery soul would be part of him.

He didn't, because she was making *him* part of her. The leg around his waist tightened, her hands gripped the front edges of his coat as she pulled him to her. One arm snaked around his neck as she rose to meet him, mouth hot and needy.

He gripped her leg—realized her gown was rucked up, exposing soft skin. His palm slid over a smooth thigh, her skin hot despite the light morning chill.

"I'm yours, Jones." Eyes so brilliantly blue he could not withstand them, she held his gaze. Lips curved up, mischievous, needy, wicked. Leg curling more firmly around him as if to steady herself, she guided his hand up, up, toward the heat. Toward the sweet center of her. "Make love to me."

She was wet, ready.

"Touch me here." She let go of his hand, arched toward him so her sex pressed against his hand. "I want it. Want you."

She was not his.

He did the only thing the pulsing in his blood and body could allow. He slid a finger into her, slow and soft, carefully. That would be the extent of it.

Still, it was all he had to be slow and soft.

She was tight. Hot. Her muscles contracted at his movement, contracted again as he moved his finger inside her.

"More." Her breath shuddered out, but her eyes fixed on his. "I know there is more. I want it."

Now *his* breath shuddered out. He would not be able to resist her plea. Her need and hunger swirled around him, echoed inside him, as if it were his own.

"I can't." Hell burned inside him to say the words, to remove his hand from feminine heat. "We shouldn't."

"We can. My uncle already believes we have."

He froze, hand on her smooth thigh, as lust gave way to ice in his gut. "What did he say?"

Face still gilded by gold sunlight, cheeks flushed, she stared at him. "That he knew a man helped me with the bags of grain. He believes we were—were—" She paused, licked her lower lip. "Together. He told me to play a virgin on my wedding night."

"Did Wycomb mention me? Specifically?" All thought of kissing her, of tasting her, was driven from his mind.

He should not have started this interlude in the first place.

Slowly, carefully, he lowered her leg, gown falling into place at her ankles. He raised her sleeve, pulling the bodice higher to cover that perfect breast. He tried not to linger over her skin, over the gold freckles on her shoulder.

"No." She shook her head, breath shuddering. Regret edged the sound. "He knows enough to be observant, I believe. That is all."

He bent, retrieved the shawl that had fallen onto grass and leaves only a few minutes before. His body still wanted her, so badly that just setting the fabric around her shoulders tested his resolve.

"We'll have to be more careful." There was too much at stake for Wycomb to see them now. He had been stupid, losing control of himself. "Go back to the house, Cat. Be careful."

"That is it?" She pulled her shawl tight. He looked to her face, unsure if she was shocked or angry.

"It must be." He rubbed a hand against his chest, trying to ease the erratic beat of his heart. "Anything more is a risk. We never should have—"

"I know. I *know*. Only, I want you. I've never wanted someone this way." The anger faded to a somber expression. She rose onto her toes, pressed her lips softly to his. "Be safe."

She slipped out of the copse and began to pick her way toward the Abbey, leaving everything inside him aching for her.

Chapter Twenty-Seven

The chair was large—larger, even, than she'd thought it as a child. Her weight was not enough to create an indentation in the leather, her width not enough to touch each arm.

So it was.

She could not fill her father's chair, let alone his footsteps or the needs of those who depended on her.

Cat shifted in the chair, trying to occupy more space. It didn't work.

"All is not lost, my lady." The soft words emanated from the doorway. Mr. Sparks stood there, framed by an ancient oak entrance.

This room, one of the oldest in the original Abbey, was not the official estate room, but the small space every baron and baroness before her had used for *real* work.

"You know me too well." Her laugh held no mirth. An expanse of wood stretched out before her, scarred and scratched and worn from years of quills and ledgers. Stuffing peeked through tears in the chair beneath her bum. Around her was paper, leather, instructions, accounts.

Nothing of comfort. Not even a fire. There was nothing here to demonstrate wealth, only dedication—in a space smaller than the butler's pantry.

It was this desk her father had sat at each day, far removed from the formal space Wycomb commandeered at Ashdown Abbey. That formal area had always been for show and for storage of old accounts.

Here, in this tiny closet, the Ashdowns toiled.

"I've known you since birth, if you count the years before I began working for your father." Light flashed over the lenses of Mr. Sparks's spectacles as he stepped into the little room. "I don't know what to tell you, my lady, except not to give up. There is always a solution if you look hard enough."

"I've looked," she said dryly. "Everywhere."

Her looking had revealed nothing but threats, contracts, and a man that warmed her body but could not marry her. Her head tipped back against the cushion, hands curled around the arms.

She did not fit the chair.

But that didn't mean she couldn't bring in her own chair. She was still Baroness Worthington. She still held the largest inheritance in Britain, and she still had power.

If she chose to use it.

Leaving behind the seat she could never possibly command, she stood, braced her hands on the scarred desktop. "Marriage to Hedgewood might be the only choice for now, but damned if I'll accept it."

"I beg your pardon?" Mr. Sparks blinked, green eyes wide.

She couldn't tell Mr. Sparks of Jones, of the investigation, of Wycomb's dealings on the docks. But— "I refuse to give in without a fight."

"*My lady.*" Alarm reverberated in voice and body, both edged with fear. He strode through the doorway as intent as any man ready to stop catastrophe.

She did not care.

"I came to a decision this morning, Mr. Sparks." Just after an honorable common man had kissed her in the woods. Jones had touched her. Not just her body, but something deeper inside. His touch lingered there, giving her strength. She had accepted the role of observer to stay safe, but she would no longer. Wycomb wanted her to marry Hedgewood so immensely he was willing to threaten her at knifepoint.

She would find out why.

"I'll not marry Hedgewood. I only have to discover my opening." She grinned at Mr. Sparks. "Can you request a copy of the marriage contracts from the trustees? Will they provide it, do you think?"

"Yes, of course." He removed his spectacles and used his waistcoat to frantically rub the lenses. "What are you planning?"

"To not marry Hedgewood."

"Do not openly defy your uncle, my lady." Mr. Sparks gripped the only other piece of furniture in the room—the small sideboard still holding the whiskey her father had preferred. "'Tis best to do it in secret, as we have been. Open defiance will only result in—well. I don't even know."

"Pain." She already knew. "So be it." She strode to the sideboard, lifted the decanter. Candlelight flashed over crystal, over amber-gold liquid. Pulling out the stopper, she sniffed at the liquor within. Yes, her father's favorite.

She flipped over a snifter. Poured.

"We'll be leaving in a few hours, I'm told. This is goodbye. But I'm not a pawn." Cat raised her glass, saluted first Mr. Sparks, then the account ledgers lining the wall and the bottles of ink scattering the desk.

"I'm the Baroness Worthington."

Chapter Twenty-Eight

"What problem are you trying to work out now?" The deep baritone voice drifted into the training room, as it had done when Jones was a boy.

He chose not to look up from the glinting metal in his hand. He knew what he would see. Angel would be leaning against the door, amusement quirking the corners of his mouth. Jones had witnessed Angel's understanding laughter more than a hundred times as Jones had dismantled and rebuilt pistols to keep his mind busy.

Then again, while Jones might clean pistols when he needed to think, Angel played the violin. One wasn't much different than the other once technique was considered.

"There is no problem at all." Jones's fingers found the familiar touchhole of the pistol in his hand. He plugged it with a small wooden pick, watched the firelight flash over the barrel.

"Mm hm." Dry humor tinged Angel's tone. "You have six pistols dismantled."

Jones did not tell him it was the second time he'd cleaned

the weapons since he'd returned to London that morning. He also did not care to talk about the problem of Cat and his spinning brain. "Is Lady Angelstone here?"

"Not today. I'm here on business, so she stayed at the townhouse with mother and the girls. But she is demanding that you come to dinner on Thursday. The Shadow and Grace will be there." Angel's footsteps were purposeful as he strode across the bare wood floor to the table near the fire. "Lilias says she has let you duck out long enough."

It meant family. They were always welcoming, but it never failed that he felt uncomfortable. Still, Jones could not refuse Lilias. "I will come."

"Good."

"What is your business?" Jones asked, reaching for the thick fabric tucked between the pistol locks he'd removed. He wrapped it around his palm and fingers, then did the same with the other hand. "Stand back," he murmured, sensing Angel stepping closer.

Angel did, keeping safely away as Jones picked up the pewter jug of water sitting in the coals of the fire. Jones carefully poured the boiling water from the jug into the barrel of the pistol, moving as far back from his own hands and the boiling water as possible. Water spilled out, stained the worn table he worked on, and dripped onto the first layer of the cloth he used to protect his hands.

The table had seen worse than boiling water. The marks scarring the surface told him that as much as memory did.

"Wycomb is my business." Angel's gaze was on the dismantled pistols as Jones dumped the water into a bucket. "I've not heard a whiff inside the *ton*. There's talk of the baroness and her engagement, however."

The jerk was involuntary, Jones's hand jumping as he poured the second round of water into the barrel. He hissed as the liquid soaked through the cloth protecting his skin.

Quickly, he dumped the water into the bucket and set down the pistol. Shaking the fabric from one hand, he set the jug onto the hearth with the other.

"Is it bad?" Angel asked, stepping forward to eye Jones's hand.

"No, just tender." The skin was tinged pink, but nothing more. "No worse than a spilled cup of tea."

"Good."

Jones could feel Angel's gaze on him. He didn't look up, not ready to meet his commander's eyes. Not ready to reveal what might be on his face.

"At any rate," Angel continued, though there was a question in his voice. "I've found nothing within the *ton* but the wedding to Hedgewood. Nothing out of the ordinary, that is."

"No. You wouldn't." Whatever was happening, it was outside that world—or at least on the periphery. "I thought perhaps something or someone would show itself, but I expected few results."

"What is happening, then?" Angel's fingers moving in a rolling wave Jones knew meant he wished for his violin.

"I'm not sure." Jones re-wrapped his hand, then moved the pewter jug back into the coals to reheat. Careful to keep his voice neutral, Jones asked, "What do you know of Hedgewood?"

"Very little. He switches political allegiances easily, depending on the topic. He is a shareholder of the East India Company, and is very vocal in Parliament regarding their sovereignty. I believe he feels they should be less regulated." Angel began to pace the length of the training room—once the townhouse's ballroom. "His fortune is vast, both estates and investments."

"His family?" Jones didn't even want to ask. He knew the answer, and he could never meet that lineage. While he waited for the water, he positioned a dry, well-used cloth around the end of the ramrod he used for cleaning.

"Ancient. Wealthy. It's a good match for her, but a much better match for him."

Jones's attention pricked. "What do you mean?"

"Both families are of old lineage, direct lines going back five or six hundred years. More, perhaps. The titles are some of the oldest in the nation." Angel reached for the cloth Jones had dropped to the floor. He began to wrap it around his hands. "Here, let me poor the water. It will be easier."

"Aye." It was a dance they had performed together since Jones was a boy. He picked up the pistol in one hand, held it steady as Angel brought the lip of the pewter jug to the barrel.

"The baroness's inheritance is larger than Hedgewood's holdings—but between them, they would control a meaningful portion of the country." Angel poured the water in, splashing very little outside the barrel. "The House of Commons is powerful in their counties."

"Ah." Jones knew just the right amount of water was in the barrel and reached for the ramrod. "A joining of two significant houses."

"Yes, though as I said, he will gain more than she will." Angel moved away, setting the jug on the hearth.

"Are you sure?" Shoving the covered end of the ramrod into the barrel, Jones ran it up and down to wash the inside. He'd already done it that day, but a weapon could always be cleaner. Black powder had a way of spreading.

"That is the word in the ballrooms, and believe me, those women do not make mistakes as it applies to income." Angel mock shuddered. "Is there any progress outside of the *ton*?"

"I've heard rumors that he has been seen in the rookeries." Jones set the ramrod and wet cloth aside on the table, then dumped the dirty barrel water into the bucket.

"But that would not be unusual. Assignments take all of us there from time to time."

"True." Angel picked up one of the dismantled locks, testing its movements. "Have you been yet?"

"No. I'm working out how best to approach that line of inquiry."

"Hence the pistols."

Jones didn't comment. The rote and routine of cleaning the pistols was as much about Cat as Wycomb.

"If you do make inquiries in the rookeries," Angel added. "It will not be Wycomb's name but his face that will be important."

"Aye." He'd already thought the same, but Angel's confirmation solidified his course. "I'd planned to have a drawing prepared and see if that elicits a response."

"Be careful."

...

She missed the feel of her lands beneath her feet. Not even twenty-four hours in London, and she missed the Abbey.

Unfortunately, she was stuck—feet neatly side-by-side on a Brussels carpet in bright Turkish patterns, bum planted on the plush silk cushion of a settee.

"Now that you have returned to the city, we may proceed with the engagement ball." Black eyes peered at Cat through an ornate lorgnette, scouring Cat's appearance from curled hair to blue leather half-boots. The Dowager Lady Hedgewood let the lorgnette fall to her lap, the thin chain looping through the ribbon beneath her bodice stopping it from falling to the floor. "I don't generally approve of redheads, but you do seem to be well-behaved."

"I try, my lady," Cat said dryly.

"Ahem." Aunt Essie perched on the edge of an elegant

salon chair. "Thank you for your patience while my niece was away. As you might imagine, it was her duty to see to her tenants during such trying times."

"Of course." The dowager angled her head in acknowledgment, gray hair and tightly wound bun unmoving. "But now we have something more important to discuss. While you were in the country, I began preparations for the ball. It will be Thursday next, and held here, of course."

Cat narrowed her eyes, unsure whether the dowager was being helpful or interfering. Either way, Cat didn't intend to marry Hedgewood, if she could help it.

The lady stood, angular body dressed as severely as her hair. Striding toward an escritoire, she slipped a stack of papers from the desktop. "I have also developed a tentative menu and guest list."

Shuffling the papers, she squinted at the thin script flowing across the surface as she returned to Cat.

"My lady—" Cat began.

"I shall leave the details to you, of course." Veined hands offered the paper without a single tremor. "Once you have finalized your choices, I shall enlist my secretary and any servants you would like to join us to write the invitations—and ourselves, of course. As this will be the match of the Season, our guest list will be extensive."

The lady sat again, spine significantly straighter than the chair back. She picked up her teacup, breathed in the steam curling from beneath the rim.

A *pfft* of irritation slipped from Aunt Essie. "You have it all planned, I see."

"As I said, this marriage is *th*e match of the Season, and it is also the joining of two very old, very great families." Lady Hedgewood sipped, swallowed. "Hedgewood is also my only son," she added softly. "I don't want to step on your toes, Lady Worthington, but I also don't want this wedding or engagement ball to be inferior. You were away."

"I see." Cat looked down at the guest list, the menu. The words were unintelligible to her eyes, as her brain was elsewhere engaged. *She did not want to marry Hedgewood.* Yet here, now, was not the time nor place to protest.

The place to protest was wherever in the vast Hedgewood townhouse its lord and her uncle were discussing the final details of the settlements.

"Thank you, my lady." Cat supposed she could not blame the dowager—she was a mother. "I shall review your suggestions. Perhaps Hedgewood has suggestions as well."

"He likely does, though if you can avoid asking Hedgewood, so much the better." Pinched lips turned up on one side. "He is a *man*, dear."

Silence.

Then, from Essie, a stifled laugh.

"I see." Cat looked to the lists again, hiding a grin that could not be stopped. "I shall endeavor to ensure the engagement ball and wedding are all you hope them to be."

Assuming she had to go through with it.

Chapter Twenty-Nine

"That went well, I think." Aunt Essie settled into the carriage seat, smoothing skirts with one hand, adjusting her reticule with the other. "The dowager seems to be reasonable."

"And has a sense of humor." Cat tapped the guest list with her forefinger, the russet leather of her glove a contrast to the cream-colored paper. Her finger jerked over the page as the horses began their work. "It says here on the guest list, *Lord and Lady Gillespie, but only if you want to be bored by petrology. Lord studies rocks.*"

"Good information to have about you, in the event Lord Gillespie asks you to dance." Aunt Essie's eyes gleamed, laughter crinkling the lines at the corners. "I think you may get along with the dowager nicely."

"So it seems." Cat glanced at her uncle, sitting beside Essie. He ignored them, riffling through a sheaf of papers of his own. Legs crossed as if in a drawing room and not in a crowded carriage, his trousers perfectly tailored—but the sharp planes of his face were tight as he read.

Essie cleared her throat, looking up at her brother's

profile. "How are the settlement discussions progressing? I know that the contracts are finished, but the details—"

"Are none of your concern, Essie." Wycomb did not acknowledge them by meeting their gazes, instead placing the top sheet on the bottom of the stack. His gaze skimmed the next page. "I shall manage them."

Anger flared, but Cat bit her tongue. Not enough to draw blood, but enough to keep her mouth closed and her eyes on the papers in his hand. What did they say? The paper was thin enough to see the slanting lines of ink from the back, but not thin enough she could easily make out the words.

The temptation to argue made her skin itch, the need to read the documents burned deep. But the fading knife mark at her collarbone burned hotter.

For now.

"Ho!" The call was loud, sharp, and accompanied by a jerk of the carriage. Thuds sounded above, horses whinnied. The door whipped open, letting in sunlight and a man wearing homespun clothes. He shoved Cat aside, pushing against her hip and ribs to move her before she could think to oblige. The door closed again, enclosing all of them with the sweet smell of something Cat didn't recognize—and didn't want to.

"You're late. Still." The man beside Cat rasped the words. Eyes fixed on a single point, he only saw Wycomb.

Cat shrank against the seat, gaze flicking between the stranger and Wycomb. In the opposite corner, a white-faced Essie clutched her reticule, worrying the ribbons.

"I told you it will take time." Wycomb didn't move. The papers he held did not waver, nor did his expression change as he continued reading them.

"We ain't got time. Customers are impatient." A pistol appeared, metallic and hard in the small carriage and pointed not at Wycomb, but at Cat.

She didn't flinch. Didn't have time to. The barrel was

pressed against her rib cage before she could blink, before she could fear.

Then fear rocked her, stealing breath and strength.

"If you kill her, there will be no reason for me to comply." Wycomb spoke slowly, looking up at his foe as if there were no weapon in the carriage.

"'Tis why my pistol's pointed at her," the intruder growled. "We know where your worth comes from."

Cat held still, but every word, every movement stamped itself on her mind. Metal pressed against her ribs, and though it was not hot it seemed a brand.

"Yes." Wycomb set the papers on his lap. Casually, he re-crossed his legs, as if they were in a drawing room. But his eyes—those were cold, blue and merciless, and were fixed on the man beside her. "What you seek will arrive soon. I swear it."

"On the life of your niece?"

"On the life of the woman who *could* provide me the money to continue our venture if other parts should fail. Our business is well beyond my niece, but she is a piece that should remain unharmed." Blue eyes flicked once over Cat, held her gaze as if to ensure she would not speak. They flicked away again. "For now."

The pistol in her ribs eased away. Sharp pain receded to a dull ache that would soon fade. Cat tried not to flinch, to dive for the carriage door and plunge through it toward freedom. She was not alone. Essie was stiff in the seat across from her, eyes wide and terrified. The white curls peeking from beneath her bonnet trembled in tandem with the rest of her body.

Wycomb calmly adjusted his cuffs.

"I know you are paid to simply deliver a message. So be it. The message is delivered. Now go. Or I shall kill you." His voice lowered—so low, so cold, it became sound coated by ice. The small pocket pistol materialized as though it had been in Wycomb's hand all the time. "*Go.*"

Death echoed in that single word. Soft, but final.

The intruder's pistol swiveled to face Wycomb, then Essie. Then the floor. "They will not accept lies."

"I do not give them. All will be well, with patience." Wycomb uncocked his weapon pistol and pointed it toward the roof of the carriage.

"It had better, or it's your hide—and both of these two." The man was through the carriage door, tumbling to the street before Cat could draw a full breath.

Even then, she could not.

"What the bloody hell is going on?" Cat's limbs flailed as she tumbled about, trying to regain her seat. "Who was that man?"

"No one of concern." The gun disappeared into Wycomb's coat. Calmly, as if the episode had not occurred, he murmured, "Do not think on it."

"*Do not think on it?*" Oh no. She would not tolerate it. Cat leaned forward, bared her teeth—though she hadn't intended to do any such thing. "I will *think on* whatever affects me, my lands, and my tenants. Every last one, from Kent to Cornwall to Northumberland."

A large fist backhanded her, sending her body and mind reeling. Pain exploded, splintering over cheekbone, jaw, eye. She fell back against the carriage seat while Essie let out a strangled cry.

Shock coursed through Cat's veins, cold and black. She leaped forward, sent a fist to Wycomb's jaw. More pain sang up her arm, then turning to pleasure as his head snapped back. He grunted, but the blow did little to stun him. Wycomb grabbed the front of her cloak, jerking her forward so their faces were inches apart. She tried to push away, but his other hand gripped her hair, yanked hard so her head fell back.

Tears welled of their own volition, but she grit her teeth and forced them back.

She could see each bluntly shaved whisker dotting his chin, the light pink veins crossing the whites of his eyes. Fear burgeoned and grew in her, but she refused to give it rein.

"Do not tell me not to think on it," she said. The vicious tone echoed the pain needling her scalp and throbbing in her cheekbone. "This is my inheritance, and I *will* protect it."

Aunt Essie whimpered. In her periphery, Cat could see her pressed stiffly against the corner where plush seat met bare carriage wall.

"It seems the little pussycat has claws." The low drawl shivered up her spine. "Do not think you can play in my league, *Mary Elizabeth*. I shall not allow it."

The grip in her hair tightened. She scrabbled to free herself, one hand in her cloak front, the other tangling in her hair. He only pulled harder, forcing her head back until her throat was exposed and she could no longer see him. Only the black fabric-covered ceiling was in her view.

Then suddenly he was there, looming large in her vision. "I will say this only once."

Essie whimpered again, terror swirling through the air, but Cat stayed silent. She would not capitulate.

"You will do as I say, and ignore everything else you see and hear." A knee forced its way between her legs. A hard thigh pressed roughly against her sex. She knew the difference between loving and force—knew, too, that she was at Wycomb's mercy. "You only have one value. Is that understood?"

"Yes—" she gasped. Her eyes watered again, this time with anger at herself for surrendering rather than any pain. "Yes. I understand."

• • •

The rookeries stunk. Day or night, they stunk.

He'd been back since boyhood, of course. Assignments led him there.

It was never a pleasure. Never a time to reminisce about the past.

Jones hunched his shoulders in the filthy, homespun coat he used for such work. It did not keep out the stench of shite or piss, nor did it keep out the memories of sleeping in the alleys—or of searching every whore's face for features resembling his own.

He was careful with the drawing procured by Sir Charles's office. Showing it to the wrong person might ruin everything—not showing it would get him nowhere. Luck wasn't running with him in the first and second pubs he visited. The patrons were too distrustful and too into their cups to be of use. The pubs only served as a place for decent ale—and the gin he avoided altogether. He'd tasted French brandy and fine wine at Angel's table. Jones might have begun life drinking gin, but he'd never go back.

The third pub he had more luck with, though it wasn't in the pub itself. He'd shown the drawing briefly to the proprietor, who simply shrugged. Abandoning the patrons as too drunk to pay attention, he stepped out into the street.

The door didn't close behind him.

Jones spun, already reaching for the knife in his waistband.

The man standing there simply put his hands up in truce, tangled ropes of gray hair twisting in the faint breeze. "Saw yer sketch there."

"Ye seen 'im?" Jones butchered the words just as he had as a boy. It was an easy patter to fall into.

"Aye, I know that face—not wot ''e comes round offen." The man spit into the gutter of High Holford Street. "But 'e's been 'ere right enough."

A rush of blood pumped through Jones, sending his heart into a frenzied beat. He kept his face carefully blank. "Why are ye tellin' me?"

"'E weren't from in 'ere." The man shrugged narrow shoulders hidden by a patched coat. "An' I didn't like 'is eyes, eh?"

"I'd think others would 'ave noticed a man from out there." Jones jerked his head toward the west, knowing precisely what "out there" meant.

"Well, 'e t'weren't dressed for out there." Fingers chapped and red from work gestured in the same direction. "'E was dressed for in here—not wot 'e fit in entirely. Clothes don't change a man."

No, they didn't. No one knew that better than Jones. A boy of the rookeries would always be a boy from the rookeries. Which mean Wycomb—however dressed—would still be an arrogant peer. "Who was 'e with?"

"Well, now." The man rubbed the back of his neck and glanced up, as though the crowded buildings and smoke-laden sky would provide an answer. "I don' like ta say."

Which was an answer in itself, and sent satisfaction soaring through Jones. "Understood, sir." If a man born and bred in the rookeries didn't want to say, then Wycomb's dealings were with a dangerous group.

"I ain't willing to risk me throat just to 'elp out, see?"

"Nor would I, sir." Jones tipped his head, touching his forefinger to the brim of his cap. "A working throat is an important thing."

The man's lips quirked up, revealing a mess of broken and yellow teeth. "Clever."

"Yessir."

"'Ere. I'll give you a bit more." The man reached into his coat pocket and retrieved a short, whittled pipe. "Ye have tobacco?"

"Sorry, no."

"Eh." He didn't remove the pipe, however, just clenched it between the broken teeth. "You don't want to cross these men, boy. They 'ave their plans, and the plans aren't falling inta place. You make it worse an' they ain't going to like thet."

Jones was getting closer. Here was a man who had seen Wycomb and those he was with. The fact that he didn't want to reveal the companions was unimportant. It only mattered that they were dangerous enough he was wary. The rookeries were full of criminals, but there were ranks.

"Where can I find them?"

"Dunno. But if you ask enough questions, they'll find you."

...

My Darling,

I have missed you since I was in the country. Not just your face and body, but your advice. We suit each other, you and I. If only we could be together.

It seems jonquil is all the rage this Season, and so I will be wearing it at the Duchess of Torland's ball tonight.

Please find me, my darling. Soon.

Yours,

Cat

"Aunt Essie." Cat folded her message to Jones, once, twice, then sealed it with wax. "If anything should happen to me, leave Worthington House."

Essie's eyes had been wild the last three hours as they

sat in the drawing room, embroidering handkerchiefs as if nothing were amiss. It was where Wycomb had put them when they returned. He'd commanded they stay until he gave them leave, and neither of them dared countermand him.

Until now.

"Mary Elizabeth?" Her aunt's voice was weak, fingers plucking at thread rather than creating elaborate flower designs.

"Not today of course. Later." Cat stood and strode across the room to her aunt. In low tones, she murmured, "Find someone you trust to stay with, or go to the countryside, the Continent. Whatever you must."

"I don't understand what is happening." Essie didn't whimper, but her voice was a very shallow step away. Fear had opened her eyes wide.

"I can't tell you. I don't know myself." Cat set her hand on Essie's shoulder, squeezed. "Be ready with clothes and pounds so you can leave if you must. Is that clear? Don't wait for me, don't fight. Just run."

"Just run." Essie licked her lips, then let out a fast breath. The thread in her lap twitched as her fingers convulsed. "What of you?"

"I am not alone." The statement was both wonderful and terrible all at once. Jones would stand with her, but could not be hers. She leaned forward, set her mouth near Essie's ear. The scents of powder and rouge and *eau de parfum* competed for dominance, but the mixture was familiar and comforting. "Run, Essie. Either somewhere nearby where you are safe, or far away where he won't find you."

"I will." Essie half stood as Cat moved away. "Mary Elizabeth? Cat?"

It was the first time she could remember that Essie had called her Cat. "Yes?"

"I know my brother." A shudder rippled her soft frame. "He will find us if he wants to."

Chapter Thirty

Her handwriting was beautiful. It flowed and dipped and soared across the page. Jones rubbed a thumb across the smooth stationery. However much he wanted to linger over the peaks and valleys of her words, there was more here than ink over paper.

"Thank you, Rupert, for bringing the note." Jones set the note on the edge of his desk. "Have you seen the baroness today?"

"Yessir." Rupert tugged at his bright hair, shades more orange than the baroness's deep red. "I saw her this afternoon, coming from a fancy townhouse. Looked a mite off."

"Off?" A common word, but it sent unease spiraling through Jones.

"Aye." Rupert shuffled worn shoes on the patterned Aubusson rug. "'Er face was all red, and she didn't walk. She near ran inta the 'ouse. The ol' lady did the same. The gov'nor, though, 'e strolled along easy as you please, though he weren't lookin' right neither."

"Mm." Jones flicked at the note on his desk, let his

thoughts shift through time and air as much as the paper shifted against wood and polish. Wycomb could hide any emotion—Jones had seen him do so. Cat could hide much, trained as she was to endure the *ton*.

If she showed strain, then something was amiss—which coincided with her love note.

He turned, studied Rupert. The boy was just on the edge of growing into a young man, all angular legs and arms. His pants were an inch too short, and one bare toe was visible between sole and cap of the shoe.

"Wait here." Jones slipped from the room, knowing the boy would do as asked. And he was about to send the boy out for more reconnaissance, along with the others.

"Here." He slipped back in, the items in his hand held out. "They should fit."

"Sir. Mr. Jones." Rupert's mouth opened and closed, a fish in the air gasping for water. "Boots?"

"Aye." The affirmative word was one he rarely said now, but it seemed fitting somehow.

"For me?"

"I thought you might need some soon and bought them a while ago when—" He stopped. Rupert's face was bright with equal amounts of joy and disbelief. Jones swallowed hard, remembering the first time Angel had gifted him with a simple cap, because he didn't have one of his own.

Terror had filled him, because Angel had cared.

Elation and pride had also filled that space in his chest, because Angel had cared.

"You need proper gear to be a spy." Jones shrugged, as if the boots were nothing more than a tool. It didn't matter that Jones had agonized over the choice before purchasing them. "You can't join our ranks if you can't learn, and you can't learn if you're dealing with wet feet. Soon enough, you'll be issued a weapon as well. *If* you decide to stay on."

The boy accepted the boots as reverently as any priest accepting the sacrament.

"They are very fine, sir." Rupert stroked the mediocre leather, chapped fingers running along seams as softly as the clouds touched the sky. "Are you certain they are for me?"

A freckled face turned up, nerves and hope mingling on blunt features. Jones understood that look, probably more than the boy himself.

"Yes. They are for you. I need my men to be ready." He set a hand on the boy's shoulder, gripped hard. "Now, tell me more about the baroness."

...

Cat could hardly bear the awareness that prickled her skin and kept her mind whirring. It was as though she were a lantern, burning day and night, with no reprieve from this state of watchfulness. It didn't seem possible to be alert at every moment, but she was living it.

The rhythm of the music continued its cheerful beat and her body performed the steps of the country dance, years of training keeping her movements flawless. But her mind was elsewhere.

No one in this ballroom knew what lived in their midst. None of them knew the man commanding the edge of the dance floor was a spy and a monster. And she must dance and smile and make conversation so that they would not know of it.

"My lady, is something amiss?" Hedgewood's brows drew together as the two of them met and separated and turned on the floor. "You appear strained. I'd prefer the *ton* believe this matched isn't forced."

The words *it IS forced* rolled onto her tongue, but she bit them back.

She sent Hedgewood an apologetic smile and shook her head. "It is nothing. Just weary of travel and worried about the Abbey and the tenants, of course."

Where was Wycomb while she danced? He had been circulating the ballroom most of the evening, though the card room had held his attention for a time. She'd noted everyone he'd spoken to, approximately how long, whether he was cold and formal or if he had turned jovial—though perhaps jovial was too strong a word. She would have termed his demeanor jovial for anyone else, but for Wycomb he simply became approachable.

She met Hedgewood, followed the dance movements, and set her hand in his.

"When you are my wife," he murmured between the musical notes. "You needn't worry about the Abbey. I shall see to it."

A few steps, a spin, and they were separated again. A chill spread over her skin, oppressive enough she could feel its weight. Cat circled the lady next to her, changed her position, and met Hedgewood again. His head was cocked to one side, the handsome face alive with enjoyment despite the speculation and discontent hovering around his eyes.

"The Abbey shall always be my concern." She smiled easily, as if they shared an understanding of the necessities of being the lord and lady. "It is my duty to be involved."

Hands gripped together, they circled once, twice, in time with the music.

"No, your duty is to attend to my wishes." The words slipped between lips tipped up in a contagious grin. He bent and pressed his lips to the knuckles gripped hard in his as they moved back into the line. Around them titters and sighs of admiration flowed beneath the violins. "My wishes are that you accept my directives."

"No." She gave him the same smile, angled her head as

they fell back, separating from the other dancers. Side by side, hands held, they faced the opposite line of dancers.

She saw him. Jones. A glimpse in the rear of the room—well away from Wycomb—behind the crowds, behind jewels and gowns and starched cravats. He met her gaze, then slipped away into the crowd and disappeared.

He was here.

It was all she needed to know.

"I'm sure your uncle has explained that I will not tolerate disobedience." Again with a smile both charming and knowing. Hedgewood spun her out, in, and leaned close in what would appear to anyone else as a lover's whisper. "Unless it is in the bedchamber, of course."

Spin out, mind whirring. Spin in, mind whirring yet more. There was nothing else she could do or say. She had Hedgewood's measure—and he was little better than Wycomb.

"Of course," she murmured demurely, as if she accepted such things. Her stomach rebelled, threatening to purge the punch and cakes she had consumed earlier. But they stayed down, and Hedgewood smiled with shameless satisfaction.

Her mother had told her the truth—the ballroom was little more than a lion's den.

But somewhere out there was Jones. Waiting for her.

Closer was Wycomb, watching every move she made.

The notes lengthened, the movements became slowed. They bowed to their partners, again to those couples adjacent. The music died.

All the while Cat wanted to run.

Hedgewood refused to relinquish her fingers. His hand tightened on hers, hard and masculine, but without that innate gentleness Jones carried about him. Hedgewood led her off the floor into the crowd, just as he should.

Pastel gowns cleaved, smug faces made way. Skirts

rustled as she passed. Everyone watched her. Nerves rose and roiled, told her she should run from the room. But she didn't. She smiled as her mother had taught her, inclined her head in acknowledgment and greeting—she was an Ashdown. Whatever she might feel, she knew the duty centuries of history required.

Still, the chill of Wycomb's gaze ran down her spine and the sham of Hedgewood's good humor raked at her calm.

He led her to Essie, her arm held possessively in his with the strength of his grip. It would appear lover-like to anyone else—and she would never again trust what she saw.

"My lady, I hope you have another set you can spare me later this evening?" Grinning, green eyes laughing down at her, Hedgewood bowed over her hand as she stepped beside Essie.

"Of course." Refusal would be idiotic just now. "Thank you for the dance, my lord."

"It was my pleasure, Mary Elizabeth." Hedgewood bowed his farewell with a smile, but the use of her name sent arrows of unease and anger through her.

He was like Wycomb.

"That young man is positively smitten." Aunt Essie said it into her glove once Hedgewood was well away, the pale silk curving over an amused smile. Still, strain had deepened the lines of her face. She looked older than she had just that morning.

"So it would seem," Cat murmured, though she knew he wasn't smitten with her as much as her inheritance. Irritation slipped in, then slipped away again as she caught sight of Wycomb. He was conversing with a short, balding man Cat knew to be their host.

Still, her uncle's gaze drifted around the room until they settled on Cat, flicked once to Hedgewood, now amongst a group of gentlemen on the edge of the room. She shivered and deliberately turned away so she faced Aunt Essie and her back was to Wycomb.

She was hunted on all sides.

The walls of the ballroom suffocated her, the laughter of the *ton* sounding unusually loud and tinny. Her stays were laced too tightly and she could not seem to draw a proper breath. Blood rose in her cheeks, flushing beneath her skin.

"Excuse me, Aunt Essie." Cat clutched her fan and reticule, fingers both numb and exquisitely painful. "I need the retiring room."

Essie looked sharply at her. "Are you well?"

"Yes, I just need a moment." She smiled in reassurance, the skin of her face brittle enough it might shatter.

With a brief nod from Essie, Cat hurried through the crowd, the distance to the door a mile if it was an inch. She nearly shoved her way through the floating gowns and laughter of the other guests until the door loomed above her.

Then she was through it, leaving the laughter and perfumed bodies behind. Turning to the left, she moved through the hallway, then down another until she found the steps.

She had no idea where she was going, but it was not the ladies' retiring room. There would be nothing there for her but competing debutantes eying each other and their mamas exchanging thinly veiled insults. Or matrons gossiping about their latest peccadillos.

Cat needed air. Air and freedom and space.

Chapter Thirty-One

She burst through the rear door and into the garden of the Duke of Torland. Gulping in air as though drowning, Cat staggered past evenly trimmed bushes and ordered flower beds to drop onto an intricately wrought iron bench.

Her fingers curled around the edge of the seat as she leaned forward and stared at the pointed toes of her dancing slippers, peeping beneath muslin. She did her best to blend into the night, but it was difficult when one wore a gown the color of bright daffodils. Still, she tried to be unnoticeable, pressing her palms against the bench.

She would have to go back in soon. She could not sit out here, self-pity holding her to the seat. But she wanted a minute, one minute when she was not on display before the entire *ton*, when there was no one who would abduct her, or threaten to kill her, or pressure her into a marriage she was not ready for and did not want.

Just one moment of peace.

"Are you well, Cat?"

She nearly jumped out of her skin at the soft, calm words.

Her head whipped up, gaze casting wildly around for Jones, but she did not have to look far.

He was there, a few feet away, where he had not been a moment ago.

She had not heard the crunch of gravel or the swish of grass as he approached. His brows were drawn down in the center, twin lines of concern and confusion. The evening jacket he wore was ill-fitting, the cravat at his neck simple and unfashionable. He looked awkward in the evening wear, though his black breeches ended in boots polished to such a gleam she could see the reflection of both the gold light from the house windows and the silver beams of the full moon above.

She thought she saw the gleam of moonlight on metal in the folds of his shirt as well, but then it disappeared and he was draped in nothing but darkness.

"Are you well?" he repeated, stepping closer. This time she heard the faint rasp of his boots on the path, but only because she was listening for it.

"Yes." She narrowed her eyes on his shadowed face, though her heart leaped at seeing him again. Her body seemed to have different thoughts. No leaps or bounds, but a pull deep inside her. "Do you never make noise?"

His lips twitched, the serious expression he usually carried flitting away. "It's a useful skill in my line of work."

"Still, it's unsettling." Her fingers reflexively twitched the seat of the bench before she let it go. With a deep breath of air that smelled of both night and man, she leaned against the back of the bench. The iron was cool, even through her gown, and the pattern dug into her shoulder blades. "Yes, I am well. It's only that I felt alone. There was no one in there for me, but out here—" She stopped, drawing in a breath and turning her face away.

The darkness had a way of drawing out confidences, but

she knew where she and Jones stood.

Nowhere.

"I needed fresh air, that is all." She didn't move. Somehow the buzz of insects and rush of wind in the trees anchored her to the seat. A part of her felt infinitely delicate, ready to shatter at the slightest touch.

Cat realized there was no answer or sound from the man standing before her. Popping open her eyes, she saw nothing but sky, moon, and tall pruned hedges.

"Jones?" she whispered, not certain she even wanted an answer.

"Cat?" He was beside her on the bench, though she'd not heard or felt him sit beside her.

She turned to face him, frowning. "Do they teach you this when you become a spy?"

"No, I learned it as a boy. A boy in the rookeries has good reasons for being quiet." His eyes flickered over her face, moving here and there, as if trying to determine what she had not said. Then he turned to face the night. Eventually he spoke, words low and easy. "Sometimes," he said, crossing one leg over the other as though they discussed chess over a glass of Madeira. "Sometimes a person can stand in the middle of a crowd and be utterly alone."

Cat didn't speak, not certain if she could even trust her own voice. *How* did he understand? What had she said or what action conveyed what she'd been thinking? She held herself still lest this moment, this precious, open moment, be lost in the darkness.

"Sometimes," he continued, looking up at the sky, perhaps contemplating the feeble twinkle of stars beyond the glow of London's lighted streets and smoke. "A person wants to scream to everyone around them that there is something bad in their midst, that unseen dangers lurk in the shadows. They must act. Run, scream, hide, stockpile weapons, food, whatever must be done to weather the advancing storm."

"Build an ark," Cat said, some part of her soul responding to his words as though they'd been her own. "Build a vessel to save everything you hold dear."

"Yes, that's exactly right," Jones answered, and though she was not looking at him, she sensed that the corner of his lips turned up simply from the tone of his voice. "Build an ark."

"How do you hold it all inside you?" she asked, looking up at the sky herself. Beyond London, beyond darkness, to those stars—where anything was possible.

"I often don't have a choice." He turned his hand palm up on his lap, and she wondered if he meant for her to take his hand. Cat turned her own hand palm up, so that they seemed to be two mirror images. His hidden beneath worn kid leather, hers just beside it on her own thigh, inches away and hidden by smooth, new kid leather. In a single moment, a shift of bone and glove, and they could join hands.

She did not move, could not. He did not move, either, not his hand or any other part of him. He was as still as one of the stone pillars guarding the entrance to the terrace.

She felt the connection, glove to glove—more, skin to skin—as if somehow they *had* touched. Her palm tingled, growing exquisitely sensitive to the silk covering it. Warm fingers slipped over her hand, slid between her fingers until their hands were joined together. One hand, but made of two, settled on the cold iron of the bench.

"You are not alone, Cat. I am here. When I am not, you will have strength enough to stand on your own. Everyone doubts their abilities until they are tested."

"Yes." But he would not be with her always, only for now, and she had yet to be truly tested. "I needed to speak with you about this afternoon."

"What?" His voice hardened—not toward her, but in the

way she knew meant espionage.

"It was after I met Lady Hedgewood today," she answered, suddenly weary. "We all entered the carriage and started home, Essie, Wycomb, and I. A man jumped into the carriage and held a pistol to my side—"

The fingers twined with hers twitched.

"He didn't hurt me. He was motivating Wycomb." She spoke quickly to soothe. "He said Wycomb was late with something and customers were impatient. Also, that they knew his worth was tied with mine, and Essie and I would be hurt if Wycomb didn't deliver—but we are fine."

"Then why is your left eye swollen?"

"It is?" She set her fingers to the tender area, probed. "I thought it appeared normal." It had been when she'd left the townhouse for the ball. Perhaps it had simply taken more time to swell than she'd expected.

"How were you hurt?" His words were so low, so guttural, she barely recognized them.

She thought about lying for less than a second. "Wycomb backhanded me, but only because I refused to let him lie to me about the man with the pistol."

Jones was quiet, his fingers unmoving in hers. Then those fingers slid away and he stood to face her.

"I will kill him." The words, low and vicious, barely floated on the night air.

"Jones, no." She shook her head, rose to face him. "I am well. It is nothing more than bruise."

"I let the knife go for the sake of the investigation. But not any longer. For that and for this—" Jones quickly tugged his glove from his hand and feathered bare fingers over the bruise. Callused skin, gentle touch. She had not wept yet because of the blow, but she nearly did now. "I will kill him."

"You cannot." Satin slipped against rough wool as she set her hand on his arm. "We don't know what he is doing. I don't know how to protect everything I hold dear."

Jones dipped his head, touched his lips to hers. Warm, bold. Tasting of Jones. Her body wanted to unfold beneath him, but they were not alone. Anyone, at any moment, could find them.

"My engagement ball to Hedgewood is next week." The words tumbled from her, as thick as the sorrow filling her chest.

He set his forehead against hers, held there. "I have wishes, Cat. I shouldn't."

There was nothing to say, nothing to do but hold her own wishes in her heart.

"I have to go. Someone will miss me soon." If her lips were ripe from his kisses, it would not go unnoticed. Still, she kissed him once more. His body was hard around hers, arms solace and temptation. "Jones. I don't know who Wycomb is working with, but he is late producing something and customers are not happy. His business partners aren't happy—and they are not of the *ton*."

Male laughter echoed, not far away. Female laughter followed. Cat ducked under Jones's arm, dashed along the path so she was well away from him.

"I must go." She wanted to stay. Still, she backed away, hands groping behind her for something solid. She found nothing but air.

"Cat." His fist clenched, held, opened again. "Be careful."

Chapter Thirty-Two

"Come play, Mr. Jones!" Maggie, Angel's niece, dropped a tin soldier into Jones's open palm. "Bonaparte will be defeated tonight!" She danced away, braids flying, to settle down on the floor of Angel's drawing room to set up her soldiers. "I've been studying Wellington's strategies."

"An intelligent undertaking," Jones answered. The words felt stilted inside his brain and sounded more so to his ears. How did a grown man talk to an eight-year-old girl? She was a little adult with an added enthusiasm and joy he couldn't understand.

"Wellington is the bravest soldier, don't you think? Except for Uncle Angel, of course." Bright eyes turned toward the Marquess of Angelstone, who was currently whispering into his very pregnant wife's ear. "He's the bravest. Did you know he was at Waterloo? So was Aunt Lilias."

"I believe I heard that."

Her shining eyes turned back to Jones, ready to spill an exciting secret. "Aunt Lilias is a soldier, sir. A great one. Can you imagine a great woman soldier?"

Clearly, the girl thought this was amazing, and Jones was quite in agreement. "I think it is wonderful," he responded. At which point, he didn't know what to else to say to this sprite of a girl.

"Here, Mr. Jones, I have set up the soldiers as they were at the battle. Uncle Angel was there, and this soldier—" She held up a tin man so worn there was no longer paint on his face. "This one is my father. These were his soldiers, and my Grandmama says this one looks just like him."

Jones peered at the blunted features. "He looks brave, certainly."

"Yes." She smiled at him as brightly as if she were the sun at midday. "Yes, he does." She busied herself resetting the formations, changing up the left flank and rear guard.

He glanced around, met the gaze of the sharp-featured and soft-hearted Dowager Lady Angelstone. She smiled slightly, nodding her head in acknowledgment. Beside her sat her widowed daughters-in-law, one of them Maggie's mother. They looked happier than he remembered seeing them before, as if some of the grief had left them in the past year or so.

"I must go converse with the adults, now," Jones said to Maggie.

"Must you?" Her lips turned down in disappointment, then smiled again in excitement. "When you are done, we can recreate the battle where Uncle Angel and Aunt Lilias met. It was very romantic and very bloody."

"Yes, I can see that." He tried not to laugh, choosing to cough into his hand instead. And realized he'd forgotten to wear gloves. No gentleman appeared in the drawing room without gloves.

He stood, setting his hands behind his back. A quick glance revealed Angel speaking to the third spy in the room. Julian Travers, Earl of Langford, had his arm wrapped around his wife's waist and an eye on the two-year-old twin girls playing on the floor. They were enamored of a set of—what were they? Rattles? Sturdy legs pumped and moved as they chased each other with crazed enthusiasm.

Jones wondered briefly if purgatory was small children with fences to keep them contained.

After a light kiss, Angel left his wife's side and strode over to Jones. "Thank you for indulging Lilias and coming to dinner."

"I appreciate the invitation." Jones's lips twitched and he shrugged. "Also, I dared not refuse her."

"Wise. It took me a little longer to learn that." Angel grinned and gripped Jones's shoulder. "I suppose it's love."

Cat's image flashed in and out of his mind, bringing with it a light ache in his chest. Angel's hand fell away, and Jones rubbed at that ache. It had lodged there, as if settling in for a long stay.

"Jones. I saw you with her." Angel's tone was low, all trace of amusement gone. "I followed when she fled the ballroom to make certain she was not in danger and saw you in the garden."

Embarrassment dropped onto Jones's shoulders, heavy as the weight of the world. "My apologies." It was all he could think to say.

"Why?" Angel frowned, cocked his head to the side. The gold queue of hair at the base of his neck shifted over his coat.

"She's not of my class. I have no right to her."

Silence could be huge and heavy, and as solid as any stone wall.

"Do you love her?" Angel asked.

"It doesn't matter if I do or not. She isn't for me." Jones flexed his bare fingers.

"I admit, there are a considerable number of difficulties lying in that direction," Angel spoke slowly. Jones knew from the pacing of the words he was choosing them carefully. "She bears one of the oldest titles and estates in England. Jones, she's—" He stopped, drew breath. "Hell. When it comes to bloodlines and lineage, she's close to royalty. She's connected to nearly every monarchy across Europe, with more blunt than most of them."

He knew that. He knew it all. A dull ache settled deep in his gut. "As I said, she isn't for me. She's promised to Hedgewood."

Angel didn't answer, presumably because there was nothing he could say. Angel knew Jones was right. Somehow that confirmation allowed Jones to acknowledge the truth to himself.

He wasn't in love with Mary Elizabeth Frances Catherine Ashdown, the 13th Baroness Worthington.

He *was* in love with Cat.

His belly clutched and his heart did a long, slow roll in chest.

"Damnation," Angel said softly. "I can tell by your face. I'm sorry, Jones."

"No reason to be sorry. The truth is the truth." He just wished the truth weren't as sharp as any assassin's knife— and though his childhood stood him in good stead as a spy, he could curse it now. Nothing would ever change the circumstances of his birth, and nothing would ever make him good enough for her.

One of the little girls toddled toward him. She held out her rattle, beads first. Jones forced a smile and nodded, which usually worked with these small beings. It didn't. She stood there, flyaway hair floating about her face, and said something utterly unintelligible.

"She wants you to take her toy," the Earl of Langford translated from across the room. There was no mistaking the laugher lurking beneath his voice.

"Very well. Thank you." Jones took the wooden rattle, folding it into his palm. The girl beamed at him as if she had just bestowed the crown jewels. What was the girl's name? He couldn't remember at first. Then, "Hello, Anna."

"This one is Sarah, Jones." Their mother came forward, her smile blooming quiet and steady as she picked the girl up and swung the child onto her hip. "They are identical. I can barely distinguish one from the other half the time. They're such a blur of feet and voices I can't tell which girl I'm chasing." Grace Travers, Countess of Langford, nuzzled her daughter's cheek before giving her an affectionate kiss.

"Yes, ma'am." Jones couldn't think of anything else to say. He didn't belong here, with these pretty families and their happy children. He knew nothing of family and children and love. Or of parents, for that matter. One of his was a mystery and the other had abandoned him.

"What is the matter, Jones?" Lady Langford spoke softly, her silver eyes going soft. "You're always quiet, but not like this." The child snuggled into the curve between Lady Langford's neck and shoulder, then stared at Jones with wide eyes the color of a summer sky.

"Nothing is the matter." What else could he say? He couldn't tell this woman of Cat, or the feelings growing inside him that he had no right to feel. Still, the small child before him became a sudden want. He could see a child with Cat's auburn hair and brilliant eyes. Or perhaps it would have his own brown eyes. There was no way of knowing.

The ache in his chest became painful. He set a hand there, rubbed, just to make sure there was nothing wrong.

"Who is she?" Lady Langford asked. "It's unpardonable of me to question you, and quite intrusive. But, Jones, all of us know how difficult it is to find love when you are a spy."

"I believe it is time for me to become scarce." Angel sidestepped away from them.

"Coward," Jones muttered darkly.

"Absolutely."

Jones was vaguely aware of Angel's wife Lilias pushing up from the settee and coming toward them, hand brushing her husband's arm as she passed him. Her belly led the way, and her smile was softer than he'd seen in her before. In fact, all of her was softer. Her smile, her skin, her eyes. She seemed happier than even the day she was married, and Jones had thought he'd seen true happiness that day.

"Don't bother him, Gracie. I can see Jones is not ready to share, more's the pity." She set her hand on his shoulder and leaned up to kiss his cheek, bringing with her a clean, bright scent. "But we all understand."

She stayed close, her face lifted toward his. Jones glanced up at Angel, then at Langford. They were talking, each of them grinning as they watched their wives with amusement. Is that what love was? They seemed to understand their partners, let her speak for herself. The child growing inside of Lilias was out of Angel's control, yet he didn't hover over her. Langford's other child—it must be Anna—ran across the room and tumbled to the floor, yet he didn't rush over and pick her up. He simply watched her pick herself back up, then grinned in satisfaction.

It was too much. All of it. The love, the family. The ties that bound them all together—husband to wife, friend to friend, parent to child—was simply too much to witness. Jones's stomach clutched and he couldn't quite draw breath.

He had to go. Now.

"Excuse me." He bowed once to Lady Langford, again to Lilias. "I have an assignment—you understand?" His mind was reeling so that he could barely understand their murmured responses.

He set a hand on the head of the child in Lady Langford's arms. Blond curls slipped beneath his palms. Her hair felt clean. It shouldn't matter that the girl's hair felt clean, but that quick brush across his palm was magical.

"I'm not meant for this life, my ladies." He sounded like a stuffed-shirt prig. "But I thank you for the invitation to dinner."

"Jones." Lilias held him in place with nothing but light pressure to his shoulder. "None of us know what to do with this life of spying and family. Just because it isn't natural does not mean it is wrong or impossible."

"Thank you, my lady, but it isn't for me. Even for visiting."

"It isn't difficult to enjoy it, Jones," Lady Langford said in her quiet way. "The difficult part is allowing yourself."

He could think of nothing to say, so he simply bowed to his hostess, then to Lady Langford, then the ladies chatting in the corner. A quick nod was all that was needed for the Shadow and Angel and he would be free.

Chapter Thirty-Three

Every stroke of the quill grated on her nerves. *It would be the pleasure of Lord Hedgewood and Lady Worthington to invite you...*

Cat hated the words. Each one brought her closer to the engagement ball, closer to marriage to Hedgewood. Yet she could not ignore that the invitations must be sent. She blotted the ink, set the completed note on a stack of a fifty or so just like it.

Across the dining table where they had spread out the invitation lists, Essie had a similar pile of stationery, though she was not writing. Instead, she fiddled with her quill, running it through her fingers as she stared out the window with unfocused eyes.

"Aunt Essie?"

The lady jumped, a squeak falling from her lips.

"Are you well?" Cat asked, though she already knew the answer. Essie had been living between nerves and fright since the incident in the carriage.

"Of course. Yes. Of course." She bent over the paper, set

the quill to it—but did not write. "No."

"I did not think so." Setting the invitations aside, Cat leaned against the chair back.

Essie lifted her face, eyes wide behind her spectacles. "How can you focus? How can you sit across the breakfast table from *him*, after what he did?"

"Because I refuse to let him win." She hadn't thought of it that way before, but it was how she felt. "I can be afraid enough to be careful, but not so afraid that he wins."

Shaking her head, Essie opened her mouth to speak, then closed it. Cat doubted she fully understood. Aunt Essie was kind, sweet even, but there was little fight in her. She simply did not have it in her nature.

"Remember," Cat said carefully, looking over her shoulder toward the door to ensure they were alone. "If anything happens to me, leave immediately. Be ready."

Essie nodded, then looked once more to the invitation in front of her. Still, she did not write.

"All will be well." She thought to add, *I promise*, but decided she could not add that to her lie.

The door opened and Essie jumped again. She made the same little sound as her gaze whipped toward the doorway. The butler stood there, expression mildly put out. She could see a second man behind him, cap removed and clutched in his hands.

"A messenger for you, my lady." Brown flicked his gaze toward the man. "He refuses to give it to anyone but yourself."

"Let him in." She turned fully in her chair to face the door.

Silently, but with mild irritation on his narrow features, Brown moved aside and let the man enter. Cat recognized him now as a footman from Ashdown Abbey.

"Jacob, hello." She smiled at him. "It is good to see you."

"Milady." He nodded to Cat, then again to Essie. "Ma'am."

"You have a message?"

"Aye, from Mr. Sparks. He said I should deliver it to no one but you." The footman reached into his coat and drew out a packet sealed with red wax. Stepping forward, he offered it to her. "Mr. Sparks said you should read it immediately."

"I will, thank you." Heart thumping, she took the packet and turned it over in her hands. There was no indication what it held beyond several papers. "Brown, see that he is provided food and rest before he leaves again for Ashdown Abbey."

"Thank you, milady." The footman beamed at her and touched his hand to his forehead in farewell.

"Please follow me, sir." Brown bowed to Cat and closed the door behind them.

Curiosity burned in her, and she quickly broke the seal and opened the outer layer. Inside was a carefully folded sheaf of papers. She recognized Mr. Sparks's handwriting as if it were her own.

My lady,

I obtained a copy of the marriage contract and have studied it at length. I am not a solicitor, but I am familiar enough with legal language that I can read it easily. I am sorry, but I cannot see a way out. The document is carefully drafted, and very much in Hedgewood's favor.

I wish I had a better answer for you.

Yr. Humblest Servant,
Matthew Sparks

Despair could be heavy, both on the body and in the soul. Cat dropped the letter onto the table and frantically read the other papers. It was the contract itself, copied in Mr. Sparks's script. Eyes quickly moving over the words, Cat read each provision.

She found nothing on the first read, nor the second. Nothing that would give her freedom.

Nausea rose in her throat, bringing with it a sour taste.

"What has happened?" Alarm shot through Essie's words. "Mary Elizabeth, you look ill."

"I must marry Hedgewood." Cat had to force the words out, pushing them beyond the need to retch.

"Yes, dear." Essie looked down at the invitations, back up again. "It will not be so bad. You will be away from here, safe, with a husband possessed of good humor—all of which consoles me, just now."

It did not console Cat.

"Excuse me, Aunt." She needed to be alone with her misery.

Her bedchamber brought her no solace. It did not soothe any part of the pain in her chest. Cat hadn't realized how much she had hoped the contract would free her until that hope was gone.

Even through the choking agony of defeat, Cat knew she must dispose of the note. Stirring the banked coals to life, she dropped the note into the embers. It smoldered, caught flame, and melted into ash. The contract she folded small. Moving to her escritoire, she opened the bottom drawer, set the paper in the back corner and covered it with the leather-bound ledgers there. They were old household accounts, written in her mother's tidy script, and no longer of any use.

Except to Cat. Now.

When she had finished hiding the note, Cat stood in the middle of the room, staring at rose-gold streaks of light from the setting sun. She would have to dress soon for the evening engagements, force herself to smile to the *ton*—perhaps even Hedgewood. Wycomb would escort her into ballrooms, lies upon lies spewing from his mouth as he murmured platitudes to lords and ladies.

Oh God. She could not do it.

Chapter Thirty-Four

The street was quiet and warm, with a light breeze. A perfect summer night. Yet the ache in his chest couldn't be fixed by the pretty gold and rose sunset or the scent of roasting meat or the laughter of families. They simply didn't know what it was like to be alone. Truly, truly alone.

He started to walk, not sure where he was going. This was the West End, where carriages bore the aristocracy to soirees and dinner parties and Parliament. This was a world he knew nothing about and couldn't even imagine beyond what he'd seen through windows. He didn't belong here.

She did.

He looked up at Cat's window, because that was where he'd walked to. It wasn't far from Langford's townhouse, and he'd spent hours here lately. Of course he would head here if he wasn't thinking. It was logical. Still, the ache in his chest was anything but logical, and he hated the feeling.

He shook it off and looked to the townhouse. The rear garden was empty and quiet, the mews behind him busy with grooms and horses and carriages being readied for the night's adventures. Was she at home? Perhaps she was preparing to attend a fancy gathering. He wished she were standing at the window and could see him. She might wave, or even open the window so he could see her face.

He was pathetic for even thinking it.

Whatever was moving through him and causing this longing and need and heat was nothing she would feel for him. She was a baroness in her own right, with centuries of blue blood behind her. He was nothing but riffraff from the rookeries, with no ability to provide for her—not that she needed him. She was an heiress.

His hand fisted, heart and mind full of more emotions than he could name. He should not be standing here in front of her house. It would do him little good to stare straight into the face of a life he wanted and couldn't have.

Langford and Angel had made it work. They had children and wives, and were by all accounts happy. They're lives were not normal and sometimes they had to leave their families. Langford was partially retired and rarely accepted an assignment. Lilias had been pulled into the family and wasn't alone when Angel was on assignment.

Cat would be alone. Even if Jones could marry her, when he left for assignments, she would be left alone. Not that there was any reason to think about it. There was no point in even considering what would happen in those circumstances.

He started as the terrace door opened, a figure slipping into the deepening shadows of the garden.

Cat was not at the window, but picking her way through the garden toward him. A light shawl was wrapped around her shoulders, its pale pink-and-white design twisting over the surface. Her hair was unbound and tumbled down her back, its waves shifting in the evening breeze.

It was not quite daylight, not quite dusk. Anyone who looked out the window would see them.

"Why are you here?" she asked quietly when she drew close to him. He could just make out her scent over the heavy, sweet blooms surrounding them.

He didn't have an answer, so he said nothing. He watched and waited, hardly able to breathe for fear she would leave again.

"Jones." His name was a sigh on her lips. "I cannot stay here long. Wycomb is at home."

"I have no reason for being here. None." It was an honest answer, yet he could not continue with such honesty. He couldn't tell her he was in love with her. "My apologies, Cat."

Her eyes were very blue as she studied his face. Twilight had fallen and any of the pale gold light left of the day had given way to blue-gray.

"You are the most exasperating man." She reached out her hand and set it against his chest. Even through the coat and shirt he wore, he could feel the warmth of her hand.

"I don't understand." But his heart was thumping hard beneath her palm.

"You're here, at dusk, when we could be seen, for 'no reason.'"

"I only wanted to see you." The words burst from him, though he had not intended to say them.

"Why?" Her hand stayed there, pressed against his chest. He wanted to lay his own over it and tangle his fingers with hers. He wanted to bring her hand to his lips and kiss each fingertip.

When she stepped closer, it took all he had not to touch her. Her face tipped up, the sweet, red mouth too close to his.

"I don't know." He could barely speak beyond the need growing inside him. Her mouth was there, full and ripe. But he did not taste. He could not.

He dared not.

Still, the need to kiss her clawed and tore at him. Desire

raged beneath his skin, consumed him. Her eyes were partly lowered as she watched him, as though she were nearly asleep. Nearly dreaming.

"Why will you not kiss me?" She breathed the words. Her gaze dropped to his lips and sent lust streaking through him.

"I cannot." A fist seemed to clutch his heart and lungs, squeezing so that he couldn't draw breath.

"Cannot? Or will not?"

He only shook his head. They were one and the same. Kissing her would only lead to the impossible.

No matter how much he wanted to.

He shouldn't even touch her. Yet her hand still lay over his heart, and he wanted that small contact between them. He wasn't certain he could touch her bare skin without aching inside in a way that would cause him to do something idiotic.

He carefully laid his hand over hers.

The contact nearly brought him to his knees. Yearning for her roared through him, brightening the dark places of his soul.

He drew her in, pressed her body to his, because he could do nothing else. His mouth met hers, and he wondered if she could taste the desperation for redemption there.

Whether she could or not, her arms came around him. Lean but strong, she held him to her. "You are important to me, Jones. Not because you are a spy, or because of Wycomb. Because you are you."

"I am nothing." Even as he said the words, he thought perhaps he wasn't. He'd never believed he would be more than nothing. But—now there was Cat.

"Oh, Jones." Her lips met his, quickly, then she drew back to look at him. "Honor is stamped into your soul. How do you not see it?"

The words flowed through him, warming something he had known was cold.

"Cat, my love." It was painful to say, and it would be more painful later when she was married to another. But he could not deny it. "I will bow out, Cat. I will not get in the way of your marriage or your inheritance, but I must say it once. Just once."

...

She was not shocked to hear the words. They had hovered in the air between them already. She'd felt them.

"I love you."

She set her lips to his, hoping she could infuse him with everything she felt for him—love, respect, desire. He was so honorable, his principles guiding him in ways so many other men forgot.

Jones leaned into her, his face pressing against the curve of her collarbone. "I wish I could take you away from all of this."

"Only if you come with me, Jones." Her laugh was giddy and melancholy, all at once. "Only if I can be with you."

His heart beat wildly, the rhythm strong but quick. It was an echo to the pounding in her own chest. She raised her face, lips seeking his. She wanted the comfort, wanted the heat. This time he met her lips, hungrily, as if he thought it might be their last.

She met him just as hungrily, her yearning for more swirling inside her. Strong arms circled her, pulled her more tightly to him. His body was hard against hers, and she felt, too, his manhood against her belly. Her breath shuddered out and she pressed herself to that hard length.

The groan that ripped from him made the blood rush through her veins. She brought her hands to his face, cupped his cheeks. The late day's stubble was a delicious scratch against her palms.

"Don't make me stay here tonight, Jones." Desperate for freedom, she met his gaze. "Please take me somewhere else, just for a little while."

"Cat, we can't. Your engagements." Dark eyes were bleak, the lines at the corners deepening with something so far from laughter it made her heart stutter. "How would we—"

"When I return from *ton* engagements. After midnight, perhaps one in the morning, the household will be quiet. I can sneak out." She slid her hands to his shoulders, gripped hard. She knew the risk if she were discovered missing. "I need to breathe, Jones. I need to feel free for a little while. Please take me away—to anywhere. Just for tonight."

He was quiet a long moment. Night had settled around them, but it wasn't full dark yet. His jaw clenched, shoulders straightened. She saw and felt both, and sensed the battle within him.

"I'll wait for you to return." His lips met hers firmly.

Cat slipped into Worthington House through the rear servant door. It led to the lower hallway and would, of course, be busy with the butler and housekeeper, cook and maids.

She didn't expect Wycomb to be in the servant hall.

The fist was at her throat, tangled in her shawl and yanking her bodice up to her chin as if it had no shape or cut. Her back slammed against the wall, the scream in her lungs cut short by the force.

"Who is he?" Wycomb shoved his face close to hers, bared even, white teeth.

Cat pressed her lips closed, though she scrabbled at the hand clenched at her throat. Dimly she heard footsteps, gasps as servants gathered into a ring of black linen and white aprons around them. She did not look at those circling faces, willing them to stay away and not intervene.

"Who is he?" Wycomb repeated, shaking her so her entire body shuddered.

She braced for the blow. He wanted to do it—she saw that in the lean features and dark brows bent upon hate. His eyes flicked to the right, the left, as if gauging loyalty from the servants watching them.

"I will recognize him next time. You will not be able to hide him from me forever. If you ruin the plans I've put in place, it will be your life, mine, and your inheritance at stake. Fall in line, Mary Elizabeth." The fist at her throat pressed harder, just for a moment, before releasing again. "Fall in line."

He let her loose. She tumbled to her hands and knees, coughed to clear the pressure against her windpipe. Wycomb turned on his heel. The steps to the upper floors were not far, but they were blocked by a wall of livery and aprons. Side by side, footmen and butler and maid and housekeeper stood—two deep. Their chins were high, and just as Cat thought to call out and tell them to stand down, Wycomb spoke.

"It is not the baroness who controls this household." He sent his gaze to the left of the circle, swung it through the remainder until he reached the end. He would have met each servants' gaze. Cat could see nothing beyond Wycomb's straight back, but she knew his methods well enough. "The next time she leaves without permission, it will not be she who suffers, but you. Is that understood?"

There was no agreement—but no one fought, either. Cat saw fear and defiance spread in equal measure between her people. Frantically she shook her head, hoping they would understand not to argue with Wycomb. A few of them glanced her way, but most stood silent and still.

"Good." Wycomb set his coat back into place. "Mary Elizabeth, we will be leaving in thirty minutes for our first engagement. Brown, have the fire ready in the estate room when I return, as I will have need of it."

"Yes, my lord." Brown held himself still, shoulders back and eyes fixed on the ceiling far above Wycomb's head.

"I expect the carriage to be waiting." Wycomb's heels struck the planked floor, every step ringing as if he were the master.

No one moved. The footsteps faded. Twenty or more people remained in the hall, and still no one moved.

They were waiting for her.

The wall was hard at her back, the cloth at her throat bunched and disorganized. Every part of her body was buzzing. But she saw them, the men and women that lived in this house. She knew each by name, could remember their family histories and often their future dreams.

They were hers to protect.

"Please, be careful and do as he orders," she said softly. "I have some measure of protection."

They began to disperse, murmuring to each other. Fear rode under the words, writhing just beneath the surface of sound.

"My lady." The butler stepped beside her, leaned close so others would not hear. "Some of us are loyal—myself, the housekeeper. We will not abandon you, but there are some in your uncle's employ. You cannot trust them."

"Thank you." Her knees buckled in relief that at least someone was with her. She gripped Brown's arm, using it to hold herself upright. "If something happens to me, care for my aunt. See her to safety as best you can, and get everyone else out. Do you understand me?"

He was silent, the nostrils in his long nose widening. "Yes, my lady."

Chapter Thirty-Five

Cat stood at the rear kitchen door, staring at the handle.

Wycomb had watched her all night, in every ballroom, every hallway. He might be watching her now—somehow, in the deep dark of three in the morning. A servant might be awake and report her actions. If so, she would lead him right to Jones by walking through that kitchen door and into the night beyond. But if she did not go, she could not warn Jones that Wycomb had seen them in the garden.

More, she wanted to be with Jones. *Needed* to be with him.

The handle was cold against her palm as she turned it. A flick of the latch with her other hand, and she was through the door and into the garden. She closed it as quietly as she could and spun to face the dark. Cool night air pulled at Cat's hair, strands of it flicking in and out of the hood. Against her back, rough brick pressed against her shoulder blades. He would come. He must. She couldn't have missed him.

Please.

She might never have seen the rear gate slide open—but

she did, because she was ready. He was there. Jones. Tall and strong in the pale light of the moon. She ran, tripping through manicured shrubs and flowers already wet with dew to reach him. Jones caught her, arms waiting, and tugged her hood closer around her face.

"Come," he whispered, holding out his hand.

She accepted it without hesitation. "Quickly, please!"

Urgency propelled her words, then Jones. He swept her through the well-oiled iron gate into the mews. They were quiet, with no signs of life beyond the soft neighs of horses and a few rays of lantern light. Beside her, Jones walked as if he commanded the shadows and their secrets. She felt each of his movements, almost as though they echoed deliciously inside her. The long stride, the shift of his shoulders. Broad shoulders. It seemed she always noted these attributes—perhaps because they personified him, somehow.

Strength. The ability to accept whatever responsibility he needed to.

"Jones." The need for his touch overwhelmed her. She turned, forced him to stop walking. "I want to be with you."

His arms came around her, bringing exactly the strength she craved. The sweet kiss on her forehead made her heart turn over in her chest. The kiss on her lips—hungry—made everything inside her become gold and brilliant.

Wrapping her arms about his neck, Cat met his lips. Longing had built in her, greed for Jones seemed to well up. Standing on tiptoe she pulled herself closer and felt his answering desire as he gripped her hips. His mouth slanted over hers, driving, compelling, reveling. All of it resonated in her body as it yearned for his touch. His body.

"Jones." She didn't whimper it, but it was a near thing.

"The hack." He didn't growl the words as it wasn't his way, but she felt the base need in him just the same. The strict control of his body as he guided her toward the hired carriage at the entrance of the mews, the low tenor of his voice.

The door closed, the horses leaped forward so that the carriage jerked—and suddenly she was in his arms, on his lap. She could feel his erection pressing against her bottom, heard the ragged breath he let out. Then his hands dove into the hood and cupped her cheeks. His mouth devoured hers, his hunger a living thing.

It was what she wanted. What she needed.

"Wait." She said the words against his mouth, turned her body. "Wait."

Scooping up her skirts, she straddled him. Knees on the carriage seat, center pressed against center. She wore no drawers and the heat of his erection through his breeches drew her close to him. Lace and silk rustled between them.

"My Jones." Her hands fluttered over his cheekbones, his jaw, even as her most private place pressed against his body.

"Cat." The word came out on a groan as hands dived under her skirt. Fingers skimmed up her thighs, but no higher. He held her lightly, as if to prevent his hands from roving higher. But between her legs, his erection twitched against his breeches. Against her.

Control coiled his muscles and he drew back from her. Hands still hot beneath her skirts, he met her gaze between the shadows. "Not here and now. I would not treat you as a common woman when I kiss you."

She smiled at him and pressed a light kiss to his lips. "I would have you treat me as a *woman*."

His entire body shuddered, the tremor running through him to tighten his fingers on her thighs. His face dipped toward hers again, but the hack began to slow, the driver above shouting out commands.

"We are here." Jones lifted her, guiding her back onto the seat with careful movements. He moved to the door and opened it, then sent her a final glance. "Pull your hood close to hide your face again."

She did, but her body was thrumming in places she wasn't accustomed to. Thrumming and beating and—lust. Love. All of it swirled in her. She gathered her skirts and stepped onto the street, then stood looking up at the townhouse in front of her. Respectable neighborhood, well-kept townhouse—nothing out of the ordinary to look at.

Still, it was a spy's residence.

He stepped beside her, gesturing to the door. "It's not mine. I only live here." Embarrassment tinged both tone and expression.

She set her hand in his. "I'm looking forward to seeing where you live, Jones."

• • •

"My mentor—my commander as a spy—owns this townhouse." Jones drew her into the front hall, part of him shocked she was here, another part soaring with approval. "I am staying on, for now."

"Are you alone here?" She peered around the dark hall. "No servants?"

"No, I do the work myself. Much of the house is closed now, at any rate. Years ago, during the war, there was a housekeeper." He reached for the tinderbox on the table beside the door and worked to light the candles there. He grinned, remembering those days, as the wick caught fire. Gold light blossomed and he turned to see Cat.

The expression on her face was enigmatic, caught somewhere between surprise, delight, and confusion.

"What?"

"You looked happy, just now. No, not happy. Lighthearted. I have never seen you lighthearted, Jones." She pushed the hood of her cloak away. Candlelight glowed on her hair, bringing life to its banked fire.

"I don't know that there is much to be lighthearted about." He took her hand and led her to the first place he could think of—the study. It had become his haven of late as he'd filled it with his things instead of Angel's. "Please come."

He set about lighting the candelabra around the room, then knelt before the fire. The room was chilled, as he'd not been home for hours. He worked the embers, set the wood out so it would light. When the flames caught, he turned back to Cat.

She'd removed her cloak and stood before him in a gown that shimmered in the firelight. She'd not changed after her evening engagements and her body was still clad in silk and lace, with gold shot through the skirt. He'd never seen anything more beautiful than Cat in her finery, red hair piled high and creamy skin rising above a low square bodice.

"You are lovely." He could barely say the words.

"Thank you." She flushed, smiled. "Jones, I—"

Quick footsteps pounded in the halls beyond. Cat whirled, terror moving over her features. She shrank back, hands searching for purchase on nothing but air.

"Do not worry." He wrapped an arm around her waist, pulled her in. He felt the terror in her rigid muscles and hoped he could ease it. "They are harmless."

The Gents tumbled into the room amid laughter and flailing limbs. Three boys skid to a halt quick enough when they saw Cat.

"Sir!" Rupert, new boots prominently on display, stepped forward. "It's her!"

"Aye." He looked down at Cat's face, at the easing of her features, when she saw that it wasn't Wycomb. "The baroness can be trusted. She is working with me."

"Are you sure, sir?" Young John popped up onto his toes, face screwed up in disbelief. "She's a *lady*."

"I don't trust fancy ladies, sir." Angus, more hurt in the past than the others, squinted at her. He folded his arms and Jones noted the threadbare elbows. He'd be shopping for a new coat soon enough.

"She's a lady, but a kind one." Jones leaned down toward Young John, then sent a quick glance to Angus. "I trust her."

"That's good enough, then." Young John waved his arms at Rupert, dismissing Cat and seemingly fully at ease now. "You tell, Rupert. You was there."

"Right." Rupert drew himself in, readying for the report by mastering his breath and tugging at his coat. "I watched the docks, sir, as you told me to. Yesterday, a man came down—not the one we're supposed to watch, but another lord. Nicer. He came down to the docks and had a talk with the cap'n of the *Anna Louisa*."

"Interesting. Any idea as to who he was or what he was there about?" Jones let go of Cat and crouched down in front of Rupert. "Here, your lace is untied."

"They keep doing that. I've never had laces so fine on me boots." Rupert frowned, but let Jones retie the thin laces. "No, sir, I don't know what the lord was about, but I thought it was odd the *Anna Louisa* was gone this morning. Left before the tide, even."

His hands jerked on the laces, but Jones made no comment beyond, "Well done, Rupert."

Jones stood again and fished in his pocket for the necessary coins.

"Jones?" Cat's voice made him turn. Her smile was warm, amused, and full of laughter. "Aren't you going to introduce us?"

"Baroness, may I present the Gents." He pointed to each as he went. "Rupert, who was the first Gent, then Angus and Young John."

"Hello." She smiled at each of them in turn. They

straightened to their full heights, shoulders back—as if her glance was enough to give them pride. "It is a pleasure to meet you."

"Milady, you sure do go to a lot of dances." Young John cocked his head to the side, earnest face full of curiosity. "You look pretty when you dance."

"Well, thank you." Cat laughed, the sound sweet and happy. Her lips remained curved, as she met Jones's gaze above the heads of the boys. A bolt of lust shot through him, tangling with a fierce emotion that was more than simple love. He cleared his throat, trying not to simply pluck her up and carry her upstairs to his bedroom. He wanted her there, under him. Around him. With him.

"Here." He flipped the coins to the boys, one by one. They caught them, even Young John. "Now, make a proper good-bye, and get some rest. Your nights have turned into your days on this assignment."

"Aye, sir. It's all them dances the lady visits." Rupert bowed, the lanky limbs he'd yet to grow into moving awkwardly. "Good-bye, milady."

Angus and Young John followed suit, and soon the three of them were running out of the room just as they'd run in.

"Is that your team of spies?" Cat continued to smile at Jones, the firelight gilding every line of her face.

"They're not much in the way of protection, but they are observant fellows. They have been checking the stone for your notes." He was not the least bit embarrassed at hiring the Gents. He grinned, thinking of those boys and their continuous joy. "They will make excellent spies someday."

"I don't doubt it, with you as their mentor." Her smile was soft, one side quirking up.

He could barely breathe. Every part of him—mind and soul and body—wanted her. Yet she could not be his. To control the lust spiraling in him, he reached for the poker and adjusted the wood and embers. When he was certain he would not do anything rash, Jones stood again and discovered her at the desk, looking down onto the pages of the book he'd left open.

His heart soared. Those gorgeous eyes would be fixed on the butterfly blue—like to like.

"What a lovely drawing." Long, elegant fingers moved over the page. Softly. Sweetly. "I like the patterns on this brown butterfly. What is it called?" She leaned forward to read the scientific name. "*Pararge aegeria tircis*."

"It is a speckled wood butterfly and can be found anywhere in Britain." Jones strode over to the desk and looked down at the page. "Do you not see this blue butterfly?"

"Of course." She looked up at him, a line forming between her brows. "The brown butterfly is just as lovely in its own way."

He could not speak. She did not know—could not *possibly* understand what it was to be that brown butterfly standing next to a woman who shone and glistened with life as vivid as any tropical butterfly.

"You said you had never seen me lighthearted." He set his hand over hers, moved it so her fingers touched the iridescent blue painting that haunted his dreams. "This is you, Cat. Brilliant and bright." He moved her fingers again, down to that dull, brown butterfly beneath. "This is me. I do nothing brilliant and bright. I live in shadow and was born in the cesspools of London. There is no comparison."

She did not speak for a long moment. Lustrous eyes held him firm, pinned him so that he could not move. The lashes fringing that brilliant blue burned pale gold in the firelight. "Why are you a spy, Jones?"

No one had ever asked him that question before. He wasn't even certain he could answer her. Angel simply knew, because he had been there at the beginning. Some of the other spies likely guessed, but it was a question a spy never asked of another spy. None of their paths were easy. If they had been, they would all be drapers or farmers or gentleman about town.

They weren't. They were spies.

He could not look at Cat, not while he chose his words, so he watched the crackling fire instead. Dancing red and orange flames flickered on the hearth, shedding their glow into the room. He found he could not look away, even as he spoke to the woman by his side.

"I'm a spy because it saved me. I was headed for the gallows when Angel found me. Not literally, but I would have been swinging in just a few years." He flicked his gaze toward Cat, and when he saw her rapt expression, he turned away again. He could not *look* at her when he told her. He couldn't bear to see pity in her eyes.

"There are many boys on the street like myself, Cat. Abandoned. Lost." His palms were beginning to dampen, so he wiped them on the coarse fabric of his breeches. "The boys band together, finding shelter in the rookeries and stealing when they need to."

He could not—or would not—tell her everything. But he must to tell her some of it, as the need had suddenly become a very real, very live thing howling in his chest. He stooped to retrieve the poker again and prodded the logs, doing nothing but moving firewood that had no need to move.

"What happened to change you from boy to spy?" she asked softly. Her skirts rustled as she spoke and he hoped she wasn't standing and coming near him. He wasn't sure he would be able to speak if she were close. He heard nothing beyond the rustle of clothing, and no figure hovered in his vision to send his heart pounding. Poking again into the fire, Jones fought to describe the moment—that life-altering moment.

"It was Angel. He was older than I, already seasoned by war and espionage." That log there, surely it needed to be rearranged. He would focus on it. "He was following another spy into the rookeries—a double agent, I learned later. My friends and I, we saw where the agent had hidden himself. It was only a tavern, one of a hundred in that area. Angel paid us for the information and set off in pursuit. My friends parceled out the money and went to buy something—gin or tobacco, no doubt—but I stayed behind."

He couldn't explain what about Angel had fascinated him, nor the overwhelming desire to follow that had sent him careening through allies in pursuit of the spy. The hurried run through the streets was still as vivid now as the day it happened. Buildings flashing by, the sound of his footsteps on the cobblestones, Angel's broad shoulders covered in homespun cloth as he wove through the drunkards and criminals of St. Giles.

"I followed him, Cat." Now he did look at her, as the revelations of that day swamped him. "I followed Angel and I saw him take down that double agent with fists and knives. I followed him when he reported to his commander, and I discovered what it meant to make a difference. To do something that would impact not only lives, but countries. *History*."

"Yes. Yes, I understand." She did not come forward. They were separated by the rookeries and the *ton*. She reached out, then dropped her hands again. "To make a difference. Be something and do something more than what you are."

"It's not only that." He shook his head, not sure if he could find the words. "It was a place and people I could belong to. I could do what was right and be something more than a whelp from the rookeries. But, Cat, that's not me. All of that, the espionage, the agents I've discovered betraying their country, the spies trading secrets—none of that is me."

He could hear the despair in his voice and hated himself for it. Shame roiled in his belly, but he planted his heels hard into the carpet and looked straight at that beautiful, soft-skinned, aristocratic face.

"I'm still that whelp from the rookeries, my lady." And oh, those words were like a knife in his belly.

"That's not true." Cat stepped toward him, her hand coming up to cup his cheek. "You might have been born in the rookeries, but you had a choice to walk away from it, and you had a choice to begin that life as a spy. To make a difference."

"Do I make a difference?" He could barely say the words, afraid of what he would hear coming from her lips.

"Yes. To England." Her other hand came up, so that his face was surrounded by soft, scented skin and he could see nothing but the depth of her eyes. "And to me."

Chapter Thirty-Six

His heart stuttered in his chest. Uneven beats driven by the love he saw on her face. More, by the love that swamped him. She set her lips to his, the kiss tender and soft.

"Be my first, Jones." She whispered it, pulling back just enough to meet his gaze. "Make love to me."

"Cat, you are still promised to another." Oh, but he wanted her. The lust was layered now with love, with longing.

"He will never have my heart. You will." She slid her hands from his face to his shoulders. "I have learned much of Hedgewood these past weeks. He is not as kind as he seems—he is much like Wycomb. I do not want to give him my body, but I will have no choice if we are wed."

Every part of Jones burned with fury, knowing that Hedgewood would marry her and have her against her wishes. Never treat her with the compassion and love she deserved.

"I want you to love me, Jones. Just once so that I will know—and I can look back and remember." Her eyes were huge, her lips curved and inviting. "Give me that gift. Please."

He was powerless to say no. Determination could

withstand honor, but it could not withstand Cat.

"Yes." He closed his eyes, leaned his forehead against hers. He would make sure she was fulfilled, teach her what it was to be loved so that she would always remember. His arms went around her, drawing her in. "Not here in the study. Upstairs, in my chamber."

Where he had dreamed of her.

She smiled softly and held out her hand. "Take me there."

Picking up a candle, he led her up the stairs and through hallways until he reached his bedchamber. Her hand was warm in his, her steps confidant and without hesitation as they entered. He raised the candle high, throwing its light over his possessions.

What would she see? What would she think of his space? His clothes were neatly stored away in a wardrobe. Stacked on a table were the books he preferred to read, beside them a pair of pistols he had been polishing. The bed—which seemed particularly large—was neatly made. The room was simple and clean, as he liked it, without paintings on the damask covered walls or the fuss of pillows on the chair before the fire.

"Here. Let me build the fire so you aren't cold."

Releasing her hand, he set the candle on the table and kneeled before the fire to stir the embers.

"I don't think I could be cold," she murmured. "I feel as if there is a fire already burning in my body."

His hands jerked as he laid wood on the glowing embers. He looked at her over his shoulder, pulse beginning to pound. The fire seemed pale compared to her hair in the candlelight, the heat filling the room less than what coursed through his veins.

Quickly, he finished at the fireplace so he could see her again.

Cat had moved to the bed. She sat on the edge of it, her

evening slippers set side by side on the floor at her feet. She ran her hands over the plain blue coverlet and pillows, as if testing them. He did not know what her sheets would be made of, but they would be softer than his, he was certain. Though perhaps not—Angel had purchased these linens long ago.

"Are you certain?" he asked.

"Yes." She stood, gaze steady and lips curved up as she looked at him. "I only want you for this first time."

Jones straightened his shoulders, breathed in, and felt some part of his soul strengthen. She trusted him. It was not *him* giving Cat what she asked for, but Cat granting him her virginity. That was the gift—*she* was a gift.

"I love you, Cat."

He pulled her close, pressed his mouth against hers. Her arms circled his neck, and though she had not removed her evening gown, she had removed her gloves. The skin of her inner arms was like silk and drove his need for her higher. He wanted to touch every bit of her skin, learn every hill and valley of her.

She leaned back to look at him. "I cannot undress myself, Jones. Will you?"

"You might be a virgin, my love, but you certainly know how to tempt a man." He had not intended for his voice to rasp, but his throat released the words as a growl just the same.

Her laugh was as bright as the candle glow. "Only because I *want* you to undress me. I might manage, but it does not seem to be as enjoyable that way."

"Then I shall oblige." Setting his hands on her shoulders, he turned her so that he could reach the cloth covered buttons running along her spine. There were only three, the same color as the ivory gown. Around them, gold thread shot through the ivory silk and shimmered in the light. When the buttons were released, he pushed the sleeves from her shoulders so the bodice pooled around her waist, revealing the pale freckles he remembered from the woods at Ashdown Abbey. He kissed them as he had then, tasting the sweetness of her skin.

She sighed, the sound so soft it barely met his ears. "You make everything inside me turn to liquid, Jones."

His heart stuttered in his chest, but his hands were steady as he set them to the ties on her stays. He worked quickly to loosen them, still more quickly on the ties of her petticoat, his mind losing its grip on his body. His cock was hard, nearly painful pressed against his fall-front breeches. Still, he tried to be gentle when his hands touched her bared shoulders and turned her again. Pulling the bodice and stays away, sliding the dress down her arms and letting all of it fall to the floor, seemed the most natural movements—as if he had performed them a thousand times before and would do so a thousand more.

She was lovely even in her chemise. It billowed around her, hiding her curves in white linen—but not her collarbones. Those were revealed by the wide scoop of the neckline. Jones ran his forefinger along the fine bones, tracing their shape. When he reached the edge of the chemise she stayed his hand, twined her fingers his.

"Here." She took his other hand, brought it up to the other side of the neckline. Her gaze met his, the blue burning bright. Together, they pushed the chemise from her shoulders. It drifted lightly to the floor, covering his boots.

Cat stood before him in nothing but lace garters and silk stockings.

He could not breathe. Small, perfect breasts, tipped by a lovely pink. Narrow hips with a slight indentation above. Long legs covered with white silk. The thatch of red-gold at the apex of her legs. All of it stole his breath.

She reached for one of the garters, hand on the ribbon to

loosen the tie.

"No, Cat." He swallowed hard, but the lust in him would not be denied. "Leave them."

"Indeed?" One brow rose. The matching smile was knowing. "As you wish, then, but I think you should make quick work of your own clothing."

...

Jones did exactly as she asked.

His clothes were quickly stripped away. He dropped each garment somewhere to the side, but she did not see where. She could only see Jones as each bit of him was revealed. The broad shoulders she so loved were more magnificent without clothing, the strength of his character matching the strength of the muscles there. The lean torso begged to be stroked, his chest perfect to rest her cheek on.

It was his manhood that held her, however. It stood before him, ready, she knew. Cat had lived in the country, had listened to maids gossiping. She was a virgin, but she understood well enough the mechanics of it.

She had not counted on the fact that his need for her would be so compelling. Every part of her filled with a yearning so sharp, so tight that her breathe came in a gasp.

"Enough," she whispered. "Do not play, Jones."

The man that scooped her off her feet had hot skin and a hard body, but was gentle as he laid her on the bed. Quickly he climbed onto the bed, but slowly he pressed a kiss to her lips.

So like her Jones.

"I will not play long," he whispered against her skin as he moved his lips to the hollow between her breasts. "But I need a few minutes. Just a few."

She ran her fingers through his hair, gripped the thick

locks as he took her nipple in his mouth. She cried out, arched toward him, as exquisite sensation shot from her breast to her toes. The laugh low in his throat sent the same thrill through her. He brought his mouth back to hers, seemed to devour her. Mouth, body. She could feel his erection, hard and hot, pressing against her core. Straining, but not entering. Oh, he wanted her. It would have made her smile, but she needed so much she couldn't move her lips in anything but a kiss. Heat. More. Lips to lips, tongue to tongue.

The hardness left, replaced by his finger. He pulled away from her, looked down at her face as it entered her. She shuddered, and a second finger filled her. They moved in and out, stretching her. Touching some place in her that made her entire body gather everything together to a single spot.

"I want to see your eyes." The whisper barely rumbled from his chest.

That deep, demanding sound matched the pounding in her blood. Matched the need inside her. His thumb touched a secret place she hadn't known she had and her body shuddered, though every bit of her being was taut and tight and waiting. She gripped the sheets, certain she would break apart—and kept her gaze on his.

So dark. So focused.

"I love you, Cat."

Somehow, she came apart. Everything inside her shattered in a glorious burst of sunrise and star set. She clung to him—this man who was strong and ready for her.

While that bright pleasure still swirled through her, Jones set his body against her core. He filled her, easily sliding in as if he belonged there. A dart of pain wove through the joy, but it was so fleeting she simply let it fly away again. Instead, she reveled in the feel of being held and loved. She wrapped her legs around him, heard him groan in response, and delighted in the slow stroke as he moved inside her.

He pressed his face against the curve of her neck, kissed her there, then met her lips as he slowly drew back and then thrust into her again. She gasped, clutched at his shoulders.

"Again, Jones. Again."

He did, still careful, but deeper. More. As if he would do his best to give her his soul. His breath came fast, but his body rocked in a slow rhythm that began to build something inside her yet again. He watched her face, seemed to draw something from her. Even now, in this moment when he could take his pleasure from her, he focused on her. Waited for something.

She knew what it was as sensation shot through her, as if gold coursed through her veins. She gasped, held her breath, but could not look away from his gaze. He thrust once more, kissed her as if she were everything worthwhile in the world, and pulled his body away from her to finish.

His lips never left hers.

Chapter Thirty-Seven

Cat lay on her side above him, cheek propped in one hand. The pins in her hair had scattered so the curls rained down over her shoulders and onto the bed linens. A few stray locks brushed the hand lying quiet on the sheets.

Jones rubbed a thumb across the ridges spanning her knuckles, then turned her hand over so he could see the palm. She was so rarely without gloves he had yet to learn the lines crisscrossing the pale expanse. They were not deep, as his own were, her skin free from wear and calluses. He stared hard at thin lines, thinking to commit them to his memory. Someday, he would not be able to touch her hands. Someday soon they would be gone from his life.

Sorrow pierced through him, into some secret place, followed by a layer of panic that slicked over his skin. *She would be gone from his life.*

"Jones."

He did not want to meet those eyes. They would drive him into the ground. Into a hell he would be forced to live for the remainder of his days.

"Jones," she said again, her voice breathless and wary—and insistent.

He did look up. And he *was* driven into the ground by eyes that were fierce and bright.

"There is a way." Her fingers curled around his, tight. "I can wait until my birthday—it is not long now—and we could marry."

Everything in him stilled. He could only stare at the face of this lovely woman who was beyond any dream he might have had.

"I could breach the contract and forfeit Ashdown Abbey." She swallowed hard and though the words held honesty, her eyes already held sorrow. "But the rest of the properties would be ours under the trust."

"No." He found his breath after all. "I was born in the rookeries, Cat. Born there, abandoned there, and should have died there long ago." Many of the boys he'd known had died, either on the gallows or in the alleys.

"I know." She sat up and set her other hand over his, so that his single one was engulfed in both of hers, protected by the soft skin. "You didn't."

"I should have. I should have died the day my mother left me on the doorstep of the foundling hospital."

"Again, you didn't," she repeated. "Because you didn't die, England is safer than it would have been, I am alive when I might not have been, and you're—" She broke off, lips pressing together as though to keep words from spilling out into the air between them. Then, finally, as if the words would not be held. "You're loved."

Despair crawled inside him, settling itself between his heart and his mind to poke fun at his dreams. "Cat," he croaked, pushing up so they sat face-to-face, naked body to naked body.

Perhaps, he thought, even bare soul to bare soul.

Her hands moved over his, fluttering, then settling again, warm and soft. He wondered if she would be able to draw his essence into her, scoop it up and hold it against her heart.

He wished she could.

"Someday, when this is over, we can—"

"There is no 'we.'" The words bulleted from his mouth, anger and sorrow filling him. He drew his hands away and climbed from the bed. "There will never be a 'we.'"

Why couldn't she see this?

"There can be," she said, rising to her knees as if she had forgotten she wore nothing but stockings. "There can be, if we want it enough."

"There is no way to turn me into a gentleman. I cannot be the man you need." The words scored his throat, his heart.

"The man I need?" She began to search the bed for her hair pins, piling them together in the center. She flicked her gaze toward his, eyes blazing and loose hair glowing in the firelight. "*Need*? I don't need a man. I *want* one. I want a man who will stand by me. One who loves me. A man with shoulders strong enough to bear any responsibility and a nobility that would put any gentleman I know to shame. I would share what I have with him."

"What *you* have." Even as the words spilled from his lips he wished he could take them back. They were unfair, but true, though it was not right to hold that against her—nor could they be unsaid.

"Yes." Cat's anger rushed from her in a single breath. Working the auburn flames of her hair, she coiled it at the nape of her neck. "What I have. Even without the Abbey, there are thousands of acres and pounds. We would not be poor."

She could not see it, could she?

"Cat." He stood naked in front of her. Vulnerable. He would let her see what it meant. "If we married, I would be a joke in the *ton*. The little plaything you gave up your inheritance for."

"That is ridic—"

"It's accurate." He shrugged, conscious of every inch of his bared skin. "I could not bear the whispers, the shame I would bring to you. We could try to hide in the country until the scandal died away, but it would resurface every time we came to town. If we had children, they, too, would be marked by my birth. The whispers would follow them."

"We could pretend you were from Northumberland. Or the Continent. A lord come to visit—"

"No." He said it firmly, ignoring the blue eyes that had become so huge in her face. "I cannot pretend to be someone I'm not. Particularly a lord. The *ton* would know—I can't even remember to wear gloves to dinner."

"I don't care. I cannot change my birth, nor can you." She spoke just as firmly as she plucked up one of the hairpins. "We can only try to find a way to make a future together. We—oh, bugger it."

Shock pushed a laugh from him.

"Jesus, Cat. Do you know what 'bugger' means?"

"Of course." She shoved the hairpin, then a second, into the coil of hair as if each one were a splinter of her frustration. "I'm a lady, not an idiot without ears. Nor am I stupid enough that I don't understand you're scared to be in love. Scared to take on a role you weren't born to."

He reared back as if she'd struck him. "Scared?"

Her arms fell away, helpless at her side. "I'm sorry. That was uncalled for."

"But true." Heart pounding, he met her gaze, then traced the contours of her face with his eyes. "I would be terrified to marry you. What if I failed?"

"What if you didn't?"

Silence. From her, naked on the bed. From him, naked

and standing beside it.

He turned away first, searching for their clothing on the floor. He found his breeches and tugged them on. The fire burned low in the hearth, washing the remaining fields of fabric on the floor with pale gold. He scooped up her gown, stays, petticoat, chemise—each one soft and sending up her scent. When he looked at Cat again, his arms full of her things, she had left the bed and stood before him in her stockings and garters. The red-gold curls above her thighs still called to him, as did the narrow but strong shoulders and the face full of resolve.

"Here," he choked out. "Your chemise."

If she didn't put it on, he would not be able to keep his hands from her.

She slipped it over her head, giving him enough space to breathe. "Why can nothing be simple?" she asked, emerging from the linen. Temper had dissipated from her words and features.

He found temper had left him as well.

"Life is not simple, Cat." He breathed deep and offered her the stays.

"You're right." She sighed, her shoulders curving inward as she inserted her arms into the stays. She reached behind her, trying to pull the laces tight.

"Let me." He dropped the remainder of her clothes onto the bed and reached toward her stays. "No one has a simple life. Not even the lowliest farmer on your lowliest property will find life to be easy."

He pulled the lacings tight for her, working them top to bottom.

"You are not a novice at dressing a woman, Jones."

His fingers froze. Looking up, he met a pair of amused lips and dancing eyes. "Ah. Mm."

"I can only be grateful, as your experience made up

for my inexperience." Her expression sobered again as he finished the lacing and she picked up her petticoat. "What would you do, Jones, if you could have a simple life? If no one expected anything from you, if you had no obligations and no one depending on you, what would you do?"

He did not have to think. He knew the answer, because he had known it since he was seventeen and had first read of it. "I would go to *Colle di Val d'Els*."

Cat paused, fingers caught in the ties of the petticoat. "Italian, isn't it? I don't speak it well."

"I believe it is the Hill of Elsa Valley. Elsa is the river running by the village." He had never seen a painting, but he'd read the description in travel journals. "The village is in Tuscany."

She cocked her head, a soft, surprised smile curving her lips. "A village it Italy? That is where you would go?"

Jones shrugged a shoulder. "The oldest part of it is high on a hill, and at least four or five hundred years old."

"Why do you want to go there?" Petticoat replaced, she reached for her gown. Jones picked it up first, shifted it so it would fall easily around her. He gave it to her, ensuring it was at the easiest angle for her to set it over her head, then worked the buttons as effortlessly as he had undone them.

"I have read that the valley and fields surrounding *Colle di Val d'Els* are green and gold with olive groves. Vineyards on the slopes lead down to the river, and you can see the entire valley from the old stone village atop the hill. Life is slow and easy, with wine and olives and sunshine filling each day. Can you imagine?" He had, many times. "Wine and olives and sunshine."

Cat stood before him, dressed but not as polished as when she first arrived. Her expression was sweet, her mouth not fully smiling but still brimming with knowledge. "Will you go there, someday?"

"If I can, yes." Though he knew in his heart he would never reach the village.

"Imagine us both there, then," she whispered. "Where life is nothing more than wine and olives and sunshine." Cat offered her hand, bare palm up. "What do we do now? Just continue as if we didn't make love? As if there is nothing between us?"

"Yes. There is nothing else for us." His fingers accepted hers. When they met that soft, smooth skin, he thought—just for a moment—that his soul sighed.

Chapter Thirty-Eight

The noise did not wake her.

She had not slept the night before because she'd made love to Jones, and had not slept this night because she was too on edge. Awake, wishing she knew less so she could sleep, Cat had listened to the sounds of the street. The window was open just an inch—silly, as she heard every carriage and horse that traveled down Park Lane. Still, she slept with it open now.

It wasn't carriage wheels or horses' hooves that alerted her, but voices. Harsh, guttural, and full of pain.

As well as familiar.

"Here, it's open." A voice she knew, but could not place. "Hell. Bleed less, will you?"

"If they hadn't..." The rest faded away as the speakers entered the house, but she knew Wycomb's voice.

Cat didn't dress in slippers or a shawl. She simply left the bed in her nightshift and went to her door. Cracking it open, she tried to listen. Voices drifted up from the entry to echo in the stairwell, though they were muted now and she could not make out the words. On bare feet, she slipped through the hall toward the main steps. She knew this house—which floorboards squeaked, the rug with the curling edge that was easy to trip over. She avoided both, trying to move as quietly as Jones would have done.

At the top of the steps, she looked over the railing into a faint glow. A single lit candle sat on the curved table beside the door. Perched on the first step was Wycomb, with another man bending over him. Cat squinted, trying to bring them into focus through the dim light.

"It's not deep," Wycomb said, probing at something. He was bent over so all she could see was the nape of his neck and shoulders clad in the layers of his greatcoat.

"You are lucky." The second man straightened, stepped away, his back still toward her. "They are out for your blood."

"If your damned ships would come in, they wouldn't be." Wycomb hissed as he shifted to lean back against the steps.

"I don't have control of the tide and winds—or customs." The second man strode toward the door, boots ringing loudly in the quiet townhouse. "Next time, don't come to me. I didn't start your little endeavor. I only fund it."

"I make you a lot of money." Wycomb bit out the words and half rose from the step, then sat back down.

"*When* you make money." The other man gripped the handle, wrenched open the door. Cat couldn't see or hear anything beyond the opening, but she sensed a shift in the air from the night wind. "If you can't control the dogs in their den, cut them loose." He turned to face Wycomb, anger etched into every line on his face.

Cat gasped, breath hitching in. It came out again in a squeak.

Hedgewood.

Even as she scrambled back from the railing, she saw both male heads jerk upward. Lungs frozen, she scooted back on hands and feet, each movement part of an awkward half crawl. Spinning into a crouch, Cat stood and walked swiftly but silently down the hall. The rug, the noisy floorboard—she avoided both again. Her mind spun and heart pounded as she quietly shut her bedroom door. Cat set her forehead against the cool wood panels and swallowed back her fear.

Hedgewood was part of it. Whatever Wycomb was involved in, whatever the *Anna Louisa* and other ships were supposed to provide, Hedgewood *funded* it.

Whatever it might be, she could not wait long. Swiftly, feet flying over plush carpets as her own shadow chased her, she made for the escritoire. She didn't dare light a candle, so she used the weak light from the moon and street lamps to guide her. Familiarity led her to the paper and ink. She did not sit, afraid to take even those few minutes.

Quill scratched against paper. She knew her penmanship was poor and didn't care as long as the ink reached the paper and the note reached Jones. She didn't blot it or sand it, didn't bother to seal it. Urgency fueled her, though there was no dawn light rising on the horizon. Either Jones or a Gent would be checking the stone soon, before the servants rose, before sunlight.

Her note must be there.

Still, she waited until she heard Wycomb's footsteps pass her room. He slept just a few rooms down the hall, with Essie between them. When he did finally pass, the steps were almost noiseless—but she was listening.

She waited longer, impatient and irritated that she could not properly see the clock on the mantelpiece in the dark. Finally, hoping Wycomb was well asleep, Cat opened the door to the hall and peered out. Dark and empty. The note clutched in her fist, she flew over the floor once more.

The golden glow was gone from below and peeking over the banister, she saw the candle had been extinguished. She waited, listening. When she continued to hear nothing but the shifting of the house around her, she moved light-footed down the steps and to the rear of the house. The kitchen was as dark and empty as the halls. She tore through it and into the garden. Cool morning air dove deep into her lungs, but she didn't stop. The wall loomed closer, the loose stone a fixed point she could focus on. She scrabbled at the stone, drew it out and shoved the note into the hollow behind. Cat repositioned it in the rough bed of mortar and ran through the garden to return to her bedchamber.

She made it no farther than the rear door. Wycomb was there, a pistol in one hand and a knife in the other.

"Good morning, Mary Elizabeth."

"Now that we are comfortable, why don't you tell me who he is? Remember, if you scream, I shall kill both of you. If you stay quiet, one of you might yet live."

Cat gritted her teeth against the wet dew seeping through her nightshift. She didn't speak. The hard ground beneath the garden bench was not enough to break her, nor was the split lip where he had hit her. Even the rope rasping against her ankles and wrists was not enough.

"Let me see, what did the note say?" Above her on the seat, Wycomb re-crossed his legs and set the pistol down on the iron bench. Inches above her head and yet miles from being useful. "Ah yes. *Hedgewood is involved.* A very interesting note."

Cat curled into herself for warmth, her mind reaching into the center of her for courage to fight the fear bubbling beneath her skin. He had stowed her beneath the bench, knowing someone would come for the note.

Like a spider, he waited for his prey.

Oh God. Jones would not know.

"A lover, perhaps? It would explain your disinterest in Hedgewood." Reasonable, even tones from her uncle. "I think we shall just wait here and see who retrieves your note."

"He is a better man than you," she bit out, unable to stop herself.

Wycomb moved before she understood what he was doing. Suddenly the knife was at her throat, pricking the skin in the hollow between her collarbones just as it had done once before. Terror coalesced to that single point, where metal met flesh.

She would not give in. Cat ignored the bindings, the rough rope, even the cold ground pressing against her shoulder. The trees above cast moonshadows over his face, twisting over an expression already threatening. A chill terror burgeoned in her, but she shoved it away and breathed deep.

"Who is out for your blood?" She didn't want to say the words, but she refused to let the panic best her.

"Questions from the captive?" The knife slid over her skin to the scoop of the nightshift's bodice. It held there, between her breasts and just below the neckline. "I think not."

"You cannot think I will ever fall in line again," she said.

"Mary Elizabeth," he snarled. The point of the knife pressed against her skin, but did not pierce it. Not yet. "You never did. If you had, I would not have needed Hedgewood."

"I am glad I ruined your plans." She lifted her chin as best she could, lying on her side on the ground beneath the iron bench.

"Perhaps you will not be so glad when you are dead."

"You cannot kill me, or you will lose Hedgewood." Cat bared her teeth, knowing that truth would win out. "He wants my properties and money."

"He—" Wycomb stilled, then straightened and spun in

a single movement, knife arcing out toward some unseen threat. It did not hit its target and Wycomb stepped back once, bumping into the bench and it's curling designs.

"Do not touch her." The sound of Jones's voice sent her heart soaring. He was here. She could not see him beyond Wycomb and the dark, but she knew his voice as if it were her own.

"Ah, Jones. I see. I am being watched by the spy that hunts his fellow spies." Wycomb's voice lowered, the chill in it much, much worse than the night air or the dew-ridden turf. "I have often wondered, does that betrayal of your comrades turn your stomach?"

"Let her go, Wycomb." Cat heard the sharp click of a cocked hammer in the darkness. "This matter is between you and I, now."

"I think not. If Sir Charles has set his watchdog upon me, he is aware of the shipping arrangement as well." Wycomb stepped back again until he was nearly standing on her. Crouching down, he set the knife to her throat. It pressed against her neck, not in the center now, but along the side. Her pulse concentrated there, hot against the cold metal. "How long has my niece been spying for you?"

"Long enough."

"She is my ward, Jones. Mine to control."

She tried not to let the fear implode inside her, but a whimper caught in her throat as she listened.

"There are also lines of decency and morality, even in espionage." Jones paused, and suddenly his voice was as low and cold as Wycomb's. "What you are doing now to my Cat would be the end."

"You call her Cat." Wycomb scoffed, the knife bouncing along the surface of her skin. "A stupid name my sentimental sister gave her."

"It is what she calls herself. Now, you can come in, I can

take you in, or I can kill you." Death seemed to slide along Jones's words. "The choice is yours."

With a feral growl, Wycomb leaped at him. There was no light to flash over his knife, but Cat saw the spark as Jones's pistol roared. They fell to the ground in a heap, one that scuffled and rolled. Grunts of pain and effort filled the early morning air. She rotated onto her stomach, digging her knees into the ground to push herself up. Off balance, arms tied behind her back, she could only press her face against the dirt.

Flesh met flesh, someone cried out. Cat rocked forward, gathered her muscles and dug her toes into the earth to lift her torso off the ground. Upright, she could see at least, but her feet were tied, her hands bound behind her back. *She could not stand. She could not help.*

One man rose and the dim light above caught enough of his features she knew it was Jones. Grim. Harsh—still her Jones. He was knocked from his feet as Wycomb charged, hitting him around the middle. They went down again, hard, a gasp of pain winging through the air.

Another hit, more grunts and wheezes, a sharp yelp—and silence.

Someone crawled toward her on hands and knees, as if he dragged his limbs. Close, then closer, until his face was finally visible in the dark.

Wycomb.

She tried to move, to flee or run or *something*. She could do nothing but flail, so the ground rose up and she landed face first in the dirt once again. Wycomb set his mouth to her ear, growled.

"You are nothing but a liability, Mary Elizabeth." He rose over her and grabbed the rope between her hands. He dragged her across the grass, then lifted her so she stood awkwardly on bound ankles. She would have fallen if he had held her upright. "This time, you will obey. There is nothing left for either of us to lose but your life."

• • •

"He's gone to ground." Jones could not breathe. The beast sitting on his chest was hideous in its never-ending pressure, its never-ending pain. "I don't know if I can find him. Find *her*."

"You may not be able to find them." Angel gripped Jones's uninjured shoulder, fingers digging hard into muscle. He never shied away from the truth, but said the words that must be said. Those words pinched and pierced Jones's heart. Yet the truth could not be changed. "Wycomb knows if he is caught, it is the end for him."

"I wish I knew more about—Ow!" Jones yelped as the feminine fingers that had been probing at his torso pressed against a cut.

"Hold still." Lilias, Angel's wife, set a hand against Jones's bared chest and pressed him back against the chair. Her hair was loosely braided for sleep, her wrapper billowing around her kneeling form, but she was no less formidable in her night attire in the hours before dawn than she was wielding her sabre. "I've seen better patients on the battlefield. This wound is nothing."

"It's in the—" Jones began, jerking forward in protest. A sharp pain pierced his side, forcing him to stop. He hissed a breath out between his teeth.

"It is not deep, but I imagine it's painful when it pulls." Lilias kneeled before him, face grim and hard. "It's a little deeper than the other cuts, but I don't believe you require stitches. A knife, I presume?"

"Aye." Jones looked down toward the thin red line crossing his ribs. "The rest of my wounds are just marks of a fight."

"'Marks of a fight.'" Lilias snorted, though her hands were gentle as she wound a strip of linen around his torso. "Scratches, a black eye, split lip—not to mention the lump where he coshed you. In fact, I would feel better if Grace looked at that injury, as most of the head wounds I managed were fatal. Are you certain you do not see two of me?"

"I don't have time to wait for Lady Langford to arrive." Jones shrugged, pulling at the bandage as Lilias tucked the end into itself to hold. He'd arrived at Angel's for assistance from the spy only to end up being administered to by his wife. "I must start looking for Cat."

"Lilias." Angel stepped forward, set his hand on his wife's shoulder. "Most of the time, I would not ask you to leave during our conversations—"

"Yes, you would, but I shall not argue today." With lumbering movements and the help of Angel, Lilias stood. She set her hands on the belly that had become huge in the last few days and watched Jones with bright blue eyes. "Good luck, Jones. Be careful."

A few minutes later the door closed behind her.

"I should not have come here." Jones lifted the shirt draped on the edge of the settee. He pulled it over his head, carefully shrugging into it. "I put your family at risk."

"We would be at risk from Wycomb regardless, Jones." Angel stood in front of him, boots rooted in the carpet as if to ensure Jones could not push past him. "Who was your commander? Your mentor? Who would you confide in beyond Sir Charles?"

"You." Despair, fear, guilt—all of it weighed on Jones, though Angel was right. Wycomb could easily come after Angel and his family. With a deep breath and ignoring the throbbing pain at the base of his skull, Jones tucked his shirt into his breeches. "I still need your advice, Angel."

"You shall have it. Always circle back to what you *know*. Not what you think or guess, but what you know." Gold eyes looked straight into Jones's. "Tell me what you know."

"I know I love Cat." The words scored his throat, hot and razor sharp. "Beyond that, I can barely think."

"What else do you know? Beyond what you feel, what do you know?" Angel scooped up a pile of black cloth and handed it to Jones. He wore nothing but breeches and the result of being Jones's sparring partner for far too long showed in the muscles of his back. "Here, your shirt and jacket."

"I know Cat is only useful to Wycomb for a short time. If I don't find her, she will probably die." The pain of it hammered at every inch of Jones's skin, mixing with the throbbing of his injuries. "I will have to live with that."

"What else do you know, Jones. Think. Wycomb is desperate—he knows you and Sir Charles are investigating him. He knows taking the baroness means you will hunt him. So why did he take her, and where did he go?"

"I know he has money difficulties." Jones slid one arm into his jacket, pulled it up onto his shoulder. Slowly. "I know he has connections at the docks."

"It is a place to start."

"The docks led nowhere." Except to nearly being shot and putting Cat in danger. "The *Anna Louisa* was emptied and has set sail again. 'Tis only a short voyage this time, but she is gone."

"What else, then? You haven't spent weeks investigating him for nothing." Angel stepped forward, face and voice hard. "Or have you been so enamored of the baroness you've forgotten your task?"

"Angel." Jones reared back as if he'd been hit again. "I haven't—"

"Good." The lines of Angel's face were still grim, but he had relaxed. "I have to ask, because even if you don't answer to me any longer, I still answer to Sir Charles."

"No. I haven't been too distracted. I've searched bank records—in my usual way, so there is no trace—and I've watched the docks. The Gents are on Wycomb as well. I have learned of chance encounters with rough men, of Wycomb going into pubs and coming out again in disguise. He's been seen in the rookeries, allegedly as a nine-foot demon."

"Really?" Angel's amber eyes narrowed. "That's interesting."

"Only in so far as drunkards hoisting too many bottles of gin." The coat was now on both shoulders and Jones pulled it closed over his belly and its wounds. He paused, mind suddenly churning and spinning. "A nine-foot demon in the rookeries. That is more to go on than an empty berth at the docks."

"So it is."

"The Gents saw Wycomb go into a tavern in St. Giles carrying a bag, but he never came out again—at least not dressed as he had been." Jones reached for his pistol and shoved it in his waistband. "Only a day or so before that, he visited the *Anna Louisa*."

"Don't forget your knife." Angel nodded toward the slim blade sitting on the polished side table beside the settee.

"I have others." Still, Jones swiped it and slid it into the narrow pocket he'd sown into his breeches. "I'm going into the rookeries, Angel. Don't come in after me yet—but if you don't hear from me in twenty-four hours, come looking."

"Of course." Angel grinned wickedly. "It's been some time since I've had a good fight."

Chapter Thirty-Nine

She could not see where they were going. The hood of her cloak was pulled too far over her face. Only her feet were visible in that small patch beyond the ring of expensive wool, and they moved so quickly in and out of her narrow line of sight she wondered if they were real.

She wondered if *any* of it was real.

The stench of sewage. The slop of mud and filth against her boots. The empty gin bottle she nearly tripped over. Somewhere to her right was raucous laughter and the sweetly bitter scent of spilled beer.

The shudder ran from Cat's shoulders, down her spine and through the arms still bound behind her back—hidden now beneath the cloak—and into the pistol pressed against her back.

"Afraid, Mary Elizabeth?" Wycomb leaned close, the pistol shoving into her ribs.

She gasped at the sudden pain, but did not make another sound. Cat refused to give him that satisfaction.

"Not far now, just a few more steps." He pushed her

ahead of him, one hand gripping her shoulder. She stumbled, off balance without the use of her arms.

Through the dim dawn light and beyond the hood pulled close about her face, she saw an open space where street after street converged, then crossed the circle to the other side as if they were seven spokes of a wagon wheel. Cat and Wycomb did not cross the circle to the other side, as the narrow streets did.

Instead, Wycomb shoved her toward a door set into the stone building. A pub shared the wall on one side, an empty building on the other. Above were floors of dark, broken windows interspersed by the occasional window with candlelight flickering. Ropes were slung between buildings on either side of the street, the drying clothes draped there silent and unmoving in the gray dawn.

The door swung open, a sickly sweet scent rushing out to swirl around her. Wycomb shoved her through the opening into a dim hallway. She coughed as the scent filled her nose and lungs, stumbled again over rough floor. The door slammed closed, shutting out the dawn and the filth of the rookeries. There was nothing in front of her but a narrow hall and planked floors fading into darkness.

She realized the windows were covered so no light penetrated the room or the stench that hung in the air. What little entered revealed a pale, writhing smoke in its thin beams.

"Oy!" Feet pounded through the narrow hall until a tall, gaunt man stood before them. "The room is— Oh! 'Tis you!" A pistol appeared in his hand before Cat could blink. "One thrashin' weren't enough?"

"I'm here on a different matter." Wycomb walked forward, the pistol that had been at her back now pointed at the man.

Cat shrank back against the wall, pressed her hands and shoulders as tight as possible to the worn panels. A whimper of fear rose in her throat. She swallowed hard before it could escape.

"I have a business proposition for you." Wycomb reached for her, gripped her upper arm.

"Yer last offer cost me money. I had ta repair me shop when yer shipment didn't come in, the men were that glimflashy. Tore the place to bits."

"Well, this offer will make you money—will make both of us a lot of money."

"Eh?" The man cocked his head. The pistol wavered. "What is it?"

"Her." Wycomb yanked back Cat's hood, revealing her face. She blinked, but lifted her chin. "I know of more than one party who will pay handsomely for her return—assuming she remains unsullied."

...

He'd had no luck at the pubs—again—and had not seen the man he'd spoken to during his last visit. Prostitutes on the street were of no help. Wycomb's picture looked familiar to a few, but the locations he frequented were lost on the girls. Despair was a heavy weight. It had been a full day, dawn to dusk, that Cat had been missing.

Jones stayed in the shadows of the narrow street, against the wall to avoid the worst of the mud and filth. The eerie, blue-black light between sunset and night hovered over St. Giles. Still, candlelight beamed between the rags stuffed into broken windows as makeshift patches. That broken gold light fell on a pack of boys running past, barefoot, heedless of the dung and piss and vomit they were stepping in.

He'd stepped in his share—and he'd be burning his boots when he returned to Angel's townhouse. Still, he had a job to do, not memories to relive.

Jones collared one of the boys, jerking him around to face him before he boy bolted. He bucked and reared, twisting to escape. Unluckily for the boy, Jones knew all the tricks.

"Do not be afraid, boy," he barked. "Just want a word." That small body was quick as a whip and nearly had his knees buckling with a good kick. "Son of a—"

"Lemme go!" Small hands scrabbled at Jones's fingers.

He jerked the boy's collar, watched his body twist and writhe to free itself. "I only have a few questions."

"Aye?" The boy peered up at him from beneath the brim of his cap. "Questions ain't good in St. Giles."

"I know. I was born here."

That seemed to give the boy pause. He stopped wriggling and hung from Jones's hand, peering up at him with blue eyes much too large for his face. "Where?"

"A whorehouse in the Dials." Bitter words. Bitter taste. Sometimes the truth couldn't be made sweet.

"Aye?" The boy looked up, wide eyes searching Jones's face—for what, Jones did not know. "You don' look it."

"I got out. Became something." He jerked the boy's collar again to bring him back to the present. "That something wants to know if you've seen a man who looks like this." Jones held up the drawing of Wycomb.

"If I have, what'll you give me?" The boy's cheeky grin was irresistible, reminding him forcefully of Young John.

"Two things." Jones let him go, and though the boy was freed, he stayed in the shadows of the building beside Jones. Eyes and ears were ready, keen interest moving over his face. "What's your name?"

"What's yours?"

It was a test, so he fell in line. "Jones."

"Stupid name. Mine's Michael, only everyone calls me Tim." He straightened, as if a simple name gave him purpose. He wore no coat, just a shirt and breeches, but he smoothed them down as if they were as fine as any lord's attire.

"Why Tim?"

"Dunno." Michael-called-Tim shrugged. "But I has a name, and it was given to me by me Ma. There's others what can't say thet."

"True. My name was given to me at the foundling hospital." Jones bent over, looked Michael in the eyes. "How trustworthy are you?"

"Very, sir." Michael straightened, puffing out his chest under the worn shirt. "Me Ma weren't no whore—beggin' yer pardon sir—and she taught me right. You can trust me, sir."

The gut feeling grew, just as it had with Rupert and Young John and Angus. He had unintentionally collared another Gent.

"Well, Michael, I might have work for you. Honest work. I need to know you're ready for it." Jones set a hand on Michael's shoulder, gripped. He held up the drawing of Wycomb. "What do you know of this man? They say he becomes a demon with red eyes."

"Oh him." Michael didn't laugh, but he did snicker behind his hand. "He ain't no demon. That's the opium, see?"

"What?" Shock reverberated through Jones. Some things he could expect from spies—murder, treason, lies. *Opium* was a word he had not expected.

"The opium. The men what comes out of the opium den—they think the sun is a fireball and the moon is ice. They think they can touch them." With eyes much older and wiser they should be, Michael leaned forward. "Those men think *I'm* a demon. It's the smoke. Once they have it, they don't know nine feet from one foot. They only know the den."

"Where is it?"

There was a long pause, a considering one. The boy looked him up and down, once, twice, with serious eyes.

"Seven Dials. Next to a whorehouse."

Chapter Forty

He waited. Watched.

The den was not far from the Seven Dials. It was a narrow "townhouse" tucked between two larger ones, all sharing walls with more ragged buildings on the block. The windows were covered from the inside and showed no light. Men staggered in, desperation etched into their features. They staggered out later in a crazed stupor.

He didn't know how many rooms it had, or how many patrons were in it at any given time—worse, he could not determine if Cat or Wycomb were inside. He couldn't even peek into the windows.

Slipping the pistol from its hiding place beneath his coat, then his knife from his boot, Jones crossed the filthy street to the door opposite. The wood was worn, black paint from long ago flecked over the surface. He opened it slowly, ready for what might come.

The stench of unwashed bodies and opium smoke filled his nostrils. Jones clenched his teeth together and tried to breathe through his mouth. Stepping into the hall, he let the door close softly behind him. The wall was rough, even through his coat. He ignored the scrape and pressed his shoulder blades against the wall.

The hallway was narrow, with open doors dotting the length of it. The light was dim, barely more than the late evening night in the streets beyond.

Cat might not be here. Jones reminded himself this, even though his gut told him adamantly that she would be. Wycomb at the docks. Wycomb interested in the *Anna Louisa* returning from India. Wycomb unable to procure the "goods" he promised and a demon in the rookeries. The connections were there, if one looked.

There would be only one more chance to save her.

He had failed her once already. Fate and Wycomb would not give him a third chance.

Drawing in air, Jones stilled his mind to clear it of fear. It was an old trick, one that usually had the desired result. The fear did not wane this time. It clung inside his chest and coated his throat with panic. If he failed her again, what would happen to her?

Before he could think so much he forgot to act, Jones turned his head and angled his body to see into the first room. His gaze raked over the scene. Men lay half propped on pillows, some appearing to sleep and others unaware of anything about them. A general air of repose wove between the wisps of smoke.

No Cat.

Instead, there was a man beside the door, watching the patrons. Large forearms crossed over his chest, and both a pistol and a knife were tucked into his waistband. A guard, it was clear.

There would be more—to guard the product, to prevent crazed patrons from rioting.

Quickly, so the guard would not see him cross the open

doorway, Jones moved down the hall to the next room. It was set up as the first room, pillows and tables and pipes strewn about, though empty. Business must not be good.

Jones continued down the hall, picking his way as quietly as he knew how, to peek into the third room. This one was also empty, though it showed signs of use. Cloth was laid out as though it were bedding, empty bowls and scraps of garbage littered the floor, but no sign of Cat.

He reached the end of the hall and found stairs leading up and others leading down to what might have once been kitchen areas. He looked up, looked down. The upper floors were dark and quiet, but pale light and the echo of voices drifted up from below. Jones crept down the stairs, testing each step for strength and sound, pistol and knife ready. Both weapons were solid in his hands.

A warren of small rooms ran the length of the lower floor, as if someone had added space as needed over time without regard to hallways or proportions. Some opened into other rooms, others were separated by narrow halls barely wide enough for his shoulders. Storage or servants' rooms, perhaps, before St. Giles had become the slum it was now.

He crept through the snarl of rooms, listening. He passed one room where a group of men were gambling on the toss of a dice. Gin bottles littered the floor beside chicken bones stripped of their meat.

Four men, plus one above.

Not good odds, but he had dealt with worse and survived.

Only he'd never had Cat with him.

He couldn't think of it. Cat dying filled him with such horror that the entire world went dark before his eyes. With a shaking breath, Jones chased the darkness away with the image of her eyes in his mind.

Butterfly wings.

The panic slicking his insides grew. He used it to fuel him, letting that panic ground him. He would not fail her again.

He passed another room where two men lay sleeping on pallets. Light snores alternated, as if they orchestrated the sounds. Jones thought one was the man who had tried to abduct Cat on rain-soaked Oxford Street. *Six men, plus one above*. He continued, and discovered a seventh man seated at a table in the next room, not facing the door nor with his back to it, but perpendicular. Various lidded pots ranged across the table, more were stacked about. Burlap bags were piled in one corner, mostly empty, with tobacco leaves spilled around them.

Ah, here was the center of production, where the opium was mixed with tobacco for the patrons above.

Behind the table, a splash of dingy white spilled over the stone floor. Cat lay on her side facing the door, face pillowed on one arm. The hem of her nightshift was grayed with dirt, the cloak partially covering her spotted with mud—and worse.

Jones moved out of the doorway to press himself once more against the wall of the darkened hallway.

No blood. He hadn't realized the fear had overtaken him until his belly loosened from the tight fist gripping it. No visible injuries, though her eyes had been closed. Had they drugged her? Laudanum? Or, worse, the opium itself? His hand curled around the hilt of his knife, fingers gripping the horn as though he could dig into it with his nails alone.

Dear God, no. *Please*.

Heavy, staggered footsteps sounded above. Someone in the den was moving. The footsteps faded amid vague grunts, but the sound reminded Jones he could not wait. He peered into the room once more to gauge his opponent. The man was bent over the table, his back not fully toward the door. Any significant movement and Jones would be seen. He seemed tall even in the chair, but lean. Emaciated.

If he raised the alarm, his skill would not matter. If he used the pistol set at his elbow, his size would not matter.

Jones looked once more at Cat to gather himself before the attack. Her sharp gaze pinned him in place. Bright and clear and focused, her eyes showed no hint of confusion or hallucination. She did not blink, did not even move, but watched him carefully. He expected to see relief reflected in her face. Instead, her features had firmed into a sort of confirmation.

Even trust.

His heart swelled as he set a finger to his lips and held it there to be certain she saw it. Satisfaction rippled through him when she didn't acknowledge him beyond a blink. She was smart enough to know her movement might betray his presence.

Attention returned to the man, Jones breathed in slow and sure, quietly enough his opponent would not hear that intake and be alerted. The quick rush of energy that preceded any attack spiked through him. He channeled it, through his muscles and joints and into his fingertips. He pushed off hard with his feet, surging into the room. Training became instinct, then instinct became action. The man heard him and spun around, already reaching for the pistol on the table. It was too late. Jones leaped, launching himself into the air and using momentum to send his shoulder into the man's chest.

Pain bloomed in Jones's shoulder, but it was nothing compared to the impact of the stone floor as he landed. He rolled, fast and quick, to be out of knife range before he was ready to fight.

In the corner, Cat scrambled to her knees and pressed herself against the wall. He saw now she was chained at the ankle. *Hell.*

The man moaned as he pushed himself up. Jones didn't give him the chance to get beyond his knees. He slammed his fist into the man's face, once, twice. He went down again, but his foot lashed out and caught Jones on the shin. Leg buckling beneath him, Jones fell to one knee.

The man rolled, much as Jones had done but clumsier. There was street training here, but not formal training.

From the corner Cat made a small, strangled sound.

Jones had to end this. Now.

He swept his own leg out and caught the man alongside his head. Soundlessly, he crumpled to the ground.

Panting, Jones rolled the man onto his back and began frantically searching his pockets. It had to be somewhere, tucked away.

"He doesn't have the key." Panic edged Cat's voice. "The other man does. The one upstairs."

Bloody hell. Jones abandoned the unconscious man and surged toward Cat, who was struggling past chains to rise to her feet. He wanted to cup her smudged and fearful face in his hands, to rub his thumb over her bruised cheekbone and smooth the pain away.

There was no time.

"I have my picks." He might not be fast enough—he was good, but he wasn't on the same level as the Flower. Unfortunately, he was the only choice they had. Jones knelt at her feet. She hiked up her nightgown and cloak to give him access to the manacle.

Blood stained the pale skin around the iron manacles. He fought back a round of rage and steadied the hand that had started shaking. The blood was so red. So fresh.

Cat made no sound as he worked. The muscles in her shin and calf flexed as her body swayed above him. Exhaustion? He couldn't be sure. The world narrowed to the small, dark opening of the manacle's lock. To the delicate implement he worked. The tumblers caught, moved, caught.

She was free. The iron fell to the floor with a loud clang.

Her breath kicked out in a squeak and Jones looked up. Cat's eyes were wide and frightened, but still full of purpose.

"We have to go. Now, Jones." Cat shook her nightshift and cloak to cover her ankles with a swoosh of fabric and lace hem. "They'll be back soon. They never stay away long."

They. Part of him longed to know who "they" were. The fact that he couldn't stay to fight "them" chafed, but there were priorities in these circumstances. He pushed to his feet and resigned himself to flight.

"How often do they check on you?"

"Every fifteen to twenty minutes. Longer, sometimes, if someone is with me." Her voice was as calm and pointed as ever, though he saw the underlying fear in her face. "But he was here just before you arrived. There's time."

Her ungloved hand slipped into his. Soft skin and strong fingers moved against his. He took comfort from it even as he turned toward the door and freedom. Cat ran with him, her footsteps not quite as silent as his own but not as loud as he would have expected from a novice.

Bursting through the doorway, Jones glance once right, once left. The network of hallways were dark, with only the faintest glow from the room where men gambled. Right would take them past that room to the stairs to the upper floor. He turned left and took the blind path, with no idea where they would end up beyond the rear of the townhouse.

There would be a window or door to the street above. There always was.

A chill permeated the air and Jones glanced back. "Cold?"

Cat shook her head, loosened hair floating in the breeze created by their passage. "Where are we going?" she whispered.

Hell if he knew. So he didn't answer, just continued his job, pistol held up and ready in one hand and Cat's fingers twined in his other hand.

There was no need for the pistol. At the rear of the hall was another series of rooms with windows. They were high as the floor was underground, but they opened to the old mews—now another extension of the rookeries. They'd emerge on the cobblestones, none the worse for wear if they moved quickly.

"Oy!" The shout wasn't far away.

"They know I'm gone." It wasn't a hiccup that cracked Cat's voice, but it was close enough. Terror had a sound all its own.

"We'll get out." Where to go from there was another matter altogether. He dropped her hand and rushed to the window. The latches were useless, rusted shut and unable to open. He pushed, jammed the palm of his hand against the latch and ignored the pain. It wouldn't budge.

Footsteps rang in the rooms beyond. Jones and Cat carried no light to betray them, so it was only their sound that would give them away. Jones looked once at the doorway behind, once more at Cat and her wide, determined eyes.

"Turn your face," he said. Averting his own countenance, he crooked his elbow and jammed it against the glass. Shards flew as the sound of broken glass filled the air. He felt one slice his face, another his forearm. His elbow didn't bear thinking of, as he could already feel the blood trickling down his arm. "Out. Now."

He cupped his hands and Cat set a foot in them, without any hesitation. He boosted her up until she could hoist herself onto the sill.

"Don't go far, but stay hidden. I'll be right after you." The footsteps were closer, faster, running now. He looked up into her face as she knelt and peered in over the wooden sill. "I'll be just one minute."

"Jones, I will hold you to it." She leaned through the

broken shards of glass, kissed him once. Hard. "I love you." With that she was gone, leaving nothing but the clear, starry sky and the stench of opium behind.

The door burst open and Jones spun, braced for attack. It was only one man who lunged and reached for Jones, his knife glinting in the light from outside the window. But he was unsteady, and hardly a match. Jones shoved the palm of his hand into the man's nose, then swept his feet out from under him. Satisfaction reigned for only a moment before the man kicked and caught Jones mid-thigh.

Pain roared through him. He landed on the stone floor with a breathless grunt, then rolled and tried to scramble to his feet. His leg buckled and the pain spiked, so he leaned against the wall to gather his strength. Then he leaped, reaching for the knife.

The man surrendered the knife easily, which should have been the warning.

The fist caught him square in the jaw and sent blinding agony and bright stars wheeling through his brain. He staggered, bracing to prepare for another blow even as he plunged the knife into his attacker's thigh, then wrenched it free.

The howl of pain reverberated in the stone room, the sound overpowering the thud of the man dropping to the floor.

Jones spun toward the window, already dismissing the opponent. His only thought was Cat, alone in the rookeries. He reached for the window sill and hoisted himself up. Tossing a leg up and onto the street, he angled his body, then threw his shoulder into the ground and rolled, bringing his other leg through the window.

The ground was wet and stunk of piss, but the air was clear of the scent of opium. He didn't pause to take a deep breath of the night. Pushing to his feet, Jones scanned the darkened alley. One end opened onto the main thoroughfare, where footsteps and shouting and other street sounds echoed. The other end of the alley he knew intersected the hundreds of other narrow alleys connecting the streets of St. Giles.

Where was Cat? He listened, trying to filter any noise that might be in the alley from other city noises. Above him, clothing flapped on strings spread between the buildings. Lights spilled out from a few windows, along with voices punctuated by laughter.

No Cat. He saw no flash of gray-white at either end of the alley. Would she go toward the street, or hide in the alleys? Either way she could be killed, or worse. There was nowhere in the rookeries a lady could hide, especially one like Cat with wealth sewn into the very stitches of her cloak and quality bred into the bones beneath her soft skin.

There was nothing to do but guess. He aimed for the wider street, thinking she might go where there were people in the hopes of greater protection. When he reached the street he saw no sign of her nightgown or cloak, or any scuffle that might indicate someone was hassling her.

He ran toward the other end of the alley where it opened into another narrow space between buildings. He looked right, left. Nothing. No sound of running footsteps, no visual sign of her passing.

"Hell." He ran a hand through his hair as fear spread a thin layer of ice in his belly. Where had she gone?

He started running down the alley, feet pounding into the cobblestones and sending fluids he'd rather not think about splashing onto his boots. He navigated the twists and turns and tried not to let memory overtake him. *Cat.* He had to find her before Wycomb did, or one of the men in the den, or some other criminal on the streets recognized her for what she was.

He couldn't see her. Nothing. Not a whiff of her soap nor a flash of her nightgown.

Chapter Forty-One

Cat waited at the end of the alley for Jones. He didn't come. Not in one minute, nor two. She peeked around the corner, saw nothing but shadows and far beyond, the light of the street. She waited longer, back pressed against the rough brick—until she heard the footsteps. Fast and hard, with such purpose it drove terror straight through her.

She ran, as quickly as she could hampered by her nightshift and cloak. Gathering them up so the froth of fabric was bundled in her arms, she set her head down and turned into an alley, then another and another. Without hesitation. The footsteps faded, but fear did not. Perhaps, just perhaps, she was safe. Desperation clawed at her lungs as she skittered down an alleyway and into the nearest shadowed corner. It was a doorway, inset slightly into a brick building.

Dismay dawned as she recognized the front door of the opium den across the street. She had returned almost to where she had started.

"Oh God, oh God, oh God." Fear had a sound—running footsteps in the dark. It had a scent as well—urine and body sweat and the stench of the opium.

She couldn't stay here. She shouldn't *be* here. Her nightshift fell once more around her ankles, dirty but still a beacon in the dark. Cat pressed herself against the door, flattening her fingers against the wood. She didn't know where to go. What to do. Gasping slightly, she grabbed the door handle behind her back and turned.

The panel fell open with a swift whoosh of air. She stumbled backward and into yet more terror.

"Oy!" The shout was harsh and full of anger. Cat spun around to discover the tallest, baldest man she'd ever seen. "Get out! This is my room!"

"I'm sorry. I'm sorry, sir." She nearly sobbed it, which was horrifyingly embarrassing. "I'll go." She should have been imperiously angry. Any woman of her class would have done so and demanded some type of respect.

Pathetically, she couldn't summon enough anger or pride to demand respect.

She shut the door and simply stood there, looking into the shadows of the alley and at the den not twenty feet away. Was Jones still in there? Squares of light formed a patchwork over the cobblestone pathway. A few people passed through them, intent on their business and taking no notice of her. Yet. Sounds assaulted her from all directions, rooms above, the street nearby, the homes and shops and pubs a stone's throw away beyond the alley.

"Missus."

When had the door opened behind her? She spun around to face the large bald man who had chased her away.

"Missus, come in." A heavy hand fell onto her shoulder and held her in place. "Dressed like that, you'll be taken for sure."

"What?" Her voice was appallingly high-pitched.

"You'll be dead by morning, or worse. Come in." He gave

her no choice, pulling her through the doorway with more strength than she could fight. The door closed behind her, shutting out the sky and stars and—as he leaned against the unremarkable wooden panel—freedom.

"What's a fancy lady like you doing in these parts?" He was huge. Taller than Jones by a foot or more. Wider.

When she opened her mouth to protest, he simply cocked his head and spoke before she could.

"Don't go tellin' me you ain't a fancy lady. Quality ain't stamped into the clothes as much as the blood, missus. You has quality." He strode across the room to the banked fire, stirred it to life with a makeshift poker resembling a bar from an iron fence found in every street of the West End.

"What do you want?" Cat set her hands behind her back and clutched her skirt, hoping her fear would transmit to the skirt and not to her captor. "I have no money with me."

The great beast of a man set the iron bar aside and simply watched her, dark eyes shadowed in the dim light. Without speaking, he settled himself on a short stool between the fire and a pile of blankets. She noticed then that there was no table in the room. Only a fireplace, the stool and blankets, a trunk that had seen much better days, and cooking utensils. All of it was clean and organized.

He was likely better off than most in the rookeries.

The man remained silent, though he was now winding something in his hands, pulling, braiding, stretching. It looked like rope.

Rope.

Terror could grab a woman with two fists and squeeze the life from her. It could send the edges of her vision into the black and weaken her legs.

"Don't go off like that." The man's hands paused their movements, the long fingers gentle on the threads despite their size. "Might want to take a breath, now, afore you keel over."

Cat drew in one shaking inhalation and found her vision clearing. She knew it wasn't this huge man and his rope that caused her fear. It was everything. Every moment of the last few days culminated with this one moment, this one man.

But she'd managed before, hadn't she?

"There now. That's better. Color in your cheeks again." He nodded once, acknowledging the change in her. "Can't see why you'd be in these parts, milady. Might be you need to be shown where to go?" He cocked his head and watched her with those dark currant eyes.

"Yes." Only she couldn't go home, so being shown out of the rookeries was nonsense.

"Good."

"No." Yet she couldn't stay in the rookeries where she was an easy mark, and where Wycomb might find her. "I don't know."

Oh God, her vision was going black again. She gulped in air and hoped the door at her back would steady her.

"Ah. It's that way, is it? Can't go back, can't go forward?" The man seated before her began to wind the rope around one hand, gathering it between fingers and thumb so it became layer upon layer of material. The light from the newly stirred fire shown over a smooth skull.

"No, I can't go back." Saying the words sent her stomach plummeting. "I can't go anywhere."

Slow and steady the man worked, though his gaze did not leave her face. "What do you know of the opium dens?"

"What?" Perhaps it was not the most eloquent response, but, "What? What?" She jerked forward in a movement that was part step, part stumble.

"You reek of opium, and as there's only two dens in this area, you must have been at one of them, though you don't seem to be the worse for wear."

"And you don't speak like a miscreant of the rookeries."

"Sometimes a man isn't born here, he ends up here by choice."

Cat wanted to ask why anyone would be here by choice, in a room with the drapes drawn and surrounded by urine-soaked streets. She didn't ask, because sometimes it was better not to know.

"May I stay here, just for a few minutes?"

"Not if you're dealing in opium." He dropped the coiled rope into his lap. "To each his own, but I don't want any of those sorts stumbling into my back room."

"I'm not dealing in opium." She was vaguely amused he thought so, and even more amused he would cast her out for it. "I was held against my will."

He pushed up from the stool and she noticed his coat was patched and frayed. "How long is this bit you'd like to stay?"

"I don't know. A few hours. Perhaps until the morning?"

"It won't be any safer out there in the morning, milady." He moved to the corner of the room and bent over the blankets. Cat couldn't make out what he was doing and unease began to spread.

"I better go now." What had she been thinking, asking this giant if she could stay? She reached for the door handle.

"Stop." The man gestured to the pile at his feet. Without his shadow blocking it, she could see the cloth, smoothed out now to create a makeshift bed. "You can sleep here. I'll sleep on the floor."

"Sir—"

"Sir?" He laughed lightly. "My lady, my name is Bill, as I'm bald as billiard ball. I'll see you out of the rookeries in the morning."

Chapter Forty-Two

Jones hunkered down in a doorway, tossing a hot cross bun from hand to hand just as he had as a boy. He let the bun cool and watched the streets. He'd spent the night searching for Cat but had found not a trace of her. He sat, waiting and watching. The bit of bun he ate was dry in his throat—with no fault to the baker. Still, he waited. The sun climbed in the east, dark blue turning to gray and then to yellow sunlight.

The rookeries appeared much more habitable in the dark.

The bun in his hands cooled with only a single bite out of it. He found he couldn't eat. Yet there was nowhere to set the bun without fouling it, so he continued to hold it—and waited. Seven streets converged here, all of them part of the rookeries. There were hundreds of places to hide, but she would not go home. The rookeries were his best hope.

Hours passed. Dawn. Midday. The evening light began to fall when he finally saw her. She walked beside a mountain of a man wearing patched but clean clothes. Jones fought the urge to rush into the street and snatch Cat away. Training stayed him, so he paused to observe her body language. Alert but not frightened. She watched the streets with avid interest, but with the cloak pulled around her so only a glimpse of her nightshift could be seen as she walked.

Jones chose his moment as they stepped out of the circle of streets and into an alley. They were less likely to be seen there, and with the windows and doors as they were, observation from above would be difficult.

"Cat."

She spun, shock and joy warring on her face. Her butterfly-blue eyes were wide, pupils dilated. She ran, jumped, and wrapped herself around him as if he were the only safe haven in London. Arms about his neck, her legs wrapped around his waist, he felt every touch of her body to his, each point of contact causing a fire in his body and cool relief in his mind. Her lips met his, hungry and scared and loving all at once.

"Jones." She buried her face in his neck, though her body slid down his until her feet reached the ground again. "I was so afraid."

"As was I." More, now that he knew she was safe. All the worry he'd pushed away during the long watchful hours seemed to coalesce to a single location in his chest. "I couldn't find you. God, Cat, those were long hours."

"Are you well, then?" The giant towered over them, arms crossed and a frown creasing his face.

"Yes." Cat beamed up into the man's face. "Bill, this is my Jones."

"Jones." Bill squinted at Jones, looked him up and down as if assessing his worthiness. "Milady shouldn't be in St. Giles or the Dials."

"No, she shouldn't." Jones nodded, both in respect for the statement as well as the man's care for Cat. "Thank you. I know exactly the dangers she might have faced without you."

"Aye. See she's safe." The man looked at Jones, then Cat, then Jones again. "If you've need for help, milady, you can call on me."

"Thank you." Cat reached out, set her small, white hand on a forearm marked with tattoos and scars. "For everything."

"Aye." The big man set a hand to his forehead, as if he were tugging on a cap out of respect. "Be careful."

"I will." Cat watched him stride back through the circle of the Dials and into an alley. A light smile curved her lips.

Everything inside him soared, just watching her expression soften. That she could appreciate a bald man in the rookeries was exactly why he loved her. He wished he could simply scoop her up and bring her inside him—not to protect her, but so that her grace would calm and soothe the dark places in him.

She spun suddenly, eyes serious again. "Hedgewood is part of it."

"What?" All thoughts of love flew from him. He pulled her into the shadows of the nearest building. Long, slim fingers clutched at his arm.

"I don't understand exactly what is happening, but I saw Hedgewood and my uncle the night he took me away." She breathed deep, swallowed hard. Still, Cat straightened her shoulders. "He is working with my uncle."

"How?"

"Money. The ships bringing in the opium. Also—" She paused, as if the next words were difficult. "Wycomb took me to the den so Hedgewood would pay to get me back. He wants more money."

"He's planning to run, then." Jones drew her close, pulled the cloak tighter so her nightshift would remain hidden. She nestled against his shoulder and he set his chin on her head. Silky hair tangled in the two-day's growth of his beard. Neither of them seemed to care.

"Cat, you are worth more than anything Wycomb could demand."

"There is nowhere safe for you." Jones set his elbows on his knees, leaning forward so that his torso folded over his thighs and his hands fell into the empty space between them. "Nowhere."

"I know I can't go home." She could not go to Ashdown Abbey, nor Worthington House. Not to any of her other estates, even those in the wilds of Yorkshire. Wycomb knew them all.

"No. And you can't stay at the townhouse, either. Neither can I." Jones lifted his head, gaze roaming the streets and townhouses in front of him as if memorizing each brick.

They sat on a bench in Hyde Park, staring at trees well away from the townhouses and hawkers beginning their day. The night had been a round of running, hiding and running again. The sun had eventually raised her face above the city, bathing it in pale gold light that would strengthen throughout the day.

Cat hoped her will would increase as well. She slipped her fingers between Jones's gripped hands, twining her fingers through his. "Is there another house we could go to? You must have dozens of places to hide in the city, in the country."

"He knows them all, Cat. Even if we move around from safe house to safe house, there is nowhere Wycomb won't be able to find you eventually. It will simply be a matter of checking the right safe house at the right time." Regret overlaid resignation in his tone. He breathed deep, fingers clenching and releasing. "Worse, I can't be certain there are any places he *doesn't* know about."

Fear spiked through her so that the rhythm of her heart rose, the blood pumping through her veins becoming a thundering, crashing pace.

"Then we don't go to a safe house." She strengthened the

grip of her fingers. "A person can disappear in London if they want to."

"Yes." His head came up, eyes latching onto hers. "But you are known in many places, simply by virtue of your status. You'll be recognized in the West End because you are the Baroness Worthington. You'll be recognized for a lady in the rookeries because you don't belong. Even in those semi-respectable parts of the city, you may be noticed for either reason."

He was right. *He was right.*

"What do we do?" The words were choked and strangled as they left her throat, leaving it barren.

Well beyond them on the public road near the Life Guards Barracks, a crested carriage rolled past. The horses moved in a steady, even gait. Once it passed, Cat could see a woman carrying a basket of bread. She shouted, trying to sell her goods. That was life in London, Cat supposed. The wealthy passed by the poor without a glance.

"I don't know what to do." The words were full of despair and uncertainty. Jones pushed to his feet to pace away from the bench, steps beating an uneven tattoo on the path before them.

Cat stared at the now empty bench beside her. That space seemed to hold all the uselessness of her life. She was Mary Elizabeth Frances Catherine Ashdown, Thirteenth Baroness Worthington. She owned thousands upon thousands of rolling green fields. She employed hundreds of tenants, men and women and children who depended on her—and her guardian would likely kill her on sight, and if he did not, he would force her to marry. She gripped the edge of the bench, fingers curling around forged iron, as the dread in her raged higher.

The seat was not enough to anchor her. Booted feet digging into the grass were not enough to anchor her. So she focused on Jones.

Just on Jones.

His back was to her, broad and strong, with weapons no doubt hidden between his body and his coat. His shoulders shifted as he pulled a small paper from his coat pocket. He unfolded it, slowly, as if the fold were momentous.

"I love you, Cat." The words wandered into the air, as though of little import. Four words that were quiet and simple, and could have meant "I would like tea."

They didn't. They meant everything.

"I—" She didn't know what to say. Didn't have the words to explain the sheer joy surging through her, tumbling around with the fear still tearing at her.

"I love you, Cat. And I know what we have to do."

• • •

It was simple, really.

He would kill Wycomb so that she would be safe.

He would set her free of Hedgewood, even if that meant killing him, too.

Jones set this thumb on the paper, marred now from repeated folding. He rubbed the drawing. *Morpho helenor achillaena.* As a young man, he'd wanted to see it fly, though he'd known the butterfly was not native to England. It was only found in the tropics, so he would never would see it.

He'd imagined the wings opening and closing, hiding the blue, then revealing it. Imagined the freedom of fluttering flight over meadows and wildflowers, through the air with nothing but a backdrop of sky and cloud.

Now, instead of finding the butterfly, he'd found Cat. Her eyes would haunt his days and nights, and all he would have left of her was the butterfly drawing.

"You tore the page from the book." Her words were

unreadable. He could not tell if she was disappointed or angry.

Either way, the pain of tearing the page was less than the pain of losing Cat.

"I wanted it with me when you were missing." The ache in his heart needed time to find a place to call home, so he took a moment to refold the page and put it back in his pocket.

When he looked at Cat her eyes were wide and lips parted, as though the shock of his words had immobilized her.

"Wycomb doesn't yet know you are free—or likely does not. And, if he does, he knows you won't return to the townhouse, Ashdown Abbey, or any of your other estates. You can't go anywhere you are recognized, because it would be too simple for him to find you. But I need to find him. I need to stop him. And you'll have to come with me."

"How will you find him? What will we do?"

"We're going back to the opium den. Eventually, he will return there." Jones set his jaw, preparing for the entreaties to come. "We're not going alone, Cat."

"Thank you for coming here. I couldn't risk your families or returning to Angel's townhouse." Jones searched the faces of those he trusted most. Angel, his mentor and Marquess of Angelstone. The Shadow, Earl of Langford. The Flower, small and lean, and wearing her customary men's clothing. Also deadly. All three were spies he would put his back to in battle and know he was safe.

Beside them in the back room of the Goose and Gander pub sat Cat, cloak wrapped tightly about her, eyes wide as she watched and listened. A tankard of ale sat in front of her just as it did the rest of them—the proprietor didn't serve anything else—as well as cheese and bread.

"Lord Langford." Her tone was flat. "Lord Angelstone."

"My lady," the Shadow replied, nodding his head as if they were meeting in a ballroom.

Angel said nothing, choosing to watch the exchange with mild amusement.

"You are both spies." Her words were accompanied by narrowed eyes.

"Indeed." The Shadow's lips twitched. "It is a pleasure to see you again, baroness. I believe you and I shared a country dance not long ago?"

"I will never believe what I see again. Ever." Cat lifted the tankard to her lips and gulped the bitter, second-rate ale. She sputtered once, then gulped again as if she had been deprived of water for weeks. "Spies are everywhere, aren't they?"

"If you know where to look." Jones set his knife to the cheese, sliding it through to carve a slice. "I've sent the Gents with a message to Sir Charles so he is aware of what is happening, but there is little time, I think."

"It must be Henri. Wycomb." The Flower leaned forward, elbows on the filthy table as if it were as clean as the table in the *ton* townhouse she now shared with her husband. She sent a fast glance toward Cat. "No one else would bring us all here."

"True." Jones set his hand in Cat's, certain she would be uncomfortable in this hovel of a pub and still wearing her nightshift and cloak. She squeezed once, then slipped her fingers out and set them on the tankard.

"He is—" Cat struggled to find the word, though her carriage did not change. She turned the tankard, a quarter turn, then a half. "Wrong," she finally said. "Everything about him is wrong. It is almost too much to tell."

"Yes. *Oui.*" The Flower crossed her arms over her coat and shirt. Satisfaction pursed her lips. "He is wrong. There are parts of him that are good, do you understand? He works hard for this country, but there is something wrong in his soul."

"That is exactly it." Cat looked to the Flower, exchanged a glance. "You know him well?"

A long silence reverberated through the room. The Shadow and Angel both looked to the Flower, then to Cat. Jones opened his mouth to respond, but decided to follow the lead of the other men and stayed quiet. They understood women better than he.

It was the Flower's turn to struggle now. Though she was adept at hiding her thoughts, Jones recognized pain rippling over her pretty features. She lifted her tankard, drank deep, and set it down with a *thunk*.

"Yes." Dark eyes glittered fiercely when she met Cat's gaze. "As well as you, I think. He was my commander for ten years."

"I see." Cat slid her hand across the table scarred with knife marks and stained by ale. She curled her fingers over the Flower's clenched fist. She spoke no more, only looked to Jones.

The Flower turned her fist up and opened it so that she gripped Cat's fingers. Jones looked at those joined hands. One small, skilled, and from the rookeries. The other was small, elegant, and from the ton.

If he hadn't loved Cat before, his heart would have fallen from his chest.

"What has he done?" The Shadow tapped his fingers on the tabletop. "He is well respected as an agent. If we are taking him down, you had better be right."

"He is dealing in opium," Jones said shortly. "Worse, he gave the baroness to the opium dealers to obtain ransom from her fiancé."

"Who is providing money to fund the opium den," Cat

added.

"Also, Wycomb is my assignment from Sir Charles." There was no longer any need for secrecy. Flicking his gaze between the Shadow and Angel, Jones recognized understanding in their faces.

"Does *he* know that?" the Shadow asked.

"As Wycomb and I fought over Cat—and I lost—" Jones added bitterly, failure settling into the base of his belly. "Yes. That was when he abducted her."

"Good enough."

"What is your plan?" Angel leaned back in his chair. He crossed his arms, long fingers tapping over one bicep. "If Wycomb knows you are ready to bring him in, he will not return to Worthington House."

"The Gents said Worthington House is in an uproar. They know the baroness is missing, and though Wycomb did return briefly, it was only to gather a few items and leave again." Jones shifted, simply to ensure his pistol was still beneath his coat. It felt as if Wycomb's gaze were on his back.

"Henri will run." The Flower narrowed her eyes and lifted one shoulder in casual confidence. "We will not let him."

"I agree." Jones nodded once, sharply. He had failed Cat, failed his commander. He would not do so a second time. "I believe he may return to the opium den—particularly as I don't know if he is aware Baroness Worthington has escaped."

"Oh, just say Cat." She waived his formality away with a laugh, shaking back her hood. "I've been walking around London wearing only a nightshift under my cloak."

"Jones." The Flower frowned at him, then looked to Cat's cloak. There were no windows in the back room, but the lamp light clearly revealed fabric smeared with grime. "You should know better."

"With all due respect, Flower," Jones responded dryly, raising a brow in impatience. "I was concerned about her life, not her attire."

"Accepted." Though the Flower's tone did not echo the word. "Still, she needs clothing. I will see she has it."

"*Merci.*" Cat spoke it with a perfect accent, as so many well-educated ladies of the *ton* did. Blue eyes warmed so that he once more thought of the tropical butterfly—one he could never catch.

The Flower laughed, bright and sweet, and pushed at the cap restraining her unruly hair. "No, my dear. I am as English as you. Only—well. I have a disguise, do you see? A French opera dancer."

"I see. The whispered rumors I've heard about Wycomb in the last few years now make sense." Cat's expression shifted, as if some fact had been settled between them. "Aside from my nightshift, we should discuss Wycomb."

"There we go. Back on topic, though no less important than nightclothes." Angel winked at Cat, then sent his gold gaze toward Langford. "Shadow, what are your thoughts?"

"As I understand it," Langford said slowly, rubbing a thumb along the rim of the tankard set before him. "We do not know if Wycomb is aware that Baroness Worthington escaped."

"We do not," Jones confirmed, blocking out the amusement he'd felt at the exchange between Cat and Flower.

"Then we must keep watch on the den. Beginning now, before he learns the truth." Langford's bright eyes moved around the table, as if seeking agreement from each of them. He pushed his ale away as if he were finished with it, though Jones knew it was nearly full.

"What if the opium dealers have already sent a message?" Cat leaned forward, setting the arms of her now filthy cloak on the tabletop. Her hair was bound in a simple knot at the nape of her neck, and there was a faint streak of dirt along her cheekbone. She'd never looked so beautiful—and he had never been so proud. "If he does not return to the den, we will be wasting our time."

"How long has it been since he left you there?" Angel asked, reaching for a hunk of the simple brown bread sitting beside the pale-yellow cheese in the center of the table.

"It was just after dawn yesterday."

"Not much more than a day and a half, then." Angel looked at Jones, nodded once before biting into the soft slice layered thickly with butter. "Your choice as to the next movement, Jones."

"The opium den." Jones was certain Wycomb would reappear there. "He will not return again to Worthington House, and even if he knows Cat is gone, he will still try to obtain his part of the ransom. Wycomb will want his money and then will disappear."

"What is your plan?" the Flower asked.

He didn't know. "I can't take Cat back into the rookeries. I can't expose her to Wycomb again."

"No. She'll be his leverage if he finds her," the Shadow agreed. "It is also not safe for her there."

"There is somewhere I can stay." Cat set her hand on Jones's forearm. Long fingers were white against the sleeve his brown coat, though dirt clung beneath the short nails. "Somewhere to hide if need be."

Chapter Forty-Three

"You're not doing anything illegal, eh?" Bill's left eyebrow tilted down beneath a bald skull gleaming in the setting sun. He looked to Cat, to Jones, back again, filling the doorway with his bulk.

"I only need a safe place to stay for a few hours." Cat was conscious of the desperate bustle in the street at her back, of the reek of urine saturating the air. More, she was conscious of Jones standing beside her. "It is important."

"I like you, milady, but I've work to do today." The scowl on Bill's face was ferocious. "I'm not inclined to share my rooms for reasons I don't understand—particularly as I'm leaving."

"I cannot provide details in full." Cat glanced to Jones, whose face was impassive as he took in the street around them—no doubt watching for danger. For Wycomb. "It is complicated."

"Aye?" Bill planted his legs inside the doorframe, as if he'd grown there. "Tell me."

She weighed her words carefully. "A man sold me to the

opium den for ransom. Jones hopes to apprehend him."

"This Jones needs to stash you somewhere while he goes about his business, eh?"

"That, and I need to keep watch." Jones jerked his head toward the door of the den.

A long silence followed. Cat held her breath, misgiving pinging through her. They were exposed on the street, on display to Wycomb should he arrive at the den just then. She rubbed damp palms on her cloak, and though instinct made her want to turn around and look for danger, her mind told her that doing so risked detection.

"Come in." Bill stepped aside, the scowl on his face only a little less ferocious.

"Thank you." Unutterably grateful, Cat smiled and crossed the threshold. As the door closed behind Jones, hiding them from the eyes of the street, she found her worry lessening.

The room was no less spartan by day than by night. Without the glow of the fire to soften it, she could see the shabbiness as well—though the smell of toasted bread warmed the space.

"Have you had supper, yet?" Bill asked grumpily. He gestured toward a bundle of cloth near the hearth and a roasting stick. "I've bread and sausages."

"We have." Jones was at the window already, pushing aside the ragged fabric to look out at the darkening street. He turned then to face Bill, brown eyes solemn. "I am indebted to you."

"Aye." Bill's lips quirked up, amusement clear in the half light of the room. "Iffen we see each other again, I'll be sure to call in that favor."

Something passed between the two men Cat didn't understand. She could almost see it in the air.

"Understood." Jones nodded, as if in acceptance of an

unspoken agreement.

"Now, I've work to do, as I said." Bill crossed his thick arms, squinted at the two of them. "I'll be back later. Milady, if Jones here leaves you for any reason, keep the door locked until I return, eh? Don't go wandering about St. Giles alone."

"I will." She smiled warmly at the tall man in his threadbare clothes. They owed him a great deal, more than she could ever repay, but she promised herself she would do what she could as soon as this ordeal was over.

"Good." He retrieved a cap from a peg near the door and settled it over his smooth head. "I'll be back."

The door snapped shut behind Bill, the finality of the sound renewing her unease. Jones snatched the stool with a single hand and immediately went to the window again. He positioned the seat, lowered himself and pushed aside the curtain so that a slim crack of blurred glass was revealed.

"Can you see the door of the den from here?" Cat asked softly, leaning close to see for herself through that long, thin triangular crack. She set her hand on his broad shoulder, let it linger there. Beneath his coat, muscle twitched and rolled against her palm.

"Well enough." He turned his head slightly, as though to determine just how close she truly was. Too close, apparently, as he drew a long breath and leaned away.

"I would have you nowhere near Wycomb when I find him." The words curled through the air, barely audible.

The dry laugh that slipped out scored her throat. "I don't particularly want to be near my uncle, either."

She did not want to face Wycomb. Nor did she want to be inside the opium den again. That door opened to nightmares, to the sickly sweet scent still lingering in her hair. To memories of Wycomb that refused to give up their corner in her mind.

Her fingers curled into Jones's shoulder, searching for an anchor. She found one. Just there, when she needed it.

A large, capable hand, callused and rough, pried her fingers loose and twined with them.

"I don't know how long we will have to wait for Wycomb." Jones's eyes were solemn when they met hers. A corner of his mouth tipped up before he spoke again, easing the fear crawling under her skin. "I'd prefer my shoulder to be in working order when we do. I might have to defend your honor."

He brought her hand to his lips, pressed them softly to her knuckles. The kiss dove straight to her heart.

"My gentleman hero."

Cat meant it, with all her being.

Jones might not believe it, but she knew what was in his heart. She wanted it. Always.

"Will you go with me? To Colle di Val d'Elsa?" The words rushed from her. She had not known they were there to be spoken, but they had been in her mind for a long time.

"What?" The hand that had been so gentle on hers tightened. Not painfully, but with strength that imparted shock. "What?"

"Come with me. We can live there, just as you imagined. No one will know us, there will be no society to snub us. No tenants, no trustees. I can—"

"Cat. Stop. We can't." His fingers fell away from hers, leaving her hand curled around nothing but cool air. The tear that now lived permanently in her heart deepened.

"We can." Desperation could be cruel. It could fill a soul so that the skin felt tight, so sound and sight sharpened to the single point of a lover's eyes. "I don't need Ashdown Abbey, or the trust. It's you that matters, don't you understand?"

"You can't give up a five-hundred-year legacy for me, Cat. I won't allow it."

"But you're willing to give up us? To give up love?" She angled her body, trying not to come between Jones and the window, yet wanting him to see her.

"It's your life. It's everything you are." He tipped his head back, closed his eyes briefly. The stool creaked with the movement and light from the street shifted over his face. "I'm nothing, Cat. We're nothing."

Oh God. Words twisted and tore at the heart, didn't they? But she set her feet into the worn planks of the floor. She knew what she wanted.

"All the tenants who rely on me can be managed by Mr. Sparks. Jones, *I don't need to be there.*" With those words, something rolled from her shoulders that she had not even known was weighing on them. "I'm not my father, Jones. I'm not his father, or his grandfather. I'm not the first Mary Elizabeth Frances Ashdown, either. I'm Mary Elizabeth Frances *Catherine* Ashdown. I'm Cat, first. The land will always belong to me, and then my children—only I am not needed to run everything."

"Cat." Jones set warm hands against her waist and pulled her forward. She went, willingly, looking down at the square jaw, at the eyes filled with shock. At the cheekbones that sharpened in moments such as this. "You don't mean that."

"I do." She smiled, with all the brilliance that shone in her heart. "We can't be together here. So, we will be together somewhere else."

"It is impossible." He sighed, leaning forward so that his forehead rested just beneath her heart. "It can't *be* possible."

"It can, if we want it to be." Every fiber and sinew that knitted her body together told her this. "Our life can be what we make it. Here in England, we will never be able live freely. There, in Colle di Val d'Els we can. It's that simple."

"Hope can be a bitter thing, Cat."

Tears formed a throbbing ache in her throat when he turned his face to the side so his cheek now pressed against her breast. Arms slid around her waist, drawing her near.

It was she who drew him in for comfort. She who circled him with love as her arms circled shoulders sagging beneath their burden. Standing here, with Jones seeking her comfort and hope a small, bright dream growing between them, the moment both tore at her and healed the chasm in her heart.

"I love you, Jones."

A relieved and terrified shudder wracked him, so that the wide, broad shoulders became momentarily frail.

"Come with me," she whispered, seeing little beyond the thick brown hair so neatly trimmed. Tears shadowed her vision and blocked that familiar sight from her. But she wasn't ready to cry yet. Not yet.

He had not answered.

He was silent for what seemed like an age. Two. Civilizations might have risen and fallen in the time that he did not speak. Only the steady drip of rain and the rhythm of their breath filled the room. Then, finally, Jones moved.

He stood, unfolding his body from the safe hollow she'd created for him, looking down into her face, searching her eyes. Cupping her cheeks, he set his mouth to hers. He gave of himself, with gentleness and sweetness, with a soft fury that stole her breath.

This was home. Not Ashdown Abbey or the townhouse in London, nor any other estate. Home was not a physical location. It was with Jones.

She moved closer, gripping the rough linen of his shirt, opening her mouth beneath his so that she could give of herself as well. His mouth devoured hers, fiercer than anything he had shown her before.

"Cat." The single word was rough with that turbulence as well as urgency. "Wycomb is on the street."

Jones pressed his lips to hers once final time, then set her away from him with great regret. "Hedgewood is with him."

Her body had stiffened with fear. He regretted that he had caused it, but better she was scared than so confident she put herself in danger. A second look through the gray-blue dusk showed Wycomb and Hedgewood both stepping into the opium den.

Now. It must be now.

"Here, take my knife." He pulled it from his boot, offering it to her hilt first. The low firelight glinted on the blade he ruthlessly maintained.

"You might need it, Jones." She shook her head, backing away from the weapon.

"I have others." Two others, just as easily accessible to him and as familiar as old friends. "I also have my pistol."

Carefully, as if she expected it to strike as quickly as a snake, she accepted the knife. It was large in her small, dirt-streaked hand. "Are you going into the den?"

"Yes, before it is too late. Lock the door as soon as I leave."

"Be careful," she whispered.

"You as well." He gave her a fast, hard kiss, aware that time was passing quickly. "Lock the door," he said again.

He slipped out that door and waited for the sound of the deadbolt on the other side. Jones closed his eyes for one second to imprint the memory of her in his mind—still wearing her nightshift and cloak, holding a knife in one hand and watching him with those butterfly-blue eyes.

The image would carry him through.

Then he set Cat aside and focused on the mission. The Flower and Shadow had positioned themselves at the rear of the den, watching the windows Cat and Jones had escaped from earlier.

Angel, who had been watching the front as well, gained

the stoop just as Jones stepped close. Training became instinctual, Angel's intent forming in Jones's mind from both memory and observation. It was a pattern they had performed before.

Angel held a pistol in one hand and a knife in the other, experience turning both weapons into extensions of his body. He nodded once to Jones as a sign to proceed and flattened his back to the wall beside the door. Jones reached for the handle, pressed the latch, and pushed it open.

The hall was empty. Dim light filtered in from the first room Jones already knew the patrons frequented, but the hall itself held no candles, no Wycomb and no Hedgewood. Pistol leading the way, Jones slowly stepped into the narrow space. He peered into the first room and saw patrons sprawled on pillows, others imbibing. Smoke hung thick in the air and wove between agitated voices, its scent sweet enough that he wrinkled his nose.

The guard was at the door, a different one this time. Jones jabbed the stock of his pistol on the spot at the temple that would keep the man sleeping for a while. Minutes, hours. It was unclear, but either way the patrons were too far gone to notice and it would gain them a window of time.

Still, Jones knew where Wycomb would go. Not here on the first floor, but below where Cat would have been held.

He gestured to Angel, pointing down to the floor below. Angel nodded in understanding, then pointed to the street behind them. He held up two fingers. Jones knew the intent of the gesture—Shadow and the Flower were already alerted by Angel that Wycomb had entered.

It was a pleasure working with his own.

Though Angel had been Jones's commander, he did not take the lead. Jones already knew the way and led Angel down the hall, past empty rooms and to the steps leading below. He pointed down, then flashed his fingers. Five. Another five.

Expect ten men.

Angel nodded his understanding and they began to descend the steps. Silently, letting muscle and joints absorb sound rather than the wood beneath their feet, they moved below. Jones heard voices, raised well beyond conversation level.

"I will not pay until I see her." Not Wycomb—it must be Hedgewood. Jones had never heard his voice, so it was only a guess.

The labyrinth of rooms and halls in the lower level spanned before him. He listened, careful to follow the sound of the voices. Doorways opened on each side, each dark though sconces were perched on the walls at intervals so they could pick their way forward.

"Just pay them." Wycomb's voice was smooth and easily recognizable, disdain dripping from the words. "Mary Elizabeth is worth more than the both of us combined."

Jones moved down the hall, pistol poised and ready, the knife in his waistband burning through his shirt as if demanding to be used. A glance behind showed Angel, face set in resolute lines. Somewhere beyond were others, but Jones could only count on Angel now. One on three. Two agents against another well-experienced agent—not including the others that would likely be in the surrounding chambers.

It was a risk.

Angel met his gaze steadily—he was ready.

"Your niece is not my concern." The words were clearly said between clenched teeth, anger infusing every syllable. "I want her estates, not her. I can find a dozen women who can give me what she can."

"We are in agreement then." Wycomb again, in cool tones. Jones moved closer to the door of the room he believed them to be in, hoping Wycomb's words would mask his footsteps. Candlelight shown through the doorway. "None of us care about her person beyond her ability to bear children. I'd think you would be concerned enough about that to pay their demands—and I cannot pay, as we both know."

Everything in Jones bristled. He stepped forward, fury coursing through him.

A hand landed on his shoulder, strong and heavy. It was as if he were in the training room, the hand on his shoulder one he'd felt a hundred times before. Jones turned to look behind him.

Wait, Angel mouthed. Removing his hand, Angel tapped his finger against his ear. *Listen.*

Jones knew there were times to rush in and moments when it was best to listen. Patience was always an advantage. He'd forgotten when they'd spoken of Cat. Breathing deep, letting all his fear center in his chest so it gave him strength, he waited. Listened. As he'd been trained.

"Your niece's ability to bear children is unimportant. There are ways around that." A pause, then, "I want her visibly intact. No scars. I want to present a wife free from marks to the *ton*."

"Of course—and if I could provide her, I would." Wycomb's sly words forced Jones to press his back against the wall. "She has been removed from my hands, however. Her fate is in yours. If you pay what they ask, she can be what you require."

"I want proof she is unsullied." Hedgewood's voice was harsh, as if he could no longer control the tone and pitch of the words.

"Well I ain't got proof," came the voice of a third man. "She's well gone, and my men are the worse for the wear. She weren't alone." A pause, a grunt. "You told me it would be easy, milord. We'd make back what we lost on the shipment if we sell her to the gent."

"Ah." Hedgewood's voice was suddenly smooth. It sent

a chill through Jones. "Is that how it is, Wycomb? You give your niece to these men and sell her back to me?"

"If it works, yes." Smooth, unworried words from Wycomb. "If you had simply persuaded her to marry you—"

Jones could not listen any longer.

Chapter Forty-Four

Jones stepped into the room, training be damned, and aimed his pistol at the center of Wycomb's chest.

"Ah, Jones." Wycomb shifted his body, ready for the assault, though he did not reach for his own weapon. "You fell in love with her, I see. A more unsuitable match for the Baroness Worthington I cannot think of—and I've already signed the contracts, so Hedgewood already owns her."

Hedgewood spun, staring at Jones with an expression ripe with disgust. "No. I will not tolerate—"

"I don't care what you will tolerate." Jones moved his pistol so it pointed at Hedgewood now. "Your claim on her is nothing but words on paper. A bullet in your heart will void any contract you entered into."

Hedgwood blanched, and despite the physique he must have honed at Gentlemen Jackson's, he shrank back—a coward when faced with a true battle. That still left the owner of the den, Wycomb, and anyone else lurking in the warrens in the lower floors.

"Don't fight us, Wycomb. If you come in without resisting,

it will be easier." Jones already knew Wycomb's answer and that blood would be on his hands that night.

"No." Wycomb dove forward, the expression on his face bereft of anything beyond survival. His body hit Jones as if it had been coiled for hours, waiting to spring.

Wycomb went for the spot just beneath the rib cage that would knock all breath from the lungs. Jones knew the same spot, but it was too late. His breath was gone and he lay on his back on the floor.

Yet he wasn't done.

Jones kicked out both legs as Wycomb rushed past. The man went down, his cry swallowed just after it was given voice. Dimly, Jones recognized Angel dealing with Hedgewood and the other man. He had little chance to think as Wycomb rose above him, fists clenched together to maximize pressure when they came down again.

But Jones knew what he planned.

He jerked to the side as Wycomb tried to thump those joined fists against Jones's chest. The blow glanced off his side and drove the air from him, but not the need to protect.

Gasping, heart pounding to remind him hadn't died, Jones rolled over. Every breath was a trial, every heartbeat beyond what his body could comprehend. Still, the figure that rose in the doorway became everything Jones hated. The man had cut Cat's skin. He'd sold her to an opium den. Wycomb had bruised her face so that a line of shadows chased her cheekbones.

Jones reached for the pistol that had dropped from his hand. Raised it.

Shot.

Wycomb went down. Screaming, still struggling, but he was down. Blood blossomed on buff-colored breeches, the stain growing each second.

Jones rolled to his knees, caught his breath in the midst

of a cloud of black powder. Wycomb gripped the door frame, scrabbling through it with one leg while the other dragged behind.

Jones sure as hell wasn't letting him disappear now.

He rose to his feet, still gasping for air, and followed Wycomb into the hallways built into the den's lower floors. Other sounds met his ears—dozens of footsteps pounding. Shouts as Angel was overwhelmed, more shouts and a shrill battle cry as the Flower and the Shadow joined him.

Still, Wycomb knew the maze of rooms and Jones did not. Jones guessed at the direction Wycomb would have turned, running through the warren of hallways and rooms. He guessed wrong, it seemed, and was forced to retrace his steps until he reached the stairs to the ground floor.

More footsteps sounded behind him, but he did not stop to determine who was fleeing the scene. Only Wycomb mattered—and Wycomb was bleeding at the top of the stairs just in front of him.

Jones leaped, aiming for Wycomb's back. They went down hard on the floor of the main hall, limbs struggling for purchase and leverage. It was Jones who found it first and drove a fist into the man's face. He tried not to find satisfaction in it, but he did. So he drove the other fist into his face and watched Wycomb's eyes roll back.

He leaned closed. "You will not touch Cat again. Is that understood?"

Jones rolled Wycomb onto his stomach, pulling a thin, strong coil of rope from the pocket sewn into the back of his coat. He wrapped a circlet around one wrist, then the other, pulled tight and formed a knot. Rolling Wycomb onto his back once more, Jones stood, breathing heavy, and looked down at the man who had hurt Cat. The man who had sold her to the opium den.

"You don't deserve to live."

"Then kill me," Wycomb rasped. Despite the words, his teeth were bared. He no longer resembled an elegant, well-dressed spy, but a desperate man who belonged in the rookeries. "We both know if I make trial I will hang."

"So you will." As much as Jones wanted to do the deed himself, he did not. Justice was not dealt in the shadows. "But you will not die by my hand."

"You've always been weak, Jones." Wycomb spat the words, thin lips pursed.

Jones did not rise to the bait—he'd learned to work with an opponent's mind years ago. "You will stand trial for what you've done to Cat." Jones could barely say the words beyond the fury writhing in him. He yanked Wycomb to his feet and pushed him forward, uncaring that the man's injured leg buckled beneath him.

The shot caught them both unawares.

The sound reverberated in the air. Wycomb jerked and Jones did the same—but only one of them had blood welling on his chest.

As Wycomb slipped to the floor, Jones looked up to find Hedgewood standing with his back to the front door and still sighting down a pistol.

"He lied to me," Hedgewood said conversationally. He looked down the pistol sight and met Jones's gaze with clear green eyes. "Whatever contract he signed, whatever he told me, he lied. The baroness is nowhere near this place—if she were, you would be rescuing her, wouldn't you? Not bothering with Wycomb."

"True enough. She's safe and under my care." Jones ignored the writhing and gasping at his feet. If Wycomb passed, it meant nothing to him but one less threat to Cat. The pistol aimed at him was more important. It was a single barrel, and though he hadn't seen Hedgewood reload that did not mean he hadn't—nor that it was the same pistol he'd already fired. "Wycomb made a mistake thinking the baroness had no spine. Don't make the same mistake."

Hedgewood paused, met Jones's gaze, then turned and ran through the front door before Jones could protest. At his feet, Wycomb clutched at Jones's boots, fingers curling around them—whether in supplication or aggression, Jones could not tell.

...

Cat could only watch and wait, the agony of the unknown coursing through her.

The street was quiet and dark, mist writhing in the shadows. Occasionally the shadows moved as someone passed the window, but in these alleys the people were fast and full of fear, trying to locate a haven.

She paced, window to fireplace and back again. Picked up the knife, set it down. She would be as likely to injure herself with it as any intruder. She strode back to the fireplace, contemplated the low flames there. Reaching for the iron bar Bill used as a poker, she moved the logs and stirred the embers.

She heard the first pistol shot from far away. It might have been someone dropping a dish in the rooms on either side. Moving to the window, she curled the curtain aside and peered into the gloom. Still nothing.

The second shot was loud and unmistakable.

A moment later, Hedgewood spilled from the door of the den as if the hounds of hell were after him. He joined the shadows, pressed against the wall beside the door as if lying in wait for those hellhounds. The door swung on its hinges, back and forth from the force of Hedgewood's push. The opening emitted dim light from inside, revealing an empty hall.

She realized just as Hedgewood did that no one was following him.

He began to creep down the street, still watching that doorway. Panic erupted in her as she waited for someone to stop him. Jones, another spy—any of them should burst through that door and stop Hedgewood.

They didn't.

"Oh, bugger that." Cat seized the iron bar and was through the front door before her mind understood what her body was doing. Somewhere in Bill's room was her cloak and safety. Somewhere in the buildings beyond was Jones and his spies.

Here, now, was Hedgewood—and Cat.

He whirled, feet scuffing on filthy cobblestones and pistol pointed straight at her before he recognized her. "Ah. My lovely bride."

"Hedgewood," she said evenly, keeping the bar behind her billowing nightshift. The metal was warm in her hand, fitting easily against her palm.

"Come, my dear. You are safe now." The pistol dropped away, aiming for the ground as he stepped slowly toward her. As if gathering his charm, he straightened and smiled at her. Light moved over a face that no longer seemed handsome to her. "I have killed Wycomb. You have nothing more to fear from him."

The words brought her no comfort.

"Am I to think you are my savior?" She gestured to the opium den behind him. "You are as involved as he."

"Not quite." Hedgewood shrugged, as if to minimize his part, all charm fading into the mist and stench whirling around them. "This was your uncle's project. I was simply his investor. When my investment failed, Wycomb paid me with your hand in marriage in exchange for additional funds to satisfy his, ah, creditors."

"I see. You recoup your investment through my lands."

"Don't forget your body, my dear." He moved close, closer, predator stalking prey in the wilds of the rookeries. "A man in my position must have an heir."

Fury lit her from within, burning in her veins. She slammed the iron bar into his chest, the resounding thud turning her stomach. He started to crumple, but she raised the bar once more and struck his side as he went down.

Jones surged from the opium den and into the street, nearly wrenching the door from its hinges. "Cat!" he shouted, then skid to a halt on the cobblestones. He looked once to Hedgewood's inert form, then again to Cat.

"Good thing Bill keeps this around." Breath heaving, Cat held up the iron bar.

A smile spread across Jones's face, lighter than any she had seen from him before. He strode toward her, his pace steady and sure. "I think you've discovered a lady's newest accessory."

Chapter Forty-Five

Jones set the snifter in Cat's hands. She curled her fingers around the glass and brought the amber liquid to her mouth. Clearly no stranger to brandy, she did not gasp, nor did her eyes water—she simply drank deep. His mouth fought a war with his mind and curved up in a grin.

That was his Cat.

"The men we could bring in from the opium den are tucked away in cells at Old Bailey. Hedgewood is below with Angel—I do not think it long before he shares his secrets." The Flower stood in front of Sir Charles in Jones's study. The shoulder of her black coat was torn, breeches dirty at the knee, but she appeared no worse for wear in any other way.

"Good." Sir Charles's brown eyes showed no sign that he had been awakened by his agents just before dawn. "What of Wycomb?"

"Langford is seeing to his body in the usual way." The Flower shifted, though her boots were silent on the thick rug. "Forgive me if I do not mourn him."

"I do not blame you." Sir Charles turned his head, pinned

Jones and Cat with his cool brown gaze. "Jones, I wouldn't mind a finger or two of brandy myself."

"Yes, sir." Jones went to the sideboard and flipped up a second snifter. Crystal clinked as he removed the stopper from the brandy decanter, the sound competing with Sir Charles's words.

"I must thank you for your assistance in this matter, my lady." The spymaster softened his tone, which was something Jones rarely heard him do. "My condolences regarding your uncle's death."

"I do not mourn him, either," was Cat's dry reply.

The Flower snorted, then turned the sound into a polite cough. Jones hid his grin as he poured the brandy for Sir Charles and replaced the decanter.

"I see." Sir Charles's reply was stilted, though Jones sensed some amusement beneath the words.

Jones turned back toward the room, smooth glass cupped in his hand. "Sir."

Sir Charles accepted the snifter, swirled and sniffed. "Jones, I expect a full report from you later today, including any information Hedgewood provides."

"Yes, sir." Jones looked to Cat, still wearing her cloak and nightshift. Her hair had lost its usual luster, though the fire of it couldn't be entirely dimmed by dirt. The stained cloak was wrapped firmly around her, but the nightshift beneath had grayed. "I will start as soon as I see her ladyship home. I'm certain she needs rest."

"I need a bath, first, I think." She sipped the brandy again. Her gaze did not leave Jones, staying level with his over the rim. "Sir Charles," she said slowly, turning the full force of that iridescent blue on him. "What of Hedgewood?"

"That remains to be seen. It may be that he is brought before a jury, or he may be released. It is not yet clear." Sir Charles frowned into his glass. "I see what you are concerned about. Your marriage."

"Specifically, the contract my uncle signed." She breathed deep, knuckles whitening as she gripped crystal. "I am unclear if it stands."

"Do you want it to?" Sir Charles asked slowly, the lines on either side of his mouth deepening.

"No," she said, words sharp. "I do not."

"I'm certain that with a little *influence*, shall we say," Sir Charles said slowly, a considering expression moving over his face. "A judge could be persuaded that Wycomb was not in his right mind when he signed it. A peer of the realm involved with opium, attempting to ransom his ward—a case could be made that the contract is void."

It would not entirely settle her future, Jones knew. She was still just shy of gaining her majority and a new guardian would need to be appointed, though perhaps by the time the contract was declared null she might have reached twenty-one. Even then, her inheritance would still be held in trust until she married—it seemed to Jones she would be at the beginning again.

And still unattainable.

Cat's features firmed, candlelight gilding the delicate planes. "If that can be achieved, I would be grateful."

"I am certain it can—I am quite on good terms with His Majesty." Sir Charles stood then and sketched an elegant bow for so stocky a man. "Good day, my lady. Jones."

"Good day, sir."

"Flower, a word before I go." Sir Charles set his empty snifter on the sideboard, gathered his sword cane, and strode from the room.

"*Au revoir*, my lady," the Flower murmured as she followed the spymaster, perfectly silent in her men's boots.

Cat's face relaxed when they were alone, and she let out a long, drawn out breath. "There is hope, then."

"You won't have to marry Hedgewood." Jones slipped the now empty snifter from her fingers and replaced it with his own hand. Twining his fingers with hers, he brought them to his lips, kissed the hands she had finally been able to wash in his chamber above.

"I could marry you," she said.

He paused, his mouth still pressed against her sweet skin, then drew away, but did not release her hand. He was not ready to, though he knew what his answer would be. "You cannot marry me, for all the reasons we already spoke of."

"Then in Italy, in Colle di Val d'Elsa." A plea edged her words. It tore at him, rending a long, thin cut through his soul.

"I cannot go to Italy with you," he said softly, sorrow layered over the words. "I am needed here."

"I don't understand." She shook her head, unbound hair moving and shifting over the hood lying on her shoulders. "I don't understand," she said again, voice rising.

He only had one purpose. One skill that gave him worth. "I am a spy, Cat. I will always be a spy." Freeing his hand, he gripped her shoulders. "Even if we went to Colle di Val d'Elsa, you would not leave your life behind. You will always be the Baroness Worthington. Part of me will always live in the rookeries. We'll never be free from our pasts." A long, slow breath shuddered out. "Neither of us."

A log snapped in the grate. Jones's hands twitched on her shoulders before they both looked over at the lick of flame and burning coals. The logs burned a dull red, the color ebbing and fading only to grow again, stronger, then flaring into life.

"I do not want freedom, Jones." Cat looked away from the coals and at him. Into him, as if she could see the scars he bore on his soul. "I only want to go to a place where our differences are not as great."

There was no breath. Not from him. Not from her.

"Where our differences are not as great." He sighed, hands falling away from her shoulders. "Colle di Val d'Elsa."

"I'm going." She spoke firmly, not asking him, but telling him. Her gaze held his, pinning him with the tropical blue. "I have a few trustworthy footmen, perhaps a maidservant, who would travel with me as chaperone. I can hire a guard."

"It is not safe. You would be in danger—"

"As if I have been safe in my own home these last weeks and months? No." She shook her head and lifted her chin, wrapping the filthy cloak around her as if it were a velvet mantle covering a gown of silk. "I wish to see it, and I will do so."

"Do you expect me to come with you to protect you? Is that what you think—that you can manipulate me into changing my mind?" He ground out the words, though he knew they were untrue and unfair, and paced away from her. He set his palms to the surface of Angel's desk—his desk—and pressed them flat against the cold, polished wood. He knew a chair sat beyond the wood, but he could not see it.

Only the woman speaking behind him seemed solid.

"I will see Colle di Val d'Elsa," she repeated. "And I will wait there for you."

"Don't, Cat." He couldn't bear the building pressure inside him and pushed hard against the desk surface.

"I will be there in two months. In four. Even six. I will be there, waiting for you. All I ask is that you send word if you do not intend to come."

"You cannot wait for me. I'm nothing." He spun to face her and found she had stepped just behind him.

"You're everything to *me*." Dirt smudged her cheek and one lock of long, curling hair had fallen over her face. A fierce light came into her eyes.

"Jones." The male voice was soft, but there was an edge. A sharp edge that allowed no argument. "Hedgewood is ready."

Angel stood in the doorway, gold hair unbound and amber eyes shuttered from his thoughts. Jones knew he had heard some of their words, though whatever he thought he did not reveal.

Time stretched thin, winding around them. Jones fastened his gaze on hers and he found himself memorizing the faint pattern of her iris. Point, valley, small point, starburst. It was a pattern he might not see again.

"Go," she commanded, expression clear. "Do what you must. I will wait."

"I can't—"

"I will promise you six months, Jones. That is all I will give you."

Chapter Forty-Six

Cat tucked her knees up and wrapped her arms around the pouf of her skirts, so that she was folded into and around herself. Laying a cheek on one knee, she gazed out at the rolling hills and ancient houses built into the countryside.

It was beautiful. Every stone house glowed in the bright Italian sun, each terra-cotta roof absorbing the heat and sending waving lines into the blue, blue sky. The dark squares of the windows marching across the sea of homes seemed sharp. Below the labyrinth of houses, the earth opened up to trees and valleys and vineyards, as far as the eye could see.

A woman could weep at the beauty of Tuscany.

Yet there was little beauty for her. Here, at the top of a hill near the house she had rented in Colle di Val d'Elsa. *The Hill of Elsa Valley.* The River Elsa snaked through the trees and stone, its shining surface just visible from the lawns of the house—the house that was full of servants and furniture, but empty of everything she held dear.

He had not come. Six months, and Jones had not come. Eight months, and still he had not come.

Cat eyed at the letter lying on the thick, verdant grass beside her. All was well at home. Without her uncle to pressure them, the trustees had become more reasonable. Ashdown Abbey was well cared for by Mr. Sparks, the tenants were secure and happy, and her other estates were prosperous. There was no need for her to return.

Only Italy did not hold her here.

Setting her forehead against the hard, flat bones of her knees, Cat sighed long and loud. It was time to go home. Whatever waited for her there would not be what she'd left, of course. The scandal of a woman traveling alone, the difficulties of society, even the humbling re-entrance to her own home would not sit well. She had left England for a man and was returning alone. Alone and abandoned.

"Very well," she said aloud, pressing her eyelids against her knees to stop any tears that might plan to escape. "I will return home. I will pull together whatever pieces of my life that are salvageable and return to England."

She flopped back onto the earth with a puff of air rushing from her lips.

Tall grass and wildflowers danced around her head as she stared at dazzlingly bright clouds scattered over the sky. The sweet scent of the blossoms surrounded her as the breeze ruffled petals and leaves. Birds chirped while a bee buzzed above. She swore the flutter of butterfly wings was audible against this background of hilltop silence.

She saw it all, felt it all, and yet something had turned cold in her heart.

"You look like a faerie, lying among the flowers."

After one gasping, shocked, breathless moment, her lungs began to function again. Her view was only of the sky and clouds and waving flowers. She couldn't see him, wherever he stood, but she knew his voice as well as her own.

She did not answer, some primitive, protective part

willing her voice to be silent lest she had only dreamed of him again.

"I'm sorry I'm late, Cat. I was detained."

Her breath hitched as the sob rose in her throat. He was here. Late, so very, very late, but he was here. He had not died by the hand of some foreign agent, he had not died during the crossing—and he had not forgotten her.

"Ass." She hadn't realized she'd harbored anger, but it was mixed with joy and pain.

"Yes." He said nothing more, no explanation or further apology.

Cat closed her eyes against the sunlight, against the dizzying relief that Jones was alive and beside her, and let the anger and fear wash away. For a moment, there was nothing but the buzz and lilt of the countryside in her ears and dark gratefulness behind her eyelids—then the grass sighed as he knelt beside her.

She was afraid to open her eyes, afraid to look at him.

Had he changed? Would he still be the Jones she'd known eight months ago?

A rough, calloused fingertip touched her mouth, skimming over her flesh as though hesitantly relearning a long-forgotten treasure. It moved to her hair, tangling in the mass she hadn't bothered to pin up in weeks. There was no one there to see it.

"I've missed you." He whispered it, even as his hand stroked the unruly locks. "Missed you. Loved you. It seems I couldn't stop loving you, even when I believed I would not come."

"Was it so hard?" She still did not open her eyes, but let the memory of his face live behind her eyelids. The dark eyes, the serious mouth.

"Not hard, but time consuming once I made the decision to come. There were missions to complete before I could be reassigned."

His hand move from her hair to her cheekbone, the work-roughened pad of his fingers smoothing over her skin. He stroked once, gently, and she could no longer keep her eyes closed.

He was the same. Leaner, perhaps, with tired shadows beneath his eyes, but he was the same. Jones. Her Jones. The dark, intense eyes, the lean planes of his face. Full lips she was desperate to kiss.

He had come.

There was sorrow around the edges of his mouth, drawing the corners down. His hand hesitated on her cheek, then fell way. His continued to watch her, as she lay in the grass and he knelt beside her. The sounds of the meadow became a low hum in her ears, barely a murmur against the steady drum of her heart.

"Has it been so long that I have lost you, Cat?"

For a moment, she could not answer. Had he lost her? She searched her mind, her heart. No. No, he had not. There was so much inside her, so much heart and love and purpose, and while she *could* live without him, and had these last months, she didn't want to.

"No, Jones." She drew a deep, long breath, the bodice of her gown pulling and stretching even as her heart stretched to love more of this man. "You have not lost me."

The relief and joy on his face was beyond measure. Her throat constricted and burned with a fierce, desperate need to cry. His breath shuddered out with the same rhythm that shook his shoulders and for a moment she thought *he* was crying.

But those eyes were dry when they rose to meet hers. Dry and bright with a turbulent darkness that called to her.

"I was afraid you would not be here," he whispered. "Every night I closed my eyes and dreamed of you here, in the golden light of Italy, but I never thought you would come."

"Jones." Cat brushed aside a daisy dancing in the breeze and reached her hand up to cup his face. "I told you I would. I promised."

"Yes." He pressed a kiss against her palm. "Yes, you did."

The sheer wonder in his voice made her want to cry again. This man—this wonderful, responsible, intelligent man—did not believe she could love him enough to wait. Her heart broke for him, then soared again. She'd kept her promise.

"There is only us, now, Jones. Here on this hillside. I waited here for you every day, because I thought perhaps I would see you sailing down the river, or riding up from the village." Her gaze skimmed over every feature, drinking in the face she'd only been able to see in her mind these last months. "Be with me here, Jones, where I waited. Love me on this hill."

Time spun out, filled with golden sunlight and the steady beat of the pulse in Jones's throat.

"It will not be our first time." She smiled at him. "But you will be the last man."

Something went tight in Jones's face—tight, but not angry. It was powerful, and so intense she shivered beneath his gaze.

"Cat. My love." His mouth touched hers, gently. Whiskers rasped against her cheek and sent delicious pleasure winging through her body.

She twined her arms about his neck and met his lips as he lowered himself to the grass beside her. Slipping a hand beneath her back, he began to work the buttons of her bodice, quickly, and with almost frantic movements—though his mouth was lazy in its exploration of hers.

"Jones," she whispered. "Let us not waste time with our clothing."

He paused, looking down at her with such seriousness

that her heart swelled with joy of being loved with a passion that excluded all else. "A very good suggestion."

They disrobed quickly, tugging at ribbons and laughing. Through it, she became more aware of every inch of her skin, of the scent of his skin and the warm Tuscan sun. When he lay her down on his spread coat, she was ready to bring him into her.

Though his body was clearly ready, he waited, setting his mouth on her breast and his tongue to her nipple. She arched up, running her hands through the hair that grown during their time apart. It layered thick around his face and gave her more to tug.

He chuckled lightly and moved his lips to the valley between her breasts. Each kiss he feathered there created a wave beneath her skin. That wave grew as he moved down her body, tasting her inch by inch. It was as if he were trying to match her body to his memory.

Finally, he rose above her. She ran her hands up strong arms to grip his shoulders. So broad, and so willing. The strength there, the smooth skin rippling over muscle thrilled her.

The intensity shone in his eyes again, darkly full of promise and love. He pressed against her core, hot and hard, his gaze never leaving hers.

"I love you, Cat," he whispered as he slipped into her, filling both her body and her heart. "I will love you always."

"Did I tell you of my new assignment?" Sated, ridiculously full of love for her, Jones reached for a strand of curling, deep red hair. He let it slip and slide through his fingers. Their happiness had been as slippery as those lovely curls, but he could no longer pretend he didn't want to capture it.

"No." Her legs were tangled in his, though her arms were thrown above her head to rest in the tall grass. She was open to him, heart and body. "Is it here in Italy?"

"No. England."

"I beg your pardon?" She sat up, quick as a flame might catch fire, to stare at him. Her breasts were exposed to the sunlight, and he could not help but run a finger from her shoulder, down the line of her breast to touch its pink tip.

"I am entering partial retirement, much like the Shadow." The idea did not fill him with fear as it once had. "Sir Charles will call upon me occasionally, as needed. The rest of the time, I shall attend to my estates."

Her mouth fell open. "I *beg* your pardon?"

"Is that all you can say?" He laughed, as it was such a pleasure to surprise her.

She only blinked at him, sun shining on her freckled shoulders and turning her hair to brilliant flame.

He sobered, though a smile still tugged at his lips. "I would have you marry me, Cat, if you are still willing. We could return home."

"How can we? The scandal will be horrendous. We'll be ostracized immediately." Her gaze flicked over his face, the blue that had haunted his dreams clouded with doubt. "Even if we manage the first wave of outrage, we'll never be truly accepted again. You said yourself, the ton will always buzz with gossip when you appear."

"I did say that." He set his arms around her, drew her warm body against his. "If we marry and lived here in Italy, Cat, what of our children? What happens when they return home to claim their birthright?"

She stilled, the breath leaving her body so that the woman he held in his arms was frozen in a single, crystalline moment of Italian sunshine.

"Our children?" The word was like a whisper of wind

through the grass.

"We'll have children, Cat. Many, I hope." He pressed his lips against hers, softly. Wanting her to feel the love spilling over inside him. Yet, beneath all that love was truth. "When they return to England to claim their inheritance, the scandal will be theirs, not ours. They will not be accepted. If we weather the storm first, they may be accepted. More—" He breathed deep, knowing he was sending himself into the lion's den of the *ton*. "More, you and I can stand together. We can provide our children with an example, so they understand love and sacrifice and strength. We can teach them to stand against those who would put money and property above others. We can show them how to navigate their birthright using the gift of love."

"Oh, Jones." Elegant, smooth hands cupped his cheek. Her gaze rested now on his, lips curving up. "That's—that's—"

"Ridiculously sentimental." He felt foolish. Moving away, he began to roll into a crouch. The hand on his arm stayed him, then gently pulled him back toward her.

"Brave." She sighed the word, her gaze meeting his. "It will not be easy."

"No." He ran his hand up her calf, down, willing comfort to flow from his touch and into her. "Though I plan to be too busy making love to my wife to notice."

She laughed, a soft, amused sound that lifted his heart. "That can be arranged, Jones."

"I don't want to live in the shadows, Cat." He'd done so all of his life. First in the rookeries, then in training, then as spy. He settled down beside her, kneeling almost at her feet. "Not with you."

The wind kicked up, pushing at the grass so it rippled and rolled across the meadow. The wind pushed at her hair, too, so the strands danced around her face. When she tipped her face up to the sky and let the gold light of Italy gild her skin, his heart simply stumbled to a stop.

She was smart and beautiful—and she was his.

"I love you, Cat."

Her eyes remained closed, her face still angled toward the sun, but her lips rose in a radiant smile.

"Let's stay here a few months," she said. "Let's enjoy a little time before we face it all." Now she did look at him, with eyes that echoed her soul. "When we go home, we'll face all the difficulties of the *ton*. We'll let the tide of scandal rage. In a few years, the scandal will not be as great, and a few years after that, it will only be whispered about. When we're old and gray, no one will care."

"In the interim, you will have to show me how to go on as a landowner and a man of the *ton*." He grinned at her, relief and pleasure swirling in him. "I would not want to wear the wrong cravat."

She cocked her head. "Considering you're not wearing anything at all, Jones, I'd say a cravat is the least of your worries."

Cat reached for him, uncurling her naked body. Running delicate hands up his forearms, she leaned forward, revealing the round loveliness of her breasts. He breathed in her scent, mingling with the sweetness of wildflowers. When she pressed her mouth to his, her fire hummed in his blood again.

She drew back to look at him, the butterfly blue alluring and filled with desire.

"Make love to me again, here in the field. Then we'll return to the house, and you can make love to me again there." She smiled at him. "Someday soon we'll return to England, we shall be married, and you can make love to me there."

It seemed to him his future wife was very wise.

"As you wish, my lady."

Epilogue

Cat wandered through the front hall of Ashdown Abbey. Sunlight streamed through high mullioned windows to create a diamond patchwork over the marble floor. A footman passed, and she drew him aside. "Have you seen his lordship?"

"He was down at the stables earlier, checking on the mare."

"Oh, is she foaling?" Chagrined, Cat thought she might have slept late and missed the event.

"Not yet, milady, but 'tis not long."

"Thank you." She smiled at the man sent him on his way. He whistled lightly as he crossed the hall to pass beneath one of the hundred stone archways of Abbey—an act Wycomb would never have allowed but that Cat found heartening.

Not bothering with a pelisse or shawl for such a warm spring day, Cat made her way across the rear of the Abbey to the stables. The building was dim despite the open window, humid, and smelled of horse and sweat and leather. Stepping through shafts of sunlight along the corridor of stalls, Cat found the foaling mare in one of the larger spaces. The horse was round and fat and happy, munching on a feed bag and flicking her tail at buzzing flies.

Two apples were lined up outside the door, and Cat knew Jones had been there, though the stall was empty of people. The mare had been ill in the fall and winter, and he had treated her with red apples to encourage her to eat. Cat rubbed her gleaming, well-curried coat.

"Good morning, my dear," Cat murmured, running her palm over the mare's swollen side. The mare barely noticed and with a smile, Cat left her.

Stepping out into the sunshine again, she walked once more to the towering house and stood in its shadow. From there she could see lawns rolling away, the edge of the formal gardens. In the distance, shimmering along the tree line, was a folly some long ago ancestor had built. Beyond that, beyond what she could see clearly, were golden wheat fields and thatched tenant's cottages.

All of it belonged to her, and now Jones.

She set her hand on her stomach, flat beneath pale blue muslin. Someday, perhaps, all of Ashdown Abbey might belong their children.

Moving back into the house through the terrace doors, she found Mr. Sparks striding through toward his office, worn account ledgers tucked under his arm.

"Good afternoon, my lady." Bright green eyes twinkled at her from beneath his spectacles as he adjusted the ledgers to sketch a slight bow.

"Hello, Mr. Sparks." Cat grinned as she noticed the spring in his step—it had been there since they had returned to Italy the year before. "Have you seen Jones?"

"He just returned from inspecting the planting in the north fields. I believe he is in the estate room."

"The big one, or the other?"

"The other," he said, pushing up his glasses with a

forefinger.

"I should have guessed. Thank you." Her heart soared and she found herself smiling. Jones always seemed to be in that little room occupied by generations of her ancestors. "Will you be joining us for dinner this evening?"

"I don't believe so." He patted the ledgers in his hand, the tanned skin nearly the same shade as the aged leather. "Your husband indicated you both would like to discuss assisting the blacksmith in the village to expand his forge. I must study the accounts."

"Yes, the blacksmith has been assisting the neighboring village since their smithy burned. We've been thinking to combine the shops and avoid future fires." She smiled at the man who had seen her through her father's death. "Your expertise would be most appreciated, however."

"Ah." Green eyes lit beneath the spectacles. "I shall most certainly attend."

"We shall see you then." She found that another smile flitted over her lips as she watched Mr. Sparks walk to his own office as if a bubble of satisfaction propelled his steps.

So much had changed.

Cat finally found Jones in the tiny room the Ashdowns had toiled in for generations. He was in his shirtsleeves, fine linen shifting as he reached for a sheaf of papers, and appeared to accept the towering bookshelves around him as ordinary rather than a mountain of history on his back. Piled beside the scarred desk was the waistcoat, cravat, and coat he'd donned that morning—she imagined he'd removed it as soon as he was out of eyesight of the Abbey, then carried it back lest he be caught.

"Hello," she murmured, heart soaring as he looked up and smiled at her. He smiled so often now, she barely recognized him as her serious Jones. "I invited Mr. Sparks to dine with us."

"Excellent." Jones ran his hands through the hair he'd continued to keep long, as she'd discovered she preferred it that way. There was so much more there to take hold of. "I'm looking over the yields from last fall to be certain the new granaries will be able to hold enough to last the winter."

"Jones?"

"Mm." He'd looked back to the documents, running blunt fingers down a column of numbers. He fit easily into her father's chair, she noticed, though she had found the seat comfortable of late.

"The physician said we are to have a babe later this year." Cat found that the joy in her could not be hidden in her words. "In the fall."

Jones stilled, then looked up at her with deep brown eyes blurred by shock. "A babe? We're having a babe? You and me?"

"Yes." She laughed aloud as he pushed back the chair and leapt across the tiny room toward her. Strong arms enveloped her, wide shoulders just there for her to lean on.

"You are well?" Jones cupped her cheeks, pressed his lips to hers with such reverence she wanted to weep. "The babe is well?" he whispered.

"Both of us are well, as far as we know." Cat slipped into that space between his torso and arm. Satisfied, she smiled to herself. His body and hers had somehow shaped themselves so that she fit perfectly there.

"I love you." His arm around her tightened—not roughly, but with the subtle protection she had discovered meant he was moved.

Cat smiled to herself. He was easy to understand, her Jones, once you knew him. He was all that was responsible, strong, silent, unyielding—except for the heart of him.

The heart of Jones was filled with nothing but love.

Acknowledgments

Many thanks to my editor, Alethea Spiridon, the Goddess Among Agents, Nalini Akolekar, and everyone in the art and marketing and editing departments at Entangled Publishing. It really does take a village!

I'd also like to give a huge shout out to Kimberly Kincaid for reading and loving Jones's book. Thanks for that eagle eye going through the first draft. And to Jennifer McQuiston—without your suggestion, Cat and Jones would never have had their HEA!

Last, but not at all least, many thanks to Kerry Keberly. My very own Eliza Jane. Thank you for plotting, brainstorming, and sending me good vibes and pretties in the mail. Without your long distance handholding, this book would still be unfinished. Most especially, thank you for taking my frantic phone call at 10 pm the day before deadline—which, after two pots of coffee followed by two glasses of wine, went something like this: "Hello-Cat-is-stuck-across-the-road-and-I-can't-get-her-out-and-who-should-kill-the-villain-because-I-don't-think-she-can-and-I-don't-want-Jones-to-backslide-and-one-of-the-other-spies-can't-do-it-and-I-can't-send-Cat-into-the-opium-den-either-and-now-what-do-I-do?" To which, my dearest moon sister, you calmly replied: "OK. Let's talk this through."

About the Author

Despite being a native Michigander, Alyssa Alexander is pretty certain she belongs somewhere sunny. And tropical. Where drinks are served with little paper umbrellas. But until she moves to those white sandy beaches, she survives the cold Michigan winters by penning romance novels that always include a bit of adventure. She lives with her own set of heroes, aka an ever-patient husband who doesn't mind using a laundry basket for a closet and a small boy who wears a knight in a shining armor costume for such tasks as scrubbing potatoes.

Discover the* A Spy in the Ton *series…

A DANCE WITH SEDUCTION

Discover more Amara titles...

HIGHLAND REDEMPTION
a *Highland Pride* novel by Lori Ann Bailey

Skye Cameron has no idea why she was kidnapped, but the last thing she wants is to spend any time with her rescuer, Brodie, the man who broke her heart. She's promised to another in a political marriage and must fight to keep from falling for her handsome childhood sweetheart again as they dash across Scotland in an attempt to elude her captors and stay alive.

TYING THE SCOT
a *Highlanders of Balforss* novel by Jennifer Trethewey

At first, Alex Sinclair, the future Laird of Balforss, has difficulty convincing Lucy FitzHarris to go through with their arranged marriage. Once Lucy arrives, she cannot resist the allure of her handsome Highland fiancé. But when Alex betrays Lucy, she is tricked into running away. Alex must rein in his temper to rescue his lady from unforeseen danger and Lucy must swallow her pride if she hopes to wed the Highlander she has come to love.

My Hellion, My Heart
a *Lords of Essex* novel by Amalie Howard and Angie Morgan

Lord Henry Radcliffe, the sexy Earl of Langlevit, is a beast. The only way Henry can exorcise the demons of his war-ravaged past is through physicality, in and out of bed. Intent on scandalizing London, Princess Irina Volkonsky is a hellion and every gentleman's deepest desire...except for one. Irina knows better than to provoke the forbidding earl, but she will stop at nothing short of ruination to win the heart of the only man she's ever loved.

To Love a Scandalous Duke
a *Once Upon a Scandal* novel by Liana De la Rosa

Declan Sinclair is devastated to discover his brother has been murdered, and he's the new Duke of Darington. Clues point to one man, and, he resolves to destroy the culprit. If only the killer's daughter didn't tempt his resolve. Lady Alethea Swinton has cultivated a pristine reputation. But she's willing to court scandal to help handsome Declan uncover the truth behind his brother's death. Until she realizes Declan's revenge will mean her family's ruin.

Made in the USA
Middletown, DE
02 December 2017